Praise for Jonathan Moore's
Redheads

"The first hundred pages or so of this damn book kept me up until three in the morning, and then it just...got better. A vivid trio of heroes embarked upon a worldwide chase, on the trail of a terrifying, brutal villain—who is also one of the most original creations in recent memory. This is accomplished and exciting work, which at times seems to channel the best of Michael Crichton in its attention to believable, telling detail. Moore drives his train with assured hands, pausing only to broaden his characters and then plunging them into darkness. Moore's a major new talent, I promise you."
—Jack Ketchum

"Part horror, part CSI, part revenge thriller, *Redheads* gets under your skin in unexpected ways. Fans of Dean Koontz and Douglas Preston will find much to love in Moore's impressive debut. Highly recommended!"
—Jay Bonansinga, *New York Times* bestselling author of *Frozen* and *Shattered*

"*Redheads* is a remarkable debut thriller that drew me in and wouldn't let go until the final page. Moore writes like a pro. The characters are real, the dialogue is slick, the action is fast and perfectly crafted and the story is highly cinematic."
—Glenn Cooper, internationally bestselling author of *Library of the Dead* and *Book of Souls*

"Jonathan Moore has created an unforgettable villain who would give the likes of *Dexter* or the *CSI* team sleepless nights. And if your hair is of a reddish hue you will definitely want to keep the lights on while reading this one!"
—Frazer Lee, author of *The Lamplighters* and *The Jack in the Green*

Redheads

Jonathan Moore

SAMHAIN
PUBLISHING

Samhain Publishing, Ltd.
11821 Mason Montgomery Rd., 4B
Cincinnati, OH 45249
www.samhainpublishing.com

Redheads
Copyright © 2013 by Jonathan Moore
Print ISBN: 978-1-61921-570-2
Digital ISBN: 978-1-61921-491-0

Editing by Don D'Auria
Cover by Angela Waters

First Samhain Publishing, Ltd. electronic publication: November 2013
First Samhain Publishing, Ltd. print publication: November 2013

Dedication

This one's for you, Maria.

Chapter One

At least once a day, Chris Wilcox got the idea there was a place he could go, an old familiar house, and if he walked into it, he would find the life he thought he'd lost. This vision was crowded with friends, their voices a blur of toasts and cheers, and at its center was Cheryl, waiting for him.

Most of all, and always, there was Cheryl.

The idea might flood into his mind at any point—while driving a rented car through a strange city, or reading a newspaper clipping about a murdered girl, or cleaning his handgun after shooting all morning at paper silhouettes—and the image would possess him so forcefully he could actually feel Cheryl's arms around him, the warm press of her breasts against his chest. He would pull to the side of the road, or put the news clipping down, or stare at the Glock as though he'd accidentally shot a hole in the ceiling. He thought there must be some maze of streets he'd never found, some twist in the roads that would fold back through time and space to that house, where everything was the way it ought to be. He just didn't know how to get there.

But as soon as the idea took hold of him, it tore itself away. He was full of bewildered hope and then he was simply alone in a foreign city with his file of newspaper stories and the weight of the gun tugging in its shoulder holster, the dry whisper of snowflakes hitting the windshield of his rented car. He'd grip the steering wheel and close his eyes, biting down on his tongue to wake himself from the dream he hoped he was living.

Of course it never worked.

There was no such house, no Cheryl with her cheeks flushed from wanting him. He'd leveled the house and sold the vacant lot. Cheryl hadn't drawn a breath in six years and would never be more than a memory; the taste of wine in his mouth was nothing but his own blood.

Chapter Two

July 2010

The dead girl's apartment was easy to spot. It was the only one on the third floor with dark windows. All the others blazed with light, and no wonder: the newspaper didn't have all the details, but had printed the worst. Chris followed the boardwalk around the side of the converted cotton warehouse. Her four windows faced the ship channel between Galveston and Pelican Islands. That was probably a factor. These things always happened close to the ocean.

Chris had flown to Houston from Honolulu that morning to break into this girl's apartment. It was another marker on a trail that began with Cheryl and twisted through thirty-six other homes and apartments and rented rooms, and disappeared into the darkness ahead. He had spent the entire flight hoping something in the apartment would light the way.

He said the girl's name aloud, just to give her another breath of life.

Allison Clayborn.

She'd lived in Galveston just two years, doing research for a green energy company called Gulf Solar. Three days a week, she taught an engineering class at Rice University. She'd grown up somewhere in central Texas.

Chris could picture her as a teenager in the scrubby Texas hills, riding in the back of a pickup truck with her red hair blowing back, the sun lighting the freckles splashed on her otherwise white shoulders.

He could picture her in a white lab coat, looking at a spreadsheet on her laptop and chewing on the end of a pencil.

He could also picture her dead.

She would have had lovely breasts, and they would have been cut off or cut up, and possibly cooked if she had a cast iron skillet in her kitchen. He hadn't seen the coroner's report yet, but he knew her liver would be gone. If she'd fought—if she'd scratched and clawed—her fingertips would be missing from the first knuckle. Her breasts and liver would have been taken to feed some kind of sick hunger, but the fingertips, he thought, were taken for a different purpose: to keep the police from finding the killer's DNA under Allison's nails. But Chris knew other places to look for that.

Her condo faced Harbor Street, where a few giant live oak trees cast wide shadows from sidewalk to sidewalk. The entrance was an ornate cast iron gate framed by gas lamps. Behind the gate, stone steps led through an archway to paired oak doors. He walked to the gate, taking out his bump key. The lock was a Yale pin tumbler no different than the latch on the front doors of most suburban houses. It wouldn't be a problem.

Chris fit his mechanical bump key into the lock, pulled the spring-loaded trigger three times to knock the vertical tumbler pins clear of the lock cylinder, and twisted the plug with a small torsion wrench. The lock opened in less than five seconds. It took his breath away to think how unguarded Allison's life had been. Or Cheryl's, or the lives of the thirty-six others he'd found.

He passed through the front gate and up the steps. Standing in the gas-lit entryway, he opened the oak door and went into the elevator lobby. The lift was a brass cage that rose through the center of a staircase. The stairs were dark wood with heavy railings, padded down the center in a long stripe of red carpet. He climbed to the third floor and found the door marked 304. There were no sounds. At the end of the hallway a polished wooden chair sat before the windowsill. No policeman sat guard in the chair. He saw no security cameras. An official seal was taped along the length of the doorjamb, and an orange sign was fastened in the center of the door with the Galveston Police Department emblem and *DO NOT ENTER BY ORDER OF LAW* in large red print.

The last forensic team had sliced the seal in half with a razor and hadn't replaced it. The police were done with the apartment. But the cut seal was still there, so the cleaners hadn't come. He thought about that for a moment. The timing was critical because the cleaners would destroy what he was looking for. He was already wearing latex gloves, so he simply bumped Allison's lock, stepped quickly inside her home, and shut the door behind him.

Chapter Three

Chris paid a private investigator in Honolulu eighty thousand dollars a year to watch every newspaper in the world for one kind of story. Mike Nakamura did this on the Internet, where his computer ran a constant sweep, searching out the right combination of words, translating articles into English, ceaselessly hunting for the particular terms which Mike and Chris were always refining. Chris knew the job didn't take more than an hour or two of Mike's time in any given day. Mostly, he was paying Mike to stay quiet. They both knew where this was leading.

The approach was limited, but was the best they could do. They were drawing a line forward from the few points they could find since Cheryl's murder. Chris knew the Internet was a repository of the present, diminishing in value the further he wanted to probe the past. It was practically useless to search for something that didn't happen in the United States in the last ten years.

Still, the search produced results.

It was how Chris first learned about Allison Clayborn.

Two and a half days after she was killed, and less than twenty-four hours before he broke into Allison's apartment, Chris was on his boat, moored in Kaneohe Bay. A thousand feet from the edge of his own backyard. Chris watched Mike's truck turn off the road and ease down the steep driveway. Then Mike was a shadow in the moonlight, crossing the broad lawn that sloped from the back of Chris's house to the dock.

They always met aboard *Sailfish* to talk about the project.

When Mike came astern in the spare kayak, Chris was waiting for him on the swim platform. They pulled the kayak onto the teak platform and took the four steps up the transom to the deck.

"You doing okay?"

"Yeah," Chris said. "Let's get below. Rain's gonna come harder in a minute."

They crossed the cockpit and stepped through the companionway into the cabin. Chris shut the hatch behind them and handed Mike a dry dish towel from the galley.

"Thanks."

"You found one?"

"Two, actually."

"Okay."

He went to the wet bar opposite the galley and pulled a beer out of the fridge.

"Drink?"

"Still got that scotch?"

He poured Mike two fingers of Talisker, and they took the drinks to the salon table and sat opposite each other.

"Let's see them, then."

Mike pulled a small waterproof case from his pocket, flipped it open, and slid a USB drive into his palm. He handed it to Chris.

"Besides these two, how many others?" Chris asked.

"That fit the basic search? Maybe fifty."

"Jesus. It's not even a full moon."

"I know," Mike said. "It happens like that sometimes. Some other days are even worse."

He sipped his drink. Chris pulled the laptop computer from its drawer, plugged in the USB drive, and began to read.

The first article was a murder in San Diego.

Neighbors on the top floor of a five-story walk-up on Seaward Street had complained to the manager about a smell that had been getting worse. It was summertime and it had been over a hundred degrees for three straight days, but even the people lucky enough to own air conditioners were sleeping with their windows open to flush out the stench seeping through their walls. After a day, the manager finally investigated, and decided the smell was coming from a unit on the fifth floor. He knocked, but nobody answered.

He shuffled back to his office on the ground floor and looked up the name of the renter: Caroline Borden. The manager called, but she didn't pick up. A day later, he finally called 9-1-1.

The officers found Caroline Borden dismembered and stuffed into her oven. The oven racks were leaning against the wall, to make room. The oven had been left on broil, but an electrical short stopped its progress no more than an hour into the job. Then the oven cooled to room temperature—over a hundred degrees—and stayed like that until the neighbors complained about the smell.

In the dish drain next to the sink, the police found a hack saw, a long serrated bread knife, and a good-sized pair of pliers, each of which had been thoroughly washed and set to dry.

There was a photograph of Caroline embedded in the newspaper article. Maybe a glamour shot from a strip club's entrance, cropped to print in a newspaper. Caroline was looking directly into the camera, her left forearm resting atop her head. Her hair was spread across a white pillowcase; she had a shy smile. Her shoulders were bare and below them everything was cropped out. She had gray-green eyes and coppery-red hair that stopped just below her chin.

Chris stopped reading.

"You do any other research on the San Diego story?"

"Standard follow-up. She had two drug arrests in the last year. Most recent was two weeks ago. Released without charges."

"Maybe someone thought she cut a deal," Chris said.

"Maybe."

"What was the drug?"

"Drugs—plural," Mike said. "Crystal meth. Heroin. Some designer stuff."

"Where's Seaward Street?"

"Nine blocks from the ocean. Industrial area, close to the wharves."

"Anything else?"

"Some aliases came up, maybe stage names. Carrie Bourbon. Celesté Bourdaine. There was a strip club in Tacoma where she might've worked a few months last summer."

Chris clicked her picture again. She was a redhead and fit the basic pattern. But this didn't feel right, even though she'd finished up in an oven. He imagined she'd run away from home and had been doomed since that day.

He closed the story again and took a sip from his beer.

"See if you can add a new filter to the program. Take out anything involving drugs."

"That could cut it down by a lot."

"It should."

"You could miss one."

"Let's just see how that works for a while," he said. He didn't think he'd miss any. Drugs had never been a factor.

"Okay."

"Pour yourself another scotch if you want."

The next story, from the *Houston Chronicle*, was Allison. The last murder Chris was sure of had been in Vancouver, and that had been eight months earlier, in November of 2009. There had been many others before that, always separated by uncertain spans of time and distance. Houston and San Diego were equally plausible as next locations. Many things could be arranged into a pattern by a patient-enough observer. Chris was finding one, but it was out of focus. He had spent years at this navigation table trying to plot these few points.

INVESTIGATORS HAVE NO LEADS IN BRUTAL GALVESTON MURDER

(AP) GALVESTON July 6, 2010 – Officials here say they have no leads in the brutal murder of Allison Clayborn, and are asking anyone with information to come forward. The July 4 slaying shocked the community. "She was a beautiful girl," said neighbor Mary Kelsey, of Clayborn who had just turned 30. "Vibrant, redheaded, full of life. Everybody loved her—and this whole thing is just terrifying."

Ms. Clayborn's boyfriend, Ben Sullivan, 38, found Clayborn's body in her Harbor Street condominium in the early hours of July 5. Police have not released specific details of the crime scene. A written statement on the department's website asked witnesses to come forward and said the murder was the most violent attack in Galveston's history. Speaking on the condition of anonymity, an official close to the investigation said Clayborn was sexually assaulted and tortured, and her body was mutilated.

The same source said the mutilation involved "elements of cannibalism".

The official release on the department website said investigators did not recover the attacker's fingerprints or DNA. The only prints inside the condominium belonged to Clayborn and Sullivan. Police ruled out Sullivan as a suspect yesterday.

Sullivan was unavailable for comment for this article and has voluntarily checked into an undisclosed inpatient psychiatric clinic, according to a statement by his attorney, James Caldwell.

Clayborn was the sixteenth murder victim so far this year in Galveston County. The incident is the only this year in which the police department was unable to make an arrest within twenty-four hours.

Chris finished the article, and the earlier ones from the fifth of July, and lowered the laptop screen.

"There's no picture?"

"I haven't found one yet."

"See if you can. Pull some strings with the Galveston police if you have to. I'll cover the expense."

He nodded. "You got a feeling on this one?"

"Yeah."

"It's never been longer than eight months between."

"No," Chris said, rubbing at the back of his neck with the cold beer bottle. "I thought there'd probably be one this month."

The wind was picking up, whistling in the rigging. Chris could hear the rain hitting the decks. The articles from July fifth said Allison had been out with friends on Strand Street and had walked home alone around ten at night. She was supposed to meet Ben Sullivan the next morning to go on a trip to New Orleans. None of her girlfriends thought she was seeing anyone besides Ben. She wouldn't have stopped in a bar by herself—she was shy unless she was in a knot of friends. The bar and restaurant where she'd eaten was no more than three well-lit blocks from her own front door. Her telephone call to Ben started at 10:27 and ended at 10:30. She called from the phone beside her bed; it was found dangling off its blood-specked cradle.

The only audible words on the recorded message to Ben were, "It's me, just calling to...hey, are you here?"

Then there was a *clunk*, the phone hitting the floor, probably. The last two minutes and forty-five seconds were nothing but Allison's screams.

But Ben didn't get that message until much later, because after he finished his night's work at Intel, he got into his Acura and drove directly to Galveston to pick up Allison. They were planning to stay at the Columns Hotel on St. Charles Avenue in New Orleans, and had reservations that night at Commander's Palace.

Not all of this was in the newspapers. Mike found a personal blog kept by one of the *Houston Chronicle* reporters assigned to the story. What few records the Galveston police made available, Mike had already gotten.

"Was there anything else you wanted?" he asked.

Chris shook his head. "I'll wait and see the picture before I book a trip out there."

He printed the contents of Mike's drive, using the little ink jet on a shelf under the navigation table. He had a drawer in the master cabin where he collected these. He didn't like to keep them in the house. When they finished printing he left Mike at the table and went to file the stories. Without anything else to go on, there wasn't much to say.

Chris spent the rest of the night thinking about Allison Clayborn, and the project. He wondered about the story Mike brought. What

14

elements of cannibalism did the Galveston Police Department suspect? If he showed them the photographs he kept, would they throw them down in shock? Was he the only one who could see the pattern?

He watched the sun come up while sitting at the bow, then rowed the dingy back to the dock and locked it alongside the kayak. In the kitchen, he made a pot of coffee and drank the first cup, walking around the house and looking into each empty room. He went to the loft above the bedroom and sat at his desk, which faced the bay. The wind had shifted and *Sailfish* had swung on her mooring to point east.

He turned on his computer and searched the Internet, finding stories about Allison. It didn't take long to find a picture. She was leaning against a bicycle in the driveway of a house, Ben Sullivan's perhaps. The photograph must have been taken this past autumn. Allison wore a black windbreaker. Leaves lay strewn across the lawn. It was windy, too: there was a leaf caught in the spokes of her front bicycle tire, and Allison's red hair lifted off to the side. She was laughing. She had a beautiful, delicate face, and her eyes were the color of a summer river: green and deep and warm.

He went down the wooden stairs to the kitchen and poured another cup of coffee, then drank it looking out the window at the ginger blossoms tapping against the glass in the wind. It was going to rain again. He went to the phone on the wall by the refrigerator, dialed Mike on speaker, and went back to the window.

"How's it, Chris?"

"I found her picture in today's *Houston Chronicle*."

"So did I. I just printed it out for you."

"Don't worry about it. I just need to decide what I'm going to do."

"Okay."

They didn't talk for about a minute. There were dogs barking outside of Mike's house, children's voices.

"You still there, Chris?"

"Yeah," he said. "Keep your cell on. I'll call you if I need anything."

"You got it."

He went to the phone and hung it up. Then he went back to his study and booked the first flight to Houston.

Chapter Four

He waited for his eyes to adjust to the darkness inside Allison's apartment.

After he closed the door, the first thing he noticed was the sharp chemical smell from the forensic team. That would be print-developing chemicals applied to the walls and door knobs and probably every sharp or hard object in Allison's apartment. A good team could lift a print from a glass that had gone through a dishwasher. With the right tinctures and tests, a careful lab technician could tell the print of a smoker or heavy coffee drinker by the chemical traces deposited with the rest of the oils in the print; a single print could yield a DNA sample. But the strength of the chemical smell told him what he also already knew: the forensic team had gone wall to wall and floor to ceiling and had not found a single print that could not be ruled out as belonging to Allison or Ben.

He crouched low, shining his dim flashlight at his feet. The floorboards in Allison's apartment were either refurbished originals from the condominium's days as a cotton warehouse, or had been salvaged from an old barn by an interior decorator. They were aged a deep brown and dented with the wear of years, but the new stains were easy enough to see. A rivulet of dried blood ran out of the living room into the foyer. He stepped to the side and played the light across the floor until it reached the red brick wall of the living room. He crept across that space, mindful the flashlight beam stayed low and well clear of the three tall windows on the far side of the room. Now, in addition to the smell of the forensic team's chemicals, he could smell something far less clinical. Blood was rotting in the grain of the wood. The entire living room reeked of it. Combined with the antiseptic bite of the print-developing chemicals, the room was close and thick with a smell like bandages peeled off an infected wound. And it was painfully hot. The police left the air conditioning off, and the living room's west-facing windows let in the sun all afternoon.

Breathing shallowly, he went to the bedroom.

It started here.

He risked letting the light shine up the wall behind the bed, then let it roam upwards. Fine blood droplets misted the ceiling; the spray was thicker as it came down the wall towards the bedframe. The mattress and box spring were both missing. The forensic team would have bagged them both and carried them to a lab, for trace analysis. A spill of semen, a single hair. He could see the things Allison stored under her bed: a Prada shoebox, a giant Tupperware container of folded sweaters, a low cardboard box of photo albums. Dust bunnies were strewn around, motionless in the breezeless air.

The blood trail started by the bedframe, crossed the floor between his feet, snaked through the living room, and ended in the kitchen. He imagined Allison being dragged by an ankle or by her soft red hair, off the bed and through the apartment. He followed the trail into the kitchen, knowing before he got there what he would find, knowing that this time he was early enough but not too late. The apartment hadn't been cleaned yet, so what he was looking for would still be here.

He knew very little about his quarry, but there was one thing about which he was absolutely certain: sometimes he came back.

It might be two days after, or even as long as five, depending on how long it took for the girl to be missed, the police to be called, and the forensic team to finish its work. Then, sometimes, but not always, he would come back to finish what he'd begun. This was the first thing Chris had learned, the primary fact that governed all of his trips.

Sometimes the killer came back to finish feeding.

Chris stepped into the kitchen and turned off the flashlight. He could see well enough by the streetlight outside the kitchen window and the green glow from the clock on the microwave oven. There was a deep cast iron frying pan on the stove. The pan and stovetop were spattered in grease. A fork lay on the countertop. Its tines were filmed in oil and flecked with blood. Next, he put the light into the frying pan.

Left-over scraps of meat had blackened to crisps as the pan had cooled.

He had no doubt these were all that remained of Allison's breasts. There was no way the police would have missed this. They didn't see it because it wasn't there during the investigation. The killer had stayed close enough to watch them, to know when it was safe for him to come back and cook what was left of the pieces he'd hidden.

He turned to the refrigerator, knowing. A lidless, empty ice cream carton lay on its side on the floor in front of the freezer. He knelt and aimed his flashlight. The white cardboard inside the container was smeared with blood. He snapped off the light and closed his eyes. His ears were ringing and his head was spinning, rolling back and back and getting nowhere, as if he'd swallowed half a bottle of whiskey on an empty stomach. He breathed the rank air and counted backwards in his mind, still kneeling on the floor. Finally, he stood. He put the fork in a wax paper evidence bag and pocketed it.

He walked with his hands in his pockets until he got back to the street, then stripped off his latex gloves. It was a humid and hot night, but compared to the apartment, it felt cool and wonderful. The air smelled of oak bark and saltwater. He took three steps in the direction of his motel, then stopped.

The street was empty except for a beat-up blue van parked illegally in front of a fire hydrant. Its sliding door was open. A dirty blanket hung off the seat and dangled over the gutter; food wrappers were littered across its dashboard.

He saw a shadow rushing up behind him and turned, grabbing uselessly for his holstered pistol. The man was wearing a black ski mask and was already reaching out to him with an object the size of an electric razor.

"Good night, asshole."

He heard this gravelly voice at the same time the stun gun crashed into his chest and the two sharpened electrodes punched through his sweatshirt. The current was like a shotgun blast, but before Chris collapsed to the sidewalk, the man had him under the arms and dragged him five more steps to the waiting van and muscled him inside. The man crawled in after him and slammed the door.

Chris was face up on the wool blanket and the man in the ski mask was kneeling next to him. Chris jerked when he felt the needle go into his neck. He fought to sit up but the man had the stun gun's electrodes pressed into his throat. His arms were pinned somehow. He felt the needle probe deeper, then gasped at the stinging heat when the man pressed the syringe's plunger. The effect was almost instantaneous. His jaw went slack and his mouth fell open. His neck felt like molten wax and his head collapsed back into the blanket. The man in the mask was pushing on his chest but let up after about fifteen seconds.

Then the man's hand was over Chris's mouth and nose, pushing down hard enough that he felt the cartilage in his nose buckle as it bent sideways. He saw purple flashes behind his closed eyelids. His arms and legs might as well have been an amputee's fantasy. He couldn't move them at all.

"I could smother you. What could you do about that?"

Chris couldn't answer. He was choking, but his stomach was a mile away and he didn't retch.

The man pulled his hand away and Chris felt a little air trickle into his chest.

"Saw you eight months ago in Vancouver," the man said. "Hanging around the docks. I couldn't grab you then. This time I was ready. Wait'll you try this."

Chris could do nothing but wait.

He was screaming in his mind, begging his arms to move. The inside of the van felt like a pool of quicksand. He was sinking. The man had a new syringe in his hand.

"It'll put you down."

He felt the second needle's sting, and this time, the wave that spread from it was black and empty.

Chapter Five

Chris had no idea how much time had passed. He wasn't in the van anymore. He couldn't open his eyes. It was cold; his skin had tightened into goose bumps. Something was squeezing his face and there was a rushing feeling in his nose. It was too cold to be blood. There was a whirring noise from somewhere behind him. He kept trying to open his eyes but couldn't. He felt himself slipping back into the drug that had knocked him out. He told himself to focus. Where was the man in the mask? There was no noise but the mechanical whirring from below and behind.

I'm going to lose this fight, he thought, and slipped back.

Later, his eyes were open. He was looking at man in a chair for a long time before he realized he was awake. He was seeing himself in a full-length mirror. He was naked and was sitting in an ancient wheeled office chair. His arms were taped to the armrests and his ankles were taped to the single column that supported the seat. Many wraps of duct tape went around his chest and held him upright against the back of the chair. His mouth and nose were covered with a clear rubber mask that was held in place with webbing straps. A flexible hose led down and disappeared behind the chair. The whirring noise came from back there.

The mirror was about five feet away and might have been the door to a closet. There was thin carpet on the floor and an aluminum stand with a canvas webbing top. A fake marble sink was backed by another mirror and he could see plastic cups wrapped in plastic bags, and a basket of sample-sized bottles of shampoo and conditioner.

The only light came from the vanity over the sink. The rest of the motel room was dark. The mirror showed him the front wall of the room and the ends of two tiny beds. The window was covered by a curtain the same wet-sand color of the carpet. The mask and its machine whirred on and on and forced cold air up his nose and down his wide-open mouth. His tongue felt rough and dry. He couldn't move it. He studied the mirror again but couldn't see his clothes anywhere. He assumed they were in the room. The man would not have stripped him before bringing inside. Of course the gun was probably with his clothes and was no use anyway when he was taped to a chair, naked, and couldn't even close his mouth.

He heard the bedsprings creak and then heard steps across the carpet. He still couldn't turn his head but he could move his eyes. In the mirror, a shadow passed on the front wall of the hotel room. He had never felt this cold, but his muscles were so useless he couldn't even shiver. He heard a quiet click.

"He's awake. White male, I'm guessing mid- to late-thirties, approximately one hundred eighty pounds. No ID. Beginning interview."

It was the same gravelly voice. It sounded excited.

"Can you talk yet?"

He couldn't. All that came out, muffled through the mask and the forced air, was a low *aahhh.*

"Subject was given a muscle relaxant. Pancuronium. Not taking any chances with this son of a bitch. It might wear off in the next fifteen minutes."

There was another click. The man must have switched off his tape recorder.

Chris didn't try to say anything. He just looked in the mirror, waiting for the man to show himself. The TV turned on. He couldn't see it in the mirror, but from the sound he presumed it was mounted on a wall bracket in a corner of the room. The show sounded like a documentary about great white sharks.

The TV switched off when the show ended. Maybe an hour had passed; he'd heard a lot of commercial breaks. He'd suspected for the last five minutes that he could talk. The numb deadness in his face had given way to tingling and then to pain. He'd managed to work his jaw shut and to move his tongue side to side. His mouth was so dry he could not swallow. The same tingling was spreading down his arms and legs, but he did not try to move them. He told himself he wouldn't get the chance; it was useless to hope for one. He told himself if the time came, he wouldn't scream. He would hold on to the picture of Cheryl in his mind and swim down deep with it and wait until it was over.

"My name's Chris Wilcox. My wife was Cheryl Wilcox. If you ever knew her name."

He heard the man walk close to the corner, just out of view of the mirror. There was another click.

"Subject says his name is Chris Wilcox. Wife is Cheryl."

The man stepped into view. He was still wearing the ski mask—or had put it back on before stepping around the corner. He was taller than Chris and bulkier, and the rasp in his voice said he was past his fifties.

"You're not what I was expecting when I took you," the man said.

Chris just looked at him in the mirror. He could see himself as well, tied to the chair and hooked to the breathing machine. The image didn't fill him with confidence.

"I watched you go in. Perfect touch with the lock. Stupid to come out the way you came in. Who the fuck is Cheryl Wilcox?"

"Cheryl Arianne Wilcox, M.D. Red hair, green eyes. Murdered December 13, 2003, in Honolulu."

"You're the husband?"

Chris just looked at him.

"Shit." The man disappeared behind the corner. Chris heard the sound of a laptop booting up.

"You say you're Chris Wilcox, I can check that right now."

"Do it," Chris said.

He flexed the toes on both feet and tried his ankles out. They were working fine again. He tried his knees and found strength there. The tape securing his ankles to the chair was too strong to break, but he could feel it stretch very slightly. He looked at the chair in the mirror. It was a rolling office chair from the early sixties with five steel wheels, a central column, and adjustable arm rests that moved up and down with the push of a thumb button on the inside edge of each armrest. The steel, painted battleship gray, felt cold and thick against his legs. He pressed the left armrest button and lifted his left wrist. The armrest slid upwards on its steel post. Another centimeter and it would lift free of its mounting bracket. He pushed the button again and slid the arm rest back to its original position.

Chris closed his eyes, held his breath and imagined he was choking. His stomach lurched and when it came, it was painful and loud. The clear rubber mask filled up with vomit, which the air tube blew back into his mouth. He coughed and heaved, then threw up again. Now he really was choking.

From his doubled-over position, eyes tearing up from the spasms, he saw the man in the mask come around the corner. Chris was struggling to breathe, retching and convulsing. Some of it was real. The man took three steps closer, then moved to the front of the chair and leaned down to pull back the mask. Chris's right shoulder was angled away from the man, so he chose that arm. The distance would give him a longer swing. He pushed the button on the armrest, and pulled it, together with its steel rod, up and out of the chair. In the same motion he leaned back as far as he could, threw his arm out to the side, and then swept it back against the man's head. The impact caught the man on his left temple. The force of the blow spun the chair all the way around. The tube to the breathing machine tangled in Chris's feet. The man had fallen on one knee and was struggling to get up. Both his hands were on the dirty carpet. Chris pushed the button on the other armrest, freed it, and clobbered the man in the nose with his left fist. He had never hit anything so hard in his life. His hand exploded in pain, but the punch was perfect. The man was down. The front of his ski mask was wet with blood. The man jerked twice and then lay still. He was breathing through his smashed nose, blood oozing from the ski mask at his nose and from his temple. Chris swiped his forearm across his face and dislodged the rubber mask with its load of vomit. He took huge gasping breaths. He wanted to pause, to just breathe and wait for his heart to stop pounding, but knew there was no time.

Chris spun in the chair and caught the wall next to the bathroom door. He looked behind himself, gauged the distance and the amount of resistance he'd get from the carpet, then pushed hard. He rolled backwards, going diagonally across the narrow hall to the bathroom. He came to the wall on the other side, swiveled in the chair, pushed off the wall, and rolled backwards to the foot of the closer bed in the main part of the room. He pulled himself along the end of the bed, then pushed across to the second bed. His things were bundled against the headboard. He pulled his way up and grabbed his clothes, feeling immediately for the heft of the Glock in the sweatshirt. The gun tumbled out but he caught it before it fell on the floor. He could tell it was still loaded by its weight, but he took a second anyway to yank out the magazine and see the cartridge at the top. Then he slammed it back into place, chambered a round, and took the safety off.

His folding knife was still in the pocket of his jeans. He cut his shins twice and his wrist once in his hurry to slice through the duct tape. Then he was free of the chair and he stood up, the pistol in his left hand and the knife in the other. The man's cell phone was on the foot of the other bed and Chris picked that up too, carrying it so he could drop it quickly if he needed to use the knife. The man was just starting to sit when Chris came around the corner and leveled the gun at him.

"Lie on your face and put your hands on the back of your head."

The man hesitated and Chris came within three feet of him.

"This is a forty-five," Chris said. "I've been shooting a hundred rounds a week for six years. Right now it's loaded half with steel jackets and half with hollow points. Your guess is as good as mine which is first. Lie on your face."

This time the man lay and clasped his hands together over the back of his head.

"Take off your mask. Easy and slow. Set it to the side."

The man complied.

"Lift your face so I can see it."

The man had close-cropped white hair and a tan face with small crow's foot wrinkles next to his eyes. Chris had never seen him before.

Without taking his eyes off the man, Chris turned on the phone, switched it to speaker mode, and dialed. Mike picked up on the third ring.

"This is Chris. I got you on speaker. You hear me?"

"Loud and clear."

"Good. You got something to write on?"

"Yeah."

"I got a guy here with me. He's going to tell you his full name, birth date, and social security number."

Chris held the phone out to the man.

"Go."

"Aaron David Westfield. September 24, 1947. Five three three, two four, eight two seven six."

"You get that?"

"Got it," Mike said.

"Good. Now Westfield is going to tell you the names of every bank that has an account in his name. Westfield, go."

The man paused, thinking. "Wells Fargo, checking and savings. Citibank, credit card. Morgan Stanley, various investments. USAA, savings."

"Mike?"

"Got it."

"Westfield is going to tell you his home address."

"1042 Thistle Way, Edmonds, Washington, 98603."

"Rent or own?" Chris asked.

"Own."

The man put his face back on the floor, resting on the carpet on his left cheek.

"Mike?"

"Here."

"Check this guy out as fast as you can. I want a picture of him. Email it to me; I can use this phone to get it. And see if the phone I'm calling on is registered to him. Send me everything you can in ten minutes."

Chris hung up the phone. When he moved to put it in his pocket, he realized he was still naked.

"Crawl into the main room and lie on your face."

The man crawled, and Chris backed up, keeping pace with him. He kept the gun leveled at the man's head. When the man was on the floor between the ends of the beds, Chris went back to the pile of his clothes. He sat on the bed and kept the gun trained at the man while he pulled on his underwear and jeans one-handed. He kept it at that, because he wasn't about to risk pulling the sweatshirt over his head with the man still in the room.

"Your man as good as you hope?"

"Yeah."

"P.I. or cop?"

"P.I. Shut up."

Chris felt in his sweatshirt pocket, finding the wax paper evidence bag holding the fork from Allison's apartment. He opened the bag and looked inside. The end of the fork was still smeared with oil. In the brighter light of the motel room, he could see tiny droplets of blood on the tips of three of the tines.

"You touch this, take it out, or anything?"

"No."

It hadn't taken Chris long after he'd come awake to decide he probably wasn't in the same room as the man who'd held this fork and used it to eat Allison Clayborn's breasts. He was pretty sure he'd already be dead if that were the case. But still, Westfield could be dangerous.

"Good. You've got no idea what I went through to find this."

The man grunted.

"Or maybe you do," Chris said. He reached for a tissue from the box on the small table between the beds and used it to wipe the vomit from around his mouth. He dropped the tissue on the bedspread and took another for his chest.

"Let me ask you something. What was the respirator thing for?"

"Precaution. I never dosed anybody with Pancuronium. Wasn't sure what it would do. They use it in lethal injections—keeps the guy from writhing around. I thought maybe it'd completely shut down your diaphragm and you'd die of asphyxiation without a little extra help."

25

Chris looked at the machine on the floor where it was still half tangled in the wheels of the old office chair. Then he recognized it as a forced-air breathing machine, the kind sold on late-night television. A snoring cure.

"Some precaution. Was it your wife?"

"Yeah."

"What year?"

"1978."

"Jesus. That's thirty-two years ago."

"I know. It's what first clued me in you weren't him. After I had you in the van and I got a look at you. You'd have been what...?"

"Three," Chris said. "Your wife was a redhead, green eyes?"

"Yeah."

The cell phone chimed and Chris looked at it. It was an incoming photo and text message from Mike. He opened it and looked at the text. *Photo is Aaron David Westfield on day promoted to Captain. From website for* USS White Plains *vets. Other sources confirm. More info by regular email in five minutes.* Chris scrolled to the picture of Captain Aaron Westfield in his dress whites. The picture showed the same face as the man on the floor, the beginnings of crow's foot wrinkles just touching his eyes. Chris guessed it was twenty years old.

The phone chimed again, this time just a simple text message.

Chris read Mike's message, which answered the biggest question he had left. *The guy was on his ship in the Strait of Taiwan when Tara Westfield was killed at Sasebo. Never a suspect.*

Chris added the unwritten last sentence: no one ever caught Tara Westfield's killer. He reengaged the safety on the Glock, tucked the gun into the back of his jeans, then bent to put on his sweatshirt.

"Can I buy you a cup of coffee or something?"

Aaron Westfield rolled over and sat up. He put his hand up against his nose and massaged it gently. It was already swollen, but the blood had stopped flowing.

"Maybe I should wash my face first."

"Okay."

"Maybe you should too."

Chapter Six

They found a twenty-four-hour coffee shop on Strand Street, empty but for the college kid behind the cash register. The cashier put his book down when they came in, giving Westfield's broken nose a long second look. They ordered black coffee and took seats around a low table in the far corner. Unframed paintings of abandoned-looking buildings hung on the brick wall next to Chris's chair. They had an unfinished quality to them, blank spaces on the canvas like overexposed photographs. The painting on the wall nearest Chris was the abandoned warehouse that eventually became Allison Clayborn's condo. Chris looked at it and blew on his coffee.

The drive over had been mostly quiet. Chris sat in the passenger seat of the beat-up van with the window down. At red lights he could hear the waves rolling onto the beach. At one point he'd asked Westfield if the van belonged to him or if he'd stolen it for the job, and Westfield said it was his. He'd only stolen the Texas plates. The discarded fast-food wrappers and old army blanket told of a long drive from Washington without many stops.

Chris took a sip of his coffee, looked away from the paintings, and saw Westfield watching him. He seemed to be waiting, so Chris said the first thing that came to mind.

"If he killed Tara in '78, he must've just been getting started. He can't have been much older than eighteen, and I'd bet he was more like in his twenties."

"Why?" Westfield asked.

"As far as we know he's not from Japan, right?"

"No reason to think that."

"If he's out at night doing his thing, he probably wasn't there on a trip with his parents. So he's definitely older than eighteen in '78."

"But not too much older than that, or else, thirty-two years later, he might not be able to stay at it."

"Exactly," Chris said. "Maybe he was military?"

"Maybe. That only narrows it down to a few hundred thousand

people."

"True. And he kills women all over the world, so there's no reason to think Japan was any more significant to him than anywhere else he's been."

"Unless it was his first," Westfield said.

"Any reason to think that?"

"No."

When Westfield frowned, the lines on his face made him look older. In the hotel room, Chris thought of Clint Eastwood. The kind of hard-ass who'd keep coming at you even after a bullet should've put him down. But now, whatever Westfield was thinking just made him look old. And tired of it.

"That's the problem with this whole thing. We're so far behind the situation, all we can do is react. That's not where you want to be."

Westfield took a sip of his coffee and winced, then stood and walked to the counter. Chris watched him talk to the kid, who bent beneath the bar and came up with a plastic cup of ice and a napkin. Westfield put a few chunks of ice in the napkin and held it to his nose. He dumped the rest of the ice in his drink.

"Hot coffee's not the ticket, huh?"

"Not with this."

"Sorry," Chris said, and meant it.

Westfield shrugged. "It's okay. I'd have done the same."

"You did. How many have you gone to?"

"Six. I know about others, but a lot of them are overseas and I don't have the funds."

"When'd you first figure it out?"

"The pattern? In '96, after I got out of the Navy. I mean, I'd never stopped thinking about it. How could you?"

"You can't."

"When I got out, I was in Guam. *White Plains* was grounded there by Typhoon Oscar. When it was over I stayed ashore. First decommissioning the ship, then a job in the staff office. I stuck out four more years. I'd been in the Navy since I was eighteen. After Tara was killed, the Navy really was a family. They closed around me like brothers. The men in Sasebo, we're talking enlisted guys—Marines—took up a collection after she was found. She was a civilian, but the Navy paid for her funeral. Then I got out, and didn't know what to do. I decided to go to New Zealand and just think for a while. I could fly free on any Navy plane that had a spare seat, and there was a seat going to Wellington. I'd worked nonstop since she'd died and then I was out and had nothing. You know what it's like."

Chris hadn't worked since the day he'd gotten the call about Cheryl. He'd left his office with half a sentence typed on a document he never thought about again. Six months later, when his partners finally realized he wasn't coming back, a secretary brought him the things from his office. He'd never even looked in the boxes. They were from another man's life.

"You went to New Zealand and before you knew it, you'd been on a barstool for a month and a half. Yeah. I know about that."

Westfield took another swallow of his iced coffee.

"I was renting a room in Wellington, near the docks. Downstairs was a bar. At first when I got there, I did some hiking. Went out in a small sailboat, fished for snapper. It all seemed fake, like I was in someone else's body. You know that silence, when you're alone on the sea or in your house and the only thing breaking it up is the wind, or a clock ticking in some other room? And you think to yourself, is this really it? Is this really what's happening to me? Then I started stopping in the bar before bed. Then, before lunch. Finally I just stood outside the door before breakfast and waited for them to open. They had a little TV in a corner. I didn't pay much attention to it. I was just drinking. I don't know how long I'd been there. Maybe three weeks, maybe a couple months. I looked up and saw a news story on the TV. They had a picture of the victim."

"She looked just like Tara."

Westfield nodded. "Like Tara. Like Cheryl and Allison Clayborn. They could've all been sisters. There's this reporter standing on the street outside the house where she'd been found. Says the police are getting counselors for officers who'd worked the scene. That it was so bad no one who'd been inside would talk about it. And that he'd—I heard this clearly, because he'd done it to Tara."

Westfield paused and looked around. They were still alone in the coffee shop. The kid behind the bar was sitting at a stool reading his book. Westfield lowered his voice anyway.

"He'd eaten her face."

Chris nodded and closed his eyes. Westfield went on.

"I learned more later. Found the doctor who did the autopsy. I didn't have to get him drunk; he already was. I just told him what I knew and he told me the rest. The killer took her face off with his teeth, just ripped it off. She was still alive. The other parts, he cut off and took away."

"And then you knew," Chris said. He didn't open his eyes.

"I knew. But I didn't know where to start. How do you explain something like that? Who do you explain it to?"

A group of five college-aged kids came in and set up laptop computers around one of the tables on the other side of the coffee shop. Chris thought they might have been medical students. He remembered with a shiver the coffee shops where he'd spent late nights with Cheryl in his last year of law school while she was in her first year of medical school. They'd thought the future was a wide-open road. He pushed that away.

"That's something that always bothered me," Chris said.

"That there's no official investigation?"

"Each one's handled by local cops who've got no idea what's going on in the town next door, let alone what happens in New Zealand or Japan or Vladivostok."

"You'd think at least the FBI would keep track," Westfield said. "What's it they have? VICAP? That computer tracking system?"

"We picked it up. The thread's just sitting there where anyone could find it."

"Maybe because we wanted to see it."

The sun was coming up. Chris looked at his watch and was surprised it was only six in the morning. He felt like it should be mid-afternoon. He drank the rest of his coffee and pushed his chair back from the table.

"I'm going to walk back to my motel, get some sleep. I'm dead on my feet."

"I'll drop you off."

Chris shook his head. "I'd rather walk. But let's talk later."

"Punch in your number." Westfield handed over his phone.

It was a mile back to his motel. He stopped in his room to drop off his Glock and pick up his wallet and cell phone. Then he went back out and bought a burrito from a breakfast truck and sat on a bench on the seawall opposite his motel. He was too tired to think coherently. He ate the burrito and felt the sunlight warm his face. When he was done he balled the foil tightly and tossed it into the trash can next to the bench. He took out his phone and called Mike.

"You all right?" Mike asked, as soon as he picked up.

"Yeah. We had coffee and then I walked back to my motel. I don't know where he is now, but I'm not too worried about him."

"I think he's legit."

"I agree."

"What do you want me to do?"

"Come to Galveston. There's a direct flight to Houston that'll get you here tomorrow morning. Can you do it?"

"I'm on it."

"Bring all the files on a laptop. We'll sit down with Westfield and compare notes. He's not as thorough as us, but he's been at it longer. Maybe he thought of things we haven't."

"You're working with him, from here on?"

"Both of us are. Call me when you get a car, and I'll tell you where I'm staying."

He moved to hang up the phone and then brought it back to his ear. "Mike, you still there?"

"Yeah."

"See what you can find out about the FBI's VICAP network. How's data entered, how's it disseminated, who has the power to make entries, who decides what goes in."

"VICAP...okay."

"I'll see you when you get here."

He went back to his room, put the *Do Not Disturb* sign on the door, and turned the air conditioner up to full blast. He took a shower and came back to the cold, darkened room, and got into the bed.

It must have been an hour later that he heard the knock. He wrapped a towel around himself and went to the door, quietly, to look through the peep hole. A redhead in her late twenties or early thirties was standing there. She was reaching out to knock again when he opened the door.

"I think you got the wrong room," he said.

"I don't think so."

He'd only opened the door enough to poke his head out, but she shouldered past him and came inside. He shut the door.

"We know each other?"

Now that she was in the room, he saw she was holding a pistol in her left hand. She was wearing a gray wool skirt, a wrinkled blouse, and high heels. The pistol looked expensive, and she held it so casually and without evening pointing it at him that he guessed she knew exactly how to use it. As usual, his Glock was on the other side of the room.

"You don't know me. Have a seat."

They sat across from each other at the round table in front of the air conditioner. She put the gun on the table and kept her hand on it.

"I saw you go into my sister's apartment building. You picked the lock. You were inside for fifteen minutes. Then you came out; you got Tasered and kidnapped. You were driven to the south side of the island and I watched you get carried into a motel room. You were there for about three hours. Then, you and the other guy went and had coffee on Strand Street. My sister got murdered last week, her fiancé is in a mental hospital, you're breaking into her apartment and getting kidnapped, and then you're having breakfast with your kidnapper at five in the morning before walking back here. So what I want to know is, what the *fuck*?"

"Allison Clayborn was your sister?"

"I just said that."

"Twins?"

"No. She was a year older than me. Nobody will tell me what's going on, or if there are any leads; I can't see her body; I can't get in touch with my parents; the detective in charge of the case hasn't returned any of my calls; I don't know where Ben is."

"Why can't you reach your parents?"

"They're on a cruise in Turkey. Will you stop asking questions and please tell me what the fuck is going on?"

"Can I get dressed? I wasn't expecting anybody."

"No. Maybe later. Right now I want answers."

He moved his hands up—slowly, so she wouldn't think he was reaching for the gun—and ran his fingers through his hair. Then he rested his elbows on the table and put his forehead in his palms. His reconnaissance from the night before might as well have been on network TV. How many other people had watched him?

"Six years ago my wife was murdered in Honolulu. She'd come home early from work to jog on the beach. No one ever found the killer. He—I'll spare you the details."

But her eyes said he couldn't spare her, that no gap in his story would veil what she already suspected. So he told her.

A police officer came to his office in Honolulu, and told him his wife had been found.

Found? He hadn't known she was missing.

He went with the officer, all feeling receding from his body. He rode in the passenger seat of the cruiser, up over the Pali Highway and down through the tunnel in the mountains to the other side of the island. It was raining by the time they got to the pass, and came harder on the windward side.

He'd asked too many questions. *How had they found her in the house? Why were they looking? Who said they could go inside?* The officer had been evasive, then finally gave answers Chris wished he'd never heard.

A neighbor reported screams.

Dispatch sent a unit to roll past the house and the cops saw blood on the front steps. The door was unlocked. No one answered when they called, so they went inside.

Later, disoriented by grief, Chris would think he'd sabotaged his last chance. She hadn't really been dead until then. If he hadn't asked the questions, it could have all been taken back.

But that chance slipped away, if it had ever been a chance. They came to the house. The yard was a parking lot for police cars, evidence vans, unmarked detectives' cars, all of them sinking into mud beneath the soaked grass. He could see the blood on the threshold of the door, still bright and wet. A man wearing plastic bags on his feet was taking photographs of the doormat. Someone took Chris's elbow and looked at another officer.

"This the husband? The fuck they bring him for?"

Chris shook off the hand, pushed past the detective, past the photographer. Inside there were more of them, technicians everywhere with bagged feet, gloved hands, and shower caps. He called Cheryl's name. Halogen lights mounted on tripods filled the living room and illuminated the kitchen.

"Grab him, don't let him past."

He made it to the kitchen and saw her on the floor in front of the oven. They dragged him away a second later, but by then he'd seen enough. He could, and would, replay that single second for days at a time.

He hadn't recognized her face. Only her hair. One eye was gone; the other stared straight up. Her breasts were cut off and gone. It looked like an animal had chewed off her vulva. Her fingertips were missing at the first knuckle. The skin of her stomach, upon which he used to lay his head, had been ripped off and her intestines hung in loops over the knobs of the lower kitchen cabinets, as if thrown there in a hurry to get to something else. Much later, he learned her intestines had been tossed aside to get at her liver, which was never found.

They dragged him outside.

Other people—line officers, forensic technicians—had already vomited next to the bushes where he knelt retching. Six months later, when the police hadn't found a single suspect, he began his search on a simple premise: anyone or anything capable of something so awful had done it before and would do it again.

His search took him first to Mike Nakamura and then all over the world. He told her the last six places he'd been: Vanouver, Manila, New Orleans, Sydney, Vladivostok, Stockholm. And now Galveston.

"You think this is what happened to my sister?"

"Yes."

"How many has he killed?"

"Thirty-six I know about. That's going back ten years, the definite ones. I don't think I catch them all. And he's been doing it a lot longer than a decade."

"When you find this guy, you'll kill him?"

"Yes."

The young woman turned the gun away from him. Then she asked a question he didn't expect.

"You still live in that house?"

"No. I had it torn down. Sold the vacant land. I bought a different house in Kaneohe. I thought I should stay close, because I thought I was looking for someone close by. Then I learned that wasn't true, but I stayed in Kaneohe anyway."

"Since he's everywhere, it doesn't matter where you live."

"That's right."

"What do you do?"

"This."

"What about before?"

"I was a lawyer."

"What'll we do next?" she said.

"You could tell me your name."

"Julissa Clayborn."

"I'm Chris Wilcox."

He held out his hand, but instead of shaking it, she took it and held it. She looked dizzy. They just sat that way for a moment, their hands together on the table. Her hand was so warm, the skin soft. How long had he been huddling by the memory of Cheryl, as if that could sustain either of them? He turned away from her green eyes, feeling naked. He went to the bathroom, took off the towel, and changed into jeans and a polo shirt.

When he came back, he told her about the meeting with Aaron Westfield and Mike Nakamura.

"I want to be there," Julissa said.

Westfield was right—they could have been sisters, all of them.

"What I'm doing isn't legal. And it isn't safe."

Her eyes dropped and he followed her gaze to the pistol on the table between them. It was a match grade Sig Sauer. The chrome plating was worn on the barrel from coming in and out of its holster in a hurry.

"You lost everything and took this up because you had to," she said.

He nodded.

"My sister was my best friend."

When he didn't say anything, she picked up the Sig Sauer and put it back into her handbag. Then she looked at him again.

"When you told me, you brought me into it. We both know there's no way back. And I could help you more than you think."

She reached into her handbag and brought out an ID card in a clear plastic holder. She slid it across the table and he looked at it. This time he nodded again, his eyes closed. She was right. There was no way back.

He'd wasted enough time looking for that path.

"We're meeting as soon as Mike gets to Galveston."

"Good," she said.

"I need to sleep," Chris told her. "I'm sorry."

"Can I stay a bit? I'm not ready to drive anywhere."

Chris nodded to the room's other bed, which was still made. "Sure."

He remembered what it was like in the first few weeks of shock. Nothing was strange. He'd just gone from one event to the next as if dragged on a rope. He got into the bed closer to the air conditioner and pulled the covers up to his shoulders. Whatever Westfield had shot into his neck was having secondary effects. That, or the adrenaline was wearing off. His face felt leaden. He was half asleep when he heard Julissa turn back the covers on the other bed and switch off the lamp on the table between them.

She was asleep when he woke that night. Her ID card was still on the table, face up. He looked at her face in the photograph above the slightly raised seal of the National Security Agency and the nononsense corporate logo of Advanced Micro Devices. He turned the ID facedown and went out quietly.

Chapter Seven

Mike Nakamura arrived at the airport two hours ahead of schedule. He sat on a bench in the Japanese garden underneath the triangle of walkways leading to the Hawaiian Airlines gates. With the koi pond behind him, it was the best place in the airport to use a laptop computer without someone walking behind him and seeing the screen. He was researching VICAP; what he was finding scared the shit out of him. He looked around again to be sure he was alone, then checked his watch. Ten hours to Houston was a long time.

He couldn't believe he'd never seen this before.

The FBI ran the Violent Criminal Apprehension Program out of its training school in Quantico, Virginia. VICAP was an electronic clearing house for unsolved murders and sex crimes across North America and Western Europe. Law enforcement agencies could input data from their unsolved cases and search the database for similar murders. VICAP sought cases where the victim appeared to have been selected at random, and where the killing was motiveless or sexual. All cases were kept in the system indefinitely, and were electronically checked against each other to compile lists of possibly linked killings. The program could identify serial killings by matching the signature aspects of each crime.

Mike knew VICAP fairly well. He'd been a Honolulu Police Department detective before Chris gave him a fulltime job working on the Cheryl Wilcox case. He uploaded Cheryl's killing into VICAP himself.

After talking to Chris, he'd called a friend who was still with HPD and asked for a favor: to borrow a Law Enforcement Online password for a couple of hours. Once he'd gotten to the airport, he'd logged into VICAP to find out what the FBI knew. In the database, he entered search parameters that would surely have picked up Cheryl Wilcox's file. A search as simple as "*victim sex: F*victim hair color: red*loc: Honolulu*MO: cannibalism*" would surely have brought up Cheryl's file and no other. But instead, the system came back with an even simpler response: *No results. Please enter new search parameters and try again.*

He searched for all cold-case murders in Hawaii and scrolled through the results. Unsolved murders in Hawaii were vanishingly rare. VICAP listed five, going back to 1988. There should have been six.

Cheryl's case was not in the system.

He searched for the New Orleans case. The young woman there, two and a half years ago, had been a Tulane student named Robin Knappe. Robin's landlady found her in the gingerbread shotgun house she'd rented for two years on Magazine Street near Audubon Park. Both of Robin's breasts, her left buttock, and her lower jaw and tongue had been missing and were never found. Even a police force as beleaguered as the post-Katrina NOPD would have entered such a case on the VICAP network. The most rookie detective would've taken one look at the case and thought to do it. But Robin Knappe was missing.

New Orleans had the highest murder rate in the country, even after Katrina when a third of its population never returned. The city accounted for over a hundred and thirty cold-case murders on VICAP, and Mike scrolled through them all to make sure he hadn't missed Robin somehow. She was simply not there.

The girl in Vancouver was a seventeen-year-old high school senior, supposedly spending the weekend with her girlfriends. In fact, she was camped out on her boyfriend's father's sailboat at a marina near Granville Street. Her boyfriend walked to a brewpub near the docks, returning forty minutes later with takeout dinners and a growler of beer. Jill Moyers was completely dismembered in that short span. She bled so much the sailboat's automatic bilge pump switched on. The boyfriend dropped his bags and sprinted to the boat when he saw the slurry of blood and seawater pumping from a bronze thru-hull fitting near the boat's stern. This was in the long-shadowed final light of a northern evening; the harbor was crowded and busy as people readied their boats for winter. But there were no witnesses, and no one even heard a scream. Three people in adjacent boats had seen Jill lounging with a magazine on the boat's bow around the time her boyfriend was getting their dinner. Police speculated the killer might have swum across the narrow channel under the Granville Street bridge and then climbed the sailboat's transom ladder. This never went any further than speculation—the killer was never caught.

And Jill Moyers was nowhere on VICAP.

The implications stunned Mike. Either police incompetence was more deeply rooted than his own experience led him to believe, or something far worse was happening. He tried to call Chris again, but his telephone was still switched off. He left another voicemail, asking Chris to call if he could. Then he closed his laptop and paced the airport walkways until his flight was called.

Chapter Eight

Julissa looked at her watch in the dark. It was four in the morning. She was alone in Chris Wilcox's motel room. She did the math and realized she'd been asleep about sixteen hours.

That made sense.

She hadn't slept much since she'd learned about Allison. Ben's call came while she was in a traffic jam on the lower deck of Interstate 35 on her way to work in Austin. She had calmly pulled off at the nearest exit ramp, parked in front of a bagel shop across from the University of Texas campus, and had tried to call Allison at home. The man who answered the phone identified himself as Detective Gonzales, Galveston Police Department. She'd told him she was Allison's sister, that she wanted to talk to Allison. He asked her where she was, if she was in Galveston. When she answered, he told her to stay in Austin; they'd call her. He took her number and hung up.

Then she drove to Galveston.

Her phone battery died somewhere between Austin and Houston. Too many calls, to too many answering machines. Ben didn't pick up. Her parents' cheerful voicemail said they were en route to Istanbul. She pulled off Highway 71 in La Grange and bought a charger and adapter for her car's cigarette lighter at the WalMart on the outskirts of town. As she drove, she called and left messages. She called her sister's phone number and a different detective answered but she didn't quite catch his name. Kentwood, or maybe Ken Wood. She got back on I-10 and headed for Houston, hitting ninety on the empty stretches. She'd stopped once in the parking lot of a Cracker Barrel restaurant to call Dave Chan. They'd been at AMD's embedded security division since graduate school. Dave was technically her supervisor, but they ran their division like partners.

Sitting on the second bed in Chris Wilcox's motel room, with her knees pulled up to her chest, she couldn't quite recall what she'd told Dave or how many days ago that had been. He was the first person she'd tried to call who not only picked up the phone, but who actually spoke with her. She was pretty sure she'd lost it. She remembered sobbing and telling him she didn't know where she was. Allison was dead, maybe. She had to say maybe because it wouldn't be real until she saw her sister's body.

"Take as much time as you need. I'll take care of everything here. And we'll do anything to help you."

She'd said thank you. Bizarrely, she'd almost told him that she loved him before she hung up, which was odd, because he was just a friend. Maybe it was the shock. Or just the gratitude that someone finally talked to her. She pulled out of the Cracker Barrel parking lot and drove the rest of the way to Galveston, crying and banging on her Acura's steering wheel.

If almost telling Dave that she loved him was bizarre, the next three days were surreal. She didn't have perfect recall, but now it seemed she spent most of the time in her car or on the phone. The police wouldn't let her up to Allison's apartment. She watched from the street as the marked and unmarked police cars and forensic vans came and left. She went to the main station and walked in, asking for Detective Gonzales. She waited half an hour and was finally told Detective Gonzales was not in the building, but that he would call her. So she drove back to Allison's place and just watched the front. Her head was thumping with a headache that part of her realized was probably related to dehydration. She had a licensed Sig Sauer match pistol in her glove compartment and at some point in the last three days she had transferred it to her lap. What could she say? She was a twenty-nine-year-old computer scientist with a Ph.D. from M.I.T., but she was also a Texan and she liked to shoot handguns. But she had never held a gun for comfort before that night in the car.

She stood from the bed and went to wash her face. She didn't like what she saw in the bathroom mirror. Her blouse was wrinkled but the wool skirt was holding up. She took off her nylons and threw them away. She put some of Chris's toothpaste onto the tip of her finger and did the best job she could at brushing. She wanted to take a shower and go back to bed. Instead, she found her car keys on the bedside table and the Sig Sauer under her pillow, and started towards the door of the motel room. Chris had taped a note to the door. *Julissa: You were asleep when I woke. I'll probably be on the beach across the street. Chris.* His cell number was beneath his name. She left the room and went to her car, locking the pistol in the glove compartment. Then she walked over the motel's gravelly parking lot and crossed the empty street. Chris was on a park bench on the sea wall; he turned at the sound of her high heels on the pavement.

"Hey."

"Hey," she said, and raised her left hand. "Sorry about that. You probably think I'm nuts."

"It's not a problem. I mean, I don't think there's anything wrong with you."

"Thanks."

She sat on the bench next to him and looked out at the waves. They rolled in and broke along the sides of two jetties made of granite blocks. The surface of the Gulf was black except for where the waves broke white and foaming on the rocks.

"You been up long?"

"Four or five hours. I took a walk on the beach and then I was just sitting here. I guess I'm awake for the rest of the day."

"Up for a drive with me?" she asked.

"Sure. Where to?"

"WalMart. I think I've been wearing this suit four or five days. And these shoes are getting to be a pain in the ass."

She extended her knees and held her feet up, soles pointing to the ocean.

"Those don't look like the best." Chris pointed southwest. "I think there's a WalMart that way. Couple miles down the seawall."

They drove in her car.

Chris told her he'd gotten several messages from his private investigator, who would be landing in Houston in a few hours. On his walk, Chris had stopped in the lobby of the Hotel Galvez and had reserved a block of rooms for them for their meeting. She nodded.

They parked in the mostly empty lot and walked to the store. Workers in blue vests ran floor-buffing machines through the harshly lit, empty aisles.

"You grow up in Texas?" Chris asked.

"Near Austin. I went to U.T. and then did my doctorate at M.I.T. It was just an accident I came back. AMD recruited me while I was still in grad school."

"What do you do?"

"I design embedded security circuits for microprocessors. I work for AMD but right now I'm on loan to the NSA."

"Codes and stuff?"

"Yeah. Sort of."

They walked to the toiletries aisle. She put shampoo and a toothbrush into her cart, then a razor. She went alone to the clothing section and picked a few simple outfits, some shoes. She thought a moment about the larger picture of what she was doing, then decided not to waste her time. She supposed the bottom line was that she trusted Chris Wilcox. If he'd wanted to hurt her, he could have done it while she was asleep in his motel room. He'd told her his story and she'd believed it.

And he was the only person in Galveston with a coherent plan.

It never occurred to her to let him go back to his life while she went back to hers. Their lives had intersected, however randomly, and now he was inviting her to join his private revenge club. Allison wouldn't have blinked.

She spent less than ten minutes picking things out, then came back to the front of the store and walked until she found Chris in the magazine section. He folded that morning's paper and put it under his arm along with a world map rolled in a plastic tube. He also had dry erase markers and a little plastic tub of colored pushpins.

"For the meeting today?"

"Yeah."

He followed her to the register.

They couldn't check in to the rooms at the Hotel Galvez until noon, so they went back to Chris's motel. She took a long shower and washed her hair. Her Sig Sauer was on the toilet tank, within arm's reach of the shower. She had a feeling that for the rest of her life, she would know exactly how far it was from reach. She stepped out of the shower and toweled off, wondering how many years would pass before she stopped discovering the daily consequences of Allison's death. Chris might be able to educate her on that.

She dressed in new denim shorts and a tank top, then yanked the tags off her sandals and put them on. She came out with a towel around her hair and tucked the pistol back into her purse.

Chris was sitting on his bed with his laptop computer open.

"Thanks," she said.

"Not a problem. Your phone rang, though." He nodded at her phone, plugged into its charger on the floor near the air conditioner. "I didn't answer it."

She flipped through the menu to see missed calls, expecting to see the number of her parents' international cell phone, or Ben, or Dave

Chan. Instead it was a number she didn't recognize.

"Galveston's area code is 409, right?"

"I think so."

"Then this must be the cops, finally."

She redialed the number and put the phone on speaker. She held a finger to her lips and looked at Chris. He nodded. Someone picked up on the third ring.

"This is Timothy Spaulding."

"Julissa Clayborn. Someone at this number called me."

"Julissa—thanks for calling back. I'm the district attorney for Galveston County and I called you with regard to the investigation of your sister's death."

"Killing."

"Sorry. I hope I didn't call too early."

"I was up."

"Good."

They could hear papers being moved on a desk, then the unmistakable sound of someone sipping hot coffee.

"I was hoping you'd come in for an initial meeting to give us background information. I know it's a hard time, but the detective said you were in town."

"I've been in town since the day she was found. No one wanted to talk to me."

"Believe me, that was an oversight. We apologize. You can imagine we're a bit overwhelmed."

"I can imagine. Look, where should I meet you, and when?"

"How about this afternoon?"

"I can't, I'm busy," she said. "How about tomorrow morning?"

"That works."

"Where?"

He gave her the address of his office in the new courthouse annex.

"All right, Mr. Spaulding. I'll see you then."

She hung up and tossed the phone into her purse.

"Why not meet him today?" Chris asked.

"First things first. Your meeting sounds more likely to get somewhere."

He half-smiled and stood from the bed, closing his laptop. "I hope so."

Chapter Nine

Just before seven in the morning, and prior to the shift change at the industrial shipyard, Seawolf Park Road on Pelican Island was quiet. Aaron Westfield was parked in a rented Crown Victoria on the grass shoulder near the gate to the submarine park. He checked himself in the mirror on the underside of the sun visor. His nose was swollen and slightly crooked, but his sunglasses hid the bruising around his eyes. He was wearing a black suit with a pressed white shirt and a cheap red tie. He carried a Navy-issue sidearm on a shoulder holster that would be visible if he slid back his jacket's lapel. He unlocked the glove compartment, put his wallet inside, and picked up the FBI badge in its leather folding case. The badge was a moderately priced fake, but most people had never seen a real one anyway. The Crown Victoria was a more expensive prop, at ninety dollars a day, but his '81 van would have given him away faster than the badge's shortcomings.

He started the car and drove back along the two-lane road that ran through the mesquite brush. Gated roadways led off to the industrial docks and offshore rig repair yards that lay out of sight on the other side of several hundred yards of blighted scrubland.

He passed a series of painted wooden signs with colored pennants stapled around the sides: *Pelican Island Bait & Tackle. Live Shrimp. Cold Beer. Ice.*

Westfield could see white oil tanks and crane towers. The superstructure of an offshore oil rig rose over the low trees. He approached a guardhouse in the middle of the Newpark Marine Fabricators entrance drive. Farther down the drive, a sign prohibited smoking, and beyond that, another sign advised that hard hats were required. Westfield had a hard hat on the passenger seat.

He held his badge out to the guard when he stopped next to the booth. Not a Hollywood flip-and-close: he held the badge out long enough for the guard to lean out the window and actually read his name.

"Yes sir?"

"I was hoping to see Mr. Broussard, get him to let me talk to the shift that's just coming off. They're not in trouble or anything."

"There a problem?"

"Just helping a local investigation. Some of the guys welding that rig might've had a good view four nights ago."

"This about the woman got killed?"

"You know anything about that?"

"What I read in the paper."

"Any of the guys say anything?"

"No. But I don't mix with the crew much." He pointed at the Wackenhut security badge on his shirt. "I'm not like a regular employee here, you know?"

Westfield nodded. "You know where I can find Broussard?"

"You hurry, you might catch him in the office. He's usually in the yard at the start of each shift. I can hear him on the radio."

"Where's the office at?"

The guard took a printed map from a cubby hole in the booth and leaned out the window.

"It's in a portable building, you know like a trailer? Here, next to the tank farm."

"What's Broussard look like?"

"Big guy. Hard to miss."

"Thanks."

He put on the hard hat and started down the drive towards the repair yard.

The shift was changing when he parked on the bed of crushed oyster shells fronting the channel between Pelican and Galveston islands. He could see men moving along the catwalks on the rig towards elevators supported by scaffolding—the night shift crew coming down. The drilling rig was at least twenty stories high, not counting the derrick that rose from the side of the platform. A helicopter pad leaned off the rig like a book on the edge of a high table. Sparks from a cutting torch cascaded through the massive steel support columns and fell onto one of the giant pontoons that held the entire structure afloat. Westfield stepped out of the rental car and walked to the dock.

A giant man in a sweaty T-shirt and suspenders was waiting for the elevator at the base of the scaffolding. He saw Westfield coming and turned, needing to take three steps instead of simply pivoting.

"You the fella from OSHA or the new EPA guy?"

"FBI, actually." He held out his badge, but Broussard didn't even look at it.

"Whatever it is, we didn't do it." He burst out laughing, then held out his hand and shook Westfield's. "Cliff Broussard. Whatcha want?"

"I was wondering if I could borrow your office ten minutes, talk to the night-shift guys. That's them coming down?"

"Sure. That's them. What for?"

"You hear about Allison Clayborn?"

"Girl in Galveston, got killed last week." Broussard now looked serious. "Look, we do background checks on every employee. No drugs, no jail time, no bad credit checks. And I keep all their time sheets myself. So I'd know if someone was skipping out nights—"

"I'm not looking for a suspect. I'm looking for witnesses."

"Witnesses?"

Westfield pointed across the channel at the renovated warehouse on the other side.

"Allison lived right over there. Third floor. Anyone working on the rig at night could look across the channel and see through her window."

Broussard looked across the channel for a moment and then back at Westfield.

"That's gotta be three hundred yards."

"It's worth a shot."

Broussard shrugged. "Take enough shots, you'll hit something."

"That's the idea."

Broussard took a handheld radio off his belt clip. "Del, you copy?"

"I read you."

"Have crew three go to the mess hall. I need you guys about half an hour. Then ya'll can go home." Then he looked at Westfield. "There's ten of them on the crew. We get a lot of turnover, but this crew's been steady the last month, so they was all up there that night. We'll go up and meet 'em. It's better than my office if you wanna talk to everyone at once, plus it's got the view."

They stepped into the cage of the elevator and rode along the scaffolding that rose parallel to one of the rig's four main support columns. Westfield had stepped aboard his fair share of colossal naval warships, but he wasn't sure he'd ever seen anything afloat as large or as strange as this rig.

"What's the yard doing to it?"

"Just reinforcing some of the welds. Took some hurricane

damage."

"The crew's mostly welders?"

"Night crew's all welders. Daylight, we work other trades."

Westfield hadn't come here with an overdose of hope, and now he was even less optimistic. If every man was wearing a hooded welding mask with a narrow, smoked-glass lens, he doubted any of them saw a thing. Even if a man lifted his mask for a few moments, or took a break, Westfield knew welders had poor night vision. He used to tell his junior officers if they had a choice between a welder and someone else to stand a night watch, choose someone else.

The elevator came to a stop and Broussard pushed the cage door to the side. They stepped onto a catwalk that ran underneath the rig's main platform. Orange spray paint marked areas on the support columns which required re-welding. They followed the catwalk to a ladder and climbed up to the main deck. As far as Westfield could tell, they were standing underneath the heart of the drilling rig. A derrick climbed skyward from a nest of pipes and machinery. Broussard led them out from beneath the pipes along a pathway painted onto the steel deck. They came to a structure that looked like a house trailer. Broussard opened the door and let Westfield go inside first.

The nightshift men were sitting around two long tables on one end of the crew cafeteria. Westfield didn't take off his sunglasses when he stepped into the room because he didn't want to explain his black eyes. The nose was bad enough. He looked at the crew. Ten tired men in sweat-stained work clothes looking at a man in a suit and wondering when they could go home. He pulled the badge from his jacket pocket, letting them all see his side arm in the process, and held it up.

"I'm Special Agent Sanderson with the FBI, assisting local police investigate the killing of Allison Clayborn."

The men stirred and looked at each other, then back at him. Now they were looking at him warily, whereas before they'd just looked tired. He waited a moment and then went on.

"Her apartment's just across the channel from this rig. I could see her windows on the elevator coming up here, and I could see them from the catwalk where I got out. It looked to me like a lot of the workspaces up here have a fair view of the apartment. It happened Friday night, five days ago. Any of you men see anything strange that night?"

Nine of the men turned and looked at the tenth. The tenth man was tall and thin. He wore steeltoed work boots, coveralls, and a denim shirt with the sleeves ripped off. A green cross was tattooed on his right biceps and was fading away into his tan. He had wispy hair that reached his shoulders. He carried the look of a man who might have cancer but kept smoking anyway.

"You saw something?"

"Yeah."

"Any of you other men?"

They shook their heads or looked at the tables where they sat. Westfield turned to Broussard, who was just inside the doorway, shifting his weight from one foot to another and wiping sweat from his brow with a wadded paper towel.

"Can I take this man and speak to him in private awhile?"

"Go right ahead. You need any these others?"

"No, they can all go."

"All right. Ya'll heard him. Hutch, you tell this man whatever he needs to hear and show him whatever he needs to see. Then you bring him down when ya'll are done."

Hutch nodded.

"Don't leave him alone up here and don't let him take off his hard hat. Last thing we need is a missing FBI guy on this job site. You think OSHA and the EPA are pains in your ass."

The other nine men on the crew left the room and Broussard stepped out and closed the door. Westfield sat down across the table from the man and shook his hand.

"David Sanderson," Westfield said.

"Jimmy Hutchinson. Crew mostly calls me Hutch."

"You know what night I'm talking about?"

"Yeah. Fourth of July. We worked that night same as any other night. But I didn't see her that night."

"You saw her other nights?"

"Sure. You see her, you *notice* her, you know?"

"You knew her?"

"Not exactly. Not her name or nothing like that. We recognized each other, is all."

"Explain."

Jimmy Hutchinson had been fidgeting with a crumpled box of cigarettes. A plastic lighter was wedged between the cellophane wrapper and the cardboard box.

"Mind if I smoke?"

"Signs everywhere say you can't."

"Let's go outside. I'll show you where I was working."

Westfield followed the man back out onto the main platform. They followed another painted pathway through the machinery until they reached a stairway that led up to the helicopter landing pad.

Hutchinson spoke over his shoulder.

"I was welding a new cargo boom up here. You know, so they can unload a chopper and swing stuff to the main deck without having to carry it down the stairs? Anyway, this is where I was that night."

They climbed the staircase and walked across the painted markers for the helicopter. Red lights on small white posts protruded from the deck around the landing circle. They went to the far side of the deck and leaned against the bright yellow railing. They were twenty stories above the greenish-brown channel water. Tug boats churned up mud as they pushed a barge around a corner into a berth. Across the water was the warehouse where Allison had lived.

Hutchinson pointed, not to Allison's apartment, but to another old brick building on Strand Street.

"I live over there. I been at Newpark since they bought out Todd's Shipyard, and I was at Todd's for fifteen years before that. Been a welder and industrial diver. Got my harbor pilot's license but the money here's better. I bought a condo over there a couple years ago, right after my divorce. Neighbors on either side seen my work clothes and figured I was trouble." He lit a cigarette and breathed out smoke. "Fuck 'em, though, right?"

"Let's talk about Allison Clayborn."

"I started seeing her around Strand Street and Warf Street right after I moved there. Sometimes on Seawolf Park Road on Pelican Island. She'd jog in the mornings, see? I put in for daytime shifts in the winter time, so it must have been winter. Sometimes I get up early and walk to work—it's only a couple miles—and I'd see her jogging. Beautiful girl. I'd wave, she'd wave back."

"Ever talk to her?"

"Later we talked a few times. You know Sampson & Son's?"

"Seafood place, right behind her condo."

"Yeah, right there." Hutchinson pointed across the channel and they could see the low concrete building. Fresh red paint advertised shrimp, crabs and fish. *Direct from the boat to you*, the sign said.

"I go in there sometimes in the morning. These days, for me, that's like dinner time. I might pick up half a pound of shrimp and some gumbo crabs. Some oysters. Stuff like that. I'd run into her sometimes. She'd be in her jogging clothes still, probably shopping for dinner. They're only open in the morning, so if you want to go there, you go in the morning."

"And you talked?"

"Sure, I'd say hi. We recognized each other by then, passing on the bridge over to Pelican Island so many times. She liked stuffed flounder.

She'd get that a lot."

"How'd you know where she lived?"

"We walked out of Sampson's once. Me with my shrimp and crabs and her with her flounders. You know, I'm in my fifties, look like a working man, just got divorced. She's in her twenties, probably educated as hell. Looks like a movie actress. I know it's not going anywhere and I'm not trying to make it go anywhere. Just passing the time of day, being friendly. She's friendly back. It's a clear morning, smells like salt and ocean. I been up all night on a rig—different rig, not this one—and I'm going back to my new place to put in some cabinets. I'm tired, but I feel good. You know, here's this pretty girl walking beside me, talking with me, next day is my day off so I can stay up late into the morning. Maybe have a shower and go down onto Strand Street and get a beer. I remember because it felt good talking to her."

"Talking about what?"

"I guess recipes. Seafood recipes. I asked her how many miles she jogs every morning, she tells me five or six. Then I tell her she might want to consider going back and getting a few more of them fillets if she's burning calories like that. She laughs. She asks how I'd cook them and I tell her, and then she asks if I'm a fisherman. No, I say, I'm a welder but I work on rigs and ships. Then she lifts her hand to wave and turns towards her building. She says something like see ya, and I say yeah. I see her around some after that, but that was probably the longest conversation we had. From up here on other nights I could sometimes see her through her windows, even from way up here and this far back, I could tell it was her. She had red hair and I could see that. But I didn't watch her like that. That wouldn'tve been right, you know, like peeping. I just looked out and saw her a few times. Knew which windows were hers. And that was fine, felt fine, you know?"

"Because you liked her."

"Yeah, I liked her. She was friendly. I see her in the window at night sometimes and she's inside and safe—probably cooking flounder fillets, pouring a glass of wine or whatever—and everything's okay. Like I got my whole world, and she's a little piece of it and—"

"—everything's as it should be," Westfield finished.

"Yeah."

"What about July Fourth?"

Hutchinson drew in on his cigarette and leaned over the railing to look at the water.

"I was up here working on the cargo boom. I'd welded its base from scaffolding underneath the landing pad the night before. I was up here using a cutting torch. Around midnight I put everything down and leaned against the rail here for a smoke. I looked across at her window and it was lit but I didn't see her. Then I looked at the water and saw something moving."

"What?"

"I guess it was a guy. I never seen anything like it. It looked like a man, swimming, out in the channel. In the middle of the night."

"Can you describe him?"

"Not really. He was in the water. I could see the skin on his back and legs, so he was probably wearing just a swimsuit. Maybe he was naked."

"Race?"

"White guy, I guess. I mean, just on skin color alone it's hard to say. He wasn't black. He could've been Asian, I guess."

"But you don't think so."

"No. You ask me why, I can't say why. He looked like a white guy, is all. Besides, how many Asians you seen in Galveston compared to how many white guys?"

"What about hair?"

"He was bald."

"Clean shaven, or bald?"

"I wouldn't know."

"Where was he swimming?"

"Up the channel, that way." Hutchinson pointed northeast towards Seawolf Park.

"What else you notice?"

"I mean, for one, I never seen anyone swim in this channel, day or night. Some divers might go in sometimes to work on the bottom of a ship. But nobody jumps in and swims. I mean, look at that filthy shit. Two, this was the middle of the night, in the middle of an industrial ship channel. But I guess what I noticed most was how fast he was swimming. I never seen anything like it. I never seen anyone swim in that...style, I guess."

"He have fins on?"

Hutchinson looked at the water and thought about it.

"No. At least, I don't think so. His feet kicked out of the water and I'd have noticed fins if he'd had them."

"What about his hands, could you see them?"

"No. He was swimming without lifting them up. You know? Not like a forward crawl. It was a—what do you call it? A breaststroke?"

He mimed a stroke, his fingertips together, palms out, arms parting and coming to his sides.

"I think so. Breaststroke."

"It was like that. His hands didn't come out of the water."

"Did he have an electric water scooter? Like the SEALS use to get into harbors?"

"Like Navy SEALS? I hadn't thought of that. I guess it's possible."

"But you're not convinced?"

"No. I saw a man swimming. He was swimming faster than I thought anyone could swim. But honest to god, it looked like he was doing it on his own."

"You see him get out of the water?"

"He stuck to the channel till he was out of sight."

"How far till you couldn't see him?"

Hutchinson pointed at a tug and barge coming towards them from Seawolf Park.

"Not far. Between us and that tug." He shrugged his shoulders. "It was dark."

There were more industrial docks on the Galveston side of the channel in that direction. On the Pelican Island side, there was another shipyard farther down the island. Beyond that lay Galveston Bay, and past that, the Gulf of Mexico.

"You sure about the time?"

"Yeah. I looked at my watch when I took a break and I checked again when I got back to work. I started working again around 12:45, so I saw him sometime after 12:30."

"How fast was he swimming?"

"That's the thing." Hutchinson pinched the end off of his cigarette and flicked the butt into the wind. "It had to be faster than a man could run. Twenty miles an hour, maybe. I didn't see him long."

Bullshit, Westfield thought. He looked at the water.

"You sure it wasn't a dolphin?"

"I know a dolphin when I see it. This was a man."

Chapter Ten

Down the beach from the Hotel Galvez, a wooden pier stretched three hundred feet into the Gulf, carrying an assortment of T-shirt stands and shell shops, the kind of seaside junk stores Chris had seen a lot of in the last six years. The last building on the pier was a snack stand. Chris and Julissa were sitting backwards on their barstools, facing the ocean. Chris had an iced tea and Julissa was drinking a Coke. They hadn't said anything for about an hour, but that seemed okay.

At five minutes till noon, they paid their tab and walked back along the pier and out to the sidewalk. It was easily a hundred degrees outside. They crossed Seawall Boulevard at the light, then walked through the gardens and into the lobby of the Hotel Galvez. Chris checked them in, retrieved their bags, and took key cards from the desk clerk for five rooms—one room for each of them, plus something that had been advertised as a corporate board room. He thought it was high time to take this thing from an amateur pursuit to a full-blown corporate endeavor. He had some hard evidence, he had some partners. There was a hint of a trail. Mike Nakamura called when he finished paying for the rooms.

"This is Chris."

"I just got to the hotel. I'm in the parking lot."

"Good. Julissa and I are already here. So we're just waiting on Westfield."

"Julissa?"

"I'll introduce her when you get upstairs. You bring all the files?"

"Yeah."

"Meet us in—" he shuffled through the key cards until he found the one for the board room, "—1020. We're on our way up now."

They rode the elevator to the tenth floor and Chris opened the double doors to the boardroom. It had a twenty-foot conference table surrounded with leather swivel chairs. Two sets of glass doors led to a curved balcony overlooking the Gulf of Mexico. There was a dry-erase board, a cork bulletin board. A projection screen could retract from the ceiling. The projector sat in the middle of the table, cables waiting for a laptop.

"This'll work." Julissa said.

"Yeah." There was a knock on the door. "Here's Mike."

Mike came in with Aaron Westfield behind him.

"Saw him in the lobby and recognized him from the pictures," Mike said, indicating Westfield with his thumb.

Then he saw Julissa and froze. Westfield was in the process of taking off his tie and unbuttoning his collar, but stopped when he looked past Chris and saw her.

"Guys, this is Julissa Clayborn. Allison Clayborn's sister. She saw me break into the apartment two nights ago, then saw Westfield take me. She followed us around all night."

"Then you split up, so I could only follow one of you," Julissa said. "From what I'd seen, Chris was less dangerous, so I followed him."

"And interviewed me at gunpoint."

"He's told you what we're doing?" Westfield asked.

"Yeah. And I'm in."

Westfield gave a slight nod.

Julissa came around Chris and shook Westfield's hand, then Mike's.

"If anyone's hungry, let's order lunch now. Then maybe I can get us started while we're waiting," Chris said. They ordered sandwiches and cold drinks from the room service menu, then gathered at the table. Chris went to the bulletin board and pinned up the map he'd bought earlier that morning. He stood at the head of the table with his hands on the back of a chair.

"I want us to start thinking of this room as our headquarters," Chris said. "I got it for two nights. If we haven't moved on to someplace else in a couple days, and if everyone's still on board, we can get it for as long as we need it. I asked you all to come because I think if we put together everything we know, and combine every talent we have, we have a better chance. Mike's a former homicide detective and a P.I., Aaron was a Navy captain and was posted all over the Far East. Julissa's a computer security expert at AMD and the NSA. I used to be a lawyer. All four of us probably still have connections in law enforcement, industry or government. We have favors we can call in. I thought maybe we could start by listing every killing we know."

Mike booted his laptop and connected it to the projector. He went to the wall near the minibar and used the switches there to lower the screen and dim the lights. Then he came back to the table.

"Chris and I developed a search program over the years. We've used it to identify thirty-seven possible victims, starting in 2000 and going up to July 4th, when we found Allison."

"But," Chris said, "we also know Aaron found the pattern earlier, in 1996. Maybe we should start with Aaron so if there are any trends that are developing over the years, we see them by going chronologically."

"Makes sense," Mike said. He looked at Westfield. "You want to take over?"

Westfield took his own laptop from his backpack and put it on the table. He opened the screen and cleared his throat.

"First one I was aware of was in 1978. That was in Sasebo, Japan. My wife. Tara."

He went to the map, found the little box of pins Chris had left on the shelf under the bulletin board, and placed a pin carefully at Sasebo.

"Two of you know this, but I'm just telling it for Julissa. I was aboard my ship when it happened. We were patrolling in the Strait of Taiwan. The Navy took me off the ship by helicopter to Kaohsiung, then arranged a transport plane to Sasebo. She was already dead three days by the time I got back. They found her in our apartment off base. She'd walked to the commissary that afternoon, then came back with groceries. They found her the next day. Her boss—she gave English lessons to a couple of kids—called the base when she didn't show up."

Mike projected a map of Sasebo onto the screen. Westfield went over and studied it.

"Been awhile since I looked at this."

"Take your time," Julissa said.

"Zoom in on this part here," he said to Mike. He stepped back and waited for the image to resolve.

They were looking at warships moored along piers in a deeply inset bay. Westfield pointed where the piers met the land.

"This is the base. I don't know about now, but in '78 the commissary was here." He touched the screen and it dipped away from him. He waited for it to stop swaying.

"She would've walked along this road, come out the eastern gate, then followed these wharves. There was a pedestrian bridge over this expressway. The apartment was here."

He lightly touched a blue-roofed building.

"Military or industrial wharves?" Chris asked.

"Industrial."

"The first thing you notice about all of these is how close they happen to the water. Almost without exception the victim is found somewhere within a mile of a major shipping harbor."

"There's always a close connection to wharves," Westfield said. He looked at the map again and then came back to the table and sat. "I'll skip what he did to her. We all know about that."

"Maybe you better not skip it," Julissa said. "What he does to the women is important. We should talk about it. Even if it's unpleasant."

Mike Nakamura looked up from his laptop. "I agree."

"All right. Makes sense I guess." Westfield looked out the window and then looked at Chris.

"The autopsy was conducted by a U.S. Navy surgeon, on the Sasebo base. The investigation itself was done jointly by local Japanese detectives and military M.P.s. At the time, the Navy wouldn't give me the full autopsy report. It wasn't until '98 that I got the whole thing. I had to hire a lawyer and file a Freedom of Information Act request. The surgeon didn't come to a full conclusion as to cause of death. It could've been blood loss or blunt force trauma. A third possibility is she died of shock, which to my mind, is a nicer way of saying she died of pain. Either way, it's certain she died *in* pain, if not from it."

Westfield swallowed and looked at them. "He made sure of that."

He spoke quietly and slowly.

"I'll start from the top and just go down. He ate off her face. There were bite marks in her facial bones underneath her nose. Which he bit off. The surgeon's report says he may have been shaking his head back and forth. That's the only way to explain the shape of the bite marks. Ever see a dog kill a squirrel? It would've been like that. He bit and shook until he pulled her face completely away from her skull. Most of it was missing and was never found. The presumption being, he swallowed it."

Julissa had turned white. She was squeezing a ballpoint pen in her right hand.

"Aaron, I'm so sorry—"

"After he was done with that, he ripped her shirt off and started on her chest. Her breasts—he ate them both. Probably at that point, while she was still alive, he raped her. The semen samples got lost in the shuffle. I checked in '96."

Chris saw that Mike was looking at him. He nodded slightly. This was news to both of them and he would bring it up.

"The surgeon speculated she was still alive for about ten minutes after the rape. Based, I guess, on the amount of internal bleeding. But by then she wasn't conscious anymore. She probably died when he ripped her stomach open and took out her liver. The skin and muscles were ripped and not cut, so he likely just tore her open with his bare hands. You want me to go on?"

"No," Julissa said. "Oh god."

She got up and went to the sliding doors, stepping to the balcony. Chris could see from the movement of her shoulders that she was sobbing. Mike Nakamura went to follow her, but Chris held out his hand.

"Leave her alone, Mike."

Mike sat down. Chris looked at Westfield.

"You say they found semen?"

"Yeah. I know. I guess I hadn't focused on it until just now. There's been none at the scenes I've investigated since '96."

"And the bite marks."

"That too," Mike said. "The victims have all been savagely attacked. But probably not with his teeth. So the one in '78, the murder of your wife, is different. We've never seen that."

"Why would he change his style?" Westfield asked.

"If it were just the semen missing, given the time that's passed, I'd say he was impotent. But it's the biting too. I bet in the last fifteen or twenty years he heard about DNA testing," Chris said.

There was a knock at the door and they all jumped. Julissa came back inside. They were all looking at the door.

Chris walked over and looked through the peephole.

"Just room service."

At first none of them would eat.

Chris was hungry and he suspected Mike was too, but Julissa hadn't even looked at the room service cart when the waiter pushed it in. Westfield looked embarrassed. Not that he should have been, in Chris's opinion. What had happened to Tara Westfield needed to be told. Maybe some good had already come from the telling. They knew the killer changed over time, adapted to avoid capture, learned from newspapers and paid attention to technology. For years Chris had imagined him as simply a raving beast, incapable of thoughts or plans or even fully conscious of anything other than his own blood lust. This was better, Chris thought. Some people might pity a rabid dog, but not this. No one would blame them for what they were going to do.

Mike, Westfield and Julissa were sitting at the table again. Julissa had found a tissue in the bathroom and was wiping her eyes. Chris went to the map and, from memory, marked the thirty-six cities in twenty countries from which he and Mike had culled news reports of linked murders. When he was finished, the pushpins were clustered in Scandinavia and along the east and west coasts of North America; they were scattered across Western Europe, and more thinly, across the Pacific and Asia. There were three in Africa: one in Alexandria, one in Lagos, and one in Cape Town. There was a lone pin in South America, in Buenos Aires. Other than the fact that each city was on the water, there was no connection between the dots on the map. Putting the locations in a chronological context didn't help at all. Mike read out the date and location of each victim, along with her name. Chris wrote each date on a small post-it note with a black marker and affixed each tag next to its correct pushpin. But this added nothing. The killings skipped from Asia to Denmark to Canada to the Caribbean. They had all come around the table to look.

"There's no organization," Westfield said.

"Maybe we can take something away from that," Julissa said. "Maybe he's not travelling all the time, from country to country like some kind of...I don't know...Lonely Planet backpacker who murders people. He has a home. He travels to kill, and then he goes home."

"That makes sense," Chris said. "If he were travelling all the time like a backpacker, you'd think we'd see a whole string of them on one continent for a couple years, then on a different continent for a few more years."

"On the other hand," Mike said, "he can't be travelling just to kill. Or at least, not all the time. I mean, if you're only interested in finding redheads, why go to Nigeria, or anywhere in Asia?"

"That's true," Westfield said. "He's probably traveling from a home base somewhere, but he must be traveling for some other reason. Trips to Western countries, maybe he's trying to find a victim. But the others must have another reason. Like business."

Chris got out one of the dry erase markers and went to the white board.

"Let's write down things we know. Maybe we can put that in one column. Then we can have another column for things we suspect."

He turned to the white board and in neat letters wrote, *Tries to hide his DNA* in the column he marked *Suspected*. Underneath that, he wrote, *Has a home base*. He shrugged. It was a start. But the column labeled *Known* was empty.

"Here's something we know: he's male," said Julissa. "The semen pretty much solved that mystery. If there ever was one."

Chris wrote it on the board.

"Victims are all redheads with green eyes," Westfield said. Chris wrote, *Redheads / Green Eyes* on the board.

"Rapist," Julissa said. "Cannibal."

"He's strong," Mike said. "I think we know that."

"It's fair to say we know he's at least middle aged," Westfield said.

"And we suspect he's probably older," Chris added. "Aaron and I talked about that."

Chris wrote all this down. He looked at them. Now they were all thinking, and that was good. Julissa was writing on a pad of hotel stationery. Mike was scrolling through files on his laptop. He thought if they could fight and move just one foot forward along the killer's trail, it would be easier to take the next step, and the one after.

"If we're talking about suspicions," Julissa said, "let's talk about why all these things happen near the water. That seems like our best lead by far."

"And if we're going to talk about the water connection," Westfield said, "I want to tell you what I did this morning."

They all looked at him. Westfield reached into his jacket pocket and brought out his FBI badge. He tossed it on the table.

"This is a fake. I bought it at a flea market in Seattle. Reason I'm wearing the suit is I went down to the shipyard across the channel from Allison's condo and spent the morning interviewing the nightshift crew. They got welders working on a rig over there twenty-four hours a day. Thought some of them might've seen something."

"You found someone?" Chris asked.

Westfield told them Jimmy Hutchinson's story, ending with Hutchinson's guess that the man was swimming twenty miles an hour.

"You think Jimmy Hutchinson is credible?" Mike asked.

"Credibility sounds like something you need in court," Westfield said. "I wouldn't bring Hutchinson to court. I wouldn't ignore him either."

"Also," Chris said, "it fits with the Vancouver case. At least a little."

He turned and looked at Mike. "Wasn't there a police theory in Vancouver—the young girl on the boat—that the killer might've come there by swimming across the channel, since no one saw anybody going down the docks?"

Mike nodded. "That's right."

"You think Jimmy Hutchinson actually saw him?" Julissa said.

"It fits. It's a strange thing to see. We can't directly connect one strange event with another on the same night, but it seems like too big a thing to ignore," Chris said.

"Maybe we can find other witnesses," Julissa said.

"I'll try," Westfield said. "There's a fishing pier out at Seawolf Park. If he swam that way, maybe someone would've seen. If anyone was fishing that night. As for Hutchinson, I believed him when he told me. He probably had a thing for Allison, but he wasn't a drunk and he wasn't a nutcase. And he didn't seem to think the story explained anything. He was just giving me what he had."

"But nobody can swim that fast," Mike said.

"Especially someone over fifty," added Julissa.

"Maybe he was wrong about the speed. It was dark, he saw a guy in the water moving fast. Maybe there's a tidal current through there that helps with the speed," Westfield said.

"Or maybe your question about the electric scooter was right. That could give him an extra five or six miles an hour. If he held it under his chest, Hutchinson wouldn't see it," Mike said.

Westfield shrugged.

"Escaping by water would be a good route, if he came here on a ship and planned to leave on a ship," Chris said. "Imagine it. He thinks the neighbors might've heard. The police might be on their way. He's probably covered in blood. The water's an easy way out."

"I can think of a lot of better things to do besides swim in the ocean at midnight while covered in blood," Mike said.

"I can think of a lot of better things to do besides everything this guy does," Julissa said.

They all looked at the white board, and after a while, Chris got up and wrote *Swimmer* in the column for suspicions.

They took a break after that. While the others moved their bags to the rooms he'd reserved, Chris descended to the lobby, found the hotel's business center, and printed the thirty-six files he and Mike had assembled. They didn't have one yet for Allison. He made four copies of each and went back upstairs to the conference room.

Mike had showered and changed clothes and was back at the conference table with his laptop. Julissa was out on the balcony with Westfield, but they came inside when they heard Chris.

Mike cleared his throat and looked at them.

"Before I came here, Chris asked me to take a look at the FBI's Violent Criminal Apprehension Program, see if I could figure out why there isn't an international manhunt on for this guy. Everyone familiar with VICAP?"

Julissa shook her head and Mike explained the network.

"Thing is," Mike said, "VICAP *should* pick up the similarities in all these crimes. All these murders—at least the ones in the U.S. and Canada—*should* be in the system. I mean, they all fit the profile. Unsolved, extremely violent rapes and murders that are totally random. It's exactly what VICAP was made to pick up. Chris and I wrote a simple search and filter program and found thirty-six of these just by going through Internet news stories. You gotta figure the FBI's program is more sophisticated than ours. If it had these cases in the network, it would've linked them in about a second. So I borrowed a friend's login and password and had a look at what VICAP is showing."

Chris felt his arms break out in goose bumps. He sensed what Mike was about to say, and what it meant. If they were chasing a rabid dog, it was either incredibly smart or incredibly well protected. Or both.

"I found only one murder on VICAP we'd expect to be there: Allison. All the others are gone. And you may think it's just police who are too stupid or too proud to work with the FBI, so they don't enter the data. But that can't be true. I was on HPD when Cheryl Wilcox was killed and I uploaded that case to VICAP myself. And it's gone."

Julissa scribbled on her pad and looked up. Chris could see she was drawing a flow chart.

"That leaves us one of three places," she said. "One: the killer's in the FBI, maybe works at Quantico, has access to VICAP, and erases each old case before he kills again so there are never two cases in the system for the computer to connect. Two: the killer has protection from someone high up with access to a person who can change the database. Or three: the killer, either by himself or by paying someone he trusts, is sophisticated enough to hack into the FBI's database and alter it."

Mike looked at her. "I think that about sums it up. I thought about it all night on the plane and I couldn't think of anything else."

"If that's true, we better make sure the FBI and the police never find out what we're doing. Our investigation has got to stay secret," Chris said.

"Why?" Westfield asked.

"Because no matter which one of Julissa's options you pick, the FBI's compromised. The killer's one of them, or they've got a mole, or the killer can hack their system. And it's clear he doesn't want anyone looking for him. So if he gets word of us—"

"He'll erase the data and then come after us," Mike finished.

Chris nodded. "That's the way I see it. And this isn't necessarily a bad development. If he's in the FBI, it gives us a suspect list. And if he's well protected or capable of hacking—that at least makes the pool a lot smaller."

Julissa's phone rang. She took it from her purse and stepped out onto the balcony. The men watched her through the glass sliding doors. When a few moments passed, Westfield cleared his throat.

"What're you guys thinking for the next step?"

"I have some ideas. I thought we should all talk about it and agree. So none of us repeats what someone else already did," Chris said.

"Divide up assignments," Westfield said.

"Yeah."

"Can you project a map of Galveston?" Westfield asked.

Mike nodded and typed at his laptop. A few seconds later the projection screen showed a satellite image of Galveston. Westfield went to the screen and pointed at the fishing dock at Seawolf Park.

"People on this pier might've seen a swimmer. Unless you guys have other plans for me tomorrow, that's what I'm going to check for. Anywhere else you think I should look?"

"What about these other two shipyards?" Mike asked. He circled the laptop's mouse arrow around two industrial yards on Pelican Island northeast of the one which lay directly across the channel from Allison's condo.

"I checked. Neither one runs a night shift anymore."

"How about the yacht basin on the other side of the channel?" Chris asked. The yacht basin had four long rows of covered slips and an uncovered fifth row, for sailboats, directly facing the channel. "Fireworks that night were on the Gulf side of the island. People might've gone over on their boats to watch. Maybe someone coming through the channel afterwards passed him in the water."

"I'll check."

The glass door slid open and Julissa stepped inside. She'd been crying again.

"My parents finally got off their ship long enough to call home and check their messages," she said. She went back to her chair and sat down.

"They coming home now?" Mike asked.

Julissa nodded. "Day after tomorrow."

She put her elbows on the table and held her head in her hands, her fingers lost in her red hair. Chris thought of Cheryl, sobbing at the kitchen counter when her father died of cancer. The muscles in his legs tensed, ready to carry him over to her so he could kneel at her side and take her into his arms. Instead he stayed in his chair and looked at a blank space on the table. Julissa raised her head, wiped her nose with the back of her hand, and pushed her hair out of her eyes.

"I'm sorry," she said. "Talking with them—it made it real again."

Chris nodded and Westfield murmured something too soft for Chris to hear.

"I'm still with you guys," she said. "I think I can probably help on the FBI hacking angle. At the very least I might narrow it till we can say for sure whether the files are getting erased from inside the FBI or from somewhere else."

"What would you need to do that?" Chris asked.

She bit her lower lip.

"A computer I pay for in cash. A dedicated Internet connection, nowhere near Austin. That's about it."

"All right," Westfield said. "So I'll follow up on the swimmer. Julissa's going after the FBI angle. Mike, what'll you take?"

"I can get the IDs and background of everyone who works in the VICAP unit. It might be hard, but with some careful footwork I can probably do it in a week."

Westfield nodded. "Chris?"

"I'll follow up on the evidence I collected from Allison's apartment."

Mike looked up and raised an eyebrow in question.

"What evidence?" Julissa asked.

Chris nodded. It was time to tell them.

"The thing I know about him, that I didn't write on the board yet, is sometimes he comes back to where he killed a woman. He did it with Cheryl. I didn't realize at first. After the murder I didn't go back into my house for three weeks. I stayed at a hotel in Waikiki through the funeral and until everyone in our families left. The police were finished with the house after four days. A detective told me I could call a cleaning service if I wanted, because they were through with the forensics. I called the next day, but it still took weeks before I went in the house. Even that was just to get a few things and leave again."

"What'd you find?" Julissa asked.

"Nothing. I didn't realize it until maybe a month later. I only saw the crime scene for a couple of seconds before they pulled me out. But I saw it in dreams. The dream was like studying a photograph with a magnifying glass. Every awful detail, a bit at a time. And then one morning I woke up and realized when she was killed, the countertops were bare. We had these new granite counters. Cheryl would polish them until they were like black mirrors. Except for the blood, they were like that. Bare and empty. But when I went into my house finally after three weeks to get some clothes, there was no blood anywhere, but there was a plate on the counter, and a frying pan on the stove and a fork and steak knife in the frying pan."

"Jesus Christ," Julissa whispered.

"I know. I didn't put it together when I saw it. I just left with my clothes. Maybe a month later, I decided to get rid of the house. At first I was going to sell it, and I had a realtor list it. She probably washed everything and put it away, thinking she was going to show the house.

But she never showed it. Instead I called a friend at the Department of Planning and Permitting and got a permit to have the house demolished."

Westfield looked up. "How do you know it had anything to do with him? It could've been one of the cleaners, even a sloppy cop, who cooked something from your freezer and didn't clean up."

"It came from the freezer all right," Chris said.

Thinking about it again made him feel cold all over. What chilled him most was the idea he'd been sharing the small island of Oahu with the killer for days. They might have passed each other on the street, or stood next to each other in the hotel elevator. Maybe they'd looked into each other's eyes.

"I don't know why I even found it. Movers were supposed to pack everything and put it in storage before the demolition. But there were some things of Cheryl's I wanted to get myself, so they didn't go missing. I went into the house to get them, and I was standing in our bedroom, looking in our safe for some of her jewelry. She didn't always wear her engagement ring. She was a surgeon. The ring wouldn't be good under a latex glove, so she took it off a lot. I couldn't find it in the safe. I remembered her joking about her grandmother, always hiding cash and stuff in the freezer. So I went downstairs and had a look. She usually kept the food she wanted to eat on the bottom shelf. Vegetarian frozen dinners, Lean Cuisines, that kind of stuff. There was a pint-sized container of vanilla ice cream at the back of the freezer. It had been there about a year. Maybe even two. I'd never thrown it out because it was hers."

He told them, speaking very quietly, about taking the carton out, prying off the frozen lid, and looking inside. It hadn't been full of jewelry. A lump of frozen red flesh had been stuffed in there. Unidentifiable, horrifying. Drops of blood and ripped tissue were frozen to the waxed cardboard sides, the pooled blood frozen into a round puck at the bottom. This was the last he ever saw of his wife.

"What I think now, and I've had a lot of time to think about it," Chris said, "is he eats his fill sometimes. He can't choke down any more. But he isn't satisfied, isn't done. And he doesn't want to walk away from the scene carrying anything."

"So he hides it where it won't be found, and comes back later, in his own time," Julissa said.

"Yes. And why would a forensic team look in the freezer if there's no blood trail leading to it, no prints on it, no connection? Why pull off the lid from an ice cream carton, or open a half-empty bag of frozen Brussels sprouts, if there's no reason to? They don't have time to turn over every stone. Just the ones they think they need to."

"He did this to Allison?" Julissa asked.

Chris nodded.

"That sick fucking son of a bitch."

"What'd you find?" Mike asked.

"A fork." He looked at Julissa's shock-whitened face and left out the grease-spattered frying pan, the empty ice cream container tipped over on the floor.

"Why would he leave something like that behind?" Mike asked. "He's so careful about everything else."

"Because he knew the police were done with the scene. He didn't think about people like us, coming in after."

"What're you going to do with it?" Westfield asked.

"I'm taking it to a company in Massachusetts, for DNA sequencing. There'll be DNA from Allison, but I'm betting there's DNA from his saliva. I'll get them to isolate it and then sequence it."

Westfield shook his head.

"That—DNA profiling isn't any good unless you have a sample from a suspect to match it to. What's the sample? They just match up a bunch of points on different genes or whatever, and compare those to the sample to see if they're from the same guy. If you've only got the one, what's the point? We don't have access to the evidence from the old scenes, before he started getting careful—stuff might not even exist anymore."

Chris nodded. He'd thought the same thing for the first year or two, until he'd done more reading.

"You're talking about DNA profiling. I'm talking about *sequencing.* They can do it now. The whole sequence, every base pair on every chromosome, start to finish."

"Then what, they'll give you a police sketch?"

"Not quite. But we'll have a description. Hair color. Eye color. Likely height and bone structure. Shape of his nose. Race. All kinds of things. I don't know, maybe we could take it to a good sketch artist."

"But sequencing must cost a fortune."

"A hundred thousand dollars. Maybe less. It gets cheaper all the time."

"You're just going to write a check?"

"Yeah. Or a wire transfer."

Chapter Eleven

A warm wind blew inland from the Gulf of Mexico and flapped the curtains in the dark conference room. Julissa stood on the balcony with her elbows on the carved stone rail. Bougainvillea grew from a terracotta pot next to her and climbed a trellis to tangle in the overhead wooden beams. She watched the lights of oil tankers moving slowly towards the coast from far out in the Gulf and sipped at a glass of whiskey.

After the meeting, she'd been able to reach her parents again. She told them she was in Galveston but didn't say what she was doing. Her mother had been hysterical in the first telephone conversation, but detached by the second. She'd either been given a tranquilizer or had tranquilized herself at a hotel bar. Her father kept asking if there was any chance it was a mistake. Had she seen the body yet? No? Then it could still be a mistake. A mix-up. He started telling her about another mix-up, a van load of girls on spring break. She told him to stop. It was real. She was meeting the district attorney in the morning; the autopsy was still underway. She didn't tell him everything she knew. But there was no point in letting her father lose himself in hope.

She'd hung up, left her hotel room, and come into conference room. It felt better in here. She looked at the map for a while, then moved out to the balcony with a drink.

When she and Allison were little girls, they lived in the hills outside of Austin, near Lake Travis. Scrubby woods of juniper and elm lay behind their house. There were limestone stream beds with the tracks of old wagons still cut into the soft stone. In one of the deeper pools of a spring fed creek, they could dive to see the footprints of dinosaurs in the petrified mud at the bottom. The best thing, though, in those summer days of running wild in the woods, was to play with the pair of brothers who lived across the creek. They had many games, but Julissa's favorite was hide-and-seek, with cap pistols. They played it all summer when she was eight and Allison was nine. Julissa would dream of it at night: new trees in which to hide, new boulders from which to ambush, her heart pounding in her sleep as her dreaming body raced down paths through the spear grass and around cactus patches, her feet sure and true as she leapt the old barbed wire fence and bolted across the pasture land that fell away to the limestone bluffs, Charlie or Dylan or Allison in hot pursuit, caps firing wildly.

That summer, her parents almost divorced. They locked themselves in a study, low conversations building to shouts. Whatever it was—she never learned, even after she became an adult—eventually passed. Her parents stayed married. But that summer's game was a good enough distraction; she was only aware for a few hours each week of the mysterious fracture cutting down the middle of her family.

Now she had Chris, Aaron and Mike to play with instead of Charlie and Dylan. They could play with real guns and DNA tests and could hack into the FBI's mainframe; they could ignore work and life and obligations and friends who didn't matter anymore, and go on an international hunt for a killer who was more animal than man. And that sounded, to Julissa, like the perfect antidote to the stifling reality she would have to face if she did not throw herself completely and unequivocally into this new game.

Allison's funeral.

All the rituals of collective grief played out, each stage of the wake and service and burial overseen by a fresh-faced stranger.

And then, when it was all over, she'd get up some morning to go back to work.

She heard the door open and she turned. Chris walked around the conference table and joined her on the balcony.

"Thought you'd be here."

"I looked in my room for the minibar and didn't notice it."

"What're you having?"

"Johnny Walker."

"Any left?"

She nodded towards the bar. He went inside, poured a miniature bottle of Jack Daniel's into a glass and came back. He stood at the rail next to her and took a sip from his drink.

"Allison and I used to play on the beach here when we were kids," she said. "Labor day, I guess. Probably Fourth of July a couple times too. I was thinking, if you knew someday your happy memories would all turn dangerous and black, would you go ahead and do the things you did to make the happy memories in the first place?"

"Yes."

She sipped her whiskey and pointed down the beach towards the old Flagship Hotel on its pier out over the water.

"We stayed there, mostly. Dad said it was the nicest hotel in Galveston when he was a kid, but by the time we stayed, it was run down. I guess you have nicer beaches in Hawaii."

"That's why we went."

"Straight out of school?"

"Cheryl was. I graduated three years before her, so I took the bar in California, worked in San Francisco and waited for her to graduate. She did her residency in Honolulu, and we stayed."

They didn't speak for a few moments. She sipped from her drink and wondered how far she could hurl the heavy glass tumbler from the balcony. If she hit the windshield of a parked car, what would happen?

"I've got to meet that Spaulding guy, the district attorney, tomorrow."

"I know."

"I don't want to."

She sat on one of the deck chairs. The lights from the oil tankers were reeling on a moving horizon. She steadied herself against the armrest.

"How many of those've you had?"

"This?" She held up the glass. "My fifth. I was down at the bar earlier."

She hadn't felt drunk at all until that moment, and then she felt it all at once. She finished her whiskey and set the empty glass on the balcony next to her.

"It's not my drink. Scotch, I mean. It's Allison's—she did a post-doc year in Edinburgh and came back a Scotch convert."

Chris sat on the balcony next to her chair. He leaned against the glass wall and put his feet out towards the stone railing. He didn't say anything, and she liked him for that. They sat listening to the wind blow off the Gulf. A dark band of clouds lay on the horizon. She could smell the rain in the wind.

"I wish you'd come with me to this thing tomorrow, the meeting with Spaulding."

"I don't know what I could do."

"Just be there. As a friend."

"All right."

They sat awhile. The clouds on the horizon were blotting out higher stars as they mounted up and moved closer. Julissa saw the first flashes of lightning, veiled in the thickness of the approaching front.

"I might go to bed soon," Chris said. He had finished his drink and held both of their empty glasses cupped in the palm of one hand resting on his lap.

"You think he's still in Galveston, this man?"

Chris thought about it for a moment.

"No. I doubt it."

"I hope not. I want to find him but I don't want him in this city right now."

"It's hard," Chris said. "Not knowing, I mean."

The wind was picking up. A few seagulls perched on the roof above them flew off and flared briefly in the white lights that edged the eaves before disappearing over Seawall Boulevard.

"Will you stay a bit and watch the storm come in with me?" she asked.

"Okay."

"We can go in when the rain starts."

He nodded.

Later, Julissa was in her room listening to the rain beat on the window and sweep against the walls of the old hotel as the wind rushed past. The lightning lit the room and then left her in a greater darkness waiting for the next flash. She imagined a swimmer, deep in the heart of the storm and far out in the Gulf, plowing headlong into the rain and breaking seas, fast as a runner, the waves showing green and steep in the flashes, great schools of hammerhead sharks parting like curtains to let the swimmer pass untouched. She pulled the blankets closer and eventually slept with the lights on and her gun on the bedspread next to her.

Chapter Twelve

Chris waited his turn to disembark from the 767 that had just landed in Boston. He walked up the jetway with his briefcase and followed the signs to the baggage claim. The fork from Allison's apartment was so valuable he hadn't risked its confiscation by trying to bring it through security in his carry-on. When his suitcase came along the conveyor belt, he pulled it to a quiet place beside a broken vending machine, knelt, and checked that the fork was still in its evidence bag. Then he zipped the suitcase and went to the rental car kiosks.

Though he'd hesitate admitting it outright to his new friends, Chris was rich.

He and Cheryl made a lot of money while she was alive and they were both working. But the heavy money came after she was murdered. As a surgeon at the beginning of a long and promising career, Cheryl had been very well insured. It was enough that Chris didn't need to worry, but more money came ten months later. Their house had been in a new gated development on the edge of Kaneohe Bay. The developer's brochures advertised it as a safe place to raise a family. A wrought iron fence surrounded the neighborhood, with guard booths at the entrance drive and guards at the walkway gates leading to the beach. Security cameras watched the common areas; each house was equipped with an alarm wired to the front guard booth. On the day Cheryl was murdered, the guard at the beach gates called in sick and the private security company never bothered to find a replacement. The guard at the entrance drive booth was asleep. To make sure no one saw him sleeping, he raised the gate to let all traffic pass, and he turned off the camera recorders so there would be no DVD from the guard booth camera showing him asleep. It may not have made a difference. The police later discovered the alarm in Chris's house was improperly installed and couldn't send a signal anywhere.

Chris had not been a tort lawyer. He never thought a lawsuit would fix anything. But when he learned how thoroughly Cheryl had been failed, he sued the security company, the developer, and for good measure, his homeowners' association. The developer had an eight million dollar insurance policy; the security company had three; and the homeowners' association had two and a half. The developer brought in its electrical subcontractor as a third party defendant; the sub was insured to the hilt. Chris negotiated a global settlement for ten million dollars, made the four defendants pay to raze his house, and got the homeowners' association to buy the vacant lot. His only concession was to sign a confidentiality agreement. He could live easily enough on what they'd saved before Cheryl was killed, and on the money from her life insurance. The rest was for revenge.

He was in Boston to spend some of that.

He drove his rental car into the city and left it with the valet at the Marriott Hotel near the waterfront. The sun was going down. He'd left from Houston shortly after returning to the Galvez with Julissa after her meeting with the prosecutor. She'd come out quietly, carrying Allison's autopsy report in a folder. She hadn't said much on the drive back to the hotel.

Now, standing in the room at the Marriott and looking out over Boston's harbor, he thought about calling her. To say what, precisely? He wasn't sure. He told himself it was because he'd gone so long with no friends. Now that he had some, he wanted them. But he knew a lie when he told it to himself. It was Julissa he wanted to call, not Aaron Westfield. He put the idea out of his mind and watched the sun go down. Then he showered, changed into slacks and a white shirt, and went downstairs.

The scientist's name was Dr. Gerard Chevalier. They met at the bar off the lobby. Chris had spoken to Dr. Chevalier on the telephone twice and had corresponded with him by email. He recognized the scientist from his picture on the company's web page. He was short and square-looking, in his mid-fifties with salt-and-pepper hair just above his shoulders. He wore golden spectacles and a dark suit. According to the web page, verified by Mike Nakamura, Chevalier held an M.D. and a Ph.D. from Harvard. He started Intelligene in 2004 after patenting a process for sequencing DNA.

Chris had been completely frank with him on the phone. Chevalier was willing to do business.

"Dr. Chevalier?"

"Yes."

"Chris Wilcox."

They shook hands and took a booth away from the other groups of people. A waitress followed them, and Chris waited until they'd ordered drinks and she'd left.

"How's Intelligene?"

"Good. We were profiled in the *New York Times* two months ago, business has been up since then."

"You own the company?"

"Technically, no. I started it. But we went public last year, so the investors are the owners."

"You're still the CEO?"

"Yes."

"You've got some freedom of action?"

Dr. Chevalier nodded. "I haven't forgotten our talk."

"Good."

"You found something? Evidence?"

Chris nodded. He opened his briefcase. Inside was a cardboard tube, the kind used for mailing photographs. Inside of that, in a wax paper evidence bag, was the fork he'd taken from Allison's kitchen counter.

Chris handed it across the table to Chevalier.

"Don't open it here."

"Understood. It's good you used the wax paper and not plastic."

"Like you told me," Chris said. He pointed at the bag. "You'll probably see two DNA sources. One's a woman, and you'll find more of her than the other. I'm looking for a man. The source for the man will be saliva, if there's any trace of him on this at all. The blood and other matter is from the victim."

Dr. Chevalier put the tube in the lapel pocket of his suit coat.

"You got this how?"

"You know my situation."

Dr. Chevalier nodded.

"You're uncomfortable, I can take it somewhere else."

Dr. Chevalier shook his head. "I just want to know where I stand."

"The fee?"

"Standard full sequence rate." Chevalier opened his own briefcase and slid a sheet of paper across the table.

"This is the escrow information. They disburse half right away, as a deposit. We'll give you the initial data as it comes in. When we give the full report to escrow, they disburse the other half."

"If you can't find any usable DNA from the male source?"

"Then I'll refund the deposit."

"Thanks."

The waitress came back with their drinks. Chris had a light beer and Dr. Chevalier had ordered a glass of pinot noir.

When she left, Chevalier took another set of documents from his briefcase.

"It's a violation of federal law to sequence a person's full genome without his consent. If you sign this waiver for me to sequence your own DNA on the sample you just gave me, then I won't have a problem."

Chris looked at the waiver and looked back at Chevalier. He hadn't considered signing anything that would link him to the evidence from Allison's apartment.

"It's all right," Chevalier said. "The simplest test would show you aren't the source of any DNA in the sample you gave me. Am I correct?"

"Yes."

"This way, I do the work after hours, but handle the fee through the books like a straight-up transaction. You get privacy, I stay clear with my shareholders."

Chris signed the waiver and pushed it back. Chevalier was right: if the waiver wound up with the Galveston police, it might help convict him of breaking and entering, or tampering with a crime scene. But not murder.

"How long for the full report?"

"A week and a half, assuming I find the right DNA." Dr. Chevalier raised his glass. "To a step forward, Mr. Wilcox."

They toasted and sipped their drinks. Dr. Chevalier held his wineglass up, between the dim overhead light and his eye. He swirled the wine in his glass and took another sip.

"I had some time to think about this after our last call."

"Yeah?"

"There are other tests I could do. Or contract out. If we can isolate a saliva sample, we can try running it through a mass spectrometer."

"What'll that do?"

"I read a paper a few months ago on stable isotope hydrology. Heard of it?"

"No."

"Basically, all ground water has a unique signature of stable isotopes. A person who lives in a place long enough builds these up in his body just by drinking the local water. Researchers put together stable isotope hydrology maps of the world."

"It works?"

"Last year, some archaeologists in London found an ancient grave. They did a spectrographic analysis of the victims' teeth and proved the skeletons were Vikings. No other artifacts in the grave, just the bones. These guys were herded naked to the edge of the pit. Then beheaded."

"Without that, the stable isotope whatnot, would there've been a way to tell they weren't English?"

"Assuming there was enough preserved DNA, maybe. But preservation of DNA in a bone over ten centuries isn't very likely. And there's been genetic intermixing between the English and the Scandinavians—even back then. Stable isotope hydrology can give proof of where someone actually lived, not where his ancestors came from."

Chris thought about it. Even if the chances of it working were one in a hundred, he thought it might be worthwhile. He imagined how much easier it would be if they could limit their search area to the cities served by one aquifer.

"I won't get my hopes up, but give it a try. Assuming you isolate anything that's his and not hers."

"We've got saliva and not bone, so it'll be different. We'll know where he's been getting his drinking water in the last couple months. If he's been traveling, it might show something different than what his bones would say," Chevalier said. "Anyway, I haven't bought time on a mass spectrometer since I was in graduate school. I don't know what it'll run you."

"You get enough spit to run the test, find out how much it is. I can add it to escrow. If it's less than twenty thousand dollars, and they'll do it without a deposit, just go for it."

"Deal."

"Email is the best way to contact me from here on," Chris said. They finished their drinks and Chris left a fifty dollar bill on the table to cover the tab. He shook Chevalier's hand, went back upstairs to his room, and booked the first flight to Honolulu.

Chapter Thirteen

Intelligene started in lab space leased from Harvard, moved to its first independent office after two years of drawn-out wrangling with the intellectual property division of the university's legal department, and finally settled into a newly built lab in the woods outside Foxborough a few months after its successful initial public offering. Dr. Chevalier had twenty-three employees, none of whom were in the lab after eleven at night. The parking lot was empty when he pulled into it, having driven to Foxborough directly after his meeting with Chris Wilcox. It didn't matter that none of the money was in escrow yet; it didn't matter that he had already put in an eighteen-hour day. He was too curious to see what he could do for Chris Wilcox.

Chevalier stepped out of his car, crossed the rain-slick asphalt, and stood with his back to Intelligene's entrance, looking at the woods behind his BMW. The summer crickets must have all taken to their burrows in the downpour. The only sound was the wind moving through the wet boughs. He placed his index finger on the print reader next to the door, waited for the light to turn green, and then keyed his personal pass code. The door silently swung open and he stepped into the reception area. Moving behind the desk, he used the control panel to lock the external doors and arm all the building's alarms except the internal motion sensors. His largest investors—the new fifty-one-percent owners of Intelligene—had insisted on this security system, and now Chevalier was glad for it. He checked the monitors and saw the entire building was empty. The receptionist's third computer monitor showed that every authorized employee had checked out of the building, the last one leaving at 8:39 p.m. Chevalier went to the break room and made a pot of coffee, then went into the main lab. Three video cameras connected to the new security system tracked him as he walked.

At midnight, Chevalier turned the fork over and refocused the microscope. He zoomed in just behind the tip of the second tine. Without magnification, the back of the fork looked almost clean. Under the microscope, it was another story. There were individual blood cells suspended in a thin film of liquid that had dried at the edges, leaving a crust of crystallized minerals, desiccated cells, and microscopic globules of oils. Under the microscope it looked like sand at the high tide line. Spread on a slide with further magnification, there would be bacteria, some still active, some dead or dormant. The portion that had not yet dried was frothed at the edges with tiny air bubbles and had a viscous sheen to its surface. Dr. Chevalier wasn't positive, but he'd have bet Chris's escrow deposit this was the killer's saliva.

After that, it didn't take long to find a cell. The epithelial lining of the mouth ages and sloughs off constantly; saliva is a DNA jackpot. Using a microscopic glass pipette, he transferred the cell to a slide, stained it, and put it under a higher power microscope.

The cell was in the early stages of mitosis, its chromosomes bunched together in preparation for cellular division. As such, they were a visible chain of rough Xs across the center of the cell's nucleus. He saw the obvious male Y sex chromosome—it really looked more like an apostrophe than the letter Y—and assumed he'd found cells belonging to the killer and not to the victim. Then he saw something that stopped him short.

The cell he was looking at could not have come from a human.

It had too many chromosomes.

He set aside the slide he'd been studying and prepared a new slide using a tiny sample of the bloody tissue from the other side of the fork. He spent forty-five minutes preparing the sample, staining it, and searching for a cell in mitosis. He counted the chromosomes twice and came up with a total of forty-six chromosomes. Human. The sex chromosomes were a woman's double-x. Chris Wilcox was not joking. The cells on Dr. Chevalier's slide almost certainly belonged to a human female. He could prove that one way or another with simple tests. But first he wanted to go back to the cells he'd discovered in the saliva.

He returned to the first slide and looked again. This cell contained twelve chromosomes more than a human. Millions of additional genes. If the fork really had been pushed into a girl's flesh and blood, and if the saliva on the fork came from an animal with fifty-eight chromosomes, what could he conclude?

Maybe the killer was feeding his victims to some kind of pet.

But what?

It had to be something exotic: dogs had seventy-eight chromosomes and cats had thirty-eight. The only way to know more would be to amplify the DNA, then feed it conservative primers from known organisms. Amplification would heat the long double-helices of the DNA molecules until they split. Each strand would separate into two halves like a zipper coming undone. Conservative primers were short segments of DNA known to be present in all members of a genus. If the primers bonded to the heat-split DNA from his mystery cells, he could start making inferences. He'd be able to narrow his search by amplifying the DNA with progressively more specific primers.

He looked up from the microscope. There were no windows in the lab, but he could see a bank of monitors in the glass-enclosed security booth at the far end of the room. Monitors pulling in video from outside the building showed the sunrise. His car was still alone in the lot. His employees would be arriving soon and he needed to be cleaned up and gone before they came. The next phase of the experiments would have to wait; there was no way he could do this with employees present.

It was 6:03 a.m. when he left.

The computer system recorded his exit and the cameras watched him go.

Chapter Fourteen

Julissa claimed her sister's body by signing a sheaf of paperwork at the University of Texas Medical Branch, then authorized a funeral home to transfer the body to Austin. Her parents wanted to come to Galveston, but she'd kept them away. Ben was unaccounted for and the police were hopeless. No one who loved Allison, and who wasn't crazy, would ever set foot in Allison's apartment again. There was nothing to do but go back to Austin and put Allison in the ground.

She'd already signed a form declaring she would not cremate the remains. The State of Texas wanted its evidence preserved. When the paperwork was done and her parents diverted home, Julissa checked out of the Galvez and started the drive back. She stopped at a branch of her bank and withdrew five thousand dollars. On her way through Houston, she pulled off at the first computer superstore she found. She paid in cash for two laptops, her face hidden from the cash register security camera by the bill of the black baseball cap she sometimes wore to the shooting range.

The rest of the drive was nothing like her trip to Galveston a week earlier. She didn't cry or pound the steering wheel. She drove straight and fast, and felt focused. She'd read the files Chris had given her, and she compared his files to Allison's autopsy report. If she'd ever felt any doubt, Chris's files told her to let it go. There was one killer, and he had left his mark everywhere with the same deliberation of a lower predator that marks its kills with its own urine. Now Julissa was planning her next move.

She'd been home for two hours, had just hung up after thirty-five minutes of questions from the funeral home, and was pacing in her study when the phone rang again. She thought it would be her parents or Ben, but it was Chris.

"Where are you?" she asked when she picked up the phone.

"Kaneohe."

"I came back to Austin for the funeral."

"Mike told me."

"I've been thinking of where I want to go for my part," she said. She wouldn't say the words *hack* or *FBI* on the phone. She'd designed too many chips for the National Security Agency, had read too much about warrantless wire tapping.

"Yeah?"

"I'll give you a call when I know for sure."

"Okay."

"What happened in Boston?"

"I gave the evidence to Intelligene. Now we're just waiting."

"What about Mike and Aaron?"

"They're still in Galveston. They talked to as many people as they could on the docks and at the marina. No luck. They thought it might be worthwhile to go back to the same places for the next few nights, see if they run into anyone new."

They were silent awhile. Julissa could hear doves from Chris's end of the connection. They sounded like they were right outside his window.

"When's the funeral?" he asked.

"Tomorrow morning. Day after that, I'll get started."

"Are you coming here?" he asked.

He was better at reading her than she'd thought. But she still hesitated, not sure she wanted to admit her plan.

"I was thinking of it."

"Good."

"It's really okay?"

"Yes."

"Okay," she said. "I'll see you then." She hung up quickly.

After the service, they carried the coffin down the aisle of the church and across the churchyard to the adjacent cemetery. Julissa was a pall bearer, along with her father, two of Allison's friends from high school, and Ben's brother. Ben was still nowhere to be found. His brother never said a word. The coffin didn't weigh much. According to the medical examiner's report, between fifteen and twenty pounds of Allison was missing. A lot of that was probably blood, but the rest was flesh, soft organs, and huge strips of skin from her thighs. Julissa knew her sister had probably been eaten in the course of two, or maybe even three separate feedings. Her still-warm tissue had been stuffed into Tupperware containers and hidden in the back of the freezer for later. Now she was carrying what was left out of the church and into the already hot sunlight of the July morning.

Like scraping a chicken carcass off a tray and into a trash can after the guests are gone. That's what she was doing: just cleaning up.

No one else in her family knew as much, though the look on Ben's brother's face made Julissa wonder. He'd probably heard the message on Ben's voicemail. She hadn't heard it, but Mike told her about it after Chris had flown to Boston. She pried it out of him, and then wished she could give it back.

Later, a limousine took her to her parents' house. Aunts and uncles and cousins showed up. Friends from high school, from college. Everyone ignored the food and went directly to the liquor cabinet. Julissa poured a tumbler level-full of scotch and went to the back porch. She looked at the juniper trees and live oaks, watched the mocking birds swoop through the branches with their white-striped wings flashing.

Her father came out, but didn't see her. He walked to a rocking chair and sat in it. For a moment he was still, and then suddenly he was pounding his fists against the side of his face and sobbing. Julissa started to go to him, but then thought better of it. He'd come to be alone, the same thing she'd done. She stood slowly and wandered off into the woods. She'd poured enough into her glass to make a real outing of it. Her feet automatically led her down the trail to the swimming hole. She sat on a shelf of limestone, her legs hanging a few feet above the clear water. Springs dripped from the fern-covered cliffs on the other side of the creek. She dropped a pebble over the edge and watched it sink to the bottom.

"I will not disappoint you, Allie," she said.

She thought about those words for a while, the terrible necessity of what she was about to do, and then she began to cry as her father had.

The next day she flew from Austin to Dallas, head still pounding from the reception. She drank black coffee from a Starbucks kiosk in the American Airlines terminal while she waited to board her flight to Honolulu. She'd never been to Hawaii. It seemed like a strange place to attempt the crime she wanted to commit. But she wasn't asking herself a lot of hard questions about anything. Her instinct said, *Go to Hawaii and work with Chris.* That was enough for now. She boarded the flight and fell asleep. When she woke, judging from the barren mountains and dry stream beds far beneath them, they were over West Texas or Southern New Mexico. Her head was feeling better and she went to the back of the plane and asked the stewardess for another cup of coffee.

Then, back in her seat, she got one of the new laptops. She looked around. The man next to her was asleep. She powered up the computer, opened a Java application, and started to program her first step.

When the plane landed, her headache was gone. She had no clear plan of what to do next. She could have rented a car, but she didn't know where to drive. Calling Chris didn't seem right either. She wasn't sure why she'd come and had been so busy programming her Trojan horse on the plane that she hadn't thought about it. At the taxi stand she got into a minivan and asked the driver to take her to Waikiki. There would at least be a lot of hotels in Waikiki.

She sat in the van and looked out the window. This didn't look like a place for a serial killer. Behind Honolulu were green mountains topped with clouds. A rainbow arched towards the ocean behind the volcanic crater she recognized as Diamond Head. But he'd been here. She saw the rain in the mountains and thought of Chris driving with the police to the scene of his wife's slaughter. Nowhere near the ocean was safe. The map in their short-lived headquarters proved that. From the overpass where the van sat in traffic, she could see an oil tanker waiting at anchor west of the airport runway. He had to be coming on a ship. If he could swim like Aaron thought, he could easily make it ashore from a tanker a mile or two out. There'd be no record of him even entering most of the countries. She wondered what to do with the idea. He might not have any records, but the ship would.

"Here on vacation?" asked the cab driver.

"Yeah."

"Meeting your boyfriend?"

"Yeah."

"What hotel?"

"The Hyatt?" she said. There had to be a Hyatt in Waikiki.

"Hyatt hotel, okay. Traffic is bad."

She wondered what he would look like. Middle aged, probably, if he'd been killing since the seventies. Built like an athlete. But he couldn't possibly look like an ordinary man. There would be something that marked him and set him apart. No one could do what he did and simply blend into the crowd. She was sure there'd be some kind of ugliness about him.

"Boyfriend already at the Hyatt?"

"Yeah," she said. She was getting sick of this conversation. She rested her hand on the suitcase next to her. Her Sig Sauer was packed in a locked travel case inside her checked bag. She hadn't brought any ammunition—it was illegal to pack it.

"On the way, can you stop somewhere I can pick up a box of .45 ACP?"

The cab driver looked around. "Ma'am?"

".45 ACP. You know, bullets?"

She paid for an ocean-view suite in the Diamond Head tower of the Waikiki Hyatt. She ignored the waterfalls and tropical birds in the open-air lobby and went directly to the elevators. She left her suitcase unopened by the door, and then went out onto the lanai with her laptop.

A little before sunset, her phone rang. It was Chris.

"You find a hotel?"

"The Hyatt, in Waikiki."

"Want some dinner?"

"Sure."

"I'll call you from the lobby in about an hour."

They walked across Kalakaua Boulevard and through the lobby of the old Moana Surfrider hotel. A banyan tree with three separate trunks spread across the patio behind the hotel and gave shade almost all the way to the beach. They took a table under the boughs at the edge of the beach. Diamond Head was to her left across the turquoise water.

"Can you explain how this works?" Chris asked.

She nodded and put down the menu.

"The program's simple. It's called a stack buffer overflow exploit, and it takes advantage of weaknesses in the target computer to upload executable code into the stack buffers."

Chris looked at her as if she'd just spoken in Chinese, but before she could explain more, he asked a question.

"How do you get it on the target computer?"

"I'm going to start my way at the bottom and work up. Each FBI field office has a special agent in charge, the SAC. The SAC's the person with the highest level of authority within the FBI intranet system, short of a deputy director. You figure an FBI agent will be more cautious than an ordinary person. So the idea isn't to try to infect her computer first, but to start somewhere else and work my way towards her through the computers of people she trusts."

"Why pick Honolulu?"

"Mike was able to get some good stuff about the Honolulu SAC."

The waiter came back and brought their drinks. She looked at the banyan tree that spread out above them. Roots starting in its branches hung down in the air over their heads. Someday they would reach the ground and would grow into new trunks.

"What'd he find?"

"Her name's Helen Barton. She's only been in Honolulu three years, so she wasn't in charge of the field office when Cheryl was killed. Her son, Scott, is in the Army and was deployed to Afghanistan ten months ago. Mike ran his background and learned he's engaged to a girl in San Diego named Brenda Johannson."

"How'd he find that out?"

"Facebook. Anyway, my plan is to start with the girl. All I've got to do is get her to click on a link in an email. That'll upload my program into her Outlook's call stack. The program will let me send a second email that looks like it came from her computer."

She took another drink from her glass of beer. The waiter came back and they ordered appetizers.

"How will you get her to click on a link? Most people just delete emails with hyperlinks from people they don't know."

"Thanks to Facebook, I know who her friends are. So I made up a Gmail account in the name of one of her friends. The link's part of a wedding invitation. If she clicks it, I've got her. If she doesn't, I'll wait a day and try something else."

"You already started?"

She nodded. "I just need to find an unsecured wireless network."

"What about here?"

"Not here. See at the outdoor bar, over the cash register?" Julissa pointed over Chris's left shoulder.

Chris turned his head and looked. There was a security camera over the cash register and their table would be in the background of its view.

"There were some others in the lobby, and we might be covered by one or two I didn't see. If the FBI traced my email to this wireless network, which they could do, they'd check the video cameras. They'd know the exact date and time the email was sent. They'd see me sitting with a laptop out. Half my projects since grad school were funded by the NSA. I've had a security clearance since I was twenty-three. They'd know who I am."

"What's your plan?"

"When we leave here I'll take a walk, with my laptop in my purse. I programmed it to look for an unsecured network, log on, then send mail. If there's a security camera wherever I link up, it'll just see me

walking past."
    "Want me to come?"
    "Sure."

    An hour and a half later, in her hotel room, Julissa opened her laptop. She and Chris had walked along the beach, past the zoo and the aquarium, and then into a neighborhood of mansions that clung to the slopes of Diamond Head. To return, they cut back across the soccer fields of Kapiolani Park and zigzagged through the side streets of Waikiki between Kuhio and Ala Wai, walking past dozens of high-rise condominiums. When they said good night at the corner of her hotel, he'd put his hand on her shoulder briefly. That had felt good. She wanted to invite him up for a drink in her room but she didn't know what he would say. So she said nothing, and leaned her head down to press her cheek against the back of his hand on her shoulder. They made plans to meet the next day at noon and she rode up the elevator alone.

    Julissa sat on the end of her bed and logged into her new Gmail account. The message was sent.

    The only thing left to do was wait.

Chapter Fifteen

Dr. Chevalier was alone in the lab again. As a child, reading French-language copies of National Geographic at his parents' winter home in Papeete, he often wondered what it would feel like to discover a new species. He'd never imagined his emotions over the last seven hours.

Self-doubt. Disbelief.

Fear.

He'd compared the DNA to primer snippets of genes from birds, fish, reptiles, insects, crustaceans, and corals. There were random links but nothing substantial. His emotional thermostat ticked into fear when he searched mammalian genes. This wasn't just a new species. It was like nothing he'd ever seen.

Now he sat at his computer and began typing an email to Chris Wilcox and his friends. The telephone on his desk rang and his hands were shaking when he answered it.

"This is Chevalier."

"I hope it's not too late. You said call anytime." The voice had a soft-spoken Midwestern twang.

"Dr. Corliss. How are you? You found something?" Chevalier said.

"The sample was small. The test consumes the sample, so it'd be impossible to reproduce the test unless you have any more of it."

"But did you find anything?" Chevalier asked again.

"Based on the ratio of strontium 87 to strontium 86 in the sample, and the fact the water content was clearly glacial in origin," Corliss said, "I'd say your subject has been drinking a lot of water from one of five countries."

"You can't be more specific?" Chevalier asked.

"No. The sample was too small to say with any certainty."

"What are the countries?"

"Finland, Sweden, Norway, Scotland and Iceland. All countries with existing or recent glaciers and similar strontium deposits. If I had more to work from, I could probably narrow it down to within a few hundred miles, but this is the best I can do," Corliss said.

"How can you tell the water's glacial?"

"It's too low in the heavier isotope of oxygen, O-18. Meaning it evaporated during a climactically cooler period."

"Such as an ice age."

"Yes."

"Write it up."

"I'll have it tonight."

"And send a list of your expenses. I'll cut your check."

Chevalier hung up and went to the globe in the corner of his office, spinning it.

Finland, Sweden, Norway, Scotland or Iceland.

A cold-weather creature.

He went to his desk and continued writing the report to his clients. He wanted to fulfill his obligation and get this project off his desk and out of his mind. This was too dangerous. And even if he could prove everything he believed, what could he expect? His respectable clients would stay away and his business would collapse while tabloid reporters trampled a path to his door in search of any information on whatever it was. He didn't even want to start speculating on where it came from or why it existed. He just wanted to lay out the facts for Chris Wilcox and call the job done. He'd even decided to give back half the deposit money.

To: Wilcox, Chris
CC: Clayborn, Julissa; Nakamura, Mike; Westfield, Aaron
Date: July 16, 2010 4:58:20 a.m. (EST)
RE: Intelligene Report (!)

Ladies and Gentlemen:
This email and the attached documents will be my report on the nuclear DNA from unknown tissue found on the piece of evidence which Mr. Wilcox provided to me on July 14. I haven't completed the sequencing of the DNA, but consider this my final report. By separate letter to the escrow company, I'll return of half the deposit and the remaining funds.

I want no further involvement.

The sample contained tissues belonging to a human female and to a male. The male cells were suspended in saliva and appeared to be stratified squamous keratinized epithelial cells, consistent with the cellular tissue of the hard palate and gums. From that, I conclude the saliva belongs to the male. On the other hand, the female tissue was muscular tissue and fat cells, possibly taken from the breast area.

My instructions were to complete an analysis of any cellular tissue belonging to a male. The male cells had fifty-eight chromosomes. By comparison, a human being has forty-six chromosomes. There is no known genetic disorder which would result in twelve extra chromosomes, and there is simply no way that the organism which produced these cells could be considered "human".

I'll tell you what I know, but it isn't much to go on.

Eighty-five percent of the organism's genome is consistent with a mammal. Sixty percent of the mammalian DNA is in common with human DNA. The other forty percent of the mammalian DNA has no direct association with any primate or other species I could find.

This creature has genes I've never seen, so I can't speculate on what they do. And it lacks genes normal organisms possess. For example: it has no telomeres, which are the genetic structures commonly associated with aging. Does that mean that it never grows old? I don't know.

It might look like a man. I found genetic markers I'd normally associate with light-colored skin. It probably had red hair, although it may not anymore, because I found a gene associated in humans with male-pattern baldness. Whether this gene would be active in this creature is, again, anyone's guess. Unless its diet or other circumstances have resulted in a different outcome, it might be quite tall—over six feet. It has a muscular build and may be extremely strong. As an aside, and this may relate to either its diet or its hygiene (or both), its saliva is swarming with bacteria. I haven't identified the various strains, but as a safe guess, anyone bitten by this thing would be looking at a fatal infection.

The genetic information for its brain is unlike anything I've seen. Is it intelligent? Almost certainly. Is it more intelligent than us? I can't even guess. A genetic laboratory equipped for comparative zoology or evolution may be better at answering these questions.

The isotope hydrologist I contacted at Harvard got some results from a saliva sample I gave him. His report is attached, and it's as specific as he could get.

If you were sitting here, you'd probably ask me what I thought this thing is. Or you'd want to know where it came from. I don't have the answers you want. But I can give you a few guesses. I think I can safely say it's not from outer space. Its DNA is similar enough to other organisms that it probably evolved naturally. The only other possibility is that it was engineered, but I wouldn't put much money on that: genetics has gone pretty far in the last ten years, but not that far. So if you asked *for my gut feeling, I'd say this: it's a natural product of evolution, something that branched off from everything else long ago.*

It's an old planet. We don't really know everything that's out there.

Why would a predator so finely tuned for killing not be more successful as a species? Why aren't there more of them? Who knows— there are a lot of reasons for a species to die out besides not being adapted to hunt and kill prey. Maybe this species is so violent that whenever two of them are in the same room, instead of mating, they kill each other. Maybe there are a couple hundred of them and they're just hard to spot. Maybe they look just like us. If I'm right that its lack of telomeres means it doesn't age, that would explain why this one is still around, even though its species as a whole has declined.

I believe nothing good could come from this knowledge, besides what you four propose to do. If this creature has done what you say, it needs to be tracked down and wiped out. It doesn't need to be researched, or understood, or, God forbid, bred. If it has cells and DNA, if it eats to stay alive, then it can be killed.

Regards,

Dr. Gerard Chevalier, M.D., Ph.D.

Chevalier didn't believe he was doing the right thing, but he knew he was doing the smart thing. The smart thing was to close the lid on this box as fast as he could, give it back to Chris Wilcox, and forget it as quickly as possible. Within two years, with enough work on other projects, he was sure he could forget this. He would come to doubt all of his conclusions and would believe that this had been some kind of strange hoax.

He hit the *Send* button and in a moment, the email was gone.

The sun was coming up as he walked across the lobby and used his access card to sign out and open the front door. A green light was blinking on the console of lights behind the security station. He assumed this meant the system was properly functioning.

Chapter Sixteen

Chris woke at dawn and went in his bare feet across the back lawn to the dock. He stepped into the dinghy, used a hand pump to bail the rain water from the night before, and then rowed to his boat. *Sailfish* was a sixty-two-foot Hallberg-Rassy, three years old when he and Cheryl bought her at Nawiliwili Harbor on Kauai and sailed her to Oahu. Now she was nine years old but in better-than-new condition. He rarely sailed her, but he kept her maintained. She was too beautiful to rot on her mooring, and Cheryl had loved her. Not a single bad thing had ever happened to either of them aboard the *Sailfish*. They had sailed each weekend, had crossed the Kaiwi channel to Molokai in every kind of weather, had made love in *Sailfish's* spacious center cockpit while sailing on autopilot under a full moon with the cloud-shadowed volcanoes of the Big Island ten miles ahead of their bow. Every time they stepped aboard, they had the same conversation and went through the same calculations: how much longer do we have to work before we can sell everything but the boat and follow the wind for the rest of our lives? They had a map of the world on the bedroom wall and they penciled in routes and highlighted places they wanted to see in the first five years. When Cheryl was killed they had six years of work left on their plan. They might have been packing to leave this week. Instead, Cheryl was dead, Chris had more money than he could ever use, and *Sailfish* lay idle on her mooring in Kaneohe Bay, collecting barnacles that he scrubbed off every two weeks with a stiff brush.

He climbed aboard, tied off the dinghy, and opened the bronze combination lock on the companionway hatch. Once inside, he checked the volt meter to be sure the solar panels were still charging the battery bank; he checked the bilge for water; and he powered up the laptop computer at the navigation station. Then he went into the galley to make a cup of coffee. With that brewed, he climbed the companionway ladder and went back into the cockpit where he sat under the bimini cover. It was only 6:01 a.m. but Julissa would be up—she'd only been in Honolulu for one night and couldn't have adjusted to the time yet. He took a sip of his coffee and dialed her number on his cell. She picked up on the second ring.

"Hope I didn't wake you."

"Not at all. I'm walking on the beach."

"Any news?"

"She took the bait and clicked the link."

"The program installed?"

"Yeah, but that's enough about that for now," she said. And then, more gently, "I'll give you the details when we meet up. Not over the phone."

"Okay."

"You checked your email this morning?"

"No. Why?"

"There's an email from the scientist you hired. Chevalier. Either he's completely insane and just stole half your deposit, or..."

Chris waited for her to finish, but she didn't.

"Or what?" he finally said.

"Maybe you ought to read the email. Read it and come see me— room 1708 You checked this guy out before you hired him, right?"

"And Mike did a full background. He's completely legit and so's his company."

"Jesus," Julissa said. "I was afraid of that."

Thirty minutes later Chris had printed the two hundred pages of attachments to Chevalier's email, locked the boat, rowed ashore and fetched a pair of flip-flops from his back porch. He took the Pali Highway over the mountains, got stuck in traffic near the tunnel and remembered that for everyone else this was just a normal workday. He risked getting a ticket by picking up his phone and calling Chevalier's cell number. No answer. Chevalier said he wanted no more involvement, but Chris didn't think very much of that. The man had shaken his hand and agreed to do a job; he'd already been paid fifty thousand dollars and apparently planned to keep half.

He was going to make himself available for questions.

Chris dialed the number again and left a message when the voicemail finally picked up. On the other side of the tunnel the traffic cleared and moved quickly all the way out of the mountains. When he got off of the highway, he followed Kalakaua Avenue into Waikiki.

He left his car with the Hyatt's valet and rode the elevator to Julissa's floor, carrying the printout of Chevalier's report. Julissa opened the door as soon as he knocked. She was wearing a tank top and denim shorts, and her hair was still wet from the shower.

"Come in. I just finished making coffee."

He stepped into her room and followed her to the counter next to the TV. He'd forgotten what it was like to be in a room with a beautiful woman who'd just stepped from the shower. It came at him from every angle: the smell of her hair, the steam in the air, the sheen of moisture on her throat. And he knew with a certainty what it would feel like to hold her close, with nothing between them, his hands plunged deep into her red hair. He studied the bedspread, embarrassed, his left thumb touching the base of his third finger, seeking the reassurance of a ring he hadn't worn in years. Her laptop was open on the bed and he could see she'd been surfing the Internet, reading about genetics.

She poured two cups of coffee from the little pot and handed him one. If she'd sensed anything that had just gone through his mind, she didn't show it. The door to the lanai was open and the curtains were blowing inward on the light morning wind. Without speaking they moved outside. Chris put the printed report on the glass patio table.

"You get through the attachments?" he asked.

"Yeah."

"Make any sense to you?"

"Some. But keep in mind I've got no background in biology. Anything more confusing than high school is over my head. And just because the attachments make sense doesn't mean Chevalier didn't make it all up. Lots of bullshit makes sense."

"Good point."

"For all we know, you come to him with this fork and this story, and he thinks you're playing a sick hoax on him. So he throws it back at you, tells you an insane story of his own."

She bit her lower lip and shrugged.

"Okay," Chris said. "That's a theory. Here's another: what if it's true?"

She looked at him, considering it, but he started to answer his own question.

"For one thing, it answers a couple questions. Namely, why he can swim so fast and why he's still so strong after all these years."

"*If* he can really swim like that," Julissa said. "That story might not even be true. And there're easier explanations for the age. Like, he was seventeen or eighteen when he killed Tara Westfield."

"Let's go through the report and see if we can find any holes," Chris said. He picked up the first printed attachment.

"You tell him about the connection to redheads?"

Chris thought about it, replaying his few phone conversations and his face-to-face meeting with Chevalier.

"No," he finally said.

"Interesting he says the man or thing we're looking for is a redhead."

"You think that means anything?"

"I don't know," she said.

For a while they sat in silence and read the attachments. Julissa went back into the room and returned with her laptop. She balanced it on one leg and held the printout on the other and looked something up. Chris's phone rang and they both jumped.

"Maybe it's Chevalier," Chris said. "I left him a message on the way over."

"I've already left him two," Julissa said.

Chris picked up his phone and saw a familiar number. He answered and put it to his ear.

"Hey, Mike," he said. He met Julissa's eyes and shrugged. "I'm with Julissa...yeah, she's in Honolulu. I'm going to put you on speaker."

He set the phone on the coffee table and hit the speaker button.

"You guys read it?" Mike said.

"We're going through the attachments now, but yeah, we read it."

"You been able to get in touch with him yet?"

"No, but we both tried."

"So did I. Office and cell. There's a receptionist picking up in the office but they're saying he didn't come in for the day," Mike said.

"Where are you?" Julissa asked.

"I left Westfield to finish up in Galveston and caught a flight back to Honolulu. I'm driving home."

"Let's meet at my house for lunch," Chris said. "See if we can sort this out."

"Fine with me," Mike said. "I think I got my wife's college biology textbook somewhere. I'll bring it."

He hung up.

"Sounds like Chevalier's keeping his head down," Julissa said.

"We'll reach him," Chris said. "Even if it means flying back there and knocking on his door at three a.m."

An hour later they had finished going through the attachments to Chevalier's email. Westfield called Chris while they were midway through, and they spoke to him on speaker phone. They agreed there was no point in drawing conclusions until they talked to Chevalier.

Julissa took their coffee cups back to the counter in her room and then they sat on the balcony together and looked out at the ocean.

"Now what?" she said.

"I don't know."

"Does it change anything?"

"If the report's bullshit, we might've just lost our best lead. Even if he actually returns the evidence, we can't be sure he hasn't ruined it."

"You think it's true?" Julissa asked.

Chris shrugged. "It'd explain some things. But it sounds crazy."

"There's still the FBI angle," she said. "We might get something good out of that."

"Where are you on that?"

"It's almost all on autopilot now. Assuming she clicks the link in the cloned email I'll be sending her, I'll be able to start monitoring her computer use. From there, I'll pick up her passwords whenever she logs into the FBI intranet. Once I have those, I can start working my way into headquarters."

"And then?"

"I'll start checking for deleted files in VICAP. I should be able to figure out when the data was removed and track where and how the commands to remove it were made."

"Basically the same investigation the FBI would be doing if they tried to track you down."

"Yeah."

Chris stood, resting his forearms on the rail of the lanai. Three surfers were kneeling in the sand next to their long boards, rubbing them down with disks of wax. He watched them for a while, then watched the way the wind was moving the fronds of the coconut trees that lined Kalakaua. He guessed it would be getting windier by the evening.

"So, for the FBI hack, you're just waiting now," Chris said.

"That's right. It's frustrating."

Chris nodded. He didn't want to tell her she might end up waiting a long time. Years. He looked at the pile of printed documents on the coffee table. They really couldn't make any sense of them, even though they'd tried. He felt like flying to Boston and strangling Chevalier.

Chapter Seventeen

Chevalier sat in his study and looked out the bay windows at the forest outside his house. Wind coursed through the poplar and birch trees and blasted rain against the windows. Every few minutes he closed his eyes at the electric-violet flash of nearby lightning, followed almost instantly by a long peal of thunder. He regretted his email to Chris Wilcox but was having trouble getting his computer to connect to the Internet, so he couldn't do anything about it. It was probably the storm. He lived eight miles southwest of Foxborough, near the Rhode Island border, deep in the woods. Maybe the high winds had knocked a tree branch into something, or lightning had taken out one of the cable company's service hubs. He still had electricity for the moment.

He lifted his telephone and listened for a dial tone, then called his office. The receptionist answered. He told her he was at home, and if Chris Wilcox called, she should route the call to his home number. Before she could say she understood, the line went dead. So much for that. He hung up the phone and picked it up again. He still had a dial tone. When he redialed his office, he just got a busy signal. Intelligene was in the woods too—a tree must have gone down on one of their telephone lines. That had happened a few times before. He hung up the phone and swiveled in his chair to watch the storm.

In the distance, he heard what must have been all three fire trucks from the new substation in Joes Rock racing east towards Foxborough. Even with the rain pounding on his roof, he could hear the sirens and the deep blasts of the horns for a long time. When he walked to his kitchen to get a cup of coffee, he could hear new sirens from the southeast. That would probably be the substation over in Plainsville, two miles through the woods outside his kitchen window. Thunder cracked overhead and when its sound rolled off into the distance, the plates in his cupboards were still vibrating. The sirens faded in and out with the rain as they grew farther away. He took his cup of coffee and went back to his study. He flipped through TV channels until he found a station broadcasting the weather report. The live Doppler radar showed a second storm coming in off the Atlantic.

The bad weather hadn't really gotten started yet.

He looked out the windows. Even though it was barely past lunch, it was as dark as dusk outside. He thought what a great day he'd picked to stay home from the lab. He could watch the storm and catch up on his sleep. He'd left his cell phone at the office and apparently no one at the office could call him from the land lines. Chris Wilcox and his friends would just have to sit it out. He put his feet on his desk and changed the channel on the TV until he found a movie.

After the second commercial break, during which he'd gone to the kitchen to make a bowl of popcorn, his electricity went off. There had been no sudden crack of thunder or house-shuddering gust of wind, though it was still raining heavily outside. With the TV off and the lights out, the study was lit by grey storm light. He picked up his phone to see if it still worked. He had a dial tone when he picked it up but he heard it cut-out as he was returning the handset to the cradle. He picked up the phone again and it was completely dead. He looked at his watch. It wasn't quite four o'clock.

He started to the kitchen for candles, and as he was turning away from his desk and towards the door, he saw something pale glide past the window behind his desk. He whipped around. It had been at the edge of his vision; now there was nothing. The only movement was the forest itself, branches whipping in the storm. Rain pelted the window glass and ran down in sheets. A rhododendron bush grew below the window but its leaves were an olive green and nothing close to the dirty white color of the shape he'd seen move past the glass.

He backed away from the window and stood by the door to the study, watching. He was sure he'd seen something. As he stood looking at the window, he heard a sound coming from behind him and down the hall. It sounded like it was coming from his bedroom. Or rather, it was coming from outside one of the bedroom windows. It sounded like—what? He listened to it and as he placed the sound, his skin erupted with goose bumps. He was listening to something incredibly sharp scratching against wet glass.

Some kind of claws.

He sprinted down the hallway to his bedroom and then stood at the closed door. For a second he considered the idea of just going for his car. His car keys were on a hook in the entry way and his BMW was parked in an open carport under the maple trees on the far side of his entrance drive. But going outside would mean being in the storm with whatever was out there. The scratching suddenly stopped. It had been insanely loud and now it was completely quiet. Every hair on his body was standing straight up. He hadn't heard any glass break. He opened the bedroom door and dashed into the room, looking at the window as he made his way to the bed.

There was nothing out there. He had to turn his back to the window and kneel at the edge of the bed, groping underneath the bed frame. The scratching started again and he spun around on his knees but the window was empty. The sound came from one of the bathroom windows. He had never heard anything like it. It was like someone was trying to wear down a razor blade by grinding it against a mirror. He was sick with terror and for a moment forgot why he was on his knees in his bedroom in the shadows of the storm. All the mattered was the scratching sound. Then it stopped. Rain pelted the roof. A lull of silence. Chevalier remembered where he was and why: his pump-action shotgun was under the bed. He reached again and found its stock, then pulled it out. He chambered a shell by pumping the walnut grip and the sound made him feel better. He had six shells of twelve-gauge buckshot. There was a full box of ammunition in the study. The sound was probably just a raccoon or something, terrorized by the storm. But the house was on a high foundation and the ground-floor windows were six feet off the ground. The window in the bathroom was at least ten feet off the ground.

It started again, this time from the windows in the kitchen. There were four tall windows behind the sink and behind a long granite counter. French doors at the end of the kitchen opened onto a wooden deck that overlooked the forest. Chevalier leveled the shotgun, took off the safety, and crept to the kitchen. On his way past the bathroom he glanced inside and saw the double-paned storm window was scored deeply with five parallel lines about an inch apart. He stood staring at that for a moment, and then the scratching from the kitchen changed into a pounding. It sounded like something huge was slamming against the French doors.

He stepped into the kitchen and rounded the corner of the oak-paneled pantry so he could see the French doors. The venetian blinds were drawn down, hiding the glass from view. Something slammed against the doors and he saw them shudder with the weight of whatever hit them. The blinds rocked back and forth as though they were in a breeze. He couldn't see outside.

"Who's there?" he shouted.

The slamming just went on, then turned into scratching again. The deadbolt on the French doors was engaged. Thank God for that.

"I've got a twelve gauge shotgun and I'll shoot through the fucking glass!"

He shouldered the shotgun again and aimed at the center of the venetian blind on the right-hand door. When the scratching turned back into pounding, and before he started shaking too hard to keep his aim, he pulled the trigger. The gun blast was deafening in the granite and wood-paneled kitchen. The buckshot tore through the blue venetian blind and blew through the square glass panel on the other side. The shot left a hole the size of a soccer ball in the middle of the door. But the blinds were still in place and he could not see out of the remaining glass. The wind blowing through the broken window moved the blinds a bit, but he could only see shadows. The smoke detector started blaring at a skull-splitting volume from the powder smoke that filled the kitchen. He ignored it and started to move towards the door. He had to have hit it, whatever it was. If he could get a little closer, he would be able to see through the hole in the blinds. He pumped the shotgun to chamber another round and stepped towards the door.

"I've reloaded, asshole!"

The gaping hole in the door was a little higher than waist level.

He was within four feet of it, and began to crouch so he could see out. The end of the shotgun's barrel was about a foot from the door and aimed straight at the hole. He stole a quick glance at the windows behind the sink and saw nothing. He looked back in front of him just in time to see a flash of pale white flesh shoot through the hole in the glass and take hold of the gun barrel. Before he could even pull the trigger the thing outside yanked the shotgun from his hands. It disappeared through the hole in the doorway. The smoke detector blared on and on. He scrabbled away from the French doors on his hands and knees and pulled himself through the door to the hallway. It had happened so fast he didn't even see what came through the door. A blood-streaked white hand? He was breathing so fast he felt his head spin.

Now the scratching started again, so loud he could hear it over the wailing smoke alarm. He ran down the hallway and opened the door to the guest bathroom. This was the only room in the house that didn't have windows. He shut the door, latched its flimsy lock and immediately understood he'd made a mistake. He sank to his knees next to the door and listened. First the smoke alarm stopped. Then, eventually, the scratching from the kitchen stopped. He didn't hear any shattering of glass and he didn't hear any door open. There was just silence, and the sound of the storm.

And then he heard something on the roof.

His house was shingled in fine gray slate and he could clearly hear the hard tapping of footsteps moving around the roof. Then the scratching started again, but in a different pitch—claws on stone, instead of glass. When the pounding started it was harder than before. He heard shingles breaking, the shards skittering along the steeply pitched roof. There was splintering as the plywood underneath the shingles caved and broke. He was paralyzed with fear, kneeling against the bathroom door and shaking. He wet himself.

There was a thump and the ceiling shook. Dust drifted down from an air vent. *It's in the attic!* His mind was screaming. *It beat a hole in the roof and it's in the fucking attic!* The footsteps overhead stopped. His eyes were squeezed shut and he was trying to stop the shaking. That was when it spoke. Its voice was thin and strangely high pitched and seemed to come from straight within his head. It was like listening to a saw blade that could speak. It was right above him.

"I...can...smell you."

His terror finally broke his paralysis. He stood up and flung open the door and tore down the hallway to his house's entrance. He snatched the car keys off their hook, threw open the front door and barely touched the porch on his way across it. He took the five stone steps to the front sidewalk in a single leap and hit the ground running. It was normally about a hundred paces to the car, but he made it in twenty five. In the dusky light and sudden flash of lightning, he saw the BMW sitting on four flat tires. He stopped short and turned to look at the house.

"Son of a bitch!"

There it was, on the peak of the roof. In the rain and steady stream of leaves and twigs blowing from the forest behind the house, he could barely make it out. It was a crouching, naked white shape that loped at incredible speed down the slope of the roof towards the lawn.

Chevalier turned his back on it and ran towards the road, two hundred feet away at the end of his driveway. He saw a black car parked sideways across the front of his driveway, blocking it. It was boxy and jet black with tinted windows. A Rolls Royce, maybe. At a dead sprint in the storm, he couldn't tell whether anyone was inside. But his instinct told him to stay away. He turned towards the trees and ran through the forest instead. He could meet up with the road in five hundred feet, could run along it for an eighth of a mile, and would be at his closest neighbor's house. Before he made it into the trees, Chevalier looked back once more and saw the thing leap from his roof and onto the grass of his yard. It came at him on all fours like a dog. Chevalier screamed and ran into the trees.

When he next looked back he couldn't see it. Without meaning to, he came to an abrupt stop to look. Then he saw the thing coming at him and understood how stupid it had been to stop: it was a scurrying blur, darting from tree to tree so fast it looked like something from a stop-motion film. How could it move like that? It was almost on him. Fifty feet. Chevalier turned and ran again. He tripped on roots and fell to his knees and kept moving on his hands and knees until he was back on his feet. Now he could hear it behind him. He didn't dare look back. He could see the road ahead of him, rain swept, dark and empty. Something shoved him from behind and he went face first into a tree. He turned around and barely saw a clawed hand as it swept across his face. Claws dug into his eyes. He screamed from the pain and at the same time the thing pummeled into his stomach, slamming him to the ground and knocking the wind out of him. He was blind and breathless.

In one swipe it had rooted out both of his eyes.

The last thing Dr. Chevalier felt before he passed out was a bone-splintering grip on his ankle, and then the ground was sliding underneath him. His head bumped roughly across a rock. The thing was dragging him back to his house.

"*I could smell you...the whole time*," the saw-blade voice said inside of Chevalier's head.

Chapter Eighteen

The parking lot beside the Hotel Galvez had no shade and was blindingly bright in the afternoon sun. Westfield had backed his beat-up van into a parking spot and now crouched between its rear bumper and the front of a Ford truck in the spot behind him. He was using a screwdriver to take off his stolen Texas license plates and replace them with his Washington plates. The van wasn't running well and the last thing he wanted was to break down on Interstate 10 and have to explain his stolen plates to a state trooper.

After everyone else left, he'd stayed in Galveston, trying to find another witness. He'd made the rounds of the yacht basin and the fishing piers, talking to anyone he found. But no one had seen a thing.

Now there was the email from Chevalier to think about.

He pulled the van out of the parking space, turned it around, and parked in the same stall, front end first. Then, behind the screen of three parked cars, he changed the front license plate. He put the two Texas plates into a paper bag that he tossed into a trash can on his way back to the hotel. He didn't have to check out of his room until the next day, but he planned to leave that evening. It would be cooler driving at night. He could make it to Van Horn or even El Paso by sunrise, and would be out of Texas the next day.

In his room, he put his duffel bag on the bed and started packing. The television was tuned to CNN and was showing a fire in an industrial-looking building out in the woods somewhere. A blonde reporter in a yellow rain slicker was standing in front of a backdrop of flames and fire trucks. He had the television muted, but from the look of things, the building was a total loss. Westfield switched off CNN and went into the bathroom to get the stun gun he'd used on Chris. It was plugged into an outlet next to the sink to recharge. He put it in his pocket so he'd remember to return it to the van's glove compartment.

He was about to turn off the television when there was a knock at the door.

"Just a second."

He went to the door and looked through the peephole. A man in a plain black suit was standing in the hall with a manila mailing envelope.

"Yeah?" Westfield said. He hadn't touched the door.

"Front desk. Envelope for Aaron Westfield."

"Just put it under the door."

"You gotta sign for it."

"Hang on."

Westfield opened the door and the man held out the envelope. As he did so, Westfield saw the pistol in the man's right hand. It looked like a semi-automatic .22, and would have been very small except for the silencer screwed to the end of the barrel. The man pointed it at Westfield and shot him in the right kneecap. The gun made a sound like a rubber band *twipping* off the finger of a five-year-old. Westfield's knee exploded in pain and he fell backwards into the room. He landed on his side and was struggling to get back up. The man stepped in after him, kicked the door shut, and then kicked Westfield in his stomach. Westfield landed on his back and the man stomped on his stomach a second time and then knelt over him, one knee on his chest. He took a washcloth out of the envelope and pressed it over Westfield's face. It was wet with something and it burned when it touched his nose and lips. He couldn't breathe from the kicks to his stomach and was struggling underneath the man.

The man's face was completely calm.

"Normally, I just shoot you in forehead. But I get paid extra to ask questions."

He pressed harder with the washcloth and Westfield felt the burning liquid go up his nose. He wanted to scream.

"You make sound, I make it worse," the man said. "You want to scream?"

Westfield tried to shake his head. No, he wasn't going to scream. He could hold it in.

The man took the washcloth from Westfield's face and held the gun at his throat.

"Who else knows you're here?"

Westfield was struggling to take a breath. He couldn't answer. He shook his head again.

"Who besides Chris Wilcox, Mike Nakamura, and Julissa Clayborn knows why you're here?"

He shook his head.

The man was using his left arm to pin Westfield's right arm against the carpet behind his head. Westfield's left arm was trapped between the man's right knee and his side. He gently explored with his fingertips and felt the stun gun in his left pocket. He pulled at the lining of his pocket to bring the stun gun closer so he could get a grip on it with his thumb and forefinger.

"You contacted the police, the FBI?"

Westfield shook his head.

"Who talked to Chevalier?"

"I did," Westfield said.

"When?"

He closed his grip on the stun gun and was able to slowly get it all the way into his hand. He swiveled it to point at the man's thigh, a few inches below his crotch. He was pretty sure the shock would make the man convulse. If he did, he'd pull the trigger.

"Yesterday."

"Tell every word you said."

"You mean besides all the stuff about what a stupid fucking asshole you are?"

As he said this, he jammed the stun gun as hard as he could into the man's thigh, and jerked his head to the right. The pistol *twipped* again and Westfield heard the bullet go through the carpet next to his left ear, burying itself in the floor. Concrete chips stuck in his cheek and the side of his head, but that was no big deal. The man toppled off of him and Westfield sat up. The man was dazed but not out and Westfield put the stun gun on his chest and pressed down hard for five seconds. The man jerked violently, then lay still. Westfield took the gun out of the man's limp hand and pulled out the magazine. By its weight in his palm he could tell there were about eight rounds left. He reloaded the gun and set it behind him.

Westfield didn't take his eyes off the man as he unfastened his own belt, slipped it off, and fastened it just above his right knee. He pulled it through the buckle and cinched it as tightly as he could. Then he wound the leather strap around his leg and tied it roughly off. He pulled up his pant leg. The bullet had gone in just to the left of his patella. He felt tenderly along the backside of his knee and felt an exit wound.

That was good.

It hadn't lodged in the bones but had gone clean through.

Both wounds were still bleeding but had slowed after he put on the tourniquet. It must have been a steel-jacketed round and not a hollow point to have done so little damage. The man had probably chosen the small caliber so the silencer would work, and the steel jackets to punch through a man's skull. It was a good set-up for executing someone, but not so good for inflicting injuries to muscles, and for that Westfield knew he'd been lucky.

Westfield picked up the gun and turned back to the man. He patted him down and went through his pockets. His visitor carried no wallet. In his inner jacket pocket Westfield found a piece of thin spectra cord that was too short to be of use for anything except strangling someone or tying someone's wrists together. He found a rental car key. Besides the washcloth, the manila envelope had a can of mace and a switchblade knife. He rolled the man onto his stomach and tied his wrists behind his back with the spectra cord. Then he brought the loose ends of the cord through the back of the man's belt and tied them. *Good luck getting your hands in front of you now*, he thought. He rolled the man back over.

The man started to stir, but Westfield wasn't ready to deal with him yet. He might have one good jolt left in the stun gun. He knew a way to find out. He pressed the electrodes under the man's chin and hit the button. The man stiffened and then went limp again. Westfield flicked open the switchblade and cut the man's suit jacket and shirt from the cuffs to the neck and then ripped them both off so that the man was naked from the waist up. He wasn't wearing an undershirt. There was a blue rose tattooed on the man's chest and it looked like he had tried unsuccessfully to remove it with acid or lye. The skin over the faded rose was blistered with scars. Westfield rolled him over again and looked at his back. He wasn't wearing a wire, unless it was down his pants.

When the man came around again, Westfield wadded the ether-soaked washcloth and stuffed it into the man's mouth. Then he used the silenced pistol and shot him once in each kneecap. The man jerked at each shot but his muscles were weak from the stun gun. The ether-soaked gag stifled whatever he had to say about it.

"Normally I'd just shoot you in the forehead," Westfield said. "But, well, you know."

The man looked at him with bulging eyes. Westfield took stock of him. He had blond hair and blue eyes and looked about thirty years old. He was bleeding out of both kneecaps, had taken three shocks at around five hundred thousand volts each, and was gagging on ether. His hands were tied behind his back. Westfield was pretty sure he wasn't much of a threat, but still—Chris Wilcox had recently taught him a lesson in this regard. There was nothing to gain from carelessness but regret. What the hell. He picked up the can of mace and emptied it into the man's eyes.

When the man stopped writhing on the carpet, Westfield pulled the washcloth out of his mouth. The man's eyes were swollen shut and his face was red and wet with tears.

"Who do you work for?"

"You already know."

"What is he?"

"Nothing you want to mess with."

"How'd you find me?"

"He gives us your name. We trace your credit card."

"Where can I find him?"

The man said nothing.

"What's his name?"

More silence.

"Do you know what he is?"

The man just coughed, leaned his head to the side, and spat phlegm onto the carpet.

"Why would you work for him?"

This time the man spoke. He had a hint of an accent, but Westfield wasn't sure what it was. Maybe Russian or one of the Baltic states.

"He pays."

"Where do I find him?"

Silence.

"I'm gonna ask you one more time. Then I'll to count to three. If I get to three and you haven't answered, I'm gonna kill you. Where do I find him?"

The man said nothing. Westfield dropped a pillow over the man's face and pressed the muzzle of the gun into it.

"One."

The gun was angled so the bullet would go through the pillow and into the man's forehead, right between his eyes.

"Two."

The pillow would catch most of the splatter and since it was only a .22, the bullet probably wouldn't go all the way through the man's head. It would just bounce around inside.

"Three."

He didn't see any other options and he didn't think he had enough time to sit around with an assassin while trying to think of better solutions. He waited for about two seconds to let the man answer. But the man didn't say anything. Westfield pulled the trigger. He closed his eyes and thought of Tara on their wedding night.

Chapter Nineteen

It was eleven thirty in the morning in Honolulu. Julissa checked her email twice more, but there were no developments either from Dr. Chevalier or Special Agent Barton. The lack of action was driving her crazy. Plus, when Chris came in from the balcony with his cell phone, he told her Intelligene's phone line was out of service. That seemed a little extreme to her, taking an entire company's phone system offline to avoid one potentially disgruntled client.

"You want to get a drink or something?" she asked him.

"Sure."

"Let's just get one beer and then go over to your house to meet Mike."

"Sounds fine. We leave early, we'll beat traffic."

They found a windowless and dark sports bar in the basement level of the Hyatt. At ten to noon, they were the only two customers. A girl who looked like she might be a college student greeted them from behind the bar when they came in. They ordered beers and carried them to the farthest corner of the bar, behind two pool tables in the back. They sat opposite each other at a round table.

"There's something I've been wondering about," Julissa said. "Assume I get into the FBI's computers and trace the person who's been erasing data from VICAP."

"Okay."

"And assume by tweaking all the geo-location software I can get my hands on, and by reversing everything he's done to cover his tracks, I track him down."

Chris nodded and sipped his beer.

"So then what?" Julissa said.

"Then we go and we watch. Like you said, whoever's doing the hacking is either the killer or someone the killer hired. So we go and figure out who we're dealing with."

"Like a stakeout."

"Yeah."

"What if we watch him and figure out he's not the killer. Just someone who works for him?"

Chris looked at her. "What would you want to do with someone like that?"

"Watch him as long as we can and get as much information as we can that way," Julissa said. She picked at the label on her beer. "And then we go in and grab him. Take him somewhere quiet and have a private conversation with him. Find out everything he knows. Then search his house and his computer when we're through with him."

"I've been thinking along the same lines."

"What I'm wondering is what we do with a guy like that after we're done asking him questions."

"Maybe we should just figure that out when the time comes. Based on the circumstances," he said.

"I'm in this all the way. I'm not taking anything off the table and I'm not going to lose any sleep over what we do."

Chris nodded. They sat in silence for a while and drank their beers. Chris finished his and set the empty bottle on the table.

"I'll go pay," he said. "Take your time."

She watched him walk past the pool tables, across the small dance floor, and up to the empty bar. The college student came and took his credit card. Julissa continued to pick at the label of her beer and finally peeled it off the bottle and stuck it on the tabletop, smoothing it down around its edges. She wasn't sure why she felt so nervous.

"Julissa!"

She looked up. Chris was waving her to come.

"You need to see this!"

Then Chris was motioning to the girl behind the bar.

"Can you turn off the music and turn that up? Please?" He was pointing at a TV behind the bar. Julissa couldn't see it yet, but something in Chris's voice had her moving fast. The bartender found the right remote controls, turning the music down and the TV up. The TV was showing CNN. A blonde reporter stood before a burning building, between two fire trucks. The building was a two-story stone-and-glass structure, half of which was completely lost in flames. The other wing of the building had smoke pouring out of the shattered windows. The firemen in the background were aiming streams of water at the flames and into the broken windows.

The banner headline underneath the image said, *Blaze Engulfs Genetics Lab in Massachusetts, 16 Feared Dead.*

"Oh shit," Julissa whispered.

Over the reporter's shoulder, the camera filmed a crew of firefighters approaching the building with a hose. They were in full protective gear and wore oxygen tanks on their backs. They entered the building through a broken ground-floor window.

Now the reporter was talking.

"...not sure if this is domestic terrorism or some kind of tragic accident. None of Intelligene's employees are accounted for. Right now the first fire crew is going inside the south wing of the building. We've been told this is an unprecedented move at this stage in a fire. They're risking it because people may be trapped in the building. Deputy Fire Chief...wait, someone's talking in my ear piece."

The reporter put a hand to her ear and listened for a moment. Behind her, the last of the four firemen entered the building. The hose trailed in through the window and black smoke poured out.

"Our mobile news truck has a scanner that can pick up the fire crew's radio transmissions and we're going to broadcast them live. We're switching over to that now," the reporter said. She stepped to her right and out of the frame of the camera's shot. A new headline appeared at the bottom of the screen.

Live feed as Fire Crew Enters Burning Lab.

Julissa hadn't realized it, but she'd taken Chris's hand. She stood next to him, held tight and watched the screen. She heard the girl behind the bar say something.

"You from there or something?"

"Sort of," Chris muttered. He didn't take his eyes off the screen.

Then the live audio feed started. The firemen's voices were muffled behind their oxygen masks and barely audible over the roar of hot air that blasted past their open microphones.

"We're in a conference room. Furniture is...melted. No bodies."

A different voice, "Can get through here."

"Watch it."

There was a long blast of static and then finally a voice emerged from it.

"We're in the main lab. I see a body behind a collapsed table. Make that two. Wait a minute...hang on..."

For a moment the sound cut out completely. The camera went on filming the burning building and the fire crews on the outside who were losing their fight against the fire on the other half of the lab. The sound clicked back on.

"...oly shit, Chief, there are at least a dozen bodies here. They're stacked in a pile. No heads. No fucking heads at all. Some are missing arms and legs...just ripped apart...Jesus fucking..."

There was a splintering crash and a roaring boom. A different voice came back.

"We gotta pull the fuck outta here. There's no survivors. This place is gonna collapse in about thirty seconds. Now! Now! Now!"

On the screen, the amount of smoke billowing from the widows suddenly tripled. The front façade of the building teetered and then fell in a flaming cascade of bricks and glass. The first of the firefighters emerged from the shattered window and turned to help the others. One by one they made it out and then ran at a crouch away from the building.

Julissa looked down and saw she was squeezing Chris's hand. He didn't seem to notice. She tugged on his arm.

"Chris. Let's go."

They went straight from the bar to the valet stand, got into Chris's car and pulled onto Kalakaua Avenue. Julissa sat in the passenger seat. She got out her cell phone, put it on speaker, and dialed Westfield's number. It went directly to his voicemail and she left a message saying to call her. Then she called Mike Nakamura. His phone rang ten times and no one picked up. The voicemail answered on the eleventh ring.

"Jesus," Julissa said, after she'd left a message and hung up. "What now?"

"We'll go to my house. We'll keep calling them."

"What about Chevalier?" she said.

"He's probably dead."

"I believe in coincidences, but this is too much. It had to be because of us." Julissa was thinking of the firefighter's voice on the radio. Everyone at Intelligene had been ripped to pieces.

"I agree."

"But how could the killer have found out about Chevalier?"

"I don't know. But if he knows about Chevalier, he knows about us," Chris said.

Julissa had already thought of that.

"Assuming that was him in Massachusetts an hour ago, we're safe for now," she said.

"Yes."

Chris pulled onto the freeway. They followed it a few miles and then took the exit for the Pali Highway. The mountains ahead of them were capped in clouds. She tried calling Westfield and Mike Nakamura again, with the same results.

"Let me ask you something," Chris said. "I already know what I think. If Chevalier was murdered because of his work for us, does that mean his email was true?"

Julissa looked out the window. There were waterfalls on some of the high cliff faces. Normally, she would have asked to stop at the lookout they were passing. They rounded a bend and sped into a tunnel.

"Yes. I think so. If the killer tracked him down and murdered him, then he was probably on to something."

"Shit. That's what I think too."

"Unless—okay, here's a weird theory. What if Dr. Chevalier just ran a genetic sequence and found enough normal information about a human being that we could have traced the killer? The killer finds out somehow—maybe Chevalier actually identified the person through known records and then made the mistake of confronting him. The killer hacks his account and sends us the email from Dr. Chevalier. Then he kills him. Now we're left with nothing solid to go on."

"Why bother sending us the email if he could just kill Chevalier and get rid of all the evidence?"

Julissa thought Chris was right. The explanation for the attack on Intelligene which made the most sense also required them to accept that the killer was not human. If they weren't willing to accept that premise, then the attack would be hard to explain.

"Maybe it was just a coincidence," Julissa said. "The reporter said something about domestic terrorism."

"A dozen people dismembered and decapitated at the same lab that was sequencing his DNA? Less than ten hours after he sent his email?"

"It's hard to swallow," Julissa admitted. "But so's the alternative."

They had come out of the tunnel and were making a sweeping turn as the road curved and clung to the side of the Nuuanu Pali cliffs. She could see the east side of the island, which she remembered from a map she'd studied in Galveston. The map hadn't shown the turquoise waters off the beaches of Kailua and Lanikai, or the darker water of cloud-covered Kaneohe Bay, but she recognized the towns of Kailua and Kaneohe, and the Marine Corps base that lay on the peninsula between them.

Fifteen minutes later they were at Chris's driveway. They pulled off the road and drove down a steep hill. Both sides of the driveway were lined with mountain ginger and banana trees, and when they reached the flat lawn, he parked under an awning beneath a giant banyan tree. They walked through the grass to the house along a path of stepping stones. The house was two stories, with decks and balconies to give it views of Kaneohe Bay, Chinaman's Hat, and the cliffs that towered over the road.

At the front door, Chris punched the code to his security system, waited for a green light, and then put his thumb over a fingerprint scanner next to the door. A second green light came on and the door opened electronically. A computerized voice, vaguely feminine, announced, "Front door. Disarmed. Ready to arm."

Julissa watched Chris enter. He looked so fit, handsome and sane for someone who'd spent years breeding paranoia and rage and thinking of nothing but revenge. A man like him should have a long beard, live in a rented room, and wear the same overcoat every day. She followed him into his house.

"Let's go up to my study," Chris said. "I'll send an email to Mike and Westfield. If they're not answering their phones, maybe they can read email." They went through the living room and up a koa wood staircase. His study had windows on three walls and looked out over the bay. She could see his boat moored in deeper water a few hundred feet from the end of his dock.

Chris woke his desktop computer from hibernation and pulled the chair back from the desk. "You can use this to look for news, and I'll email the guys from my cell phone."

Julissa nodded. "It bothers me they're not answering."

"Me too."

Julissa put her purse on the desk and sat behind Chris's computer. The purse had a laptop computer, a cell phone, two hundred dollars in cash, her ID and credit card, and her Sig Sauer with two extra boxes of .45 ACP rounds.

"It's summer vacation—Mike could be snorkeling with his kids. Westfield's probably driving across Texas out of cell phone range."

"Too many coincidences," Julissa said.

The doorbell rang and they both looked at each other.

"Mike?" Julissa said.

Chris picked up a remote control and turned on the TV mounted on the only wall of the study not covered with windows. He turned it to channel two and then scrolled through a list of security cameras. He selected a camera labeled *Entry*. The screen showed an image evidently filmed by a tiny camera mounted in the front door's peephole. A man wearing an aloha shirt and khaki pants was standing on the doormat.

He was carrying a manila mailing envelope.

"Know him?" Julissa asked.

"No."

Chris went to the phone on the desk and put it on speaker.

"Morning," Chris said.

On the screen, the man looked up, then looked around. The intercom speaker must have been well hidden.

"Help you with something?"

"I got a delivery for a Chris Wilcox," the man said. He had a Russian accent.

"Leave it on the door mat. I'll pick it up later."

"You got to sign for it."

"Who're you with?"

"City Express."

"Supervisor over there still Doug Hirayama?" Chris asked. He opened the drawer to the left of Julissa's leg and took out his Glock. She watched him take the safety off.

"Yeah, that's him," the man said.

Chris put the phone on mute.

"I've got no idea who the supervisor at City Express is. Neither does he. Doug Hirayama's an attorney I used to work with."

Julissa pulled the Sig Sauer from her purse.

The man outside clearly did not know there was a camera as well as a microphone. They saw him take a silenced pistol from behind the envelope and shift it to his right hand.

"You gonna sign for this thing or what?" the man said.

Chris took the phone off of mute. "Be down in a minute. I gotta get dressed."

"Okay," the man said. They saw the right corner of his mouth go up in a half-grin. "I'll be right here."

Chris turned off the intercom and then flicked the remote control until the TV screen showed small shots taken by all the exterior cameras around the house. He pointed at the screen.

"I'm going out the back door. You'll see me here, here and then here," he said, touching the video feed from each camera he'd pass. He dug into his desk drawer and found an earpiece for his cell phone. He put it on and clipped the phone to his belt.

"Call me now. Talk to me while I'm going around. If he moves, tell me where he's going. Just say the number of the camera feed."

Julissa took out her phone and called Chris. She was too focused to feel fear.

"And if you get behind him?"

"I'll tell him to drop the gun and put his hands in the air."

"Okay." She dialed his cell number.

Chris left the room and trotted quietly down the stairs. He

answered her call and whispered to her.

"I'm at the back door, going out now," he said. "See me?"

"Yeah. And the guy's still on your doorstep."

She saw Chris from above the back door. He walked along the wall of the house, stepping between the flowers in a bed. He turned the corner, disappeared from the frame, and appeared again on the edge of the next camera's shot. There were ginger plants growing along that wall of the house, so he moved farther out and walked in the grass. He was at a low crouch and had the gun in front of him, both hands on its grip.

"You're doing fine," Julissa said. "He hasn't moved."

Chris came to the next corner. Julissa was pretty sure when he turned this corner, he'd be on the same side of the house as the gunman. She saw Chris pause, peering around the corner. Then he ran forward, low to the ground. He disappeared from the shot. She could hear him breathing as he ran.

"You're off the screens," Julissa said. "But he hasn't moved."

"I'm fifty feet from him. I've got some cover behind the banyan tree. You'll see me when I move in."

"Be careful," she said.

"Anything goes wrong, call 9-1-1 and don't leave the house."

"Unless I can help you," Julissa said. She did not intend to cower in the house.

"He still facing the door?"

"Yes."

"I'm going now."

She saw Chris running in from behind the banyan tree. There was no cover for him at all. He had the gun out and was twenty-five paces from the man when he stopped. When he spoke to the man, she could hear it through the cell phone.

"I got a gun on your back and I could drop you. Toss the gun and put your hands in the air."

Julissa watched. The man was still staring at the door. His grin disappeared. She could see Chris over the man's left shoulder.

"I'm not even going to count to three," Chris said. "Drop the gun now!"

Julissa had no warning. The man's face didn't change at all. He just spun around, raising his gun as he went. She didn't hear a shot, but the pistol was silenced, so she didn't expect to. She had no idea how many times he fired. Chris's gun came through loud and clear. One shot. Julissa threw down her phone, held her gun out in front of her, and ran for the stairs.

Chapter Twenty

You have got to be kidding me, Westfield thought.

He was sitting on his bed, looking at his phone. There was no visible damage, but the goddamned thing wouldn't turn on. It must have gotten crushed between the floor and his hip when got shot in the knee. On top of that, the bullet that had gone through his knee without hitting any bones had hit his laptop computer, which had been sitting on the floor next to his duffel bag.

Un-fucking-believable, Westfield thought.

The TV was tuned to CNN, which was still showing the Intelligene fire in Foxborough. He'd first turned it on so anyone who overheard the fight in his room would think he'd just been watching a movie. But then he saw the banner headlines on the screen and stopped what he was doing to watch. He'd taken his eyes off the screen only long enough to pull the trash bag out of the waste basket and put it around the dead man's head. Best to keep as much blood off the carpet as he could. The room was already going to be a disaster. There were two bullet holes in the carpet, blood near the entryway and thick pools of blood under the man's head. One pillow had a hole all the way through it and was soaked with blood. He had opened the window and turned the air conditioner up full blast to try to clear the room of gun smoke before someone noticed the smell in the hallway.

With his phone and laptop destroyed, he had no immediate way to contact Chris, Julissa, or Mike. He'd only stored their numbers on his phone and he had no idea what they were.

He hopped on his good leg to the nightstand next to the bed and pulled out the drawer. The Galveston yellow pages sat on top of the Gideon bible. He found a taxi company's number, and picked up the phone on the nightstand.

The first dispatcher listened to his request and told him no way. They didn't do jobs like that. He hung up, then picked another company. This time he was talking to an independent cab driver. The man repeated Westfield's request back at him. Could he stop at a drugstore, buy a pair of aluminum crutches, some hydrogen peroxide, some gauze and a couple of ace bandages, and deliver them to a room at the Hotel Galvez for two hundred in cash? Hell yes, he could, and he could do it in thirty minutes. Westfield hung up and hobbled back to the end of the bed. At least he'd solved one problem.

He rested a minute and then set about dragging the dead man into the bathroom. The man probably weighed two hundred and fifty pounds. Westfield's right knee wasn't any help. He dragged the man by his ankles while hopping on his left leg. He got him into the bathroom, kicked his arms until the door would close, and then turned to look at the room. It still looked pretty much like a murder scene. He decided for the short term, the easiest way to deal with it would be to just make it messier. He pulled the bedspread off the mattress and dropped it on the floor at the foot of the bed to hide the biggest blood stain and the splattered pillow. He dropped a bath towel over his own blood stains nearer the doorway. Then he opened the door, checked that the hallway was empty, and spent a moment staring at the hall carpet until he found the shell casing from the bullet the man had put through his knee. It was about five feet away from the door. He picked it up and went back into his room. There were four other shell casings to find.

The taxi driver was true to his word and knocked almost exactly thirty minutes after Westfield's call. By then Westfield had changed into clean pants and a T-shirt. He pulled on a pair of socks to cover the blood that had dripped down his leg onto his foot, and then went to the door. On the way over he tucked the silenced pistol in the waistband of his pants and pulled his shirt over the bulge. He checked through the peep hole. The cab driver was an old man in a John Deere gimme cap and a sweat-stained plaid shirt. He was leaning on the crutches and holding a plastic shopping bag from Walgreens. Westfield opened the door with the cash in his hand.

The cab driver looked at him and saw the folded twenties.

"Guess this is the right door."

"Thanks, buddy."

Westfield took the crutches and the bag, then handed over the cash. He looked in the bag and saw that the driver had bought everything he'd asked for.

"Thanks again."

He shut the door before the driver could ask any questions or get another look at the room behind him. Then he hobbled into the room on his crutches and sat on the bed. Normally he'd have gone to the bathroom to patch up a wound, but the corpse occupied most of the space. He'd feel weird about that. He hadn't decided how he was going to handle that problem. He had until eleven the next morning to figure that out—unless the dead man was supposed to report to someone, which seemed likely enough. As long as the man's handler wasn't waiting in the lobby, he'd probably have a few hours to sort this out before he had to worry about reinforcements.

The more immediate problem was to figure out a way to contact Chris, Julissa and Mike. If he were planning an operation like this, he'd take everyone down at the same time. Otherwise the targets would figure it out, and then why bother? But he wouldn't be able to warn anybody until he could get himself in a condition to leave the hotel room. He took off his pants and spent the next half hour working on his knee. He used the entire bottle of hydrogen peroxide, all the gauze, and two ace bandages. Then he dug into his duffel bag, found his toiletry kit, and dry-swallowed a couple of Excedrin tablets. He dressed again and checked himself in the mirror on the closet door. He didn't see any blood. He took another look around the room and almost laughed when he realized it had been reserved in Chris Wilcox's name, with his credit card.

No matter how well he cleaned, Chris was probably going to be paying for a new carpet.

It wasn't too bad moving on the crutches, at least not at first. He made sure his room's *Do Not Disturb* sign was well fixed to the door handle, and then crutched his way to the elevator lobby. He saw a sign for the business center behind the concierge desk, and he went through a set of glass doors to a small room with three desktop PCs set up on tables. He ran his credit card and logged into his webmail.

Julissa, Chris and Mike—

If you get this, get out of your houses or your hotel rooms. Now. Make sure no one's following you and find someplace safe to hole up. DO NOT USE YOUR CREDIT CARD TO PAY FOR A HOTEL. He can track you that way. That's how he found me. That's all I'm going to say about that in writing. My cell phone got broken in the scuffle, but I'm okay. Mostly, I was just lucky. I'll contact you again in a bit. Right now I've got things to take care of.

If you haven't seen the news out of Foxborough, you need to check it. Then you'll understand what we're up against.

A.W.

This would have to do, though after he sent the email, he spent five minutes using Google to see if he could find home numbers for Chris or Mike. He wasn't too surprised that neither of them had a listed number.

He left the computer room and hobbled outside. A bellboy hit a switch that automatically opened the door. Then, outside, a uniformed valet left his kiosk and came up to him. He looked like a high school kid with his first summer job.

"Sir, you need some help?"

He shook his head. "No thanks, son. I'm doing okay."

That was going to be a problem, later, when he was taking certain items out of his room and to the van. An enthusiastic kid might insist. He'd have to think of a way to deal with that. For now, he just hobbled to the parking lot across the street and got in his van. It was two in the afternoon; the inside of the van was holding steady at a hundred and thirty degrees. He settled into the seat, cranked down the window and drove onto Seawall Boulevard going south. For a moment, the heat and the pain in his leg had him seeing swarms of black specks. He held the wheel with both hands and drove straight ahead until the wave of dizziness passed. After that, he was okay.

At WalMart, he thought about taking a handicapped space close to the entrance, but he didn't have a sticker and he figured today probably wasn't the best day to attract any kind of attention at all. He found a spot near the back of the lot. By the time he got into the store, his leg was pulsing in pain and he was seeing the black spots again. At least it was air conditioned inside. Along the back wall, next to a coin-operated gumball machine and a vending machine that sold generic Cokes, he saw a row of three-wheeled shopping scooters for handicapped people.

Fuck it.

People used those things in WalMart all the time. He'd bring more attention to himself if he passed out, or if all the jostling broke open his bandages and his knee started bleeding again. He got on one of the scooters, balanced his crutches between his thighs, and took off. *This is going to be a really weird shopping trip*, he thought. He headed to the sporting goods section.

It turned out the largest suitcase WalMart sold was only twenty-nine inches high and twenty-four inches across, hardly large enough to solve Westfield's problem unless he also bought a hacksaw. He knew he didn't have the stomach for that, plus there was the mess to consider. He already had enough on his hands. He had to get the body out of his tenth-floor hotel room and across the street to his van, and he had to leave the room looking like something other than a slaughterhouse. In the end, he spent half an hour rolling his shopping scooter up and down the aisles until he thought of a solution. He went through the beauty aisle and the business supplies section to pick up the small items he'd need. Then he went back to the home furnishings department and found a clerk.

"I was wondering if you could give me a hand, because I need to buy that futon and I threw out my knee," he said. He was pointing at a folding bed that doubled as a couch. It had a metal frame and a black mattress. The important thing was that it was packed into a cardboard box that was six feet long, three feet wide and two feet deep. The clerk disappeared and eventually came back with a large dolly and told Westfield to meet him up front.

In the end, Westfield tipped the clerk ten dollars to load the futon into the back of his van.

Once he was in the van, he had to talk himself into going back to the hotel. With the *Do Not Disturb* sign in place, it would be nearly twenty hours before the maids found the body. He could be out of Texas by then. But his fingerprints were all over the room, and the room was irretrievably linked to Chris. And he'd used his credit card to pay for room service his first night. So he had to go back and finish this. Shooting the guy was the right thing to have done. It didn't put him any closer to getting the thing that had gotten Tara, but he felt better. That was something. He told himself he would only regret this if he got caught. And he'd only regret getting caught because then he'd have come so far for nothing.

On his way back, he took a left on 61st Street and drove towards the bay. He'd seen a U-Haul rental shop down there when he first came into town. He pulled into its parking lot, limped to the office, and asked to rent a dolly. It was fifteen dollars a day. He filled out the rental form, used his credit card for the deposit, and waited for the clerk to bring a dolly out from behind the counter.

The van started on his second try. He drove back to the hotel, circling the parking lot until he could get the space closest to the hotel. After he set the parking brake he crawled between the seats to the back, to pull the futon from its box. The mattress came wrapped in a giant plastic bag. He pulled this off and put it into the empty box, then crawled to the side door. He opened it and tenderly let himself down to the asphalt. From here and for the next hour, he was going to have to go without the crutches. The one-hour limit was arbitrary. He'd given himself that much time, and no longer, to box the body, clean the room and haul everything back to the van. It was definitely time to get out of Galveston.

Chapter Twenty-One

Chris was sitting on the grass with his gun on his knee. He watched as Julissa opened the front door and surveyed the scene. She lowered her weapon, stepped over the body on the doorstep, and walked to him. She knelt on the grass next to him and put her hands on his shoulders.

"You all right?"

"Yeah."

"Where'd he hit you?"

"He never got off a shot."

She looked at Chris's body and ran her hands along the sides of his torso to his hips.

"Thank god for that."

"It won't look much like self-defense."

Julissa looked back at the body on the front step. Chris's single shot had hit the delivery man on the bridge of his nose. The bullet took most of the back of the man's head with it on its way through. Blood and brain tissue were spread across the front door.

"It's all on video," she said. "I don't know if that's good or bad."

"Probably bad."

"Can you stand?"

"Yeah."

She took his hand and they walked over to the body. With the corpse at their feet, they both instinctively looked across the front yard to see if there had been witnesses. The street was up the hill, obscured by trees and climbing vines. High rock walls and tangles of trees blocked the view to the neighboring properties. Someone may have heard the shot, but there were wild boars on this side of the island. People hunted them. A single loud bang wouldn't draw any attention.

"Before we touch him, we should decide," Chris said. "You want to call the cops?"

"No."

"You're sure?"

She nodded. "Think about it. The guy we're looking for killed everyone at Intelligene. He probably sent this guy for us. We can't reach Aaron or Mike, so he might've sent people after them. If we call the cops, he'll get the advantage. We'll be tied down for days answering questions. You might get arrested. He'll know exactly where we are and what we're doing. He'll have all the time in the world to plan his next move. Right now, we've got the advantage. You killed the guy he sent, and he probably won't know that for a few more hours."

Chris gestured at the dead man with his Glock. "How do we know this isn't the killer right here?"

"You think it is?"

"No. I guess not. From what we heard on the news, it sounds like he might've done Intelligene himself. And he had a reason to do that himself, because of what Intelligene knew. Which puts him in Massachusetts right now."

"This guy was a hit man."

They looked at him. There wasn't much left of his upper face or his head. Chris knelt and picked up the manila envelope and the silenced pistol. He handed the pistol to Julissa and opened the envelope. It had a washcloth that smelled like ether or nail polish remover, a switchblade knife, and several large-sized plastic zip ties. He handed the envelope to Julissa and she looked through it without comment.

He patted the man down and felt a key in one of his pockets. He reached in and found a Dodge key on a Hertz fob. The man had no wallet or other identification. He'd sounded Russian on the intercom. He looked like he'd been in his thirties. His shirt was a brand Chris had never heard of, and his shoes were old and worn out. Deep cuts were healing across the knuckles of his left hand and on the outside of his left wrist. As though he'd been in a knife fight, days ago. He'd probably come out on top in a lot of fights before today. He had shaved that morning and there was a bit of dried shaving cream or soap on his right earlobe. Beyond that, there wasn't much to conclude about him.

"He might've parked up the road out of sight, then walked back down here," Chris said.

"We've gotta get in touch with Mike. Or go find him. Aaron, too."

"We need to get this guy off my doorstep first," Chris said. "In case a real delivery man comes. I'll do it, if you want to keep calling Mike and Aaron."

She nodded and went back inside. Chris trotted around the side of the house and unlocked the gardening shed. He stepped past the lawn mower and the workbench and reached to the top of the shelves to pull down the insulated fish bag that had come with the boat. It was a blue canvas bag, six feet long and three feet wide, with a zipper opening on the long side. The inside was insulated with an inch-thick layer of silvery plastic-coated foam. It was perfect for keeping a freshly caught tuna cool on a long sail back to port. But it would fit other dead things.

Back on the porch, he dropped the bag alongside the man, unzipped it, and rolled him inside. Then he zipped the bag closed and dragged it into the grass along the side of the house. He came back to the front, uncoiling the hose from the front flowerbed.

So little time had passed between shooting the man and cleaning up, it was easy to spray the blood off the door and the porch. It would show up under Luminol and black lights, and if he ever had the chance, he intended to get out here with a bottle of detergent and a scrub brush. The bullet, upon exiting the man's head, had lodged itself in the door just below the peephole. He had no immediate way of taking care of that, so he ignored it. He thought it was pretty likely that after today, he wouldn't see his house again for a long time.

Julissa came out as he was using the high-pressure stream of water to chase bits of skull and brain matter off the porch and into the flowerbeds where the ants could take care of them. She'd been gone about two minutes.

"Any luck?"

She shook her head. "Mike's phone just rings and rings, and Aaron's goes straight to voicemail. You done here?"

"One more minute."

He turned off the hose, then dragged the fish bag to the garden shed. Inside, it was ninety degrees and humid. If he didn't come up with a more permanent solution soon, the smell would take over. He had no idea when the gardeners were supposed to come next, but the lawn looked recently mowed. He hoped they weren't coming today. He dragged the bag to the back of the shed, grabbed a pair of cotton gardening gloves off the shelf, then went out and locked the doors. Julissa was waiting by his car.

"Mike's house?" he asked.

"We've got to."

He nodded and opened the passenger door for her. She was carrying her purse, which was unzipped. She had kept the silenced pistol and the manila envelope. Undoubtedly her Sig Sauer was in there somewhere, too. His pistol was tucked into the back of his pants. He hoped they had enough.

A quarter mile up the road they came to a red Dodge Caliber parked in the ditch. There was a sticker with a rental company's bar code on the back bumper. Chris slowed and stopped. He took the man's key from his pocket and hit the unlock button. They saw the Dodge's tail lights flash twice.

"You drive my car," Chris said. "Follow me. I'm going to leave it in the parking lot at Shark's Cove. I don't want it anywhere near my house when the rental car company reports it missing and the police pick it up."

"Okay."

Chris got out of his car and went to the Dodge. He opened the trunk, but it was empty. He put on his gardening gloves, opened the door and got inside. There was an envelope with the rental contract in the console between the seats. He took that and put it in his pocket. There was nothing in the glove compartment or under the seats. Then he started the car and pulled onto the highway, checking behind for Julissa.

Mike lived in Pupukea, above Shark's Cove on the rural north shore of Oahu. The way to get there from Chris's house was to follow the Kamehameha Highway, a two-lane, curving road that clung to the thin strip of flat ground between the mountains and the ocean. It ran up the east side of the island to the shrimp farms in Kahuku, then turned west to follow a string of surf beaches to Pupukea. On big surf days in the winter, traffic could back up for miles in both directions. In the summer, the ocean was calm and the crowds stayed away. The drive took forty minutes, winding around horseshoe-shaped bays and down stretches of road that came so close to the turquoise water that in winter, when storms came, Chris had seen waves surge all the way across the road.

He signaled at the Shark's Cove parking lot, turned in, and found a space. He rolled down the Dodge's windows, left the keys in the ignition, and got out of the car. His best guess was that a rental car in a north shore lot with the keys in the ignition would last about half an hour. By nightfall it would either be stripped and sitting on its axles at Kaena Point, or parked behind a surf shack in Haliewa with a tarp over it until the kids figured out what to do next. Either option was fine with Chris. Julissa pulled in behind him and he got into the passenger seat. He directed her back onto the highway, and then they took a left onto Pupukea Road. They followed the road up a series of switchbacks until it leveled and ran flat along the ridge overlooking Shark's Cove. Mike's house was at the end of the road, across the street from an old Boy Scout camp.

There were always cars parked on the street in front of Mike's house, because a hiking trail and boar hunting area began where the road ended. Three of the cars looked like rentals. Julissa parked at the end of a row of cars and killed the engine.

"How do we do this?" she asked.

"If we walk down the trail, we can cut through the forest to the right and circle around to Mike's backyard. There's a spare key taped under a picnic table back there."

Chris had seen the key two months earlier while eating barbecued chicken with Mike and talking about the files.

"So we sneak in through the back door."

"Then we check the house. If we find Mike and he's okay, we get him and his family out."

Julissa nodded. She got out of the car and put her purse over her shoulder. The hiking trail began as a dirt road, muddy in the tire ruts from recent rains. They climbed over the locked gate that spanned the road and kept car traffic out. Then they walked a hundred yards through the forest of ironwood trees until Chris led them off the trail. They walked without speaking until they reached the slight ridge behind Mike's house. A fawn-colored dog was hiding in the bushes at the edge of Mike's yard. It heard them approach and slinked into the forest.

"Mike's dog," Chris whispered. "One of them, anyway."

Mike's picnic table was in the middle of the back lawn, next to a brick barbecue pit. The back door was at the end of a wide porch.

Chris started for the picnic table at a run. Julissa followed him. They had both taken their pistols out and held them low, pointed at the ground. Chris dropped to one knee by the table, reached underneath it, and came out with the key. He wasn't sure it would fit the lock in the back door, but it seemed like a reasonable guess. They reached the house and Chris opened the screen door, then slipped the key into the lock. It turned easily and the door opened into the kitchen. They stepped inside and let the screen door shut behind them on its rusty spring. It batted back and forth for a moment and then stilled.

A TV was on somewhere, playing what sounded like a cartoon. The lights in the kitchen were off and there were dirty dishes from lunch on the counter. There was a shattered glass on the floor, a pool of what might have been Coca-Cola, and a few ice cubes that hadn't melted yet. Chris held his pistol with both hands, still aimed at the floor, and walked around the kitchen counter into the dining room. Julissa was behind him, checking the corners. They went towards the sound of the television.

The living room couch faced away from the door Chris and Julissa came through. From behind, the family looked like it was watching a Donald Duck cartoon. Mike's wife and his two youngest children were on the couch, facing the TV. They didn't move at the sound of footsteps. Their heads were rolled forward, but they weren't asleep. Chris looked at Julissa. She was wide-eyed but not panicking. She turned her back to the scene in front of them and raised her weapon, covering the two doorways that entered the living room. Chris moved around the couch to see the rest.

Mike was on the floor where the overturned coffee table had been. He was handcuffed at his wrists and there was a leather belt buckled around his ankles. His eyes were gone, cut out. Chris couldn't tell whether that had happened before or after his throat had been slit. His wife had been garroted and his kids had been shot, once each in the forehead. The couch and the hardwood floor beneath it were soaked in blood. Mike's laptop computer was open on the floor next to him, turned on. The screen showed a security dialogue box that prompted the user for a password. Chris recognized it as the screen that Mike went through to access the walled-off files associated with his work on the redhead murders. The prompt on the screen said, *Incorrect login or password. Please try again.*

"He tortured them," Chris whispered. "Mike didn't give the password and he killed his family. Then he killed Mike."

Only the youngest child wasn't wearing handcuffs. A girl of about five. Chris understood it, then. The man had burst through the door and put the gun on the little girl's head. After gathering the family in the living room, he'd made the little girl cuff them. Then he'd have told her how to wrap the belt twice around her father's ankles and buckle it, before shoving her on the couch. He'd have shot her first. Probably the older boy next. Then he took his time with Mike's wife, strangling her slowly while he asked the questions.

Why didn't Mike just fucking talk?

On the television, Donald Duck was trying to catch fish on a mountain lake, but he was having trouble with an outboard motor and was throwing a fit. Mike's youngest daughter succumbed to gravity and post-mortem contractions. She slumped over and fell off the couch, landing in a fetal position on the floor.

"Let's get out of here," Julissa said.

He looked at her and nodded. They retreated from the house the way they'd come, dashing across the backyard and into the trees. They left the back door unlocked and open. Chris paused just long enough to use his T-shirt to wipe the door knob, which was the only part of the house he'd touched.

"You touch anything inside?" Chris asked Julissa when they were back in the forest. She was pale and shaking. She'd put her gun back into her purse, though. Chris tucked his back into his waistband and pulled his shirt over it.

"I didn't," she said.

They came out of the forest and back onto the path. They didn't speak again until they were in Chris's car, winding down the switchbacks of Pupukea Road.

"What about Aaron?" Julissa said.

"I know."

Chris handed her his cell phone and she tried calling. The call went straight to voicemail. Chris took a right at the traffic light and accelerated down Kamehameha. Julissa left another voicemail message for Westfield and then hung up. She tried to hand Chris his phone but her hand was shaking and she dropped it in the foot well.

"You gonna be okay?" Chris asked.

"Yeah," she said. "Give me a minute."

They drove in silence, racing past Sunset Beach, which was empty on this surfless summer day.

"I need a pay phone," Chris said. "Mike's got three other kids. I need to call 9-1-1. The cops gotta be there before the older kids get home."

They pulled into a gas station in Kahuku. There was a pay phone next to the newspaper stand out front. He dialed 9-1-1 and waited for the operator to answer.

"9-1-1 emergency, how can I help you?" the woman said.

"You need to send some squad cars up Pupukea Road. My buddy and I were hiking back there and when we came through the gate next to the Boy Scout camp, we heard shots from the house across the street. 2611 Pupukea. There were screams too."

"Sir, can you tell me your name?"

"It was about ten minutes ago. I found the first pay phone I could. I was too scared to go up to the house. It says Nakamura on the mail box. You gotta send someone right now. They were screaming. The kids were screaming."

He hung up the phone and went back to the car. Mike had been his only friend for the last six years. But he'd always kept Mike at arm's length and never let him in. Maybe he'd kept Mike at bay for years because he was jealous. Mike had a wife and a houseful of kids and family all over the island. Chris had his fine house by the bay and nothing but anger to fill it with. And now Mike and his family were just a mess for someone to clean up. A report to go in a file that might be erased later. He shut his door and started the engine.

"They're coming?" Julissa asked.

"Yeah."

He put the car in gear and they got back onto Kamehameha Highway.

"You find anything in his car when you drove it?"

"I forgot," he said. He reached into his pocket and pulled out the envelope with the rental contract. "He had this."

He handed it to her and kept his eyes on the road. Julissa opened it and read it.

"He rented the car under the name Alex Fairfield. Fake, I guess. He only rented it for two days." She flipped through the papers and a smaller strip sifted out and fell into her lap. She picked it up and studied it.

"Oh shit, Chris."

"What?"

"This is a baggage claim receipt," she said. She held it up and Chris glanced at it. There were three stubs stapled to what looked like the flap of an airline ticket envelope.

"Yeah?"

"There're three names. Fairfield, Jackson and Caryl. Chris—he came with two friends, and they each checked a bag."

"Shit."

Julissa turned to look through the rear window. There were no cars following.

"Christ. Alex Fairfield came for you. Jackson or Caryl went to Mike. The other one's probably waiting in my room at the Hyatt."

"Seems likely."

"What do we do?"

Chris drummed his fingers on the steering wheel and accelerated through a straightaway. He was doing eighty-five when they passed a roadside stand selling pineapples and Kahuku sweet corn.

"We need to get off Oahu. Now."

"We're going to the airport?"

"Too dangerous. Even if we got there as fast as we could, we couldn't hope to get on a plane for at least three hours. After they figure out we killed their third man, they'll assume we're running. There've only got two security checks at the airport. One guy walking between the lines is all it'd take to spot us. If they don't kill us in the airport, all they'd have to do is see what flight we board and make a phone call. Plus, there's a body in my shed and the gardeners will find it in the next day or two if I don't take care of it."

"Where's that leave us?"

"We'll go back to my place and leave Oahu in the next half hour— on my boat."

"Okay," Julissa said. "But hurry. Because the other obvious thing they might do, when Alex Fairfield doesn't check in, is come to your house."

"I know."

Chris pulled into the left lane to pass a VW van that was puttering along at thirty-five miles an hour.

"There a faster way to your house?"

"No."

They were driving past shrimp farms; a little later they passed the Mormon enclave at Laie. Then they were racing next to the ocean, passing through villages at seventy miles an hour. Hauula, Punaluu. Chris slowed when they passed bridges over streams because there were children lined on the rails fishing for tilapia in the mangrove roots. They rounded the steep bends at Kahana Bay and Chris slowed to the speed limit when he saw a police cruiser pulling out of the Crouching Lion Inn. It passed him going the other direction and did not turn around to give chase. He hoped it was heading to Mike's house.

"Not much farther. Twenty minutes." He took his eyes off the road long enough to look at her. She was focused again, not scared. He liked the way she measured every situation. When the time came, he could count on her. She was holding her cell phone.

"That thing get internet?"

"This?" She held up the phone. "Yeah."

"Try logging in to a travel site, see what kind of flights we can get from the other islands."

"Which island?"

"We got overseas and mainland flights from Kona on the Big Island, from Maui and from Kauai. We could sail to any of those islands in under twenty-four hours."

"What's the fastest island to sail to?"

"Fastest is Molokai. Thirty-seven miles that way." He pointed towards the ocean. "No overseas flights, but we could maybe catch a single engine plane to Maui or the Big Island from there. It might take five hours to get to Molokai. We could cut that to three and a half or four if the wind is good and we run the engine full bore."

She looked at her watch, then back at her phone.

"If we get to your house in twenty minutes and we don't take longer than thirty minutes getting ready, could we make Molokai by seven?"

Chris thought about it. It'd be a race, but *Sailfish* was a fast boat.

"Yeah. We could make it to the harbor by seven. Tack on another thirty minutes to the airport."

"There's a flight from Molokai to Kona at eight thirty. Should I book it?"

"Wait'll we get to my house. See which way the wind's blowing."

"Okay."

She bent back to her phone and thirty seconds later gave out a cry that made Chris swerve to the side of the road and hit the brakes.

"What is it?"

"Aaron—he's alive. He emailed us and he's okay." She explained the email to him.

He pulled back into his lane and sped up again. Even the good news about Westfield didn't dull his urgency to get off the island. Or take away the image of Mike and his family, the youngest daughter slumping off the chair.

"He said they're tracking our credit cards?"

"Yeah," Julissa said.

"How much can you find out doing that?"

"Depends on their level of access. If they traced him to the hotel, they must know at least where he's making purchases. He must've bought a meal in the restaurant, since the room was on your card."

"Would they know what he's buying, or just where he's buying it?"

"Both."

"Hold off buying the plane tickets. If they trace our ticket purchases, they'll have someone waiting by the time we get off the plane, wherever we end up."

Julissa put down her phone and looked out the window.

"Shit. I didn't even think of that. You got a way around that?"

"Yeah. I'll show you when we get on the boat."

"I'll email Aaron, let him know what's up," she said. "But I'll keep it vague. Jesus. For all we know, they've got our emails hacked too."

"Okay."

Chris concentrated on driving. He had never liked speeding, but he was doing a decent job of it today. He passed a pickup truck stuffed full of local teenagers and gunned the engine until they reached the macadamia nut farm opposite Chinaman's Hat on Kaneohe Bay. Then he slowed to thirty-five.

"Let's keep a lookout for rental cars."

Julissa dropped her phone in her purse and started watching. They reached his driveway without seeing any cars at all.

"I'll pass my drive and go a quarter mile in the other direction, in case they parked that way."

"Good idea."

They made the check down the road south of Chris's house, and when they didn't see anything, Chris did a quick U-turn. As they rolled down the driveway, Chris saw Julissa's hand go into her purse. Holding her Sig Sauer, likely.

"I'll park in front of the door and we'll go straight inside. Anyone's been monkeying with the house I'll know right away from the security panel."

"Okay."

"If everything's okay, I'll grab my ID, a couple other things. We'll take the body out of the gardening shed, get on the dingy and go to the boat."

"How can I help?"

"Get on the phone and tell your mom and your dad to go away for a while. Camping in Wyoming, something like that—whatever, as long as it's far from Texas and no one knows about it. Tell them to take a shitload of cash and not use their credit cards. If we get away, if Westfield gets away, your family is the only leverage he'll have. I don't have anyone left. Neither does Westfield."

He didn't say the last part: *Mike's gone.* That wasn't real quite yet.

He watched Julissa nod.

He could tell from the flick of her eyes and the turn of her mouth she hadn't thought of that problem.

"Jesus, this gets worse and worse," she said.

"I know. We're all in, now. He's not going to give us any choice."

He killed the engine. They both got out of the car and dashed for the front door. As he worked the security code, he felt Julissa press her back against his. He knew she'd taken her gun from her purse and was holding it ready, waiting for whomever or whatever was out there.

Inside, Chris went to the security panel in the hallway. He hit the *Report* button and the electronic voice calmly said, "No incidents since last command to arm."

Julissa was looking at him.

"No one tried to get in. I can't say for sure no one's watching."

She looked out the kitchen windows.

"I'll hurry," he said. "Just call your folks."

Julissa nodded and sat on a stool by the kitchen counter. She put her Sig Sauer on the countertop and got out her phone. Chris left her there and ran up the stairs to his study. The safe was built into the floor under the desk. He fell to his knees, lifted the floor panel, and dialed the combination. There were a lot of documents in the safe, but the two things he wanted were both in padded mailing envelopes at the top. The first was a collection of papers and documents that had belonged to Cheryl. The second was a package he'd put together in contemplation of a day like today. It had a passport, ten thousand dollars in cash, two credit cards, and an Iridium satellite phone.

When he came downstairs, Julissa was hanging up.

"They'll go?"

"I didn't let them say no. They'll drive to San Antonio tonight, then Santa Fe tomorrow. They've got a friend they can stay with until I call to explain more."

"You ready?"

She tossed her purse over her shoulder and grabbed her gun.

They went out the front door and Chris locked his house. Then they went to the garden shed. Crossing the lawn, Chris felt how exposed they were. One of the other two men could be in the trees, hiding in the undergrowth or in one of the deep stands of ginger. They moved quickly and Chris kept himself between Julissa and the trees.

The fish bag was where he'd left it. They loaded it into the gardener's wheelbarrow, one of them on each end of the bag. It hung off the front of the wheelbarrow but didn't tip out. Chris pushed it from the shed, and led them across the lawn to the dock. Then they dropped the body into the dinghy. The little boat listed enough to take on a few gallons of water, but Chris jumped in quickly to right it. Julissa climbed in after him and sat on the gunwale, looking at the water.

"At least we don't have far to row," she said.

"You get seasick?"

"Don't know. I've never sailed."

He rowed until they reached the transom of the sailboat where he tied the dinghy's painter line to a cleat at the swim platform. He stepped aboard and held his hand out to help Julissa.

"Why aren't they here already? That's what I don't understand," she said.

"Westfield said they were tracking us with credit cards. I just used my card for the beers at the Hyatt. My card, your hotel. Maybe they put two and two together, think we're both in Waikiki."

Julissa took his hand and stepped to the boat's swim platform. They pulled the dinghy alongside and, lifting together, brought the fish bag aboard. Chris used a length of rope and a bowline knot to secure the bag's nylon handles to the boat. Then he hoisted the dinghy to its davits.

In less than ten minutes, they were underway. Chris had not unfurled the sails yet; Julissa was steering the boat between the channel buoys under engine power.

He slid back the companionway hatch and went down the stairs into the salon. The things he'd brought from his house safe were in his pockets; he pulled them out and put them in a drawer in the galley, except for the new satellite phone, which he took out of the envelope and put back into his pocket. He opened the envelope with Cheryl's old documents and looked at the contents. He never thought he was keeping them for any useful purpose. Just something to take from the safe at night after he'd had a couple glasses of whiskey, so he could turn her old documents over in his hands, feeling their edges, the places she touched. He put the envelope into the drawer and slid it shut, then climbed the steps back into the cockpit.

"You okay?" Chris asked.

"Yeah."

Chris came behind her and looked at the row of instruments behind the wheel. The wind was blowing steady at twenty knots and they'd already had a gust up to thirty. Looking ahead of the bow, out in the channel between Oahu and Molokai, he could see white caps on the waves.

"It'll be a wet ride once we get out there and get the sails up."

Julissa nodded. For now, they were still in the ship channel leading out of Kaneohe Bay. The water around them was calm and clear.

Julissa pointed at one of the flat-screen displays behind the wheel.

"What's that?"

"AIS—an automatic identification system for shipping. The transceiver shares with the VHF antenna. It broadcasts the ship's name, course and speed and picks up the same from any ship with the same system. It's a good way to avoid collisions."

"That's what I thought," she said. "Can we turn it off?"

"Why?"

"Maybe we shouldn't be broadcasting our name and position for the whole world on this trip."

"Shit, you're right. Turn that off."

"The transceiver won't keep broadcasting if I just kill it with this switch?"

"No."

They were just one stupid mistake from getting themselves killed. How many others would he make? Everyone on Chevalier's email was being hunted down and murdered, and who had given Chevalier the list of names and email addresses in the first place? Now that Mike and his family were gone. Mike, who hadn't even blinked when Chris asked him to retire from HPD and help him track Cheryl's killer. Who'd sat on this boat with him and helped him map a path to revenge. Whose kids called him Mr. Chris and whose wife sometimes left home-cooked dinners on his doorstep.

He blinked out of it. Now wasn't the time for this.

"When we get to the mouth of the channel, hold this course, dead to windward. I'll raise the sails and then we'll fall off the wind to the southeast. That'll give us a heading straight to Molokai and we won't have to tack."

Julissa nodded.

"Weather's okay for this?"

"It's kinda stiff, but it'll be okay. Nothing this boat can't handle."

Julissa steered to the right side of the channel as a sport fishing boat came in from the sea. The two vessels passed port to port, thirty feet apart. The men on the flying bridge of the other boat were looking at Julissa and not the bulging fish bag on the swim platform. The man driving the other boat, a local charter captain whose face was familiar but whose name Chris couldn't remember, flashed them a shaka sign. Chris returned it, thumb and pinkie out, a quick shake of the wrist.

"Is it true you can track a person with his cell phone, even if it's not being used?"

"I already threw mine over the side, while you were getting the boat ready," Julissa said. "If that answers your question."

Chris took his cell out, checking to be sure it wasn't the satellite phone. Then he tossed it over the rail.

"Cell phones and credit cards, most bank transactions. Smart phones are the worst because they have GPS installed, so if anyone hacks your phone, they can figure out exactly where you are. They can track you with your email if you don't take precautions. You mentioned you had a laptop on the boat, but don't bother bringing it. We can find a new one somewhere, with a unique ID number not already associated with you."

"Okay. You should be an FBI agent or something."

"I do contract work for the FBI. Or I used to. I don't know how that's going to work out after all this."

"One thing at a time, I guess. You okay with steering?"

"Yeah."

Chris sat next to Julissa on the bench behind the helm. For a while, he just sat there, his eyes closed and his thumbs on his throbbing temples. He felt Julissa's hand on his left shoulder. When he looked, she was crying noiselessly. He nodded and she leaned against him, resting her cheek on his shoulder.

They didn't speak because everything that mattered was unspeakable. Allison and Cheryl. Mike and his family. The dozens or hundreds of murdered women; the dark path ahead. After a moment, Julissa lifted her head from his shoulder and corrected their course, centering *Sailfish* in the channel.

Chris counted his breaths and watched the boat's progress. If he'd been calculating and cold for this long, he could keep it up a little longer. There'd be time later, but only if they made it out of Hawaii. For now they had a difficult sail in front of them, and he still had to find a way out of the islands. Chris took the satellite phone from his pocket and showed it to her.

"It's an Iridium I bought a couple years ago. Paid cash and set up an account under a false name, billed to a credit card that's also under a false name. That card gets paid from an offshore account under the same name. There's nothing to trace it to me."

"You set this all up—for what?"

"I've spent years tracking someone down to murder him. So at some point I started planning what happens the day after I get him."

"We pick up the rest of our lives. In a world without him. Without *it*."

"What if we murder him in broad daylight in front of a crowd of witnesses? Or get caught on video? Or we don't have time to hide the body, and the police start following the traces we leave? Or his hit men are still looking for us even after we've killed him?"

"So you've been planning all along to disappear afterward, under a fake name."

Chris nodded.

"For the short term, I have an ID you can use. We probably shouldn't count on using it too long, but it'll get us out of the country."

"What ID?"

"Cheryl's passport. It's in the galley. How old are you?"

"Twenty-nine."

"She was twenty-nine when the picture was taken. You look almost exactly like her."

"It's still valid?"

"For two more years. They don't cancel a passport when a person dies. A lot of countries do, but the U.S. doesn't."

"Because we have no national ID database, so there'd be no way to keep track." She nodded her head, understanding his plan. "It'll work, if I really look like her. What about you, what's your new name?"

"Jarrett Gardner."

Chris held up the Iridium phone. "Let me take care of our flight."

Chapter Twenty-Two

It was half an hour to midnight when Westfield pulled off Interstate 10 at a truck stop sixty miles east of San Antonio. He drove to the far corner of the lot, out of the glare of the bright fluorescent lights that lit the pumps and the area around the diner. He parked on gravel next to a dark tractor-trailer rig. He leaned back in his seat and looked at the stars through the bug-dotted windshield, listening to the hood and the engine tick as the hot metal cooled and contracted in the night breeze. He'd been driving across Texas in the dark with the windows down and the radio off, keeping to the speed limit and watching the rear-view mirror for state troopers. For the last two hours there had been hardly any traffic on the road at all. Just the amber eyes of deer reflecting his headlights back at him from the side of the highway. In the hours since leaving Galveston, he'd had plenty of time to think about everything that might have gone wrong.

First there was the clean-up job he'd done in his hotel room. The hydrogen peroxide got the smaller stains out of the carpet, but the biggest one, from the man's bleeding head, had been impossible. Westfield used half the bottle of peroxide, half a gallon of hot water from the sink, and all the washcloths in the room. He called it quits when the stain started to look like someone had spilled a pot of coffee on the rug. Inspired by that, he brewed a pot of coffee with the little machine next to the TV, took a few sips for himself, and dumped the rest onto the stain. Maybe the smell would throw the maids off for a while.

There was no hope of fixing the hole in the rug from the bullet that barely missed his head when he'd hit his attacker with the stun gun. Instead he pried loose the slug with his pocket knife, then used a cigarette lighter to burn the edges of the hole. He'd picked up a cigarette butt in the parking lot and he left it in the burned spot. The room was going to look like a rock band stayed overnight.

After that, he took care of the body. He wrapped it in the futon's plastic covering, tossed in the dirty washcloths and the blood-soaked pillow, and then wrapped everything in the bedspread. He used a couple of wraps of clear packing tape to keep everything in place before sliding the body into the futon's cardboard shipping box. He closed the flaps of the box, taped them shut, and then taped a blank piece of paper to the front of the box. With a red permanent marker he wrote, *ANTIQUES—FRAGILE.*

Getting the box onto the dolly had been difficult. Eventually he realized the man's legs were lighter than his upper body, and the solution was to stand the box on its end with the man's head facing down. If that caused more bleeding, so be it. The plastic, the pillow and towels, and the bedspread would catch it all before it started to leak out of the box. He gave the room a once-over to make sure he hadn't left anything behind, then wheeled the dolly to the elevators. He had to favor his left leg while walking, and his right knee could hold his weight only a few seconds at a time before the pain got to be too much. In the elevator, he leaned against the handrail at the back. The car stopped at the sixth floor and an old woman in a mauve-colored pantsuit got on. She studied Westfield and the box carefully until they reached the lobby. He waited for the woman to exit. Then he wheeled the dolly out, limping to the front entrance. The teenaged valet opened the door for him and Westfield came out into the late-afternoon heat.

"You need some help, sir?"

"No thanks."

Now he was in the parking lot of the truck stop. He had been thinking about murder pretty much nonstop since 1978. But he'd never given any thought to hiding bodies because that wasn't something Tara's killer did. For the first couple of hours, while driving through Houston, he'd planned to dump the box in a ditch on a quiet stretch of highway. That seemed like a good, no-nonsense plan until he realized his fingerprints were all over it. He was into dry country now, far from any deep water, and sinking the body in a rancher's pond or a shallow creek wouldn't do any good. It would likely be found in a matter of weeks. The clear packing tape binding the dead man inside his wrappings would probably hold on to Westfield's fingerprints for months underwater. Burying the body on the side of the road wasn't going to work either. Out here the topsoil was just a thin layer over the limestone bedrock. He didn't have a shovel in the van, and digging with a bad knee injury didn't sound too good either. He'd dropped off the dolly at the U-Haul store on his way out of Galveston, so whatever he did with the box was going to have to be within a few feet of the back of the van. The last thing he wanted was a state trooper to roll up behind him while he was using a hubcap to scrape out a grave next to the highway. That would raise an eyebrow.

If he lived here and knew the country, he'd be able to think of a better plan. He'd know a cave or an abandoned well. If he went a few more hours west of San Antonio, there might even be an old mineshaft in a ghost town tucked back in the shadow of a mesa. But he couldn't find these things because they weren't marked on the highway map. The only good option was to get somewhere isolated, pull the box out of the van, douse it with a couple of gallons of gasoline, throw a match, and take off. The fire might not destroy the body but it would certainly eradicate every trace of Westfield on the box. Someone would probably find the fire in half an hour, but by the time they put it out, Westfield would be over the horizon and the fingerprints would be history.

Westfield opened the door and got out, bringing his crutches with him. He wished he could talk to Chris, Julissa and Mike. He was sure there was something to learn from what happened today. Before he'd shot the man in the forehead, he'd said he worked for the killer, that he paid well.

The man didn't sound like a contract killer. Maybe he was something more like a fulltime employee. That suggested what all of them had already suspected: whoever or whatever they were looking for was wealthy. Wealthy enough to send the fulltime hired help on a business trip to Galveston to eliminate a potential threat. Wealthy enough to pay to have someone tracked by his credit transactions— maybe by the same person who was hacking into the FBI.

Westfield got to the convenience store and found the aisle with automotive supplies. He took a two-gallon portable gas can, then went to the cashier. There were open coolers full of ice and soft drinks next to the register and he picked up a bottle of Mountain Dew and a bag of beef jerky. He could eat better later. He prepaid in cash for two gallons of gas, then went outside to the pumps. He was running low on cash but hadn't used his credit card since Galveston. He supposed the best thing would be to stop at a bank in the morning, take out a few thousand dollars, and then drive like hell in a new direction.

He figured he'd drive another three hours past San Antonio and get off the main road before he dumped the body and burned it. The interstate would be quiet at three a.m. in West Texas; a rural road would be plain dead. Back on the highway, he opened his bottle of Mountain Dew and took a long swallow. He wished he could use his credit card and check into a motel. He'd take a long shower, turn down the air conditioner, and sleep. Whenever he slept in a dark room with the air conditioner blasting, he could fall asleep pretending he was in his bunk aboard *White Plains*—in an hour he'd relieve the watch officer, steering the ship as close as it could go to the Chinese line without crossing. And in those thoughts, just before dreams, the radio telegram would never come. The ship's XO would not take the folded paper from the radio ensign, would not read it silently and ask Second Lieutenant Westfield to step away from his station and come out on deck for a quick talk. Of course, replaying the moment in his mind wouldn't change anything. Neither would wishing for a shower and a night in a motel.

"I'm still not sorry I shot you, you son of a bitch," he said.

After another thirty minutes, he finally broke down and tried to find something besides Jesus or country western on the radio.

San Antonio was asleep when he passed through it just before one in the morning. A police car came down the entrance ramp after the Alamo Dome and stayed on his tail for a mile and a half. Westfield kept the van at exactly fifty-five miles an hour. The cop was just coasting along in his draft, maybe waiting for dispatch to come back with a report on his plates. Then, without signaling, the cop pulled into the far left lane and shot past Westfield's van. In another ten minutes he was out of the city and back into the darkness of the dry countryside. He stopped at a rest area, walked to the barbed-wire fence at the edge of the mown grass, and relieved himself into a scraggly live oak growing at the fence line. The stars were bright and the air was as dry as the rocks. He could smell some kind of night-blooming flower, a cactus maybe.

He walked back to the van and drove an hour until he turned onto U.S. 277 in Sonora. He went north on this smaller highway, winding between eroded buttes and mesas, and after ten miles veered west onto an unpaved, unmarked county road. After a mile he stopped, turned the van around, and parked on the side of the road, facing the way he'd come. He got out of the van and went around to the back, not using his crutches. There were no lights and no houses in view. Each side of the road was closed off by a barbed-wire fence. Low cedars and scrubby oaks and mesquite trees grew in the pasture land spread between the mesas silhouetted against the stars. The grass along the side of the road was so dry it crunched when he stepped on it. He opened the back doors of the van and took hold of the cardboard box with the body. He slid it along the bed of the van and then let gravity do the rest. The box fell onto the grass, balanced briefly on its end, then tipped onto the gravel road. He closed the doors, got back into the van, and drove three hundred feet towards US 277. As a kid, he'd seen one of the dumber children in his Scout troop pour about a cup of gasoline into a camp fire. The explosion from a cup was bad enough; the kid lived, but did it without eyebrows for a good while. Westfield didn't want to end up stuck on a back road because he'd accidentally blown up his van.

He got out and limped back along the road with the gas can. If they came out here with fire trucks and squad cars, they'd likely drive all over his foot prints. Otherwise, if they had a tracker, they'd be able to study his tracks in the dust and figure out they were looking for a tall guy with a limp. He got to the box, unscrewed the top of the gas can, and emptied it onto the cardboard, covering it from end to end. He was careful to keep the gas from splashing onto his legs and feet. He left the gas can on top of the box. No need to get pulled over in the next couple of hours with an empty gas can in the back.

He walked back to the van and lifted the ancient, ratty carpet covering the spare tire compartment. In there, amongst the jack, the tire iron, and the reflective triangle, was a red flare, probably as old as the van itself. He took it, shut the door, and went back towards the box until he was standing a hundred feet from it. It was as far as he thought he'd be able to throw the flare with any kind of accuracy, but closer than he'd like to be. If he'd had time to plan this, he'd have a remote detonator or some tracer rounds for his pistol.

Then again, if he'd had time to plan this, he wouldn't be in West Texas in the middle of the night with a man he'd murdered.

He pulled the plastic cap off the flare, pointed it away from his face, and struck the tip of the flare against the sandpaper on the end of the plastic cap. The flare sputtered like an old match, but then caught. Its flame was red and smoky. He put the cap in his pocket so he wouldn't drop it in the chaos he was about to set off. He considered the distance to the box, looked at the wind in the branches of the trees, and then threw the flare overhand. It spun in an arc through the air, its fire tracing a curving cycloid line as it went. Westfield figured it would do the job if it landed anywhere within twenty feet of the box. It hit the ground five feet from the body. The result was an instant explosion. Flames erupted fifty feet into the air and then mushroomed into an expanding ball. A circle of blue flame shot from the box and expanded along the ground, igniting the grass, trees and fence posts on both sides of the road. Westfield himself was nearly knocked down by the heat and shock of the explosion. Before he even saw how far the flames would spread, he turned and hobbled for the van, ignoring the pain in his right knee. When he reached the van he patted at his back and the back of his head to make sure he wasn't on fire. His shirt was so hot it may have been smoking. The keys were still in the ignition and the engine was running. He got in, slammed the door, dropped the transmission into gear and floored the accelerator.

The road ahead was bright as midmorning from the fire; the van cast a long shadow ahead of itself. He didn't need his headlights until he reached U.S. 277. He spun the wheel and skidded onto the pavement, heading south towards Interstate 10. The fire was still visible out his right window. He pushed the van to ninety. It wouldn't go any faster. No cars came from the other direction and he couldn't hear any sirens. When he saw the sign for the interstate, he slowed, signaled for the entrance ramp, and merged onto I-10 doing sixty-five miles an hour. He could still see the fire on the horizon, miles away. It took him ten miles to stop shaking and twenty miles after that to stop looking in his rear-view mirror every couple of seconds. His face felt like he'd been out in the desert all day and he realized the initial blast had given him an instant sunburn.

Chapter Twenty-Three

Almost any other day of her life, Julissa would have enjoyed every minute sailing across the channel to Molokai. *Sailfish* was fast and powerful, heeling from the force of the wind in her unfurled mainsail and genoa, her sharp hull easily slicing through the ocean waves. Behind them, Oahu had receded steadily, revealing the curves of its shoreline and the serrated cliffs of its mountain ranges as they drew far enough away to see it in its entirety. Sea birds raced alongside the boat, angling their wings to the wind before diving into the clear water. When they hit the surface, schools of flying fish were scared up into flight, skimming the wave tops for a hundred feet or more. She listened to the sounds of the wind in the rigging and the foaming wake that started on the lee side of the hull, and felt the warm touch of Chris's hand on her shoulder as he taught her how to steer up into the wind gusts. Mid-channel, when she should have been enjoying it most, Chris left her alone in the cockpit to find the spare anchor.

They needed something to weigh down the body before they dumped it.

She told herself it was a beautiful day to start a new life. Chris came heavily up the steep stairs from below, carrying an anchor that must have weighed eighty pounds. He set it on the cockpit floor and then disappeared again, emerging a moment later with a long length of thick, welded chain in a canvas bag.

"How deep is the water here?" Julissa asked.

"Thousand feet or so. Any boats around?"

"Just us."

"Okay."

Chris carried the bag of chain to the stern and stepped to the swim platform, just above the water. When he knelt, she couldn't see him anymore. If he fell overboard, she might not even realize. She angled herself on the helm seat to watch their wake. She tried to steer a straight course by keeping the line of froth and bubbles behind them on an even track. Two minutes passed and she wondered if Chris really had gone overboard. Then his head came up and he climbed over the stern rail and came back to the cockpit.

"I unzipped the bag, tied the chain around his ankles, then wrapped him with it. I'll shackle the anchor to the chain, zip it up, and shove it overboard."

"You think he'll ever come up?"

"No."

Chris took the anchor, stepped carefully out of the cockpit onto the stern deck, and started towards the transom. Julissa watched him disappear onto the swim platform. Less than a minute after he ducked beyond view, she saw his hands come up and untie the rope that secured the fish bag to the deck. Then, seconds later, she saw the bag in the water. It floated momentarily like a buoy, its un-weighted end up in the air. But it lost is buoyancy as it filled with water, and it sank before it even disappeared behind the first wave. Chris came back to the cockpit and joined her on the bench behind the steering pedestal.

"This heading okay?" she asked.

She was aiming for southwest tip of Molokai. According to the chart on the screen behind the wheel, the end of Molokai was ten nautical miles from *Sailfish*'s current position. They were hitting fifteen knots in the strongest wind gusts, and averaging over thirteen.

"This is a good course. Keep up like this, we'll be in Haleolono in an hour."

Julissa looked at the chart. Haleolono was an abandoned barge harbor three miles down the coast from the tip of Molokai. Chris had said it would be safe to anchor the boat there and leave it. He said there were bluffs above the harbor with a dirt road that came down in switchbacks. If the killer's men found the boat, they'd likely watch her from the bluffs until they were sure no one was aboard. Then they'd swim out and either set her afire or sink her, just from spite. Julissa hoped they wouldn't find the boat at all.

Chris went to the companionway, then into the salon. He emerged a moment later wiping his wet hands with a paper towel. Julissa thought he'd been washing away blood. It would have been impossible to wrap the chains around the corpse without getting blood on him somewhere. He looked tired and angry; shooting the man might have bothered him until they saw the scene inside Mike's house. Since then, he hadn't said much.

Chris sat next to her and she brushed her fingertips over the back of his hand. She wasn't sure why. Maybe just to show she didn't mind if his hands had been bloody. Maybe to say she could go six years, or ten, or twenty, without letting the fire die out.

"I'll take the helm if you need a break," he said.

"Okay." She'd been steering for two hours.

"Galley's got cold drinks, and there's a head—bathroom—right under us."

Julissa let him take the wheel and she went below. The inside of Chris's boat was finished in brightly polished teak. She'd seen pictures of expensive sailboats before, but she'd never been aboard anything like this. *Sailfish* was probably bigger than the studio apartment she'd rented in Boston as a graduate student. The boat had the unmistakable imprint of Chris's touch—spotless, organized, carefully set up for any kind of occurrence, the safety systems seamlessly built into the beautiful woodwork. She found some sunscreen in the medicine cabinet and put it on. Then she went to the galley and found two bottles of ginger ale in the refrigerator. She held them by their necks and climbed back up, feeling a little queasy from being below. It was better once she stepped onto the deck, with the fresh wind and the steady horizon. She handed Chris a bottle of ginger ale. He twisted the cap off and pocketed it, then weakly clinked the base of his bottle against hers.

"Sorry I—"

"Don't apologize," she said. "I wanted to be here. I'm sorry for Mike and his family. I'm sorry you lost your friend. When we stop and you can rest, you should mourn him. All of them. And then we'll pick up and keep going, and we'll get the son of a bitch. We've got more information now than ever."

"Yeah."

"However long it takes, Chris," she said.

She met his eyes and didn't look away. She saw he understood. Chris trimmed the sails closer to the centerline and steered the boat just south of the point at the end of Molokai. She could tell he was trying to keep himself under control. She could see the way his jaw was trembling, the grip he had on the wheel.

Half an hour later, Chris furled the genoa and then the main sail. Julissa steered for the mouth of the harbor, the engine vibrating gently beneath her bare feet. Chris was on the bow, sorting the anchor chain. She followed his hand signals when she got into the harbor. In its center, she put the transmission into neutral. The boat slowed to a drift, heading into the wind. At the moment they stopped, Chris released the anchor. Then he was walking along the side deck and stepping back into the cockpit.

"You ready?" Chris asked.

"Yeah." She looked at her watch. It was six thirty in the evening.

The day was still hot and there were at least two hours of light left.

"They'll be here soon."

He'd told her he wanted to leave the dinghy on its davits to make it seem they were still aboard. He had a yellow dry bag with their few things. Chris took off his shirt and shorts and stuffed them into the dry bag. He stood in his boxers and handed the bag to Julissa. She took it, turned her back on him, and stripped down to her bra and panties. She stuffed clothes and sandals into the bag, sealed it, and handed it back to Chris. Then she stepped onto the teak deck and dove over the rail into the water. She went down deep, eyes open. When she came up, she turned to the boat, hands over her breasts to be sure her bra had not come off in the dive. Chris was locking the companionway. She treaded water and watched him. She could hear the sound of the surf on the breakwater, birds singing in the mesquite trees that overran the land between the harbor and the cliffs, and then, quietly at first but finally asserting itself as the dominant noise, the sound of a helicopter approaching.

Chris heard it and stepped out onto the deck, looking up. He pointed and she nodded. He tossed the dry bag into the water, and jumped off the side of the boat, feet first. He came up near her, swept his hair back with his hands, and then swam over to the bag. They swam around the front of the boat and towards the flat strip of land between the harbor and the ocean. Chris climbed the rocky slope and pulled the dry bag up after him. Julissa followed, and when she got to the thorn-covered ground beneath a mesquite tree, Chris handed her the towel and then her pair of sandals. She covered herself with the towel, put on her sandals, then turned away to dry herself and dress. She handed the towel back to Chris and then stepped out of the cover of the mesquite tree and stood in the clearing, zipping and buttoning her shorts. The helicopter was close enough to see its blue paint. She pulled a thick mesquite thorn from the sole of her sandal and turned to see Chris, dressed now. He raised his hand to the helicopter and she did the same.

"Your boat'll be okay?" she asked.

Chris shrugged. "I'd call some guys to take her back, but that'd put them in too much danger. Like asking someone to house sit for me right now."

He turned from the helicopter and looked at *Sailfish.* Then he turned back to the helicopter, which was coming straight at them. The pilot must have seen them. As the helicopter approached, they backed into the trees again and waited for it to land in the clearing. The dust hadn't settled and the blades hadn't stopped turning when the door opened and the pilot stepped out and jogged toward them. He was

144

wearing a mechanic's one-piece jumpsuit and a baseball cap.

"You Jarrett?"

"That's me." Chris held out his hand and shook the pilot's. "This is Cheryl. Thanks for coming on short notice."

"Not a problem. That's your baggage?" The pilot was looking at the dry bag and glancing behind them at the boat.

"Just this."

"Plane's in the hangar in Kahului and they're fueling it up right now. She'll be ready to go the minute we land."

"Then let's go," Julissa said.

They followed the pilot back to the helicopter. Chris took a seat in the back and Julissa took the copilot's seat. The pilot handed them headsets after they buckled their seat belts. When he spoke into the microphone on his headset, Julissa could hear him clearly over the rising whine of the rotors.

"Thirty minutes flying time to Maui. Forty-five minutes, you wanna go the scenic route past Kalaupapa and the north shore of Molokai."

"Let's just go the fastest way," Julissa said.

"No problem. Here we go."

The helicopter rose above the level of the mesquite trees and then above the top of the *Sailfish*'s mast. The pilot executed an about-face turn so they looked along the wind-swept coast of Molokai. He lowered the nose and they sped above the beach. Julissa saw the bleached skeleton of a whale that had been tossed from the ocean onto an inaccessible and rocky shore.

Chris had been afraid if they went to the airport in Molokai and waited for a regular flight, the killer's men would find them. There was too much risk. If their goal was to stay alive, then money wasn't an object. So he'd called a jet charter service and arranged for a helicopter to meet them at the harbor. He'd asked if there were empty-leg charters available, and agreed immediately when the company offered a Gulf Stream V bound for Bangkok with a fuel stop in Manila. The plane could leave any time in the next three days; Chris instructed them to have it fueled and ready to fly no later than eight that evening. Julissa had winced inwardly when she heard him arrange the payment. He hadn't dickered over the terms, but had simply recited his credit card number.

Though he didn't tell her what it cost, Julissa dealt with enough Silicon Valley executives to know they would be burning at least seven thousand dollars an hour between now and when they got to Manila. She did the math in her head. Even if the charter jet averaged five hundred miles an hour, Chris was looking at sixty-three thousand dollars just to get out of Hawaii. But either of them would have spent every dollar they owned or could borrow to find the killer and finish him. She turned and looked at Chris in the backseat of the helicopter. His hands were folded in his lap and he was looking out the window at the passing sea.

They passed between Lanai and Molokai, then flew low past the tiny, crescent-moon sliver of Molokini. Then they were roaring over the pineapple fields of Maui, hurtling across the central plain at a hundred and ten knots. At the Kahului Airport, on the north side of Maui, the pilot approached a white hangar and touched down gently just to the left of its gaping doors. Julissa saw their jet inside.

"They radioed ahead, told me she's ready. Pilots are waiting."

"Thanks," Chris said. He was unbuckling his seat belt. A ground crewman ran from the hangar and approached the helicopter, bending low to the earth as he came beneath the still-spinning rotors. He opened the door for Julissa, who stepped out into the grass and trotted away from the helicopter, towards the plane. Chris was behind her. Once they were on the tarmac and away from the wind and roar, they slowed to a walk.

"Been to the Philippines?" Julissa asked.

"Just Manila. He killed a girl there, four years ago. So I went. Didn't find much. You?"

"No. Other places in Asia, sure. Japan, Taiwan, Hong Kong. Just business."

The Gulf Stream V was upholstered in tan leather, richly carpeted, paneled in nautical teak, and lit by windows four times the size of a commercial airliner's. Julissa waited for the copilot to comment on their lack of luggage or the fact that her wet bra had soaked through the front of her tank top. But after touring them through the plane, he went forward to the cockpit, where the pilot was already starting the engines. Julissa went to the galley and had a look inside the miniature refrigerator.

"You want a beer, a glass of wine or something?"

"Sure. Whatever you're having."

She took two bottles of beer and looked for a bottle opener. Then she joined Chris near the back of the plane, sitting on a leather settee that faced him. She handed him the beer. The plane had taxied out of the hangar; out the window, the sun was turning orange as it sank to the horizon. She tried to picture where she'd be in a month and couldn't. She wasn't even sure about the next twenty-four hours.

Instead of asking Chris questions he wouldn't be able to answer, she took a long drink from her beer. It had been hot on the boat, and the beer felt good. She thought of Allison. When they were teenagers they would stay up late at night in the downstairs of their parents' house, wearing their pajamas and sneaking beers out of the back of the refrigerator, just talking. Teenaged sisters were supposed to hate each other, but Allison had always been her closest friend. Even in college, they'd talked on the phone almost every night. Never once, in all her life, had she considered she could lose Allison.

"When we get there, I'll pick up where I left off," Julissa said. "I should be inside the FBI's computer in a couple of days."

"Okay. We'll make our next move based on what you find."

The plane accelerated down the runway and was in the air much faster than a commercial plane. Julissa supposed it was a matter of weight; they were on the run with nothing but a single bag that was on the seat next to Chris. The pilots banked to the southwest until the sunset was visible out the windows on the right. She could see the channel between Oahu and Molokai, lit orange now in the fading light. The sky overhead was fading to a translucent purple. The two men left on Oahu might be waiting by the elevator of her hotel with their silenced pistols and their manila envelopes. But that would only last so long. Sooner or later they would smash into Chris's house. And inside, it would only take one mistake to bring everything down. They were going to be airborne for the next nine hours—how far ahead would they still be when they stepped off the plane?

"What's in your house that could connect you to the ID you're using?"

"Nothing."

"The credit card statements—where do they go?"

"They're electronic statements, emailed to a Hotmail account. Which I only checked from my phone."

"The one you threw over the side?"

"Yeah."

"No photocopies of the ID or anything with that name in your house?"

"No."

"Nothing on the boat?"

"No."

"And that includes emails? I don't know where you got the ID, but were there any emails with whoever made it for you?"

"Nothing like that."

"When they can't find us, they're going to tear your house to pieces."

"They'll probably burn it to the ground, too."

"Any friends they could go after?"

"They already did. Mike was the only person who knew anything. And he didn't know my other name. So he couldn't have given it up. Not that he would've anyway. It looked like he held out." Chris finished his beer and put it on the table beside him. Then he looked up at her. "Anything in your hotel room that ties you to the FBI thing?"

"No. Everything's on the laptop I have here."

"Then we're still a step ahead of him. It. Whatever he is. I'm still having a hard time getting my mind around that."

"Me too."

Chris took his empty bottle and rolled it back and forth between his palms. "I imagined getting close to him, tracking him down. I spent so much time thinking about it, imagining my hands around his throat. Strangling him. But I couldn't picture his face, so it was always just a blank in my dreams. Like a man who wasn't really there. Just a shadow. Now I guess it isn't even a man."

"You'd strangle him if you could?"

"That, or a knife. I'd like it to be slow. I'd like him to look me in the eyes, so I could tell him who I am. Why I'm killing him. But it doesn't have to be that way. In the end, I just want him dead."

After dark, when they'd eaten, Chris carried their tray back to the galley, and returned a moment later with two blankets he'd found. Julissa wrapped herself and sat with her legs crossed on the leather seat. Chris poured the last of the wine and they drank together, looking out the windows at the dark sea spread out forty thousand feet beneath them. The horizon was lit by the moon and Julissa could see the curve of the earth. Traced to its completion, it was a curve that defined their hunting ground. He could be anywhere in the world.

She fell asleep against Chris's shoulder, wondering where they would eventually find him. Up a deep river that cut into the pulsing heat of a New Guinea jungle, buried in a lair under the stone-encircled heart of a medieval city. Fifty stories up a glass office tower, overlooking an industrial port. She dreamt of Allison screaming as she was eaten alive, her telephone dangling off the hook in a pool of blood on the floor. In her sleep, she wrapped her arms around Chris and held him tightly. He held her back.

Chapter Twenty-Four

The girl with the flaming red hair stood at the center of the small stage, holding the microphone stand with both hands. She wore an off-the-shoulder black dress and was lit from above by the single spotlight recessed somewhere in the dark rafters of the club's ceiling. The club had been a church for three hundred years, then spent forty years abandoned with the remains of its caved roof scattered in the bomb craters on the flagstone floor. Only recently had it been rebuilt as a club. The girl was too young to have seen any of this. Besides that, she hadn't grown up in this country. She closed her eyes and held the microphone close to her lips and sang in French.

The stage behind her was dark, but he could see the musicians in the shadows perfectly well, in spite of the sunglasses he always wore in public to hide his eyes. The man playing the upright bass was tall and had an elongated neck that bobbed in time with the rhythm line. His skin was specked with acne and he had blue eyes the same color as the buttons on his black shirt. The drummer and the saxophone player were either brothers or close cousins and wore the same white shirts and black pants. But it was the girl who held his attention. He listened to her voice. He spoke French but he didn't care about the words of the song.

In truth he had no interest in anything she might say in any language.

He was at the back of the club at a table by himself. He had put out the candle by holding the palm of his hand over the glass holder until the flame suffocated. In his dark corner, a hundred feet from the girl, separated from her by a span of room filled with cigarette smoke and plates of food and spilled beer and the breath of men who'd been drinking spirits and table wine, he could smell the perfume she had sprayed at the base of her throat—the warm scent of orange blossoms carried into a deep wood. He closed his eyes and smelled her, not just the perfume but all of her. Her hair and her skin, the tiny beads of sweat between her breasts, the creamy sweetness of her thighs.

A waitress passed and he put his empty wineglass on her tray. She looked past his shoulder as though she did not quite see him. She only registered the empty glass and his unspoken order to fill it. He was drinking red wine tonight. He had not eaten in eight days and was so hungry he felt dizzy. But that was part of the pleasure. He dismissed the waitress with a thought and gave his attention back to the redhead.

The perfume on her throat smelled sweet but its taste would be bitter, briefly, until he bit through her skin and washed her clean with her own blood. This would be late in the night, after everything else, because that bite would probably kill her. She was so young and healthy and he'd seen over and over how much a young and healthy person could endure. He would take her to all of those places before the last bite, and if ever she thought she could not make it all the way, he would be there to give her a little push.

The waitress returned with another glass of wine and set it on his table. She still did not really see him. If he took off his sunglasses and flashed his claws in her face—if he made her see, by yanking her out of the mental fog he threw around himself like a cloak—she might die of a burst blood vessel in the brain.

But there was no sport and little pleasure in that kind of killing.

He finished his glass of wine while the girl finished the song. She stretched the last note until it seemed she should have run out of breath. The club was silent and the musicians behind her had stopped playing, so it was only her voice that filled the room, fading as she pressed the last air from her lungs, the wavering elongated note weakening as she ran out of air. He felt himself stir. She would do this for him and him alone, and his ears would be the last to hear as her voice weakened and went silent.

The club burst into applause. He stood and left.

The night air outside the club was warm and smelled of the ocean. He had hunted in this very spot once before, but there would be no records of that. The club had been a church then and the girl he'd found in its congregation could not have been any older than seventeen. He smiled at the memory. She had begged for her life in a horse stable, her country accent and her skin the only things he hadn't stripped from her.

She'd had neither by the end of the night.

He closed his eyes and steadied himself against the heavily buttressed stone wall. It did not take him long to pick up the singer's scent and untangle it from the many paths on the street. He followed her invisible trail up the dark street, across an empty plaza. She'd lingered by the fountain. At some point, he opened his eyes again. He stood in front of her car, a cheap-looking Fiat. From the sidewalk, he could smell her fingertips on the door handle. The car's tires were old and the rear two were balding. He breathed deeply and took in the scent of sun-baked, decaying rubber, and then trotted up the street. After a hundred meters, he stopped and sniffed at the air and then crossed the road and turned right at an intersection, following the winding street into the heart of the city. He had suspected the trail would end at one of the university's dormitories and he was not surprised to find himself on the edge of the campus. He came to a parking stall, now occupied by another car, and he cast around its perimeter until he found her smell again. Then he followed her hours-old trail to a five-story stone dormitory. It was two thirty in the morning. He had not seen more than five cars in his jog across town. His long coat was the same coal-soot color of the old stone. Without another thought he mounted the sheer wall with his bare feet and his claws. He climbed to the first row of windows, four meters above the sidewalk. Moving on the vertical wall was as easy as walking on the sidewalk. He skittered sideways along the wall, beneath the line of the window ledges, but didn't catch her scent. There were other interesting girls here, though. He paused at one window and drank in the smell of the sleeping girl on the other side of the aged glass. But he wasn't ready to change his plan this far in. He was set on the girl in the club, on the smell of her throat and the way her voice had trailed off into the darkness of the crowded room. He climbed another four meters to the next row of windows. He caught her scent on the third window. It was unlocked and slid open easily. He stepped into the room, shut the window after himself and sat on her bed in the darkness. He had been too focused on her scent when he entered. It wasn't until after he sat that he noticed the second narrow bed on the other side of the room.

She had a roommate, and he'd come in too quietly to wake her.

He stood and moved to the edge of the other bed and looked at her. She was on her side with her face to the wall, but the spill of red hair across the pillow and the warm fragrance that rose from beneath her quilted covers explained everything.

Of course the scent here was so strong: they were twins. Their paths had begun in the same womb, at the same time, and had led them both, inexorably, to him. They had one last thing to do together, and he would lead them through it. It would take the rest of the night, possibly until the sun was high and hot. He walked to the bureau drawer and quietly slid back the top drawer, looking for socks, panties or a bathrobe tie.

Because there were two of them, and because he was in no hurry, he'd need a gag.

Chapter Twenty-Five

The beach was wide and empty, curving away for five miles in an unbroken strip of sand as fine and white as sugar. At the far end, karst cliffs rose from the water. Thatched-roofed houses and green bursts of jungle competed with each other for horizontal purchase on the cliff faces. Chris walked in the wet sand at the shell line, following his own footprints, which were the only tracks on the beach. The sun was just rising and the shadows of the coconut trees stretched far over the water. He'd woken at five in the morning, left a note under Julissa's door, and had set off to see the lay of the land. They'd arrived in Boracay in the night, after an hour's flight in a propeller plane from Manila and a five-minute boat ride from Panay. A man with a tricycle taxi had taken them from the ferry landing along a winding road and deposited them at a beachside hotel. All they knew about Boracay was that it had dozens of hotels and plenty of Internet connections.

July was the beginning of typhoon season in the Philippines. The hotel was empty except for a few families who had probably come down from Manila in between storms. The other hotels along the beach looked just as dead. The beach itself was beautiful, but the waves told of approaching bad weather. They were rough and began breaking far from the beach, and the foam was tan with churned up sand and flecked with clumps of seaweed brought from the bottom. He could see whitecaps miles out to sea. He knew from the map in his hotel room there were other islands close by, but they were all hidden beneath towering gray clouds. There would be a thunderstorm by lunchtime.

When he got back to the hotel, he stopped in the lobby. An old computer occupied a desk in the corner. A handwritten sign in English said, *Internet For Guest Only*. He sat in front of the computer. Julissa told him it was safe to check his Gmail account, so long as he only read email and didn't send any. She had promised to teach him how to send email without the possibility of being traced. If Westfield had emailed again, he should at least find out. He logged into his email and scrolled through his inbox, which was mostly filled with junk. There was nothing from Westfield.

But one email caught his attention.

The sender was someone named John Smith, emailing from a Hotmail account. It was the subject line that stood out.

I ATE YOUR WIFE

The message was barely fifteen minutes old. The file size was almost five megabytes. He hesitated to click on the message. What if the attachment held some kind of virus? Julissa had mentioned geo-location software. His finger hovered over the mouse button, but after a moment, he decided the risk was too great, especially with Julissa so close at hand. Chris logged out of Gmail, cleared the web browser's history and stood. He went to the back of the lobby, exited through the French doors, and followed the flagstone path past the gardens and swimming pool. A maid with a watering can was tending to the orchids that grew from the trunks of the coconut palms lining the garden path. He had rented side-by-side bungalows for himself and Julissa. Hers was still dark, but he climbed the three steps to its porch and rapped on her door. She opened it a crack, saw it was Chris, and let him in. She was wrapped in the bed sheet.

"Just a second and I'll get dressed," she said. She went into the room's bathroom and shut the door.

"There's something I need to show you," Chris said. "You get wireless in here?"

"Haven't tried yet. I didn't even turn on the laptop—I just went straight to sleep."

She came out wearing clothes from the day before.

"If we can't get wireless, let's go find a private place where we can. Somewhere no one'll be looking over our shoulders."

Julissa sat on the bed and took the laptop off the bedside table. She turned it on and waited for it to boot up.

"What's up?"

"I checked my email this morning. I wanted to see if Westfield had contacted us. He hadn't."

"But someone or something else did, is that it?"

"I haven't opened the email yet. It has an attachment. I figured I should bring it to you."

Now Julissa looked completely awake. "That was the right thing to do."

She played with her keyboard for a moment, then handed the laptop to Chris.

"Here, there's wireless. Log in and show me."

Chris took the computer and logged into his Gmail account. He passed the computer back to Julissa who took it and looked at the screen.

"Jesus."

"Is there a way to find out if it's safe to open?"

"Yeah. I need to download a program off the net. It'll capture the email byte by byte so we can view the contents along with any hidden code. But it'll keep everything in a secure environment and won't allow any embedded code to execute."

"Okay." Chris wasn't sure what most of that meant, but Julissa sounded confident enough. "You want a cup of coffee? I saw an urn in the lobby."

"That'd be good."

She spoke without looking from the screen. Her face was lit pale white by its glow and she was absorbed in her work. Chris watched her a moment before leaving, feeling not just friendship, but also close kinship. As if he'd been marooned on an island for six years and had suddenly discovered he shared it with another person. Now that he knew she existed, he needed her. He turned and left the room, walking through the garden and back to the lobby in a light rain. A frond had fallen from one of the coconut trees and was floating in the swimming pool. In the lobby, Chris nodded at the two girls behind the reservation desk, and went over to the coffee urn. He filled two cups and then went back to Julissa's room. He let himself in without knocking, set one of the coffee cups on the bedside table for her, and then sat in one of the two chairs by the window. From that vantage point, he could see a small outrigger sailing canoe coming in from offshore and having a hard go of it in the wind and chop. The crew handled the boat well, flogging the oversized mainsail by sheeting it out all the way, so that the boat powered towards the beach on the force of the small jib. Behind him Julissa stirred and he turned to her.

"It's a damned good thing you brought this in to me without opening the email."

"Yeah?"

He sat next to her on the bed. The screen showed blocks of incomprehensible code. Julissa ran her finger under a line of type.

"This is clever. There's a large file embedded in the email. It looks like a picture file, but a really big one, probably a photograph in raw data format. You get that from high-end digital cameras. Pro stuff. The file would've stayed on the Gmail server until you opened the email, and when you opened it, this line of code would have written over the stack buffer and installed the rest of the program."

"I don't get it."

"The program is simple—it writes your computer's unique ID number and your Internet server information onto the metadata of the sent email every time your computer connects to the Internet. So whoever sent this email can just continually check the email in his sent box, scroll down to the metadata, and get an update of what computer you're using and where you're logging into the net."

"Is there any text to the email?"

"No. Just the picture file."

"Can we look at it?"

"Yeah. Here."

She typed a few lines of code. A pop-up screen appeared, slowly filling as the computer processed the photograph.

"Oh dear god," Julissa said.

The image made Chris's stomach churn. The half-cup of coffee he'd drunk lurched in his stomach, but he kept it in.

"Has he ever done anything like that before?" Julissa asked. Her voice was just a whisper.

"No."

"I can't look at it anymore." She snapped the laptop screen shut. "I'm sorry."

The killer, the thing, had sent them a high-resolution, full-color photograph of a murder scene. Two young women sat on a narrow bed with their backs against a white wall. Their arms were around each other, and they wore nothing but gags that looked like they had been made from a fuzzy pink bathrobe tie. One of the girls was missing her entire face and one eye; the other's throat had been eaten all the way to her spinal column. Their stomachs had been ripped open and their intestines were piled in slick coils on the wooden floor. Their thighs had been stripped all the way to the bone. The flesh, what was left of it, was on the floor. A lot of it appeared to be missing. The mattress was soaked in blood. The photograph captured a long runner of blood as it fell towards the floor from one girl's flayed ankle. Only their red hair had been untouched, and was, in fact, bloodless and clean. Chris thought the killer may have actually washed it before posing the bodies for the photograph.

But it was the wall behind the girls that Chris was thinking about after Julissa had closed the screen. The killer, dipping his hand into the ample pallet of the girls' open abdomens, had written a very simple message on the wall in careful print that had only just started to drip when the photograph was taken.

WHO'S NEXT?

Chris went to the window. He was trembling. The girls died holding on to each other for help that neither could provide the other. He pressed his forehead against the window glass and felt the tropical heat outside.

"What now?" Julissa asked.

"Does he know where we are?" Chris asked. "Could his code have done its job?"

"No."

"Then we stick to the plan. You work on the FBI. I'll see what I can make of this picture. I need to figure out where this happened so we can keep track of his movements. I can try to get something like Mike's old program up and running again to watch the news."

"We've got to find him soon, Chris."

"I know."

"This can't go on."

Chris nodded. He wanted to keep them on track and keep the momentum up. He thought of Westfield again.

"Somewhere in all this we need to figure out a secure way to get in touch with Westfield. And if he got blind copied on that email we need to figure out a way right now to warn him not to open it."

"As for warning him, the email's only twenty minutes old so we might still have time. I can set up a random Hotmail account in my name and send an email to his address through a proxy server so that it can't get traced to Boracay. I can just put a warning in the subject line telling him not to open any emails. He might notice it first."

"If he has any reason to be suspicious, he'll play it safe."

Julissa went to work. When she was finished, she closed the computer and stood.

"I need some air," she said.

"It's going to storm out."

"That's okay with me."

"You want to see if we can find a place to buy some new clothes? Also I need to buy a cheap laptop so I can do my work."

Julissa hesitated, then said, "Yeah, I'd like that. But, Chris—I don't have any money."

"That's not a problem."

"I'll pay you back."

"You don't have to."

They locked her room and walked into the rain. The wind was warm but the rain drops, now as big as dimes, were cold. They walked to the empty lobby and asked the girls at the reception desk where to go shopping.

Chapter Twenty-Six

Westfield just wanted to drive home to his own house. He had a glassed-in back porch overlooking Puget Sound. He liked to drink his coffee there in the mornings, reading the papers. He could watch ships making their way south to Seattle and Tacoma and could see submarines running on the surface to the base at the end of the Hood Canal. What little he'd patched together to call a life was in the house. Instead, he was at a motel on the edge of the desert outside of Carlsbad, New Mexico, watching the window-unit air conditioner drip water down the rotten plaster wall. The carpet smelled of mildew and the brown wallpaper in the bathroom was coming unglued. He'd stopped at a Bank of America in Midland, Texas, and had then paid cash for a new laptop at a Radio Shack. Then he'd driven without stopping again until seeing the motel. The motel had exactly one thing going for it: the sign on the highway said, *Free Wi-Fi*.

He spent two hours in the filthy bathroom, washing the wound on his knee and re-bandaging it with fresh gauze and antibiotic cream. He took three aspirin and considered driving to the liquor store on the highway and buying a bottle of whiskey. He was out of the habit of drinking but he'd never be out of the habit of thinking about drinking. That first glass of whiskey in the morning, when he was drinking more or less professionally after getting out of the Navy, that glass was his sacrament in the Church of Sour Mash. He used to pour it into whatever cup he could find, and stand in the window of whatever motel room he was then occupying, and drink it slowly while watching the sunrise. He'd add a handful of ice, if he had it. If he didn't have ice, he'd drink it straight, letting it sit on his tongue before swallowing, then feeling it burn all the way down. Years later he would realize being an alcoholic was a lot like being religious. It took faith to believe if you kept doing the same thing over and over, things would eventually get better, despite all evidence to the contrary. Now he had stopped drinking and he didn't think it was possible to make things better. But evening the score was about spreading pain, not erasing it. So he was a realist.

He sat on the bed in his undershorts and unpacked his new computer. Maybe if he had been less tired and in less pain he would have done what Chris had done. Maybe if he scrolled through his email all the way to the top, he would have seen Julissa's email warning him, and he would have stopped. But he didn't see Julissa's email and he clicked on the other message. How could he not? The subject line called up all his rage and refused calm reflection.

I ATE TARA WESTFIELD

He clicked the email and watched the photograph slowly fill the screen. A million pixels of horror. He stared at the bloody message on the wall behind the poor girls. For a second, he could have gone either way. He could have stood, taken his keys from the end of the bed, driven down to the liquor store, and bought the biggest goddamned bottle of Jack Daniel's they sold. He felt so alone and so empty, it wouldn't have mattered if he kept on fighting or just fell flat on his back in his shithole room and drank until he blacked out. In desperation, he put his hand over his right knee and jammed his thumb into the bullet wound, digging through the gauze until his fingernail squeezed into the hole. The pain was as bright as noonday sun reflecting off broken glass. He closed his eyes and went with the pain, and when he opened them again, he stared at the picture for another five minutes. He closed the window, and the next email he saw was Julissa's warning.

Westfield sat in the plastic chair outside his hotel room door and watched dust devils in the desert on the other side of the highway. Already, by using the bank in Midland, he'd let them know his general whereabouts. Now, he'd probably turned his computer into a homing device for the killer's men. He'd turned it off and for good measure had taken out the battery. He sat in the heat, where at least the air didn't reek of mildew and decaying wallpaper, and considered his options. He could pack his things back into the van, leave the new computer in the trash, and run. But to what end? He was trying to find the killer, not run away from him. Which left the second option: he could wait, and be ready. He'd been caught entirely by surprise in Galveston, but made out all right. They would be expecting to surprise him, not to walk into an ambush. Maybe he could find out more about them. If not, he could kill another one of the thing's employees. Either option sounded better than just running blind. He limped back into the room, and got the

Carlsbad phone book from the bedside table.

He still had twenty-five hundred in cash from his stop at the bank. That wouldn't buy an arsenal in Carlsbad, New Mexico, but he suspected it would be enough to induce serious second thoughts about coming into his motel room.

He wondered how long he had. The nearest airport with commercial flights was hours away, in El Paso. By now they probably knew exactly where he was, but it would still take time to get here. Even if they came by jet, they would have to rent a car and drive the rest of the way. Unless they chartered a small plane and landed on a strip nearby, in which case they could be on top of him in half a day. He had his service side arm, the silenced .22 and switchblade he'd taken from the man he'd killed in Galveston, and his stun gun. But he wanted something with more reach. After what happened in Galveston, they wouldn't bother knocking.

He limped back to the chair outside his door and looked at the desert on the other side of the highway. There was a low, boulder-strewn hill. Creosote and prickly pears and tufts of brown grass grew between the rocks. At the top, there was a stand of yucca with high flowering stems. Some of the boulders were as big as cars. The range wasn't bad. Maybe a hundred yards from the top of the hill to his doorstep, the highway in between. The wind would probably be coming east to west, down the highway. He'd have to account for that.

This was as good a spot as he could ask for to make a stand.

At the moment, anyway, there was no one else staying in the motel. The clerk was an old man with hearing aids in both ears who sat in the room behind the counter watching a small television at full volume. The hill on the other side of the highway would have a view of both sides of the road for more than two miles. If he missed the men at his hotel room door, he could shoot at their car for two minutes, which ever direction they chose to run.

He went to his bed and put the battery back into his computer, then turned it on and let it automatically log itself onto the Internet.

The program he'd accidentally installed would take care of itself.

The gun shop was just outside what passed for downtown Carlsbad. Across the street was a gas station and a liquor store. The store stood alone in an asphalt parking lot crumbling back to gravel. It was built of sun-baked adobe bricks and had bars on the windows. Westfield parked in front and walked in just as the shop owner was reaching to flip the sign from *Open* to *Closed*.

"You stay open fifteen more minutes, I'll make it worthwhile," Westfield said.

The man nodded and held the door open. Westfield went to the back of the shop and looked at the rifles standing in the racks behind the counter. He leaned on the glass over the six shooters and automatic pistols and studied the rifles. As a boy he'd had a Winchester model .270 with a walnut stock. He and his father hunted in the dry hills of eastern Washington. Then, at the Naval Academy, he'd qualified with a Garand M-1 and had been the third best in his class.

"Looking for something in particular?"

"I'm gonna get a good long-distance piece. Get ready for antelope, come November."

"What caliber you into?"

Westfield didn't really care.

"In in the service, I learned with a .30-06. But what we mostly used was fifty caliber BMG."

"Fifty caliber would just about blow an antelope to pieces."

"Something smaller's okay, long as it's got the distance and some punch."

"Bolt action or auto?"

"Auto."

The man pulled a rifle off the rack. It had a black carbon fiber stock and a flat black barrel, and when he took it from the store owner and felt its weight, he could tell it was well made. He ejected the clip and turned the rifle upside down to look into the firing chamber. It was a .30-06 semiautomatic, made in Italy. He held it to his shoulder and sighted along the counter at the wall on the far end of the store. The rifle was heavy but had good balance; the barrel carried its width all the way to the muzzle. He would probably have it propped on a rock when he was shooting, so the weight wouldn't be a problem. The clip held five rounds, but he could buy a couple of extra clips, just in case. It had the natural pointing, good feel of a rifle that shot in tight groups at long range.

"This'll work. How about a scope?"

"Over here."

Westfield picked out a low-light scope, the biggest one in the case. Its objective lens was fifty millimeters across to gather light. He also picked out a laser sight that mounted to the side of the scope, and two boxes of match-grade ammunition.

Everything totaled just over two thousand dollars. Westfield counted it onto the counter in new hundred-dollar bills, fanning them across the glass top above faded Polaroid photographs of dead ten-point bucks and mountain lions, while the dealer stood on the phone, on hold with the FBI's instant background check hotline. Westfield looked at the pictures and kept his eyes down. The dealer hung up the phone.

"You're good to go."

He limped back to the van, put his purchases into the passenger seat and took a bottle of Excedrin from the glove compartment. He dry swallowed a couple of the pills, worked his throat to get them all the way down, and then started the van.

There was an hour of light left. Enough to find a quiet spot and take thirty shots at a boulder from a hundred yards, adjusting the scope after each round. It would be better if he could bench mount it and practice with it in an indoor range. But he had been making do with what life dealt him since 1978.

Chapter Twenty-Seven

Chris sat on the porch of his bungalow with his new computer on his lap. It had not taken long to get some semblance of Mike's old program running, searching the back alleys of the Internet for news of a killing. There had been plenty of mayhem in the world since he'd last checked, but there was no sign of another redhead murder. Let alone a double murder. He and Julissa read the stories together over lunch and eliminated them one by one. If the killer emailed them the photograph on the morning after the killing, then perhaps there was nothing in the news because the girls hadn't been found yet. They had no idea where the girls might be, rotting away on the bed in their final pose. They could be in any city in the world, closed up behind a locked door, missed by their friends and family but not yet missing in the official sense. So Chris turned to the photograph.

He sat with his back against the wall of the bungalow and studied the picture. Zoomed to a nearly microscopic level, he could stand to look hours at a time. On the other hand, looking at the scene in its entirety was a mistake. The monstrosity of it was more than he could bear. And he thought the word was apt: they were on the trail of a monster. Chevalier had been right. The thing was inhuman.

He was looking at the upper left corner of the photograph. At this level of zoom, the picture would probably be bigger than his bungalow. He couldn't see the girls at all, though there were two spots of blood in this section of the photograph. One was high on the wall and the other was on a ceiling beam, a droplet that was pregnant with weight and about to fall.

Just looking at the spot where the ceiling beams came up against the wall, he could draw some conclusions. The building which held the dead girls was old, probably several centuries old. Chris was neither an historian nor an architect, but he was used to paying attention to small details. The wooden beam was hand hewn. A modern beam would have the lightly curved marks left by a sawmill's circular blade. An older beam would have been cut with a cross-cut saw wielded by two men, and would have diagonal marks. This beam bore the chips and pockets of an adze and didn't have a saw mark on it. Then there was the wall itself. It was built of handmade bricks, each one slightly more than an inch thick and ten inches long. The kind of bricks the Romans made by the millions and stacked across their empire. The bricks were covered with plaster that had fallen away in a few patches near the ceiling. At the highest level of zoom, Chris could see small brown hairs coming from the broken edges of the plaster. He would have been willing to bet almost anything it was horse hair. Medieval plaster was made of horse hair, lime and bone ash. That would narrow their search down to, roughly speaking, the borders of the old Roman Empire, and helped about as much as saying they could forget about anywhere but Europe, the British Isles, North Africa and the Middle East.

He scrolled through the photo, purposely averting his eyes from the girls' faces as he passed them, and then refocused his attention to the shadows beneath the bed. He had started by looking under the bed, but hadn't been able to make out much because of the shadows. In the last several hours, though, he'd learned a lot about how to see into this photograph. He opened a control window and used it to adjust the lighting. Because of the photograph's file format, he could manipulate it endlessly, almost as though he held the camera and could retake it from the same angle, but with any camera setting he wanted. He played with the lighting until the shadows beneath the bed receded. There was less light under the bed, so objects there were grainy at high levels of zoom. There was a violin case under the bed, and on its handle was a leather luggage tag. It was facing away from him. No amount of toggling would turn it around. There was a glint of reflection from the brass clasps on the violin case and he guessed the picture was taken with a flash.

To have a view under the bed like this, the room must have been either very wide, so the killer was standing far back when he took the picture, or he had been sitting on the floor. Chris guessed the killer was sitting on the floor. If the ceiling was five hundred years old and supported by wooden beams, it had to be a narrow room. He didn't think that knowledge was going to do him a bit of good. Maybe, after eating half of two girls, the killer had to sit down to rest a moment.

There was another shadow under the bed, to the right of the violin case. Chris scrolled the picture over and brightened the area. A corner of bloody bed sheet hung down from the mattress, and though it did not directly block the thing next to the violin case, it cast an additional shadow under the bed. Also, whatever it was, it was farther under the bed.

Chris played with the light and then sat back when he finally had it.

A book.

It was a hardcover college textbook, three inches thick; its spine was facing towards the room. The lettering on the spine was nearly the same color as the glossy binding. He turned his head and tried to make it out. It was like trying to read the headline on a newspaper drifting beneath the surface of a river at night. He closed his eyes and let them rest awhile, then opened them again. He used the mouse to select the area around the book, then flipped that section on its side so that the book appeared to be standing on its end. He stared at the words. *Fondamenti di Chimica.* Then, in smaller print that was almost impossible to read, he made out one other word: *Bianchi.* The wooden floor under the bed was dusty, but there was a long clean streak leading from the edge of the bed to the book.

He thought about that. The book had been sitting on the floor but had been kicked under the bed. Recently. Perhaps it had been kicked during the struggle.

One of them had been using the book, probably on the day she died.

He went to Google to see what he could find about the book and the author. The first three links were Italian websites selling college text books. The fourth was the American site of Amazon.com. The fifth link, in Italian, was a .pdf file. He clicked on it and found himself looking at the current syllabus for a summer semester chemistry lab at Università degli Studi di Napoli Federico II. The professor was teaching from Bianchi's book, the book underneath the dead girls' bed. He looked again at the name, Università degli Studi di Napoli Federico II. He thought that was probably the University of Naples, and when he checked it on the Internet, he saw he was right.

He pulled up a map of Naples and looked at the university, which was less than a quarter mile from the ocean in the heart of the old city. In the satellite photograph, he could see cranes unloading a cargo ship and a nest of warehouses in the port district not far from downtown. It was the same story he'd seen roughly three-dozen times before.

He went back to the photograph, resized it to fill the computer screen, and then just looked at it. Maybe ten minutes passed before it hit him. The floor was made of heavy wooden planks, likely supported from beneath by hewn beams like the ones in the ceiling. The bed was framed in wood. Counting the furniture, the room probably had three tons of wood in it. The creature could disable security systems; it would have no trouble taking out any other kind of alarm. The wood in the building would have been ancient heartwood, heavy and hot burning.

Chris went back to the Internet and began searching Italian news sites. It didn't take long.

When he found it, he used a web-translator to convert the page into English. The story was ten hours old; the fire started at 4:45 a.m. in a girls' dormitory at the University of Naples. The journalist speculated it may have begun in the basement, where there was a boiler. But there was no room to speculate the fire was a freak accident. Someone had locked the front entrance and the back exit from the inside with chains. The doors were made of cast bronze and would have been impossible to break down without a medieval battering ram. People on the street had been able to do nothing except stand and listen to the girls scream. The fire was well underway by the time anyone outside noticed it; all the electrical and telephone lines to the building had been cut, and the main fire control system had been disabled not from inside the building, but from the central circuit breaker in a utility duct under the street in front of the building. Twenty-five girls were unaccounted for. The death toll would be even higher if any of them had boyfriends sleeping over.

Of the twenty-five, twenty were summer students from abroad. Chris found another website, a blog by a student journalist at the University of Naples. This student had posted a list of the missing. He scanned through it and saw the names of two who could only be sisters: Claire and Elaine Rochelle, who had come for the summer from Montreal.

There was really only one thing left to check. He went to Facebook, that giant yellowpages of the world, and typed in their names. It didn't take him long to find them. They were twins. They were beautiful. They were redheads. And, though their Facebook pictures showed them alive with all of their flesh and skin intact, fully clothed and without gags, they were surely the dead girls in the photograph.

Chris closed the computer and went to find Julissa.

He found her at a table under a cluster of coconut trees, facing the ocean. There were storm clouds on the horizon. A young girl in dirty shorts and a white T-shirt was holding a handful of white seashells for Julissa's inspection. He watched Julissa take a coin from her purse and hand it to the girl, who left the shells on the table and scampered down the beach looking for more.

"How's it going?"

Julissa turned to him. The wind coming off the turquoise waves blew her hair around her face. She tossed her head and gathered her hair behind her, taking a tie off of her wrist and making a ponytail.

Chris saw how white her neck was, saw how the thin gold chain she wore sparkled in the stormy sunlight. She was wearing a simple cotton dress she'd bought at the outdoor mall they'd found that morning. It was wet six inches up the hem of the skirt; he supposed she had taken a break from her work and walked down to the water. He imagined her gathering the dress above her knees and walking into the water, watching sailing canoes transit the horizon, her brow furrowed as she thought through a problem. Her computer was on the table and showed lines of code on a white screen. It would be easy to forget how dangerous she was. Her beauty could eclipse her other qualities. He remembered the casual way she'd held the gun on him in his motel room in Galveston.

"It's going like I thought it would. I got into Special Agent Barton's computer—she accepted the e-vite I disguised as coming from her son's fiancée. Once I could use her computer, it only took an hour to find her VICAP login and password. It took me awhile to figure out how to navigate their system. They've got an information structure that's kind of dated. Looks like they've just been adding to it since they first started the network. It's not very secure. In fact, it violates about half the security protocols we've set up since 2001."

"Can you find out anything about how the data has been altered on all the redhead murders?"

"Have a seat and I'll show you."

She took her feet off the other chair and pulled it out for him. He sat next to her and looked at the screen. He could make no sense of the code.

"The system keeps a chronological index of all changes to the data. So I've been going through and checking all the entries within a week of each killing." She pulled up a list of dates and names. Chris recognized it immediately as the long string of murders. "Three days before a new killing there is always a large-scale deletion."

She touched the screen on the entry that read *July 4, 2010 — Allison Clayborn (Galveston, Texas, USA)*. Then she pulled up another table she had created, which showed killings in one column and deletions in a parallel column. On July 1, 2010, someone penetrated VICAP and deleted the information for Jill Moyers. She had been killed on November 12, 2009, dismembered aboard a sailboat docked near Granville Street in Vancouver.

"The information on Jill Moyers is still on VICAP," Julissa said. "Whoever did this didn't delete the files. He just deleted the table entry, so when someone runs a search for victims, Jill won't show up. As far as the search program is concerned, it's deleted, because he deleted the file path."

"But you can find it?"

"Yeah. Because of that chronological index I told you about. It logged the change. Basically it's like a trash can, and I can open it up and see the file path he threw away."

"Can any of this help us?"

"Maybe not directly. But there's more."

She opened another window, another screen of incomprehensible code.

"What's this?"

"A log of who's on the system and when. And you see these long number strings broken up by periods?"

"Yeah."

"Those are router addresses and this one's a unique device ID number. The VICAP server detects and blocks proxy servers. That's no surprise. But what is a surprise is that they're recording device ID numbers. Most servers don't do that, and this one does it so subtly a person logged in doesn't even know it happens."

"Can you single out just the IDs that were logged onto VICAP when the deletions were made?"

"That's what I just finished doing when you walked up. I think I've got him. For the first eight deletions I found, up to 2006, this was the number."

She pointed at a 128-bit number on the screen.

"But from 2006 to 2010, it was different?" Chris asked.

"Yeah. This one." She pointed at a different number on the screen. "I guess he bought a new computer."

"What now?"

"I download some geo-location software, modify it a bit to make it better, and track down the routers he used. Then we go find the son of a bitch."

"How long will that take?"

"If I had all the stuff the NSA's got, it'd take about a minute. But I'll just be using this cheap laptop and modified software, so figure a day or two. The hard part will be after we find the routers."

"Okay."

Chris looked at the screen again and felt a shiver when he realized how much closer they were. Having the device ID number was like having the cell phone number of the person who'd been hacking into the FBI. As long as he was still using the computer, it would be possible to physically track him down. Maybe not easily or quickly, but that was fine. And this person, whoever he was, would know more about the killer than anyone else on the planet.

"There's just one problem," Julissa said.

"What's that?"

"I told you before every new killing, this person hacks VICAP and erases the most recent victim of the redhead killings."

"Yeah?"

"Well, we know he just killed those two girls in the photograph, but I checked, and Allison's VICAP entry is still on the system. He didn't erase it."

Chris nodded. That made sense to him, considering what he'd just figured out about the sisters murdered in Naples.

"I think maybe he's moved into a new phase," Chris said. "Maybe now, instead of leaving the victims out in the open to be found, and covering his tracks by altering data on VICAP, he's doing something else."

He told her what he'd found in the photograph, and how it had led him to the story about the dormitory fire and the names of the girls. When he finished telling it, they sat in silence for a while. The little girl in the stained white T-shirt came back from the water's edge, carrying another handful of shells. She set them on the table and looked at Chris without speaking. The shells were light purple cowries, polished by tumbling at the surf line. Chris dug in his pocket and gave the girl a ten peso coin.

Finally, Julissa spoke. She was not whispering, but her voice was quiet. "You thought through what this means?"

"Yes."

"Unless he does us a favor and sends an email every time he kills, it'll be almost impossible to track him."

"I know."

"We can keep scouring the Internet for news stories, but what are we looking for? Every house fire, every train wreck or factory explosion? If we're looking at the whole world, there are probably hundreds of arsons *every day*."

"I know," Chris said. "And there are thousands of other ways he could hide the bodies, or destroy them so we wouldn't know it was him. We can't keep tabs on every redhead on the planet."

They were quiet again for a while. There was intermittent lightning on the horizon, violet-white streaks between the clouds and the dark green sea. They would have to retreat to their rooms soon to stay out of the coming thunderstorm.

"He was taunting us even more than we realized," Julissa said. "He wasn't just showing us the bodies. He was telling us he's going to keep on killing and we won't be able to keep track of it."

Chris thought about that.

"Did you think of a way to reach Westfield?" he asked.

She nodded. "I set up a Skype account and emailed him a clue to the account."

"Skype's secure?"

"The NSA would ban it if it could. It's been trying to set up backdoors but hasn't been able to."

"What's the clue to the account?"

"I told him it's the last name of the man who first told us about the swimmer. Backwards."

"Hutchinson reversed?"

"Yeah."

"Good idea. Even if the killer is reading our email he won't get that."

"Yeah—except Aaron hasn't answered."

"Are you worried?"

"Aren't you?

Chris nodded.

A few drops of rain blew in with the next gust of wind. Julissa closed her laptop and put it into her purse. They didn't get up from the table, but sat watching the waves. Chris thought of the creature, and of chess. They were in the early stages of the game now, exploring each other's defense lines, making cautious moves to see how the other responded. Were they seeing the truth from its actions, or only what it chose to show them? A skillful chess player might sacrifice a few pieces for the right purpose. Maybe their gains were not so great after all.

Chapter Twenty-Eight

In the moonlight, the desert was silvery gray, cut down the middle by the highway, a black strip winding through the rocky hills and arroyos. The van was one of two cars in the motel lot. The other, an old Ford truck, belonged to the night manager. The light in Westfield's room was the only one shining. In the rifle scope, he could see the TV through a crack in the curtains. It looked like a war movie. He'd left the sound up, but of course from over a hundred yards away, he couldn't hear it.

He'd been in his hunting blind since sundown, having made it as comfortable as he could. He ripped the ratty blue carpet from the back of his van and spread it on the hardpan between the two biggest boulders at the top of the hill. Then he'd moved smaller rocks into the gap between the boulders, both as a shield and as a balance for the rifle. From the parking lot, the nest was invisible, just a tumble of boulders amongst the creosote at the top of the hill. He'd lugged up a gallon jug of water, a couple of gas station burritos, and his laptop. It was a clear line of sight from the hilltop to the motel, and he could get a weak wireless signal. The reception was poor, but would serve his purpose: the viral email would ping out his presence and draw them in.

How could he be sure they would come? That was his main worry. Maybe they would wait and watch from afar, monitoring his laptop's signals from some distant country and studying their chances. Meanwhile he'd be drying out on the hilltop, getting nowhere. He resolved to wait through the night and then through the next day. If they hadn't come by then, he would ditch the laptop and move on. He drank some of the water and wondered why he hadn't thought to bring any coffee.

He sighted through the rifle scope and activated the laser sight, projecting a tiny red dot on the door knob to his room. He checked the rifle again to be sure a round was chambered and the safety was off. Then he rested the butt of the rifle on the ground and leaned its stock against the boulder. He listened to the night noises: wind moving through the giant open spaces, a pack of coyotes miles away, something small scurrying close by.

The sound of the wind brought up a long-forgotten memory, which lay on his chest like a heavy stone. On a week's leave during his first overseas deployment, he and Tara had hiked along a lagoon and pitched a tent in the coconut trees somewhere in the Marshall Islands.

He tried to remember the name of the atoll and couldn't.

Instead, when he closed his eyes, he remembered the propeller-driven cargo plane landing on the crushed coral strip, Tara squeezing his hand until all three sets of gear were on the ground. Getting out in the hot sun and walking over the too-bright white gravel, blinking in the blazing light, and buying cold Coca-Cola in returnable glass bottles from a man whose house was across the dirt path from the landing strip. He remembered making love on a straw mat on the beach one morning after bathing in the ocean. Her inner thighs were salty, and when he kissed her there, and higher, tasting the clean ocean water that clung to her in tiny beads, she had cried out and said his name, her hands on the back of his head.

Now he crouched on the hilltop with the rifle next to him and remembered it bitterly. It was the beach of Maloelap Atoll, September of 1976.

From that day, she had no more than eighteen months left. He'd spent most of it at sea.

He lifted his head above the rocks and looked down on the parking lot again. Still the same: just his van and the old truck, and the crack in the curtains letting out the light of the television. He saw headlights in the distance, winding toward him. He watched to see how close the car had to be before he could hear it. At what he judged to be a thousand yards, he first heard the tires on the asphalt and the low purr of the engine. But he was downwind of this one. If they came from the other direction, he wouldn't hear so quickly. The car passed the motel without slowing and he watched its taillights, marking the spot when he could no longer hear it. He thought he'd have twenty seconds warning from one direction, and maybe only ten seconds if the car came from downwind. He shifted on the carpet and found a good position for his back against the boulder and closed his eyes.

When he woke, it was darker than before. A thundercloud in the west covered the moon. The only light came from the stars overhead. The hands of his watch, glowing dull green, showed 3:55 a.m. Some sound had woken him but he couldn't remember what. He was dazed with sleep, and cold. He picked up the rifle and rose to look over the low rocks. There was a black SUV in the motel lot. Its headlights were off but its brake lights and backing lights were on. The door to his room was ajar. The TV was dark but there was a light coming from the back of the room. Westfield crouched behind the rocks and watched, not through the rifle scope, but with just his naked eyes so that he could take in the whole scene. Then he shouldered the rifle and looked through the scope at the door. He could see the splintered wood next to the deadbolt slot and there was a rough boot print on the face of the door next to the knob. He pulled his face away from the scope and looked at the whole parking lot again. The SUV hadn't moved, but its brake lights were still on.

He looked through the scope again in time to see a shadow move behind the curtains. So there were at least two of them. A driver and the guy who'd kicked in the door to his room. That must have been the sound that woke him. He wished he had a silencer. If he did, he could shoot the man in the room and maybe the driver wouldn't know. Eventually he'd get tired of waiting and would get out of the SUV for his own bullet.

Instead it would have to be more complicated. There was no guessing what the driver would do when he heard the gunshots. He might get out and try to help his partner; he might drive around to the back side of the motel for cover and then try to flush Westfield on foot. He might just drive off, or try.

Westfield sighted through the scope again and watched the doorway to his room. A thought came out of nowhere like a jolt of electricity. What if, instead of coming after him themselves, they had simply called the police? It'd be so easy. He looked through the scope again at the inside of the hotel room. If they were cops, and if they'd made a call to the Galveston Police Department, there'd be a crowd of them by now. There wouldn't be just one shadow in the motel room and one SUV in the parking lot. They'd have backup, and backup for the backup. Every light in his motel room would be on, and the curtains would be open.

Then he had a second thought. If they weren't police, and if they tracked him here with his computer, by now they knew this was a setup. His van was outside his room and the TV had been left on. But he wasn't in the room and neither was his computer. If they didn't see the trap now, then they weren't very good at what they did for a living. And either way, they weren't going to live very long. Through the scope, he saw a shadow walk in front of the curtains, and then, suddenly, a man stood in the doorway. He was dressed in black combat pants and a black T-shirt, and if there was any further doubt about whether he was a cop or not, Westfield saw that in his right hand he was carrying an Uzi.

Westfield aimed at the center of the man's chest. Through the scope, he could see the laser sight's tiny red dot just over the man's heart. There wasn't time for anything else. As the man stepped over the threshold and onto the sidewalk, Westfield pulled the trigger. The bullet traveled faster than sound and the man never looked up. The shot was high and caught the man squarely at the base of his throat. He fell backwards into the room and lay bleeding on the carpet with his boots sticking out the open door. Westfield looked up from the scope and watched the scene below. He half expected to see ten men rush from his motel room, but none did. No lights came on anywhere in the motel. The SUV hadn't moved. All four of its doors were still closed. The man he'd shot lay absolutely still.

That was coldblooded, premeditated murder, Westfield thought. *My first for tonight.*

He turned the rifle on the SUV and looked through the scope. Maybe the driver was listening to the stereo and hadn't heard the shot. The SUV was parked facing the motel, so Westfield was looking at it from above and behind. It had Texas plates. They must have flown into El Paso and rented it there. He aimed at the roof, guessing if he put a bullet five feet from the front, it would angle through the back of the driver's-side headrest. He wondered if New Mexico was an electric chair state or a lethal injection state. Probably lethal injection, he decided. Most states were. He fired four shots into the SUV's roof as fast as he could pull the trigger. The sound of the shots rolled out over the desert silence and came back in echoes. The SUV's brake lights flickered and then went out. But the transmission was still in reverse and the SUV rolled backwards across the lot, tracing a curve. It came to a stop when it rammed the side of Westfield's van, its high back bumper slamming into the driver's door.

Westfield ejected the clip and inserted a new one. Then he put his laptop computer into a duffel bag, slipped the silenced .22 into the waistband of his pants, and started picking his way down the rock-strewn hill, trying to stay clear of the patches of cactus and lechuguilla that hid in the shadows of the boulders. When he reached the bottom of the hill, he crossed the sandy arroyo and then climbed the embankment to the highway. Now he was close enough he could hear the SUV's still-idling engine. Other than the wind, that was the only sound. Between the road's edge and the parking lot on the other side there was no cover at all. He crouched at the side of the road and just watched the scene for a minute. Nothing changed and there were no headlights on either horizon. He stood, clenched his teeth against the coming pain in his knee, and approached the SUV at a fast walk. He had the rifle in front of him, not at his hip, but shouldered and with the laser sight tracing its dot on the driver's side door.

As he crossed the parking lot, the motel's single streetlamp, which had been blinking on and off all night, finally went out for good. Westfield's shadow disappeared from beneath him. The SUV had black-tinted windows, opaque as obsidian in the darkness. Westfield reached the SUV and tried the handle of the driver's door, keeping the rifle's muzzle leveled at the window glass. The door was locked. He moved three steps down and tried the handle on the rear passenger door, but it was locked too. There was just the low purr of the engine. Someone would drive past soon. Someone who would slow down, see trouble, and make a call. He had to get the SUV off of his van and clear out. There was evidence everywhere that would connect him to these killings. This had been stupid, nothing more than lashing out with rage and now he was stuck with it. He was only just realizing the consequences. He set the rifle stock on the pavement and leaned its barrel against the side of the SUV, then took the pistol from his waistband. It would do no good to shoot out the window glass with the rifle; he could only expect the night manager to sleep through so much. But the pistol was silenced.

He went back to the driver's door and leaned close to the glass, cupping his hands around his eyes and pressing them to the glass. He tried to peer in and at first saw only darkness, perhaps the reflection of his own wide eyes.

And then, swimming up as his eyes focused, there was a dim white form on the far side of the SUV, blurry with speed as it came towards him.

He took three quick steps back from the window, raising the pistol as he did so. At the same time that he fired, his knee finally gave out. The shot went high, missing the SUV completely, but the window exploded outwards without any help from the bullet. The thing from inside came flying out in a star-spray of shattered glass. He had time only to see the outlines of the shape coming at him. Then it was on him, knocking him flat onto the ground. The rifle and the duffel bag went cartwheeling away. He slammed into the asphalt, head bouncing with a hollow *thunk* off the pavement and back into the howling, biting face of the thing on top of him. He saw its eyes, yellow as rotten teeth and glowing in the darkness like a wolf's. There was no chance for the pistol. It had yanked it away from him and crushed all the bones in his right hand before he'd even hit the ground. It wore a glass-tattered black overcoat and was otherwise naked as an infant, wet with blood and screaming. It raised its pale face up at the night and screamed once more before it dove into Westfield's chest with its teeth. Then its mouth was full of his flesh and it was silent.

But Westfield could still scream, and he did.

Chapter Twenty-Nine

Julissa woke to the sound of a strong wind blowing across the thatched roof of her bungalow, and she lay listening to it, thinking of the nightmare. It was another variation of the nightmare she'd been having since Allison was killed. In the dream, she was incorporeal, trapped in Allison's apartment, able to watch but unable to do anything as the door opened and a shadow came inside. She tried to see him, or it, but couldn't. It was like a gap in the air, a burn mark on a photograph in the vague shape of a man. It ripped her sister apart and she watched, the same way every night, until she woke soaked with sweat, afraid she may have been screaming in her sleep. But who would hear if she did?

The lamp on the bedside table was already on, casting a warm circle of light on the exposed beams of the bungalow. A small gecko crossed overhead, paused on the beam and appeared to do pushups as it clicked out its mating call. She told herself the dream was false, an invention of her imagination; she could learn nothing from it. There were no hidden clues, no revelations waiting to be found if she let it interrupt her sleep every night for the rest of her life.

She got up. She was wearing cheap cotton panties she'd bought on their trip to the department store. Other than the panties, she wore nothing else. She crossed the bedroom and stepped into the bathroom. She put on a white T-shirt that came just past the curve of her hips, then went to the door of the bungalow. It was three in the morning. The garden was dark, windy, and empty. She stepped onto the porch, went down the steps, and crossed to Chris's porch by following the path of stepping stones, rain wet and smooth under her bare feet. Drops of rainwater slid from the curved leaves of the banana trees and wet her hair and her shirt. Chris's lights were off. She crossed his small porch and tried the handle of his door. She did this very quickly, because she knew if she paused she would just go back to her room and get into her own bed to wait out another sleepless night.

His door was unlocked. The handle turned and the door opened.

She thought about that. Chris secured his house like a bank vault, and he'd told her on their sail to Molokai that sometimes he slept aboard *Sailfish* when even the house didn't feel safe enough. But now his door was unlocked and she knew it was for her. He wouldn't come to her but he'd known she might come to him, and he'd left his door unlocked in the hope of it. So she stepped inside and shut the door behind her. Despite the darkness, she could see him. He lay asleep on his side, atop his sheets, wearing only a pair of boxer shorts. She pulled her T-shirt over her head and let it drop onto the floor. Then she stepped around the bed and got in beside him, putting her palm onto his chest and her lips against the back of his neck. He stirred, waking.

"Julissa," he said, and she was glad there was no question in his voice. He put his hand over hers and then turned to face her.

"Is this okay?" she asked.

He kissed her, his hands running up her back and into her hair. Then his hands found her breasts, cupping them from underneath. She wanted him as badly as she had ever wanted anything in her life, and when at last she slipped out of her panties, pulled his boxers off, moved on top of him, and guided him inside of her, that first thrust made her gasp as though she'd just come to the surface after too long under the water.

"I need you," she whispered.

He didn't need to answer. She understood his response, in the way he held her and moved with her and the way he kissed her throat and breasts. The geckos in his room made their mating calls, and the walls of the bungalow shuddered in the wind. She cried out in her first orgasm and then held her face to his chest as they moved more slowly. She knew he could feel her tears falling onto his skin and was glad he just held her, and rocked with her slowly, and said nothing. What could he say? He made love to her, gently, and after a while she stopped crying and rolled with him so he was on top of her.

The second time she woke, it was daylight. Chris was still next to her, awake. He kissed her when he saw her eyes were open. Somehow he'd disentangled himself from her without waking her, had brushed his teeth and shaved, and had then come back to bed. She let her hand linger on the back of his neck after their kiss.

"Is this going to screw anything up?" she asked.

"No."

"We can hunt him and kill him, but still be like this?"

"Yes."

Later, she went back to her room wearing a towel from his bathroom. In her own room, she dressed in shorts and a tank top, then grabbed her laptop and stepped back out to meet Chris by the pool. They walked to the beach and then down it, heading north towards the cliffs that came from the water. Chris walked beside her, carrying the yellow dry bag that had been their only baggage coming to the Philippines. It looked empty except for the rectangular bulge of the computer he'd bought the day before. Shore birds ran along the sand in front of them, finally taking flight and escaping over the breaking waves. She let herself imagine buying a house here, atop the cliffs, loving Chris and having nothing to do each day except snorkel over the reef looking for lobsters, or sail with him to other islands. After a few moments, Chris took her hand and she leaned against him. For someone whose entire life was dedicated to revenge and murder, he was one of the least complicated people she'd ever known.

They cut across the beach and went into one of the restaurants on the sand path and asked the girl sweeping the floor if they could order breakfast. The girl showed them to a table and came back with menus. Julissa took out her computer and Chris moved his chair so they could both see the screen.

"I finished this last night," she said. "It's a geo-location program that should work with Google maps."

"We'll use it to find his address?"

"I wish. We've got the unique ID number of the guy who's been hacking the FBI. That's how we'll ultimately get him. First we find out where he's been getting onto the Internet. If he's smart—and we have every reason to believe he is—his computer's a laptop and he's logging on to the net from free hotspots."

"How do we find those?"

"The FBI stored the router address every time he logged on. So we start by tracking down the routers. That'll give us his point of entry to the net. After we know that, we'll have at least a general idea of where he is."

"You done this before?"

"No."

She opened the program she'd downloaded and modified, then took a piece of hotel stationery from her purse. She'd used a pencil to write the last five router addresses their quarry used to log into VICAP. She typed all five 128-bit numbers into her program's input prompt and started the search algorithm with a keystroke.

"It'll take a little while," she said. "It's searching every major hub on the net for a listing with these router addresses. It's not like a Google search. Private wireless routers are just entry points to the net, not pages with content that people search for, so they're not indexed in directories."

"You want breakfast?"

"Please."

Chris waved to the girl, who came from the other side of the restaurant and took their orders. The morning was still cool, the clouds over the sea laden with rain that would come in the afternoon. They waited for their breakfasts and waited for the search program to do its job and watched the sea and the sky. She thought about the afternoon, when they would have to go inside to keep out of the storm. That gave her a good feeling, knowing where they would go and what they would do. She took his hand and brought his fingers to her lips.

Chapter Thirty

The container ship M/V *Tantallon* steamed through the rising waves two hundred and fifty miles northeast of Miami, en route to Amsterdam, with no crew on deck and only one man on the bridge. The crew had been removed by helicopter a hundred and eighty miles from port, the order coming from headquarters via single-side band radio just minutes before the helicopter's red and green running lights appeared on the horizon. Now Captain Bryce Douglas was alone on the *Tantallon*'s wide bridge, standing behind the main wheel and looking ahead at the spray that whipped across the bow four hundred and ten feet in front of him whenever the ship broke through the bigger waves. The waves weren't a problem. The problem was what the helicopter dropped off before it picked up the six crewmen and swept back towards land, leaving him alone on the ship.

Well, not exactly alone. There was the VIP.

The girl's screams came again, as loud as before, shrieks of terror and pain that pierced through the steel bulkheads and made him shudder. It was a wet sound, as though she was forcing it through her own clotted blood. He'd thought her ordeal was over two hours ago. It had been quiet for a while and he had hoped it was finished, chanting it under his breath as he stood at the helm, *It's over please god let it be over it's over please god no more please god let her be dead and let it be finished.* But it wasn't. It was starting again, as horrible as when it had first begun half a day earlier.

Captain Douglas checked the doors for the tenth time. There were two ways onto the bridge: a gangway ladder from the quarters below, and a steel door that led into a hallway cluttered with fire control equipment. The other end of the hallway opened outside, at the stern of the ship's superstructure near the top of the track that launched the main freefall lifeboat. He'd locked the trapdoor to the gangway and had sealed off the steel door to the hallway, and for the last thirteen hours he'd been standing without relief at the helm, gripping the bridge fire axe in his right hand and pressing the flat side of its red blade to his chest.

Of course he'd taken the VIP on board before.

The call would come by scrambled satellite phone once or twice a year, always the same procedure. The crewmen would drop whatever they were doing, go to their quarters, and sit on their bunks. Steering from the bridge, he was the only one who'd see the helicopter settle atop the high stack of cargo containers on the deck; the only one to see the VIP scurry from the helicopter's unlit cabin, a shadow that would quickly disappear down the side of the stacked containers and into the hull of the ship. Then the pilot would switch on the helicopter's interior lights, a signal to the captain, who would use the ship's intercom to order the crew to walk in single file across the stack, carrying their sea bags. Two hundred miles from the coast, headquarters would tell him when the next helicopter would meet him, the crew having flown across the Atlantic in a charter plane.

Either the VIP would slip back into the dark helicopter once the crew was back aboard, or he would stay hidden in the ship. It was impossible to be sure.

In the first three hours after the girl started screaming, he had thought about unlocking the doors and running down the stairs into the dark underbelly of the ship, ready with the fire axe and a D-cell flashlight. But his terror had stopped him and he had done nothing. He thought about steering the ship off course and smashing the controls, sending out a distress signal and making a run for the lifeboat on its launching track at the stern. But he had been too scared to take even that cowardly step. Not scared of being alone in the lifeboat on the ocean, but terrified of the fifty-foot hallway from the bridge to the lifeboat. He couldn't face the forty seconds it would take to get to the lifeboat, climb into it, and trigger its release. And although the fiberglass lifeboat hatch would latch closed, there were no locks. He'd thought about the shadow scurrying head first down the vertical wall of cargo containers as the ship pitched in the dark.

The VIP.

What had he been carrying back and forth across the Atlantic?

This trip had been different from the moment the helicopter touched down on the stack. By moonlight, he saw the VIP emerge from the cabin, like the darkness that grows across the ground at dusk. No man could move like that. It slithered to the edge of the stack, arms and legs a black blur, so fast he wouldn't have credited it had he not seen it before. But when it was gone, the helicopter's cabin lights did not come on. Instead, the pilot hailed him on VHF channel 16, a breach of the normal procedure. There were three quick breaks on the microphone key to get his attention, and then the pilot spoke one sentence only.

"Stand by for additional offloading."

There'd been no need to respond. The captain stood in the shadows and watched out the bridge windows.

The helicopter's sliding passenger door opened farther and two men stepped out. Men who walked upright on two legs, whose faces were visible by moonlight. They wore black combat fatigues like members of a SWAT team, and they took their bearings on the deck before turning back into the helicopter to pull out a bag, a black bundle six feet long that they carried between the two of them, one at each end. They crossed the stack towards the bridge and disappeared with the bag. He heard them inside the ship a moment later, speaking in low voices and not in English. He'd made enough deliveries in the Baltic to know Russian when he heard it, even at a whisper coming up through the open spaces in the ship.

Then they were out again, back onto the deck and pulling a second bag from the helicopter. They brought it into the ship, but only one of them trotted back to the helicopter. When he was inside, the cabin lights switched on. The captain keyed the intercom and ordered the crew to the deck, single file as always. He watched them duckwalk across the stack and move into the helicopter at a crouch beneath its spinning rotors. He watched the door shut and the rotors pick up speed, the helicopter lifting off and hovering over the deck a moment before it tilted forward and moved off into the night, its red taillight blinking into the growing distance.

About five minutes later he'd heard the first animal roar and then the girl's first scream. That was when he locked the doors and grabbed the axe. The VIP had been busy with her for the last thirteen hours and it wasn't over yet. He looked into himself for the strength to go and do something for her and came up with nothing. He cursed himself and his cowardice, the shame of finally knowing, so late in life, that he wasn't the man he'd thought himself to be. He knew men who wouldn't have had a second thought. But he had locked the doors against his fear and had stood by doing nothing. Not even a radio call.

The girl screamed again.

"No please no please please n—" the last of it was cut off in a strangled cry that needed no translation.

He tightened his grip on the axe and waited for it to stop. Five minutes went by and then she was silent again. He looked down at his hand and saw blood coming from under his fingernails, his clench on the wooden handle so tight he'd burst all the capillaries in his fingertips.

He heard a sound and whipped around, his back to the helm station and the axe blade over his left shoulder, ready to swing.

It came again: tapping on the thick steel door. *Click-click-click-click, click-click-click-click.* He placed the sound and froze. He was listening to four, long-nailed fingers rapping in succession against the steel. *No,* he thought, *not fingernails.*

Not fingernails at all. He was listening to claws.

He was shaking all over, facing the door, trying to keep the axe steady. The clicking went on and on. Then the clicking stop and the VIP spoke to him.

"*Stand in the corner by the chart table, Captain.*" The voice was low and came to his ears by shivering up his spine like the tip of a rusty nail.

"I've never done anything to you," the captain said. He thought of all the times he'd carried this thing across the ocean without questions. Wasn't that loyalty?

"*Stand in the corner by the chart table.*"

His feet took him across the wide bridge and he stood between the chart table and the thin metal drawers that held charts for every deep water port and channel in the western hemisphere.

"*Put the axe on the floor and put your face in the corner.*"

He watched himself put the axe under the table. He was too unsteady to keep on his feet, so he knelt in the corner and rested his forehead against the bulkhead, eyes closed. He could feel the uneven motion of the ship as it broke through the waves. Behind him, the steel door blasted open with a loud *bang* as it swung the full arc on its hinges and slammed into the bulkhead. He cowered into the corner but did not turn around. The door opening was impossible, of course. The bridge had been retrofit less than a year earlier, prompted by the M/V *Arctic Sea* incident. The steel doors could be locked from the inside and the glass in the windows was bullet proof. Sealed off with the crew inside, the bridge was supposed to be able to keep pirates out for five hours, even if they had cutting torches and grenades.

The VIP had opened the door just by hitting it.

He could feel it standing behind him, hot breath on the back of his neck.

"*Stand up.*"

He did as he was told.

"*Turn around and open your eyes.*"

He turned slowly, taking a step so that his back was against the bulkhead. He opened his eyes, expecting to see the monster, but the bridge was empty. It must have been standing on the port wing, over by the recessed windows that looked out to the stern. The trapdoor to the gangway stood open.

"Go down to the galley."

Yes, it was behind him on the port wing. He didn't know how it could have opened the gangway trapdoor and then moved to the port wing at the same time he was feeling its breath on the back of his neck. He was dizzy and he realized he might have passed out. Maybe time had stretched farther than he realized. He took hold of the handrails and went down the steep ladder. An hour ago his bladder had been an urgent bursting pressure and now he couldn't feel it. Then he noticed that his khaki pants were soaked all the way to his socks. He didn't remember letting go. He was at the bottom of the ladder now, moving down the greenish-gray hallway in the direction of the galley. He knew the VIP was right behind him but he couldn't hear anything. No sounds on the steel ladder, no steps behind him in the passageway.

He turned and entered the galley. If he hadn't already emptied his bladder into his pants, he would have done so at that second. There was blood on the floor and blood on the stainless steel countertops and blood across the teak mess table. One burner of the gas range was lit, turned all the way up. He looked at the ring of blue-and-yellow flame under one of the bigger cast iron skillets. Smoke poured off the overheated pan and the lumps of blackened, leftover meat inside it. He felt the hot breath on the back of his neck again, and then that rusty-nail voice scraping into him like a sickness.

"Clean it."

He stepped into the galley, dizzy again. The smoke alarm went off. He walked to the sink and thought, *This is a nightmare this isn't real, this is a nightmare—*

The dishwater in the sink was backed up, so he reached in, numb, to find the drain stopper. He touched something soft and slimy and pulled it out. At first he thought it was a filthy dish towel, but it was worse than that. He was holding a handkerchief-sized swatch of human skin.

"Clean it," the thing said again, directly into his ear. He could smell its rancid bloody breath.

This is a dream, this is a nightmare.

He dropped the skin into the trash can and watched the pink dishwater drain from the sink, staring at the bits of flesh and the old soap suds that clung to the sides as the water went down.

An hour later whatever was left of Captain Douglas was hidden in a back corner of his mind, crouching in the shadows and looking through his own eyes as though looking through the wrong end of a telescope. Everything was far away and removed. The only thing that got all the way inside was the voice. It told him what to do and he did it. He cleaned the galley and ran the filthy mop water down the sink and bagged the skin and bits of meat and the charred skillet. At the voice's bidding he carried the bag to the stern rail and threw it over the side, into the ship's wake. And then the voice told him what to do next. There was no question of disobeying the voice.

"Engine room. Go."

He went. The steel staircases leading into the ship's belly were lit by bare bulbs inside steel cages. When he passed them, he could see the thing's shadow on the catwalk, mixed with his own. The angles were wrong and the lights would dim as thing's body blocked them. The hidden part of him, who was still Captain Douglas, realized the VIP was following him from above, crawling on the underside of the catwalks like a spider.

The engine room was dominated by two diesel power plants, each two stories high. There was a black body bag on the no-skid rubber floor in between them.

"Get the first-aid kit on the wall."

He went to the bulkhead at the rear of the engine room and took down the metal first-aid box next to the fire extinguisher. He backed up with it and stood by the body bag.

"Open the bag."

Captain Douglas knelt and unzipped the bag down its whole length. He thought of field spiders, the big black and yellow ones that wrapped their meals in neat packets of silk to save for later. He pulled the zipper to its end and parted the canvas to see the contents. There was a man inside, wrists and ankles cuffed. The thing's prey was badly wounded, but very much alive. He had duct tape wrapped across his mouth, but his eyes were open. His face was swollen and purple and his chest bore deep bite marks in his pectoral muscles. Captain Douglas saw the man's eyes focus near the ceiling. The man's eyes widened. He lay still but alert. The shadows in the engine room moved and darkened as the thing crossed another light.

"Clean the chest wounds."

He looked into the bound man's eyes and saw something that called him forward from his hiding place. For a few minutes he was all the way back again, Captain Douglas of the M/V *Tantallon,* a man who had stood on the bridge during hurricanes and who had been the first lieutenant on a submarine in the Royal Navy and who had once carried himself with pride. And here in front of him was a man who would not have hesitated where Douglas had. Here was a man who'd have rushed from the bridge with or without a weapon when he heard the girl's first cry. Douglas opened the first-aid kit and took out sterile gauze and a bottle of rubbing alcohol. He met the man's eyes again and an understanding passed between them. Douglas knew what he had to do. It was a tiny act and he did it secretly while he was cleaning the infected bites. The thing was above them on the ceiling, but Douglas could block its view of the case by leaning in close. He understood when he was finished here, he could retreat back into hiding, and there wouldn't be much time after that. He didn't know if what he was doing now would keep him out of hell—he suspected it was nowhere near enough—but he did it gladly. It was quick, and he went back to his work, cleaning the long tear below the man's navel. The man didn't even stiffen when he poured the alcohol directly into the gouge, but his eyes met Douglas's for a second. They understood each other.

"That's enough. Close the bag."

Douglas looked at the man's eyes a last time and then zipped the body bag closed. He could already feel the room receding, reality backing off as his mind withdrew down a long tunnel.

"Go to the steering room."

He went, dizzily, a wind blowing in his ears that couldn't have been there. The steering room was at the back of the ship and held the hydraulic gear that controlled the rudder. The second body bag was here, zipped closed. The room was covered in blood, the rubber flooring slick with it.

"Mop it down."

He did, for thirty minutes, and then the thing told him to stop.

"Get the bag."

He picked it up from one end, and it wasn't that heavy. Part of him knew why.

"Drag it up to the stern deck."

He went back up into the air the way he had come down after throwing the garbage bag overboard. The thing followed him and then it was there, right behind him, speaking with its breath on his neck.

"Open the bag."

He hesitated.

"Open it."

He unzipped the bag and she was in there, the girl whose murder he didn't try to stop. She looked to be no more than twenty. Neither her face nor her red hair had been touched, but the rest of her was mutilated. One arm was missing and both breasts were gone. A pair of handcuffs was locked onto the wrist of her intact arm, one cuff locked around her wrist and the other cuff free and dangling. He understood then, and the thing's voice told him what he already knew.

"The other cuff is for you. Put it on."

He knelt and reached into the girl's open stomach and took out the cuff. He put it over his left wrist and clenched it. *This is a dream, this is a nightmare. None of this is real.*

"Pick her up."

He held her to his chest and stood, lifting her out of the bag. The sun was setting and the ocean was a deep jade green shot with white in ship's the churning wake. It looked cold.

"Jump."

He let himself fall forward, the weight of the girl carrying him over the rail and thirty feet down into the water. He hit head first with the girl still held in his arms. Now he was out of the reach of the thing and its voice, and he was Captain Bryce Douglas again. He was all the way back. But there was no point in trying to come to the surface, so he kicked his legs to propel himself downwards. His last thought before he took in a searing lungful of cold green ocean was of the man in the body bag, the thing's prisoner. They had understood each other, he was sure of it. Maybe he wouldn't go to hell. Maybe he had seen his moment and taken a chance to do the right thing, like a man. He held the girl tightly and opened his mouth for the last time.

Chapter Thirty-One

They finished their breakfasts and lingered over their second cups of coffee, and then Julissa brought the laptop back to the table and turned on its screen.

"We've got him," was all she said.

Chris leaned close to her and looked. The computer showed a street map with red circles where the routers were located. The map was a city he knew well.

"San Francisco," Chris said. All five circles were clustered within about six blocks in the Inner Sunset. "He must live nearby, walks out to find free Internet when he wants to do his work."

"It's a good bet."

"If we were in San Francisco, could you find him?"

"If he's still there, using his computer, we've got a shot," Julissa said. "Finding the routers was easy, but finding the computer will be a lot harder."

"I'll book our tickets as soon as we get back to the hotel. If we leave Boracay this afternoon we can probably be in San Francisco in twenty-four hours."

It didn't take long for Chris to pack his room after he booked their tickets. He put the duffel bag with his clothes on the porch and sat down next to it, waiting for Julissa. It worried him they hadn't heard from Westfield. For that matter, it worried him that it was so easy to trace the hacking to a neighborhood in San Francisco. And then there was Julissa. Maybe he was worrying about San Francisco to avoid worrying about her. He thought about their night, how perfectly they had fit together. He thought about the way she had ridden him, her hair spilling across his face and her breasts brushing his chest, and thinking through the memory of it, he realized throughout the entire act of their lovemaking, he had thought only of her and not of Cheryl. It was too early to wonder if they would still be together after they were finished with this.

That sort of thought had too many presuppositions—that they would finish at all, that they would both be alive at the end of it.

At every step of the trip, Chris felt their safety slip away: when they showed their passports to the guard at the airport entrance and then a second time to the guards at the metal detector and x-ray machine, and yet a third time when they paid their airport tax. Then they were on the propeller plane to Manila, and upon landing their bag was searched and their passports inspected again. They paid their airport exit tax and took a taxi to the international terminal and went through the same process to reach their next flight, except here, in the capital, their passports were entered into computers instead of ledgers.

Then there were the cameras.

There were video cameras at the security checkpoints and at passport control, and video cameras at the jetway where they would show their tickets the last time to get on the plane. The cameras' gray wires snaked to the ceiling and disappeared, carrying the video feed with them, perhaps to the Internet. An American in khaki pants and a Hawaiian shirt stood at a newsstand and stared openly at Julissa and only turned away when Chris caught his eyes and started to walk over. The American turned and disappeared into the crowd.

They found a cafe in another part of the airport and he left Julissa at a table in the back, out of the view of the crowded terminal hallway. He went to the counter and ordered coffees, paying with his credit card. Chris looked for the American in the Hawaiian shirt but didn't see him again. He told himself it was normal. Julissa was beautiful; therefore, men would stare.

They sat across from each other with their laptops. Chris searched the Internet for any sign of Westfield. A simple Google news search for Westfield's name brought him to the story right away. It was a video on the website for KRQE News Channel 13 out of Albuquerque, New Mexico. The thumbnail image on the link to the video showed Westfield's beat-up blue van parked in front of a rundown motel. Police tape cut across the front of the image. Under the image was a headline: *FBI Investigates Double Murder in Carlsbad.*

"You'll wanna watch this."

Julissa moved to the other side of the table and looked at Chris's screen.

"Oh shit."

Chris clicked on the link and waited for the video to load. They both leaned close to the laptop so that they could hear the audio over its small speakers. Chris lowered the volume so no one else in the cafe would hear.

The video opened with a newscaster sitting behind a desk in a studio. As he spoke into the camera, a newsreel played in a box to the left of his head.

"Yesterday's double murder in Carlsbad took a new twist today when agents from the Federal Bureau of Investigation announced the FBI is taking the case off the hands of local officials."

The newsreel showed video of the murder scene, presumably shot the day before. Policemen and crime scene teams were moving in and out of the hotel room beside Westfield's van. The camera panned to show a white-sheeted stretcher being loaded into a black van.

"The FBI made the announcement today after two of its agents removed the bodies of both victims from the Eddy County morgue."

Now the video cut to a shot of a man in a blue FBI windbreaker standing in front of a concrete Federal building in Albuquerque. There were other news crews around and the man was in mid-sentence.

"—all we can say at this time is that there's an FBI interest in this case. Both victims were preliminarily identified as persons of interest in an ongoing Federal investigation—"

"There any terrorism connection?" an off-screen reporter asked.

"No comment."

"How were they identified?"

"The victims' profiles matched information in the State Department's biometric database."

"You know the victims' names?"

The FBI man blinked. "That's an ongoing investigation. I don't have any comment on that."

"Is Captain Westfield a suspect?"

"Captain Westfield is a person of interest and we would like to talk to him. That's all." The man turned and went up the steps. The shot cut back to the newscaster in the studio.

"Our field reporter Kate Bledsoe is on the scene in Carlsbad with more."

Now the video cut to a feed from the motel parking lot. The reporter Kate Bledsoe stood in front of the motel. She wore a tight khaki blouse and blue jeans and her booted foot was on the curb. In the desert behind her, Chris could see the neon sign for the Caverns Motel and below that the plastic letters that spelled out *Free Wi-Fi* and *Vacancy*. This story was starting to make sense. Their warning had been too late.

"I'm standing on the scene at the Carlsbad motel where police responded last night to a shooting. They found two unidentified men dead in the parking lot and in one of the rooms. One had a gunshot wound to the throat and the other to the back of the head. Police reported both men were wearing black combat fatigues and were armed with illegally modified sub-machineguns."

She pointed, and the camera panned across the desert and focused on a low, boulder-strewn hill.

"Police say the shots were fired from this hill. Investigators found a sniper's nest and recovered cartridges from a 30.06 rifle."

The camera zoomed on the hill and Chris could see a low rock wall built between two boulders. He imagined Westfield crouched behind it. Then the camera turned and focused on Kate Bledsoe again.

"One of the victims was found halfway inside room 109, which was registered to Aaron David Westfield. Investigators recovered Westfield's blue 1982 Ford van from the hotel parking lot. According to the clerk, Westfield checked into the hotel that afternoon and paid in cash. Westfield was an officer in the U.S. Navy and retired with the rank of captain. Investigators are looking for any leads as to Westfield's current whereabouts. They believe he's from Washington State, but have no information on recent employment or activities, and no information on why he was involved with the men who were gunned down. Back to you, Dave."

The video cut back to the newscaster in the studio. Kate Bledsoe was reduced to a little square over the newscaster's shoulder.

"Kate, have the local police gotten any fingerprints off the shell casings they found?"

"No. They said that would be unusual. Firing the shell burns the prints off."

"Does anything connect Captain Westfield to the murders?"

"Only that one of the bodies was found in his motel room, and his van and all his things were left at the scene, and the 30.06 rifle in the parking lot was sold in Carlsbad yesterday to a man using Westfield's ID."

"What're the local authorities saying about the FBI's sudden involvement?"

"The local sheriff's office never asked the FBI to step in. According to the sheriff's office, two FBI agents arrived in the morgue without warning and took both victims' bodies into Federal custody."

"What happened to the bodies?"

"They were loaded onto a plane and flown to Quantico, Virginia."

"Does the FBI have a theory about who these men were, or why they were gunned down in Carlsbad?"

"No, Dave. The FBI hasn't released any statement at all. Local police tell me they're looking for answers and would appreciate any information from the public."

Kate Bledsoe's image disappeared from the screen and was replaced by the same picture of Westfield that Chris had first seen in Galveston: Westfield as a younger man, in his Navy dress whites.

"Police say this man, Aaron David Westfield, is a person of interest in the Carlsbad killings. Anyone with information on Captain Westfield is encouraged to call Crime Stoppers, or you can submit a tip online at www.tipsubmit.com." The image of Westfield expanded to take up the full screen, while the website and phone number scrolled across the bottom in yellow lettering.

The video ended and Chris closed his laptop. Julissa had gone pale and was holding her coffee in her lap at an angle. Chris took it from her and put it on the table before it spilled on her legs.

"Maybe he got them both and switched vehicles?" Julissa said.

Chris shook his head. "He wouldn't have left all his stuff."

"When they came for Mike, they killed him and left him there. If Aaron's body isn't in the hotel, where'd it go?"

"Maybe they wanted him for something," Chris said. "If they took him, he's probably still alive. Otherwise, why bother?"

"Jesus. They want to use him to find us."

"Yeah."

They sat in silence for a minute.

"That guy said something about the State Department's biometric database," Chris said. "Any idea what that is?"

"Imagine a giant database full of photographs of people's faces, with each photograph broken down into twenty or thirty unique reference points."

"Like a fingerprint?"

"Yeah. A video camera with an infrared illuminator can scan people's faces and compare them against a biometric database to ID people in real time."

"They do that?" Chris asked.

"More than you'd probably want to think. The algorithms can tell the difference between identical twins. If you're looking for terrorists or known criminals, one way to find them is to put biometric ID cameras in high traffic areas—airports, subway systems, toll booths on a turnpike—you get the idea. Anyway, the State Department started the database. It uses it to check entry visa applications, but it's an open secret they share the database all over the intelligence community."

"You've done work on it?"

"Not directly. But biometrics is a hot thing, so it's something I ran into a lot."

Chris stared at the tabletop and thought about Westfield, alone in the desert and waiting for the killer's men. He must have been a good shot. Chris tried to picture what would have happened after Westfield was gone and the police were on the scene.

"So, someone in the morgue took photographs of these guys Westfield killed and uploaded them to the Internet, probably by putting them onto some kind of law enforcement missing-persons database. And that raised a red flag on the FBI computers because the faces matched people they were looking for."

"That sounds right," Julissa said.

"If the FBI has an interest in these guys, there must be a file on them somewhere. Think you can find it?"

Julissa nodded. "If it's on the FBI server, I can get it."

She went back to the other side of the table and started to work on her laptop. Chris sipped at his coffee and turned around to watch the crowd in the terminal. There was no sign of the American in the Hawaiian shirt. Were any of the cameras in this airport actually biometric scanners? That seemed unlikely in the Philippines, but he supposed the U.S. might pay to install them in foreign airports too. They had been so safe in their bungalows on the beach in Boracay. Safe, but too far removed to stay in the chase. In San Francisco they would be leaving tracks everywhere, no matter how hard they tried to stay unseen. And the killer might not be the only one looking for them; by now he could be wanted for murder in Hawaii. Then he had an even more troubling thought. He turned to Julissa.

"If he took Westfield alive, we have to consider the possibility he knows what you and I are up to."

Julissa looked up from her computer.

"You mean if Aaron talked because he was tortured."

"Yes."

"You want to change the plan?"

"No."

"Good, because neither do I. We don't have a fallback position and I won't sit and do nothing while Aaron gets killed."

Chapter Thirty-Two

Chris had insisted on buying first-class tickets from Manila to San Francisco, reasoning they would want the privacy. They had seats next to each other at the front of the plane, and Julissa discovered he had been right. In the three hours before their flight, she had worked her way into the FBI computers and downloaded three gigabytes of files from a network that could only be accessed by FBI station chiefs or higher. Now they sat in their first-class seats, thirty-nine thousand feet over the Pacific, reading the dossiers she'd stolen. She would lose her job, her security clearance and serve time in a Federal prison if half the things she'd done in the last four or five days came to light. And they were barely getting started. Their goal was simple: to kill an animal. But to get there they would almost certainly kill half a dozen other people; forty-five minutes with the documents made that clear. It was also clear there was no going back. She dimmed her screen, so no one behind her would see the document, and went on reading. She found Chris's hand in the darkness and held it.

The files she'd stolen consisted of nine dossiers on foreign spies and criminals, one top-secret memo from something called the National Biometric Counterintelligence Joint Task Force, and a redacted list of intercepted communications that were so secret not even the FBI had access to the files it referenced. She had scanned everything quickly and now went back to the memo, because it ran a thread through everything else.

"See if I've got this straight," Chris said. His computer was open on the tray table, its glow lighting his face. "The FBI and the CIA set up a joint task force because five guys who shouldn't even know each other were having secret meetings."

Julissa nodded.

"Looks like it was pure chance," she said. "They had biometric cameras in the Port of Copenhagen and ID'd five guys going past the checkpoint in fifteen-minute intervals. Three of them were retired GRU or SVR agents from Russia, one of them was German BND."

"Disgraced German BND," Chris said.

"Yeah. The last one in was a British MI6 officer who went AWOL in Basra and hadn't been seen since 2006."

Chris looked at the memo, then switched files to look at one of the dossiers.

"They knew they were on to something. They just didn't know what. So they started watching. They programmed the database to pick up any meetings between any of these men."

"It makes sense," Julissa whispered. "I mean, guys like that, meeting in shipping ports in the middle of the night? The FBI must've thought they'd stumbled on to a terrorist cell or an ultra-secret foreign intelligence operation."

"Or a trafficking ring," Chris said. He pointed at the other four dossiers, the German, British and Italian smugglers who were somehow caught up with the ex-intelligence agents.

"Then two of these guys turn up dead in New Mexico and the FBI is scratching its head, trying to figure out what's going on and why someone like Westfield is caught up in it," Julissa said.

She looked across at Chris's laptop. He'd opened the file of one of the Russian GRU agents, Anatoli Shurikov. Three photos lined the top of the screen. Two were cropped closeups of Shurikov's face, taken from security cameras, and one was a blowup that was probably taken upon his graduation from the Spetsnaz officer training school.

"It's him," Chris whispered. "The man I shot."

Julissa nodded.

Chris went on in a low voice. "Between us and Westfield, we got four of them. We got Anatoli Shurikov. Ilya Vishnyakov must be the one who came for Westfield in Galveston. Westfield must've gotten rid of him like we did with Shurikov, which explains why the joint task force memo says there was a .22 at the New Mexico scene with both their prints. Then he got these other guys—"

"Strasser and Voinovich."

"—yeah—he got them in Carlsbad. So maybe we've cut their core group down to five."

"The core group of what?" Julissa asked.

Chris shook his head. "It doesn't look like this joint task force has any idea either—we might even know more than them. If they know about the connection to the killer, it isn't in these documents."

"No. It looks like just dumb luck," Julissa said. "I think this creature needs help to do what it does. Help crossing borders maybe, or help cleaning up and hiding its tracks."

Chris scrolled to look at a collection of nine photographs—a mix of surveillance photos and mug shots—that comprised the nine men who were being tracked by the U.S. joint task force. "So he hires the kind of people who can do that—smugglers and intelligence agents."

"Not just agents," Julissa said. "These guys were all killers, too. The Spetsnaz is the Russian equivalent of the SEALS. Strasser came to BND from GSG 9, the German federal tactical SWAT team. You've heard of the British SAS, and that's where Kent started. When the creature hired them, it was probably just looking for their skills without realizing all nine had faces that would register on intelligence radars and raise some eyebrows if anyone noticed they were hanging out together."

"Makes sense," Chris said.

"Maybe the FBI overlooked something because they didn't understand the big picture the way we do. And we should consider there's probably a tenth employee involved the FBI doesn't know about," she said.

"The hacker."

"Yeah. I haven't seen any mention of him. But that makes sense. They've only been monitoring camera feeds, and those photos would mainly be of people in transit. Hackers don't get out much. He probably does all his communication online, so he may have never met any of the people he works for."

"We'll have to check all the files. See if we can figure out when these guys were spotted in which cities. If the dates match up to any of the killings, that may tell something," Chris said.

They sat in silence for a while in the darkened plane. Around them the passengers were either sleeping or watching movies on private seat-back screens. Chris was looking at the photograph of Shurikov, and Julissa recalled how quickly and easily Chris had gotten behind him and taken him down with a shot to the head. Chris must have picked up on that thought.

"They underestimated us the first time," he said.

She squeezed his hand and knew he was right. Would Chris really have been able to do that if Shurikov had been paying attention?

Probably not.

"We must've looked like soft targets. An ex-lawyer, a computer programmer, a washed up Navy captain, and a retired Hawaii cop? Jesus, they probably thought it was a joke," Chris said. "Next time we won't have that advantage."

"True," Julissa said. "They might also lay low a while."

"Why's that?"

"That news clip is on the Internet and wasn't hard to find. If they've seen it, they know the FBI's interested. They know they've been tracked for over a year. They're probably holed up somewhere right now, trying to figure out how big a breach they've got. Also," Julissa said, liking this thought more as she whispered it quietly to Chris, "I'm guessing their employer is not a nice thing to work for. And I would guess it's extremely pissed."

Chris turned now so that he could whisper into her ear. What he said gave her no comfort.

"That's true," he said. "Which makes me very scared for Aaron Westfield right now."

Chapter Thirty-Three

Westfield had woken in the stifling darkness of the body bag and had immediately understood from the sound and sense of motion that he was in a helicopter. He couldn't say how long he'd been unconscious but the dryness in his mouth and the hazy pain calling in from all over his body told him he'd been drugged, and heavily. He could think of no advantage to letting anyone near him know he was awake, so he lay still and listened. The pilot was flying in radio silence and there was no conversation or sound of other passengers. But there was a person next to him. Of that he was sure. He could feel the distinct press of an arm against his arm, a hip against his hip.

Some ache in his heart felt that touch and sounded out a question: *Tara?*

Of course not. But there it was: he knew he was next to a woman.

He tried to recall anything after the SUV's window shattered, but he could not. There was the whirlwind of the thing coming at him, its yellow eyes, its teeth ripping into him. But afterwards there were only snatches of nightmares and bright bursts of pain. He tried to stay absolutely still, and sent his mind to remember anything he could. Whatever drugs he'd been given were clearly still with him, but they weren't as bad as things he'd poured into his body willingly. He went all the way back to meeting Chris, Julissa and Mike in Galveston and then went forward from that point to the night in the desert and the thing's explosion from the pane of tinted glass, and it was all there. So he was just missing a matter of hours. He thought about it and admitted it could have been days.

Then the helicopter had started its descent. He felt it first in his ears and then in his stomach as they dropped altitude like an elevator. They slowed, and just before the hard touchdown, he heard the sliding door open, and he was able to smell the ocean. That hint came through the small air hole over his nose, faint but clear, the smell of a breeze that has blown for countless unbroken miles over a clean sea. He caught it over the smell of the helicopter's fuel and the smell of the rubberized plastic bag, and for an instant he expected to be thrown out the door and into the ocean. But then he felt the skids hit a metal deck and he knew it wasn't over for him yet. He fell into a daze of pain when they carried him into the ship and dropped him in front of the throbbing engine, then fought his way out of it when he heard the young woman's voice.

"Please let me out. I can't breathe."

She was right next to him; he could hear her struggling just inches away, probably inside her own bag. And then he heard the tapping. His heart sped up and his skin tightened. His body knew what it was before his mind placed it. Claws on steel, pacing. He lay still but the girl still fought. She didn't know.

"Please, I'll do anything!"

The pacing stopped, next to his head. Westfield could actually feel the creature's body heat through the vinyl wall of the bag. He heard the long, slow pull of a zipper.

It went on for a minute. The thing was taking its time opening the girl's bag. When it finally stopped, the screaming started.

Westfield fought to get out, but was hopelessly bound. Steel cuffs bit into his wrists and ankles. The wrist cuffs were attached to something around his waist so he couldn't move his hands above his stomach. He tried to explore with his fingers, but could barely move his right hand at all. It felt swollen to the point of bursting.

The girl's screams went on and on, and between them, Westfield could hear the thing's low voice. Its words weren't clear but their intent was obvious. It was taunting her, deliberately driving her into a frenzy of terror.

Then he felt pressure on his face. The thing's clawed hand lay across the top of his bag; its voice whispered directly inside his head.

Listen, it said. Its voice was an awful scratch. *You always wondered what it was like for her. What she went through. How long it lasted. Now you'll know.*

The thing moved away from him then, back to the girl, who redoubled her screams. She screamed until she ran out of breath and then the only sound she could make was a low keening.

The thing gave a wet chuckle, like a drain coming unclogged.

And then it roared and tore into her and the girl's shrieks went so high Westfield could only hear them in his heart. He fought at the cuffs until his wrists were bleeding and he had used all the air in the bag. He was dizzy and his head was pounding in pain, but the girl's screams would not allow him to stop, and he fought until long after he had lost any sense or conscious thought.

Then he was in the scorched and ruined landscape of a nightmare. He struggled across this wasteland, where screams came from the darkened sky, and he felt his chest explode with infection. The thing's mouth was as rotten as its mind. The moon was overhead, lighting his agony with its heatless glow. Dark tendrils of slime mold extruded from the bite marks in his chest and clung to his pale skin like the placenta of some second birth. He thought it would cover him until he was enveloped in its gelatinous cocoon. He tore at it with his hands, but his fingers stuck to the wounds and the slime crawled up his arm, black and burning. He writhed in the bag, half blanketed by the dream. Next to him the thrusting and pummeling never stopped, and neither did the screaming.

When his fever broke, hours later, he came to a kind of dazed consciousness again. The girl must have died. There was just the sound of the ship's engine and the movement of the hull through waves. He lay in the body bag, shivering and soaked with his own urine, and waited again. When the bulkhead door opened, he listened to the footsteps and then heard a voice that could only belong to the thing.

"Get the first-aid kit on the wall."

He heard footsteps moving around him and creaking from overhead. Someone set a heavy-sounding metal box on the floor next to him.

"Open the bag."

The thing sounded like it was right above him. Then the zipper over his face came down. After untold hours in the bag, the light of the engine room was overpoweringly bright. He squinted to focus and made out the face of a man. Just a regular man, kneeling over Westfield. He wore a white uniform shirt of the British Merchant Navy, which was stained with water and spots of blood. His brown hair was in disarray, and his eyes were blank with terror. When Westfield's eyes grew accustomed to the light he looked beyond the man and focused on the catwalk that ran over the engineering space where he lay.

The thing was there, practically hovering above them by clinging to the underside of the catwalk. Its neck was twisted impossibly around so that its yellow eyes met Westfield's.

"*Clean the chest wounds,*" the thing said. Its voice came snaking out of its leathery lips, which never moved at all. The merchant man went to work as if hypnotized, and Westfield ignored him, staring at the thing.

You could stuff it in a suit and put it behind a desk, he thought, *and it would pass for human.*

In low light, if you couldn't see its hands.

But no one would ever mistake it for anything but a monster as it clung to the catwalk, naked, its pale skin pulsing and bulging at its stomach from the meal it had just taken, its taloned fingers and toes easily holding its contorted body in place. He stared into its yellow eyes while the man poured searing alcohol into his wounds and reached into them to clean them with pieces of sterile gauze. There was more here to resist than just the pain and the fear. The man who was tending to him was already destroyed, and Westfield understood this creature had more weapons than just its claws and its teeth. Its eyes searched his and he could feel the way it was pushing into him. The yammering madness of its thoughts now hummed inside his skull. But he gave it nothing more than his own hatred, and when he felt it slipping past that and deeper, he thought of Tara.

Tara on their wedding night, standing at the foot of the bed and reaching behind her neck to unclasp the hook at the back of her gown. Tara on the street without an umbrella on a rainy day in Tokyo, her wet and red hair standing out in a sea of black umbrellas, the crowd parting around her as she stopped to take a photograph. Tara, whom he would never see or speak to again, whose horrific death had been reenacted for him here on this ship.

Tara, whom he loved and missed.

The thing blinked.

And that was when Westfield felt the man slip two metal objects under his left hand. He briefly met the man's eyes and used his fingers to slip the objects, whatever they were, into hiding beneath his wrist.

"*That's enough. Close the bag,*" the thing said. Westfield was grateful when the zipper was shut and he was in the dark again, away from the creature and its probing, lantern eyes. He heard the pair of them move off and listened to the bulkhead door slam shut. Then he gently explored the objects with his left hand and discovered a pair of tweezers and a small steel scalpel. The fever came buzzing back then, worse than before, and he knew he couldn't fight it. He tucked the scalpel and tweezers between the cuff and his left wrist so they would not fall out of his reach and then he lay his head down and closed his eyes to let the wave of sickness take him. The chills turned to a fierce sweating heat, and his tongue swelled with thirst, and eventually, in spite of all his struggles against it, he lost consciousness again.

He woke in blinding light. He squinted and took deep breaths of the relatively fresh air. The bag was open, zipped down just past his sternum and the tape was gone from his mouth. That could mean only one thing, and he'd been expecting it, but he still felt a quick jolt of fear when he remembered the tweezers and scalpel he'd been slipped. He relaxed when he felt them still against his wrist, held in place by the steel cuff. Either they hadn't searched him or they knew about the pitiful instruments and wanted him to hold on to some hope. Not that he had any illusions after what he'd seen in the engine room.

He let his eyes focus on the ceiling—catwalks, conduits, and caged light bulbs that threw more shadow than light—and then tried to look around. He was no longer in the engine room but had been taken to another place inside the ship. It was quieter and cooler here. The fever had passed again but he was weak and dehydrated so at first it was difficult even to raise his head from the floor to peek over the edge of the body bag. He persisted and forced himself to sit all the way up. On the other side of the narrow space, seated at a machinist's workbench, was a man. This was no merchant seaman. He wore black combat pants and a black T-shirt and was facing away from Westfield, but turned quickly when he heard the noise of Westfield's body shifting.

"Welcome back," he said. He had a cheerful voice and a gentleman's English accent.

Westfield just stared at him. The man was clean-cut and would have been handsome but for the half-moon bite mark on his left cheek and the fingernail scratches trailing away from his right eye. Both wounds were puffy and pink, but if they bothered him, he didn't show it at all.

"A pleasure to meet you, Captain Westfield. I've been hearing all about you from my colleagues."

Westfield wasn't sure he could talk if he wanted to. His mouth was so dry he couldn't put together the motions to swallow.

"We just have a few things we need to sort out before we weigh you down and toss you over the side. What do you say?"

He opened his mouth and breathed out an answer in a rasp that was barely audible over the ceaseless rhythm pulsing from the engine room, "Have at it."

The man stood from his stool at the workbench, picked up a leather case the size of a shaving kit, and came to a casual crouch next to Westfield. He put one big hand on Westfield's chest and pushed him down to the floor. Then he started to talk, his hand still pushing the wind out of Westfield's lungs.

"You probably remember Ilya. From Galveston? He and I never saw entirely eye to eye so I don't hold it against you, whatever you did to him. But he did bring some good things to the table, now and then."

He held the leather case and opened it over Westfield. It held five small glass syringes, each needle capped by an orange plastic cover. The lettering on the syringes was in Cyrillic.

"This for example. Probably the only thing the Russians ever made on their own, aside from vodka, that has a real spark to it. You wouldn't credit them with being able to come up with something so delicate and so *useful*. You ever heard of Ivan Rybkin?"

Westfield just stared at him. The man's hand was back on his chest, crushing him. Westfield didn't dare open his mouth for fear that all of his remaining air would be pushed out. The man was clearly waiting for it, ready to pounce and slam down on Westfield's sternum and leave him gasping. But it was also obvious that this was only a game he was playing until he got to the main event.

"No? Well, it's your loss. Great story. Sex, spies and videotape. All that. And it's where Ilya learned how to use this. Which he then taught me."

Now he slammed the palm of his hand into Westfield's chest and punched the air from him in a single, painful burst. Westfield felt as though his lungs had collapsed and stuck together; no matter how hard he tried to suck air through his dry and swollen throat, it would not come in. He lay writhing in the bag, and as he struggled, the man calmly took one of the syringes from the case, flicked the orange protective cap off with his thumbnail, and jabbed the needle into Westfield's jugular.

Westfield fought in agony against his airless lungs and could do nothing to stop the fire spreading from his neck. Inside the bag he made a desperate effort to wriggle the scalpel free from the cuff so that he could slit his own wrists and bleed out in the bag before the man noticed. Anything to end this now. He pulled the scalpel free but it fell from his weak fingers and slipped past his reach. When he finally got a breath of air into his lungs, the drug hit his brain like a depth charge. He saw a flash of blinding of white light and felt himself fall backwards, as though the hull of the ship had opened and dropped him into a whirlpool. The man was still with him, falling alongside him. His eyes locked on Westfield's, and he grinned.

Chapter Thirty-Four

Chris walked out of the Marriott on Post Street and got into a taxi next to the valet stand. Julissa was on the twentieth floor in their adjoining rooms, programming the software for their next step. She'd sent him out with a shopping list written on each side of two small sheets of hotel stationery.

"Let's go to Fisherman's Wharf," Chris said. The driver nodded and turned on the radio. N.P.R. was covering the Intelligene murders in Foxborough. Their route took them over Nob Hill, then over Russian Hill and down towards the north end of the city. It was raining and the streets were slick but the driver never slowed. They passed a row house Chris and Cheryl had considered buying when they were thinking of staying in California. On the radio, the news host went through all the details that Chris already knew: the dismemberment of the entire staff of scientists and interns, the pyramid of body parts found in the center of the fire, the fact that Chevalier had been found in his home, ripped in half. There were no known motives. The company was profitable, its books clean. Chevalier had been admired and liked, even by the people he'd left behind at Harvard when he started his company. There were none of the usual academic jealousies or accusations of intellectual theft. Chevalier had been a genius in his own right, had been generous with his ideas. The mystery was wide open and the police had no leads. The story moved to the economy and Chris looked out the window and thought about other things.

When they arrived in San Francisco, Julissa had asked him to stand in a separate line going through immigration. She didn't want him nearby if she got arrested for traveling on a stolen passport. He'd been one line over and had watched the ICE officer clear her into the country. It had taken about a minute, the officer looking at Julissa's face and then typing into his computer. There were cameras all around, at least a dozen just that he could see, half of them backed by UV illuminators that Julissa said would help the biometric algorithm make faster identifications. Surely they were both in the State

Department's database, their real names matched irrevocably to their faces. But they both passed through immigration without incident, walked quickly past the customs check and then out of the secure area of the airport. They had taken the first taxi they found, not wanting to spend the time to rent a car, not wanting to spend another minute in an airport crawling with law enforcement and enmeshed with wires and lenses and microphones.

So now, Chris was on his way to rent a car. He paid the taxi driver and stepped out on the sidewalk next to Fisherman's Wharf. There was a Hard Rock Cafe and a Bubba Gump Shrimp Company, both closed this early in the morning. Seagulls stood on the roofs, each balanced on one leg, oblivious to the cool morning rain. Chris could smell sourdough bread in the ovens of a bakery, and then there was the smell of the bay itself, like the water inside a freshly shucked oyster. He walked over to the rail and looked at the sailboats tied up at their docks. The owner of a fifty-foot ketch had left his dinghy in the water, and a young female sea lion had climbed inside to sleep on the floorboards. He had built his entire life around this one task, and had dedicated himself to it daily with a focus that had frightened Mike. But he was not so single minded that he could not dream of a gentler future when the thing was dead. He thought of Julissa diving off the side of a sailboat and into the turquoise water of a lagoon in the Tuamotus, as gracefully as she had plunged into the harbor at Haleolono. He thought of the way she had turned to him, treading water with her hands lightly cupped on her breasts. Chris turned his collar up against the rain, checked his pocket for Julissa's shopping list, and then headed across The Embarcadero and up Beach Street to the Avis storefront.

After he got his car, he sat in the driver's seat on the third floor of the parking garage with his computer open on his lap, using Google to track down the things he needed to buy for Julissa. He'd been afraid that for some of the stranger electronics parts, he'd have to drive all the way to Silicon Valley at the south end of the bay, but he found a store on University Avenue in Berkeley that sounded promising. Berkeley was just across the Bay Bridge; he could be there in half an hour if traffic wasn't bad. He used his satellite phone to call the store, and when he had a clerk on the line, he read down Julissa's list and confirmed everything was in stock. She'd been up late in the night drawing circuits and doing calculations on her computer. He didn't entirely understand what she was building, but he knew it would help them find the hacker's computer.

They didn't have much of a plan after that. Chris drove out of the parking garage and followed Beach Street to The Embarcadero. Assuming they could get the guy without killing him, they would need a quiet place to do the interrogation. There were isolated areas along the coast just south of the city on Highway 1. They could drive him down there, leave the car at a scenic lookout, and force him down into a gully near the ocean. It would be nighttime and there would be no pedestrians on the highway, and even if there were, the sound of the waves and wind would keep his shouts from reaching the road.

He assumed they would have to hurt him to make him tell them anything, and he thought about that for a while. Here, in cold blood, driving down The Embarcadero in the rain in a rented Chevrolet, he could picture hurting this man. Cutting him with a knife or smashing his fingers to pulp with rocks. What if the hacker turned out to be a woman? That was a complication he hadn't thought of, and it changed the emotional calculus. If they were to be successful, they'd have to deal with any number of things they'd never planned for.

And then he considered the fact that the whole idea was dependent upon the shaky assumption that the person would either talk willingly or that coercion would make him tell the truth. Chris thought it was fairly common knowledge that a person will say anything to make torture stop. Even if their plan worked, Chris was still concerned about what to do with their man after they'd gotten what they wanted out of him. Killing him would be the most logical thing to do. Any information he gave them would be worthless if he ran off and sounded a warning before they could act on it. What of the tricky question of how tight a leash the thing kept on its pet computer hacker? Did he have to check in every day? Maybe the best thing would be to incapacitate him and then clone his hard drives, search them at their leisure, and never interrogate him at all; surely a hacker would store most of his useful information on a computer drive, and Julissa would find a way to read it.

He thought about these things as he circled up and onto the bridge, crossing the suspension span to Yerba Buena Island and then the second stretch across to Oakland. He had a sense it would be a day of troubling thoughts without real answers. It happened often enough he'd learned to roll with it. But he wished he hadn't left Julissa alone. He would finish this as fast as he could and get back to her.

In Berkeley, he found parking and walked along University Avenue until he came to the store, which was a dimly lit warehouse of steel shelves and dusty cardboard boxes. He handed Julissa's list to the college student working as a clerk. He wore a black apron over his street clothes and the nametag on his shirt pocket read *David*.

"I talked to you on the phone. Can you find all this stuff for me?"

David looked at the list and used one finger to push his glasses farther up his nose. "You building some kind of transmitter?" he asked.

"I don't know. I'm just picking this up for a friend."

The clerk shuffled through the four pages of Julissa's neatly scripted list and looked up at Chris. "I hope she's gonna pay you back, because just to warn you, this's gonna be at least two thousand dollars worth of stuff."

Chris smiled. "She mentioned that."

"You wanna go somewhere for about half an hour? It's gonna take a while to find all this." The clerk gestured at the store with a sweep of his hand. "This place isn't exactly in alphabetical order."

"Sure," Chris said.

He walked out of the store and back onto University Avenue. It had been ten years since he'd been in Berkeley and he'd never known the town well anyway, so he walked without a plan or a destination. He just wandered. There was plenty to think about. He'd been hoping the police investigating the Intelligene murders would leak something useful, but so far, there'd been nothing. He and Julissa had never talked about how the killer had tracked down Chevalier. After it found Chevalier, it picked up the trail leading to the four of them and their investigation in Galveston. They'd been so busy running from the consequences of that disaster, they'd hardly had a chance to consider how it had come to pass.

Chevalier had emailed some of his results outside of Intelligene—his last letter to them mentioned a researcher at Harvard who'd done isotope hydrology tests on saliva from the fork—so there had been at least one breach to the outside. It was impossible to know how far downstream the information had run. Then there was the chance, which Chris considered more likely, that Chevalier had contacted the FBI. Chevalier couldn't have known the killer had a direct conduit into that database. He tried to think of any other plausible explanations and couldn't.

He took out his phone and called the hotel room. Julissa answered on the first ring.

"Yes?" she said.

"It's me."

"Okay. God. I was scared when the phone rang. I thought—well, I don't know. I'm just jumpy."

"I wanted to check and make sure you're okay."

"I'm all right. I've got the chain on the door and I kept the butter knife from breakfast this morning because it's the only thing I've got."

"I'm in Berkeley. I found a store that has everything on the list. The clerk's getting it together now."

"Did he know what it's for?" she asked. Her voice was so gentle on the phone. He thought, again, about the way their bodies fit together when he held her.

"He asked if it was a transmitter."

"Yeah. It might look like that. Good."

"Listen," Chris said. "I had an idea about Intelligene. I think Chevalier might've tried to contact the FBI. Maybe he got scared after he thought about what he'd found. It's the only thing that makes sense."

Julissa was silent and Chris could picture her thinking about it, tapping the end of a pencil against her chin and picking his idea to pieces.

"It makes sense. But they can't be *that* aware of what goes on at the FBI, or they would've known about the joint task force looking for them. If they knew about that, why risk of sending those guys into the U.S.?"

"But they didn't take a risk. The FBI doesn't have a clue how they got into the country."

"So you think maybe they know about the task force and they don't care?"

"It's a thought. Can you think of any other way he could've found out about Chevalier?"

Now he actually could hear her tapping a pen against something, probably the leather-topped desk in the hotel room.

"We know Chevalier emailed that researcher at Harvard, the isotope hydrologist. That guy might've spread results to other scientists, and scientists talk a lot. The killer might have a few on his staff somewhere, or might have a few he's watching."

"Why would he have scientists on his staff?"

"Maybe he wants to know more about himself."

Now Chris was silent. Julissa had just hit on something he'd never considered before, and he was disgusted when he found the smallest pull of sympathy for the thing. He saw it out there, alone in the world, wondering: *What am I?* And then on the heels of that thought he had another that was more disturbing still: what if it tracked scientists not because it wanted to know more about itself, but because it wanted to find another creature like it? What if it had some reason to believe that it *wasn't* alone in the world? Could it be searching for a mate?

"Chris?"

"I'm here." He paused. "Just thinking. I'll be back in the city in about an hour and a half. Can I bring you anything besides the stuff on the list?"

"No. I'm okay. Just nervous being in the hotel alone."

"I'll be back soon."

He hung up and continued walking along Berkeley's side streets, lined with neatly kept professors' houses. He thought about Intelligene and the killings in Foxborough. There was more to it than they were seeing. Maybe more than they would get from the hacker they were tracking, but he couldn't see it clearly yet. He put his hands in his pockets and looped around one more block before coming back to the store. The clerk, David, had loaded everything into two cardboard boxes on top of the counter next to the cash register.

"What's the damage?" Chris asked.

"Worse than she predicted. Twenty seven hundred and change." He handed Chris an invoice and Chris gave him a credit card.

Driving back into the city, stuck in the traffic at the toll booth to get onto the Bay Bridge, he thought about Julissa alone in their hotel rooms. She had every reason to be scared. They still had no idea how it was tracking them. If it found them the first time, it could find them again. And now they were defenseless because they'd been forced to leave all of their weapons aboard *Sailfish* when they abandoned her on Molokai. They would have to think of a way to protect themselves. It was next to impossible to legally buy a gun in San Francisco. They would have to improvise. He looked at the two heavy boxes on the passenger seat next to him. A solder gun lay atop the plastic-wrapped pile of capacitors and oscillators and god knew what else. At least he could put himself to good use by finding them some weapons while Julissa somehow put all that together.

Chapter Thirty-Five

Westfield was having a hard time staying on his barstool. He was holding on to his drink with both hands and staring down into it, focusing on the disk of liquid that vibrated gently in time to the music. He must have closed his eyes there for a little while, but now he was back and he focused on the drink. When he thought about it, he could remember ordering it a minute ago. It was Jack Daniel's, neat. Two fingers' worth in a tumbler, the way he always got it. The bartender was standing at the other end of the bar talking to another customer. There was a voice from the stool next to him, a man asking a question, and he turned and looked at him. Another drunk, sitting on the stool next to his. He looked like he was drinking the same thing as Westfield. Maybe they'd ordered this round together at the same time. Yes, that was it. He remembered it now and turned back to the man. The room spun a little as he turned, the mirror behind the liquor bottles spinning nicely, the neon lights it reflected going into a good swirling blur. This was his favorite part of getting drunk: those fine hours when he was truly wasted, yet capable of drinking infinitely more without any real effect at all until much later when he simply blacked out, usually, but not always, in his own bed. As always, he felt elated to have achieved this state. *I did it!* he wanted to shout. Instead he finished his slow swivel on the barstool and looked at the man next to him.

"You say something?"

"You go away there for a second, pal?"

"Yeah. I guess I did." He set his drink down.

"You were telling me about your friends."

He remembered his friends. God, it was good to have people behind him again. Good people he could trust.

"I don't know where they went. I wish I had their phone number or something. Could get 'em to come over here. Chris is a really good guy. Julissa's drop-dead beautiful, but she's got a dangerous mind, you know?"

He reached out with his right hand to pick up his drink. His fingers fumbled it and it almost spilled onto the bar. He looked at his hand and couldn't quite focus on it, but his fingers looked bent sideways at each knuckle. That couldn't be right; in fact, that was so fucked up it was almost funny.

"My fingers look bent out of shape, you know?" he said to his new friend. He held up his hand. Moving his right hand made his left hand sting around the wrist. That didn't make much sense either.

"Don't worry about that," his friend said. "You look okay to me."

"Okay."

The Jack Daniel's was warm and sharp, the only truly familiar thing in this whole place. He couldn't remember coming in here. What city was this?

He must have said it out loud because his new friend answered.

"Galveston, Aaron."

He tried to remember how he got in here and couldn't. He could remember Galveston. He remembered some flashes of a different bar. A girl in leather chaps and nothing else, dancing against a polished brass pole. His new friend was shouting and trying to wave her over with a handful of hundred dollar bills. Had they really been in a strip club? He tried to think of it and just had that one flash, the whole memory a scene about a second long: the girl dancing against the pole, his friend shouting, the glare of the spotlight. He couldn't see her face. Her head was turned away from him and he could just see the way her flaming red hair spun through the air as she moved. That was all. He remembered walking down the street, afterwards. This man, who was his new friend, was propping him up at the elbow and telling him he shouldn't have grabbed at the girl that way. That it was okay to look but not to touch. That he'd take him somewhere quieter to get a drink and then maybe they could try another place after he calmed down a little. But that memory swam in and out and he wasn't sure if he was looking at it straight on, or if he was just seeing its reflection on the surface of his drink. That didn't make sense, but he thought for a second he was on to something. It slipped away. The man was talking again and he looked up.

"I asked you if you remembered what Chris and Julissa were going to do when they left the hotel."

"Julissa went home. Chris went to Boston, and then they both met in Hawaii."

"Why?"

He remembered the man picking him up off the sidewalk when he'd tried to stop. He'd wanted to just lie down on the sidewalk and sleep on warm concrete, but the man helped him up, told him that the cops would come and put him in the drunk tank if he did that. And he didn't want to end up in a drunk tank in this town, the man promised him. *You want to land in a drunk tank in Texas? Are you kidding me?* But that memory was as hollow as the strip club.

"Why?" the man asked again. "Why'd they meet in Hawaii?"

"We were looking for the guy."

"What guy? The killer?"

"No, not the killer, the other guy. Look, you need another drink. I need another drink. Let's get another drink."

"We just got this one," his friend said.

He looked around and saw the drink. That's right. Jack Daniel's, neat. Two fingers' worth.

"Then let's drink it."

"Okay."

Westfield picked up his drink with both hands and finished it in one long, burning swallow. As he did so, his sleeve fell down on his left wrist and he saw a handcuff there. No chain, just the cuff. There was a pair of tweezers jammed under the cuff, so tight against his skin that the sharp tips were drawing blood. When the whiskey wore off a day or two from now he was going to have a lot of questions about tonight. That struck him as funny and he laughed.

"What?" the man said.

"Nothing."

"C'mon, don't hold back on me. I'm your buddy. Who else pulled you off a sidewalk tonight? Or got you out of the way before bouncers beat the shit out of you?"

"I was just thinking this is gonna seem pretty fucked up tomorrow when I get up."

"I'll say."

Westfield looked down at the bar again. His glass was full to the brim now. The bartender must have come up behind him and filled it, but he'd never seen any bartender fill a tumbler level full with whiskey.

"Who were they looking for?"

"The computer guy, you know, whoever's changing the VICAP data on the dead girls. I talked to Julissa before she got on the plane in Austin."

"You think they can find him?"

"Julissa? Sure. She's dangerous. Did I say that already?"

"When they track him down, what are they going to do?"

"Ask him questions."

"In person?"

"What, do you think we're going to call him up on the phone? Ask him to take a survey? We'll go in person. All of us."

"Let's drink on it."

They raised their glasses and drank. Whiskey sloshed over the sides of Westfield's glass and ran down his fingers and wrists and burned the cuts and broken bones like boiling acid, but he held on to the glass and drank it dry. The room was spinning, the good way it did when he was all the way down in the deep well of Jack Daniel's.

He looked at the man, his new friend, and saw him do a strange thing. He reached into the pocket of his black pants and took out a phone. It was big for a cell phone these days, its antenna thick and boxy. Westfield recognized it for what it was: a satellite phone. The man dialed a number, put the phone to his ear and waited. He locked his eyes on Westfield's.

"It's Kent," he said. "The girl's looking for our technician. Wilcox is following her. They'll be in San Francisco, if she's any good." He listened for a while longer and then put the phone back into his pocket. Then he stood, turned around, and walked away from the bar. He passed the jukebox, and headed towards the door.

"Hey!" Westfield said.

The man didn't turn around.

"Hey!"

He opened the heavy steel door by turning a wheel and pushing with his shoulder. Then he stepped out onto the street, straightening his clothes. The sound of traffic roared into the bar and then quieted again when the door slammed shut. Westfield watched the wheel spin as the man sealed bar's door from the other side. That had to be the craziest bar door he'd ever seen. He sat on his barstool and tried again to piece this night together. He tried to remember what had led him into a strip club, but now he could only remember the idea he'd been in a strip club. It was all words. His friend explaining how the girl was dancing on the pole, explaining how he'd been right there next to him, shouting and waving the cash. Explaining how the bouncers came running when Westfield had tried to grab the dancer. That's all he had now, just the memory of the words. *Like he was feeding me*, Westfield thought. He pushed up his sleeve and looked at the cuff on his left wrist. It was so tight it was cutting the circulation to his fingers. *I'm going to need to get that thing off pretty soon*, he thought.

The bar was empty now. Closed, in fact. The only light came from the red glow of a neon Budweiser sign the bartender neglected to switch off. It was reflected in the mirror and the shuttered windows and a hundred more times in the bottles lining the back wall. Westfield thought about going around the bar and pouring himself another drink, but instead, he pushed off his stool and tottered carefully to the pool table. Its felt was protected by a faux-leather cover that was probably blue but looked black in the red light. He climbed up onto the table, lay on his back, and passed out.

Chapter Thirty-Six

The device took shape faster than she'd expected.

When Chris came back from Berkeley, he stood on the bed with masking tape and a shower cap from the bathroom to seal off the smoke detector so she could use the soldering iron without setting off an alarm. Then he'd gotten out of her way, walking into Chinatown. They decided there was too much risk buying a gun in a store, because of the background checks. Getting something on the street, or stealing guns from an empty police car, were out of the question. Julissa didn't need to point out if he got arrested, and disappeared to jail along with his access to safe sources of funds, she would only last about as long as the cash in her purse. So they decided Chris would see what he could buy just by asking around in shops.

When he left, she kept working, but it was harder when she was alone. At every sound in the hallway, she stopped and stared at the door, expecting it to be kicked in. There were the usual hotel noises, like the soft whir of the elevators running up the central atrium, and the rattle of a housekeeping cart. She was listening for padded footsteps that stopped outside her door, and she was thinking of men in cheap suits who had killed for their countries and who now killed in the name of the thing. She was thinking of the thing itself, wondering how it might come at her. Maybe it could slide through the air vents and spill onto the floor like an uncoiling snake; maybe it would come through the twentieth-floor window after scurrying up the wall like a spider. She thought of picking up the phone to call Chris on his satellite phone, but stopped herself. She had work to do.

And in spite of her fears, she got it done. She had a polished version of the software by the time Chris came back with a black duffel bag, which he unzipped and unpacked on the bedspread. He'd found two Tasers, four bottles of pepper spray, and half a dozen stainless steel throwing knives in leather sheaths. The knives were serrated and heavy, and reminded her of the kind of junk they sold in border towns along the Rio Grande. Chris shrugged, embarrassed. He said he'd found this cache in the back room of a basement-level Chinatown shop that sold pirated pornographic DVDs. It wasn't much of a defense against the thing hunting them, and she could tell by his face he knew it. She took him and held him close. His hands slipped low onto her back and she kissed him.

"We'll just have to be extra careful," she said, close to his neck. "Anyway, it's not like we're in Texas. I didn't expect you to come back with a machine gun."

When he went out an hour later to bring back coffee and food, she had started assembling the device. On the beach in Boracay, she had come up with a simple and elegant solution to a hard problem. The problem was this: she had the unique device identification number for the hacker's computer because it had been logged on the FBI server along with the router addresses he'd used to access the system. But a laptop only transmits its device ID while establishing a connection with a new system, so even if she could somehow listen to every wireless transmission in San Francisco, she wouldn't be able to unwind the right stream of data from that tangled web unless she caught the hacker's computer at the exact moment it connected with a wireless router and broadcast its ID. So her solution was to build a device that could tackle two jobs, one after the other. The first was to transmit a disruptive signal that would knock offline every wireless device on every channel within its radius. Then its antenna would switch to receiver mode, to scan all sixteen channels and listen as every computer tried to reestablish a connection with its router. If she could get close enough to the hacker's computer to knock it offline, she would pick up its unique device ID as the wireless card automatically tried to reconnect to the router. The transmitter would disrupt every wireless signal within three hundred feet, and her receiver would pick up every computer trying to reconnect within the same radius. After she narrowed it to three hundred feet, which could still be a couple of thousand apartments in a city as dense as San Francisco, they could sift it further by isolating the signal, reducing the antenna's reception quality, and rotating the receiver dish to see when the signal faded or strengthened.

She'd thought it through on the beach, watching a storm blow toward their island, a little girl racing along the beach gathering shells in hope of getting pesos. She'd perfected it and mapped the circuitry in her bungalow, listening to the geckos in the ceiling and trying to stop herself from going to Chris's bed. Drawing it on the airplane and in the hotel room had been easy, and when Chris came back with the parts and she already had a working version of the software, the pieces fit together perfectly. Her laptop's network window showed twenty wireless networks within reach of her room. With that many access points, there would surely be a few computers actually logged in. She'd be able to test her creation without even leaving the hotel.

A few hours later, Chris came in with two cups of coffee he'd bought in the shop across the street from the hotel. He handed one to her and sat on the foot of the bed. It was six in the evening, but there was still plenty of light. From one of the windows in the corner suite, Julissa could see the Transamerica Pyramid. Through the other window she could see one of the upright supports of the Golden Gate Bridge. She watched a ship disappear behind the cityscape as it steamed towards the bridge. With water on three sides, and wharves along the entire bay side, the thing would be comfortable almost anywhere in San Francisco.

"How's it coming?" Chris asked.

"It's done."

She sipped her coffee and looked at the device. It had been a while since she'd built anything from scratch, but she'd done a good job. She'd stripped apart sixteen wireless routers and run them on parallel circuits through a handmade motherboard that would control the interference burst and then coordinate a scan for Internet devices trying to log back onto the net. A USB cable led from this to her laptop, so she could control everything from its keyboard. At the moment, her creation was spread all over the hotel desk in a mess of wires and green printed circuit boards.

"I can pack it all into one of the cardboard boxes you brought from the store. It'll fit on the backseat. You can drive and I'll control it from the passenger seat."

"How long will it take to run a cycle?" he asked.

"Maybe ten seconds. Some of it will depend on how fast the computers getting knocked offline are able to try to reconnect."

"Can I drive at a steady pace?"

"In theory, yeah. As long as it's a *slow*, steady pace."

She packed the device into a box, putting a lid on it so the valets downstairs wouldn't wonder what it was. She put her laptop into her purse and then went to the bathroom to change clothes. It was cool in San Francisco, but Chris had come back from his trip to Chinatown with a pair of jeans, some running shoes and athletic socks, and a sweatshirt for her. The sweatshirt was embroidered with the logo of the San Francisco 49ers. When she was dressed to go out and had run a brush through her hair, she looked at herself in the mirror and thought she looked like a tourist. A sleep-deprived and very worried tourist, maybe.

"I'm ready," she said, stepping back into the main room of the suite.

They rode the elevator to the lower lobby, passing through the to the valet stand. Chris handed his ticket to a young woman in a red jacket and they waited for the rental car. When it came, they loaded the box into the backseat, and while Julissa got things set up in the passenger seat, Chris drove them slowly onto Post Street. At the first red light he turned on the GPS mounted to the dashboard.

"When it's up and running, I'll turn on the track function. So we'll know what streets we've covered."

"Good idea."

Julissa dropped the car's cigarette lighter into a cup holder and plugged the device's power cable into the empty jack. Then she turned on her laptop and started the program. They heard a low whine from the box in the backseat as the sixteen parallel rows of capacitors built up a charge for the first interference burst.

"Here it comes," Julissa said. "Let's hope no one calls the FCC right off the bat."

The capacitors in the backseat reached their full charge and then they heard a *click*, like the sound of a flashbulb going off. A popup window appeared on the GPS screen with the message <<*SEARCHING FOR SATELLITES*>>. The green numbers on the dashboard clock glowed brighter. Then she looked at her computer screen and watched the column on the left-hand side. One by one, 128-bit ID numbers filled the screen. The device was scanning all channels and picking off computer ID numbers as they tried to reconnect to wireless routers.

"It's working," she said. "Thirty computers on the first sweep. We're between two hotels so a lot of people are online."

"How will you know when we find the right one?"

"There'll be an alarm. I'm monitoring the laptop to make sure nothing crashes, but I won't have to keep a sharp eye on the numbers."

She looked up and saw they had turned onto Market Street. Chris was taking them west, away from the Bay and across the tip of the peninsula towards the ocean. The GPS found its satellites again, but as she watched, it blinked out as another burst of interference from the backseat cut out its reception.

"All the coffee shops he used were on Irving Street, so I thought I'd start us there," Chris said. "Soon as we hit Inner Sunset, I'll slow down and take it street by street."

She nodded. The street was packed with cars leaving downtown. A streetcar crowded with riders passed them on the left. Julissa noticed several people on the streetcar and two women in a crosswalk take smart phones away from their ears and stare at them blankly. The GPS was on the fritz again. A few seconds later, ID numbers began to scroll in.

Chris turned north on Van Ness, then took them towards Golden Gate Park. By the time they edged past Haight Ashbury and entered the park, she had collected over a thousand device numbers. Her invention was working beautifully. Chris sped up as they drove through the park, passing huge green lawns and stands of Monterey Cyprus and joggers out with their dogs. Even in the park, Julissa picked up two computer IDs, probably from one of the museums. Then they turned onto Lincoln Way, which ran along the southern boundary of the park. A neighborhood of two- and three-story row houses stretched away for blocks on their left. This was the beginning of the Sunset District. One block south was Irving Street, where the hacker had gotten online at five different coffee shops and wine bars.

"We can start in the center and work out, or we can follow Lincoln all the way to the beach and work back in," Chris said. "You choose."

"Center."

Chris nodded and made a left turn on Ninth Avenue. There was an Irish pub on the corner of Ninth and Lincoln. Julissa picked up three computers as they passed it. Then Chris slowed to a pace not much faster than a walk. He pulled to the curb to let another car pass and they worked down Ninth towards Irving at five miles an hour. Julissa's device was grabbing computer IDs from both sides of the street. She looked at the digital clock just as its numbers began to glow brightly from the interference surge. It was 6:45 p.m.

"I bet from now until eleven a lot of people will be online. We'll probably get a hundred computers on every block," Julissa said.

"Will it make sense to keep looking after that? Or should we go back to the hotel and call it quits for the day if we don't find him before midnight?"

"After eleven we should start again and re-cover the same ground. That way, if our guy's a night owl, we won't miss him by driving past his house too early."

"Makes sense," Chris said. He crossed Irving Street and Julissa could see one of the coffee shops their hacker had used. It was tucked between an organic grocer and a Thai restaurant. There was a chalkboard sign on the sidewalk that said *Free Wi-Fi* and *Live Music*. The sidewalk was crowded with people walking out to dinner or drinks, and as they passed through the intersection Julissa saw scores of people at outdoor tables in front of the cafes and wine bars up and down Irving. She hoped their quarry lived on a quieter street. She doubted things would stay quiet once they found him.

Then they continued south on Ninth Avenue, grabbing computer IDs by the dozens. Chris pulled to the side once to let a police car go past and then pulled back into the lane and kept driving at the same slow pace.

"If we get pulled over because it looks like we're casing the neighborhood, I'll say we're moving to San Francisco and trying to decide where to buy."

Julissa glanced at the mess of wires and antennae poking out of the box in the backseat.

"Maybe focus on not getting pulled over."

Chapter Thirty-Seven

When Westfield woke, the faux-leather of the pool table cover was gone and instead he was in the stifling rubberized darkness of the body bag. It had been zipped closed again and the stench of his urine was what had finally brought him back to consciousness. He must have been given a drink of water, though, because his tongue wasn't swollen, and he could swallow. He remembered the bright light of the room and the man with the English accent crushing his chest, and something about needing to sort out the answers to a few questions before he got thrown over the side. The dream of the pool table slipped away.

He couldn't remember anything after the man crushed the breath from his lungs.

Then he remembered the tweezers. Something about the dream tried to surface, then sank away. The tweezers might have had a place in the vanished dream, but they had been real too, hadn't they? He bent his left wrist and felt a sharp object pushing into his skin underneath the cuff. Now he remembered there'd been a scalpel too, but he'd lost it somehow. He rolled his body slightly to the left and could feel the scalpel under his left buttock. There was no chance he could get it. But the tweezers, maybe. That would be the first step, and he went to it.

The fingers on his right hand were all broken. That much was clear when he tried to use them to pry the tweezers from under the left cuff. He remembered the thing flying at him from the window of the SUV in the motel parking lot outside of Carlsbad, the way it had smashed the pistol out of his hand with one crushing blow while it was still entirely airborne. But his right thumb was mostly okay and he could use it to push the tweezers up towards his left palm. He realized he would have to sit up a little in the last moment so the tweezers would fall into his palm instead of away from it. Until that moment he hadn't wondered whether anyone might be watching. Maybe the thing itself was there, hanging like a prey-swollen spider from the underside of the catwalk, watching with its yellow eyes.

He could only hear the engine's steady throb. It went on and on the way ship's engines do, stretching out a noise with such constancy that it just became a new kind of silence.

There could be twenty people standing around him in a quiet circle, for all he knew. He imagined that for a moment, then let it go. Hanging above him however many hours ago, the thing had touched his mind somehow, but it hadn't gotten in. At least, not all the way. He'd caught it at the threshold and forced it out. It was like finding a white worm in a shovelful of turned earth, a hidden thing, used to its secrets and stunned to be caught in the light. He would know when it was watching him; he'd be able to feel the way it wriggled and squirmed behind his eyes.

But it wasn't here.

If the man with the English accent had drugged him and questioned him, but he was still alive now to consider all these things, then they were checking whatever answers he'd given. There'd be no sense in throwing him overboard before that. They might need another session. So he was alone.

Without wasting more time, he sat up halfway, used his right thumb to push the tweezers free of the cuff, and caught them in his left hand before they fell away. Then he lay back and held the tweezers in his hand and listened again, but there was nothing. With the tweezers secure between his left thumb and his palm, he felt the edge of the right cuff until he found the keyhole. He then held the tweezers between his thumb and forefinger, pushed one tip into the keyhole until it was no more than a quarter of a centimeter in, and used the keyhole as leverage to bend the tweezer tip to a forty-five degree angle. He did all of this by feel and without allowing himself to stop and think. He owned handcuffs for his own pursuit of the killer and had tested them at his breakfast table overlooking Puget Sound. It was good to know the limits of whatever you depended on. Handcuffs only went so far.

When he'd bent the tip to the correct angle, he reinserted it into the hole, twisted it, and pulled back on the tweezers.

The cuff fell off his right wrist. Even so, he couldn't pull his left arm free, because the cuff chain was bound to something at his waist that felt like a leather belt. So he gingerly transferred the tweezers to his right hand, holding his tool awkwardly with his thumb pressed against the shattered knuckle of his forefinger. The left cuff was harder to open but manageable because at least he had the freedom to move his right arm. In thirty seconds he had his left arm free, and in another two seconds he had found the scalpel in the cold puddle beneath him.

He sliced the bag open from head to foot, and sat up. Now he was sure he was alone, because the compartment was dark except for the red and white lights of an electrical switchboard on the bulkhead, and the glow of LCD monitors. He cut away the rest of the bag, saw his ankles were cuffed with a regular set of handcuffs, and had them off in under a minute. Then he stood slowly, taking off the leather belt that had been clasped around his waist. The cuffs fell into the remains of the body bag.

It might have been days since he last stood on his feet. A slight shift of the deck nearly tossed him across the compartment. He caught himself against the bulkhead and then got his bearings, noticing first the chill after the swampy heat of the bag and then the fact that he was utterly naked.

He thought he was in an electrical control room just forward of the main engine room. He assumed the watertight door wouldn't be locked if they'd gone to the trouble to keep him cuffed in a body bag. When he tried the wheel, it turned freely. He hesitated over the threshold, considering another echo of the dream he'd had. But it was too faint, so he set it aside and stepped into the engine room, closing the door behind him. He still carried the scalpel in his left hand, though he knew it was perfectly useless as a weapon. There would be tools in the engine room and at least two ways to reach the deck.

There was a mechanics' locker behind the main power plant. He stood in the warmth and roar of the engine and went through the crew's belongings until he found an oil-stained engineer's jumpsuit. He put it on and zipped it up the front. His chest was a patchwork of bite marks, each one a scabbed-over hole from which white tendrils of infection spread under his skin. No wonder he'd been delirious with fever. There was no time to look for shoes, but in the sliding drawers of the machinists' area he found what he really wanted: a twenty-inch cast-steel pipe wrench. He'd have preferred a gun, but the wrench would work well enough in close quarters.

The moment he'd unlocked the cuff on his right wrist, he'd started working out a plan. It was unfinished, but he knew he needed to find the steering room before he went topside. That would be aft of the engine at the stern of the ship. He didn't expect to come across any crewmen, but he walked quietly anyway, bare feet silent on the non-skid rubber matting. He clung to the shadows on the right side of the passage, so he could swing with the wrench in his left hand. But he met no one.

He'd inspected plenty of container ships in the past, and though the machinery had evolved somewhat over the years, he had no trouble recognizing the steering gear when he found it. There were hydraulic levers port and starboard that turned the rudder post, which was heavily mounted just forward of the transom. He saw no security cameras, but knew they could be mounted anywhere. There would certainly be a few cameras topside on the stern. Any big cargo ship that ran shorthanded on the high seas would have them.

But that was a worry several minutes in the future.

What he needed to do now was sabotage the steering gear so it would fail if someone tried to turn the ship around. The tools for repairing the gear would be kept in this room, and what could be used to fix that equipment could rig its failure. He found a supply cabinet next to a workbench and opened its drawers one at a time until he found what he was looking for. He gave himself five minutes to do what needed to be done, measuring the time by counting to three hundred as he drilled holes in the main hydraulic lines and weakly patched them with hose clamps and cardboard which would burst at the first rise in pressure from a major movement of the rudder. He didn't want to simply drain the fluid from the system because the loss of hydraulic pressure would set off an alarm in the bridge. That alarm couldn't come until later. In the last sixty seconds of his countdown, he went to the wall-mounted fifty-five gallon drum of spare hydraulic fluid, and punched through its bottom with a hammer and a screwdriver. The viscous yellow liquid began to spread across the floor of the steering room. If they had a good engineer aboard, they would get the rudder working again—but it would take hours.

He was done in here and looked for the exit, finding a ladder welded to the transom that led into the darkness. This would reach the deck, right at the stern rail. He mounted the first rung and began to climb, one handed. He kept the pipe wrench locked under his right armpit. The thing could be flying headfirst down the ladder towards him in the darkness, its mouthful of infected teeth coming at him with the gathering speed of a falling stone. He looked up the rungs and could see nothing. After a while he put thoughts of the thing out of his mind and focused on climbing.

When he got to the hatch, he balanced himself by locking his right elbow around a steel rung while he leaned backwards with his weight on the rusty wheel. When it finally gave way, he spun it counterclockwise and then pushed the hatch up with the back of his neck as he climbed through.

After the darkness and dim artificial light inside the ship, the daylight struck him blind. For a moment, he shrank back into the hatch. He'd expected night. But the sun was either rising or setting, and the sky on the horizon was lit a pinkish gray. If he lived long enough, he'd find out whether this was dusk or dawn. When he adjusted to the idea there would be no cover of darkness, he came entirely out of the hatch and stood on the stern deck. He was in between two canyon-like stacks of cargo containers that rose ten high and five deep between the stern and the superstructure that held the bridge. Then he looked up and saw he'd come to the deck directly beneath the thing he'd been praying the ship would possess: a free-fall lifeboat.

Chapter Thirty-Eight

Chris methodically worked through the straight and flat streets of the Inner Sunset, and then, while Julissa slept next to him, he started on the curving, steep streets that led up to and around Grand View Park on the southern edge of the neighborhood. In the amber light of the streetlights he could see waves of fog blowing through the stand of cypress trees on the dark hilltop to his left. To his right, down the slope, there was a row of fine houses. The computer was on Julissa's lap and her head was leaning against the window. Light from the streetlights made a halo from the small circle of vapor where she had breathed against the glass in her sleep.

The alarm went off thirty seconds after he turned onto Fifteenth Avenue. The alarm was just a slowly repeating beep, not very loud. He drove another five seconds before he realized what it was. Then he gently applied the brakes and parked against the curb. It was three o'clock in the morning. The cars parked on the street were covered in a glittering layer of dew. A light rain had been falling, but had stopped for now. He let the windshield wipers go through one more sweep, then turned them off. Some of the houses had lights over the doorsteps or above their garage doors, or low ground lights set amongst the bushes of their steeply sloped and small front yards. But there were no windows lit. He put the transmission into park, set the brake, and dowsed the headlights.

Julissa woke and looked at the computer.

"It's him," she said.

Chris nodded and watched as she leaned into the backseat, reached into the box containing her device, and came back holding the main receiving antenna on a long cable. Then she opened a programming window on her laptop and began to dial down the antenna's sensitivity. Chris watched silently, taking his eyes off her face only to scan the street and the rear-view mirror. Julissa switched off the alarm and the car was hushed except for her fingers tapping on the keyboard and the quiet purr of the engine idling. Julissa covered one side of the circular antenna with a sheet of lead foil and then rotated it slowly. The uncovered side of the antenna was facing backwards when the alarm began to ping again.

"Back up about a hundred feet."

"Yeah."

Chris put the car into neutral and released the parking brake. They coasted silently backwards down the hill with the headlights off. When they'd gone past two houses, Chris turned to the curb and parked again.

The third time the alarm began its ping, Julissa's antenna was facing the house directly to their right. It was a two-story house made of unpainted redwood planks. Its garage came nearly to the edge of the street and there was a deck built on top of the garage accessed from sliding doors giving passage to what may have been the master bedroom. Though curtains were drawn across the glass doors, Chris could see a faint blue-white glow. Otherwise, the house was dark.

"Is this the one, or is it possible there's a house behind this?"

"I don't think we could get reception beyond fifty or sixty feet. This is the place."

They looked at the house, at the cold illumination seeping through the bedroom curtains.

"Now what?" Julissa asked.

"Stay here," Chris said. "I'm just going to check it out."

He saw she was scared and he leaned across the seat and put one hand on the back of her neck. Beneath the spill of her red hair, her neck was still warm from sleep and he wished he could simply take her back to the hotel and make love to her and then sleep next to her until well into the morning. He wished he could let go of revenge and just take Julissa to a safe place where they could live quietly and love one another. But even though she was terrified, he knew her heart was locked into this just the same as his. So he pulled her gently to him and kissed her, and felt both longing and ferocity in the way she kissed him back.

"I'll be right back. I'm not going inside. I just want to see what kind of alarm he's got."

"Okay."

He reached into the glove compartment and took out a black shaving kit full of things he'd picked up in Chinatown. Then he stepped from the car and pulled the hood of his black sweatshirt against the light rain. He crossed the street and walked into the narrow side yard between the hacker's house and the one next door. No motion light came on and no dog barked. He opened the shaving kit, found the pair of black spandex gloves, and slipped them on. Then he took out one of the throwing knives and a penlight. He unsheathed the knife and held it in his right hand, keeping the penlight in his left hand. He did not turn on the light yet, but walked quietly between the low juniper bushes, the legs of his jeans soaking through from the rain in the branches. He came to the kitchen window, which was about three feet square. Its outer sill was above the level of his head, but there was a plastic trash can against the house just under the window. Now he turned on his light and saw several things at once. There was a pair of wet boot prints on the lid of the trash can, and there was a six-inch diameter circle of glass on the ground in the bushes. He shone the light carefully up the window. Someone had used a diamond-bladed glass cutter to cut a circle from the pane's upper edge. The window was closed. He turned off the light and held it in his teeth while he climbed up onto the trash can. When he stood, the circular hole in the glass was right at his face. Without even using the light he could see it would be possible to reach through the hole and unlatch the window. As for an alarm, the window was wired with a sensor. When the sliding pane of glass was opened, a magnet on the moving pane would lose contact with the stationary sensor on the casement, triggering the house alarm. But when he flicked on the penlight, he saw this sensor had been overcome in the same way he would have done it. A small piece of black magnetic tape was stuck over the sensor, so that no matter what position the window was in, the alarm system would believe it was closed because the sensor would never lose contact with a magnetic pull. There were no vibration sensors on the window, probably because the hilltop was too windy.

He heard a rustle of clothing against branches behind him and he dropped to a crouch on the lid of the trash can, bringing up the knife. Julissa was standing five feet away, hidden in the shadows except for her face.

He lowered the knife and slipped down from the trash can.

She stepped up to him and leaned to whisper in his ear.

"What'd you find?"

"Someone's broken into this house," he whispered back. "Probably tonight."

He used the flashlight to illuminate the boot prints on the trash can and the circle of glass on the ground.

"The prints haven't washed off yet, and it's been raining on and off for an hour."

"Who'd have gotten here before us?" Julissa whispered.

"I believe in coincidences, but not this time."

"You think it sent someone."

Chris nodded. He led them farther into the shadow between the two houses. There was a low redwood fence partitioning the backyard from the narrow side yard. At least in the darkness he didn't feel so exposed, though he realized if people expected them to come, he and Julissa may have been watched from the moment they rolled up. He needed to think fast. If they made a run for the car, they might get shot crossing the driveway. A man with a rifle could be standing behind the curtains in the bedroom, or hiding in the shadows on the hill where they'd never stand a chance of seeing him. But if there were gunmen in either place, why didn't they get shot the second they stepped out of the car? The killer and his hired men obviously knew what they looked like.

They came to a second window that lit the living room. Chris risked raising his head to the level of the sill so he could look inside. The room was in perfect order. A few small spotlights over the bookshelves showed the space. There were leather couches facing a gigantic flat-screen television, dark wood-and-glass display cases housing vases and jade carvings. The walls were adorned with framed paintings showing scenes from Guilin—steeply peaked mountains rising above the mist, rivers flowing between stands of bamboo. A potted orchid sat alone on the coffee table. Nothing was tipped over, there were no books strewn on the floor, there were no bullet holes in the furniture or blood splatters on the walls.

"What now?" Julissa said. She was whispering so quietly he heard her words more by the brush of her breath against his ear than by the sound of her voice.

Maybe the only safe thing was to hop the fence into the backyard of the house next door, move into the yard of the house past that, and then run on foot in the shadows until they could catch a cab or hop a bus. If the killer sent his men to break into his own hacker's house, then it was likely the hacker was dead and whatever evidence he'd possessed had been destroyed. Perhaps the hacker knew too much, or his usefulness had ended and his only remaining purpose was to hang as bait. If that were the case, then the best thing they could hope to get from this situation was to stay alive. Chris thought about it a second longer, and saw by the look on Julissa's face that she was reaching the same conclusions.

"Is there anything in the car that could trace us to the hotel?" Chris whispered.

"Not on my computer. Did you rent the car under the same name that you used to check into the hotel?"

"Shit."

If the killer's men got the car and traced it, they would find the name he was traveling under, which was also the name connected to his source of nearly endless funds. It had been unbelievably stupid to park out front and walk up to the house. Part of his mind wanted to ask how he could have known. But the facts were simple: he'd been stupid and may have killed them both. He and Julissa just looked at each other, crouching in the shadows with their hands on each other's shoulders so that they could whisper into each other's ears.

"Then let's go in," Julissa said. "I mean, if we're fucked either way, we might as well do the one thing that has a chance of getting us somewhere."

Chris nodded and they went back to the kitchen window. He climbed onto the trash can, checked that the magnetic tape was still in place over the sensor, and then slid the window open. To climb inside he'd have to step into the kitchen sink and then down to the floor. Before he did, he handed Julissa a second pair of gloves from the shaving kit in his sweatshirt pocket. As she put them on, he ducked through the window and into the kitchen. He still had the throwing knife in his right hand. When Julissa stepped into the sink, he held her left hand to help her silently down to the floor. The kitchen had a recently cleaned citrus smell. Chris went to a small throw rug in front of the stove and wiped the soles of his shoes so they wouldn't squeak on the hardwood floors. Julissa did the same.

As they reached the living room, they heard a thud directly above them. This sound was followed by the scratch and drag of a man clawing his way across a hardwood floor. Then the house was still. Julissa had taken a big Chinese-style cleaver from the magnetic rack in the kitchen. She was looking across the living room to the staircase that rose up into darkness. She nodded at it with her chin, and Chris raised his own knife and led the way.

Chapter Thirty-Nine

For the first time since he got out of the body bag, Westfield really believed he was going to make it. He'd climbed the steel ladder to the aft-end of the freefall lifeboat. The lifeboat was set on sled-like davits that tilted it steeply over the stern of the ship. He had never used a lifeboat like this, but was counting on the idea that emergency equipment should be easy to figure out. The hatch at the back opened easily enough, and when he looked inside, he immediately recognized the wheel and lever that released the clasps on the transom so that gravity could take over.

There was a 220-volt power cord that connected the lifeboat to the ship. He bent to look at it. It would be easy to unplug, but after that, everything would have to happen very quickly. If he knew anything about ships, it was that everything had an alarm wired to the bridge. Disconnecting the free-fall lifeboat from the ship's power source was going to be one of those things. He grabbed on to the cord with his good left hand and yanked it out. Then he stood and climbed through the orange hatch into the lifeboat. The interior lights were on—unplugging it must have activated the internal systems. Now he could see the ladder he would have to climb to reach the raised helmsman's seat. He turned to shut the hatch and as he did so, he slipped on the tilted deck and tumbled backwards. He somersaulted down the steeply sloped aisle, all the way to the bow. The bulkhead that stopped him was well padded. He got to his knees and then pulled himself up by holding on to the headrest of one of the backwards-facing seats.

The Englishman was there. Westfield reached the hatch just as the man jammed a pistol at Westfield's chest. Westfield ducked to the side and slammed the hatch. The man fired three shots, none of which hit Westfield. They were eye to eye with the hatch's reinforced glass window in between them. Westfield had his right arm locked through the wheel and was pulling the door closed. Because of the boat's tilt on the davits, he had gravity on his side: he could put all his body weight on the door just by leaning back. The man's hand was still trapped inside the lifeboat, but he had dropped the gun. The man was shouting, probably asking for help, but Westfield wasn't listening. He was too busy using his left hand to turn the wheel on the aft bulkhead that unlocked the release lever. Then he found the lever. His eyes never lost contact with the man's. The Englishman must have realized what was about to happen, because he started to beat on the window glass with his free hand.

"Hey!"

Westfield nodded at him.

"That's right," he said.

He released the lever.

The motion was immediate. The lifeboat hurtled forward on the sled and then was airborne off the high stern of the ship. All the seats faced backwards to give the crew the best chance of surviving the impact unscathed. Westfield rode down standing at the back of the enclosed boat in its aisle, his arm locked through the steel wheel on the hatch. He braced his arm and held on to the wheel with his left hand. As the boat cleared the davits and started its freefall to the ocean, its bow tilted nearly straight down.

Westfield felt himself flying, his body parallel to the deck and his feet pointing at the bow. Then there was the jolt of impact as the bow hit the waves and the entire boat submerged.

He held on as best as he could, feeling his right elbow stretch and pop, and finding what purchase he could with his feet on the backs of the first row of seats. The light went blue green as the stern drove under the water from the force of the drop. Westfield slammed into the floor as the boat righted and popped back up to the surface. He got to his knees and turned the wheel hard to the right with his left hand, sealing the aft hatch. Five or six gallons of water had splashed in when the boat submerged, but no more than that. The blood all over the hatch explained that. The man's hand must have been severed on impact, and then Westfield's weight pulling on the hatch kept it closed while the boat was underwater. His eyes followed blood trail to the bow: the Englishman's arm, sliced unevenly midway up the forearm, lay next to the pistol. Two sharp bone ends poked out through the skin and muscle. He remembered the pistol shots, supposing he'd know in a moment whether they hit anything important.

The short ladder to the helmsman's seat was a challenge. He felt as if he'd spent the last week on a medieval torture rack being pulled apart. The relief was that the control panel was straightforward. There were meters showing battery charge, a main breaker, a fuel meter, an oil pressure gauge, a tachometer, and an engine temperature gauge. He found the throttle and pressed the rubber starter button. Down below, the engine turned over once and then purred like a sewing machine.

"Thank you," he said, looking down where the engine must have been. If it started and ran like that, it couldn't have been hit by a bullet.

He put the transmission into forward and revved the engine to four thousand RPM. Right then he was more interested in putting distance between himself and the ship than in worrying about the engine's health. It probably wouldn't blow a gasket or overheat right away. The helmsman's seat was in a raised turret at the back of the enclosed lifeboat. By turning around he could see to his stern, through reinforced windows. Looking aft, he saw two satisfying things. The ship was steaming away without any sign of turning, probably going twenty knots. And there was a body in the water a hundred feet from the lifeboat, floating facedown.

The Englishman must have been knocked unconscious by the impact and the shock of losing half his forearm. If he hadn't already drowned, he was in the process of doing so. Westfield watched the ship for five minutes and it never tried to turn. Either he'd knocked out the steering so completely that it could do nothing but plow across the ocean in a straight line, or its crew hadn't noticed the lifeboat was gone. Either option was fine with Westfield. He wondered if the creature were still aboard. If it had come aboard the ship by helicopter, it may well have left the same way once it was finished with the girl.

The pain flared in his chest and his thoughts turned from the creature to the infection it gave him. The creature had provided Westfield at least a rudimentary cleaning. Apparently it wanted him alive long enough to answer the Englishman's questions, whatever they had been. Now Westfield decided to try to finish the job. The lifeboat had no autopilot, but the steering wheel had a lock, and he engaged it to set the rudder amidships. Then he climbed down the ladder to find the lifeboat's medical supplies. The boat was made to hold eighteen men; it was well stocked, and its first-aid kit was in good order. Westfield took what he needed and then climbed back into the helm seat, working on his chest with antibiotic ointment, then using finger splints and white medical tape to bandage his mangled right hand. Finally he used his left hand and his teeth to rip open a vacuum-sealed Z-pak of azithromycin. He swallowed two of the tablets with a long pull from one of the liter-sized bottles of water he'd found stored in plastic crates under the seats. The instructions on the back of the package told him to take one of the remaining tablets a day for the next four days.

"If you live that long," he told himself.

That thought brought his eyes to the stern again. The ship was so far towards the horizon, he could only make out its superstructure as a faint white blur. In another five minutes it would be gone entirely, and he would be alone on the ocean. Then it would be time to throttle back and conserve fuel while he tried to figure out where he was. As he looked around, he realized he didn't even know what ocean this was.

Chapter Forty

They were looking at a man who should have been dead.

Julissa had followed Chris up the stairs, keeping her hand on the small of his back so she wouldn't lose him in the shadows. When they reached the landing, he switched on his small flashlight. He'd turned the throwing knife in his hand, holding the blade in his palm. Maybe he knew how to throw it. Then she let her eyes follow the circle of light as Chris worked it across the floor and along the walls of a richly decorated study. She saw the oiled wood paneling and the carefully placed paintings, the desk in front of the bay window with its leather-padded writing surface and a laptop computer open at the center; she saw these things, but without any immediacy, because what she was truly seeing was the blood splashed on every surface touched by Chris's light. It was dripping from the desk onto the floor and there were splashes and spots of it on the walls and across the fronts of the paintings, and there was a wide trail of it from the desk to the bathroom door, and that was where the man who should have been dead had finally tumbled to the floor to finish doing the only thing left for him to do.

Chris did not go to him right away, but instead played the light along the walls into all the corners of the room and then crouched to shine it beneath the desk. There was plenty of blood, but there was no living man to be seen. Chris went across the room, shining the light at their feet so they could step clear of blood. He stepped over the man and shined his light into the bathroom, then turned again and crouched close to the man. Julissa stood with her back near the wall, watching Chris with one eye and the staircase with the other.

"His throat's been slit," Chris said to her.

She looked down and saw the two rough slashes across the center of the man's throat. Chris briefly let the light roam around the room again. As she watched it go from the leather chair, to the walls and then to the trail of blood that led to the body, she understood the chronology here. The man's attacker cut his throat while he was sitting in the chair; in his struggle the chair had spun, jetting blood from his jugular all over the room. The attacker must have left him for dead, but he wasn't. The thump they'd heard was him falling out of the chair and dragging himself across the floor to the bathroom. When Chris knelt next to him and put the light in his face, the man's eyes rolled back and tried to stare past the beam. They were unfocused and registered no expression.

"Can you hear me?"

Bubbles of blood came from the man's slit throat, but there was no sound of his voice.

"He can't talk," Julissa said.

"Were you the one hacking into the FBI?"

The man closed his eyes for a few seconds, and then opened them again. He was so thoroughly covered in blood it was impossible to tell anything about him. He had black hair and brown eyes, but even the shape of his eyes was obscured by the clotting blood on his face.

"Is that a yes?" Chris asked.

The man blinked.

"Do you know how to find him?"

The man blinked again.

Julissa saw that the man's fingers were scrabbling against the floor weakly. She and Chris must have had the same realization because as she was turning towards the desk, Chris said in a low whisper, "A pen. Get him a pen!"

She stopped when she saw what the man was doing. He bent his elbow and dipped his finger into his own slit throat and then reached out to the wall in front of his face and drew a diagonal slash. He made a second diagonal slash in the other direction and then a small horizontal dash in between. He'd written an upper-case "A". Chris and Julissa stared at him as he reached his finger back into his neck to re-wet it with his blood. He reached back to the wall and made an upper-case "I" next to his first letter. As he was dipping his finger into his wound a third time, a spasm overtook his body, starting at his feet and moving upwards until it had all of him. He tried to steady himself and get his finger to the wall to paint another letter, and he died just as his finger reached the wall. It was as simple as that: he stopped shaking and lay still on the floor in the spreading pool of his blood, his finger outstretched and pointing at the two letters he'd written. The wet blood, heaviest at the corner of the letter A, ran slowly over the baseboard towards the floor.

"Let's get out of here," Chris said.

"I'll grab his laptop."

Julissa was still trembling when they got into the car, but she stopped by the time Chris drove them down from the hilltop and made a right turn onto Lincoln Way. There were cars parked along both sides of the street, but there was no other traffic. Chris drove at twenty-five miles an hour. He hadn't said anything since they'd left the house. She had so many questions she couldn't even think of where to begin. She looked at the computer and tapped at its keyboard for three blocks, then shut the screen and tossed it into the backseat. Chris looked at her. They were stopped at a red traffic light; its glow lit the left side of his face.

"The hard disk was scrubbed less than half an hour ago," she said.

"We walked in right after his killer walked out."

"Except we don't know if he ever walked out. We never searched the whole house," Julissa said. "If they came here to kill him so we couldn't get anything out of him, don't you think they'd stick around and kill us too? Isn't that what you'd do?"

Chris nodded. The light turned green and they started rolling.

"They left the laptop on even after they scrubbed it, probably to draw us in. They know what I do for a living. They knew I'd find him."

"Maybe they didn't think you'd get here so fast."

Chris glanced into the rear-view mirror and then turned his head to look at a car that was overtaking them in the left lane. She followed his gaze and saw they were being passed by a black sedan, driving without its headlights. As it pulled alongside, Chris slammed the brakes at the same time the passenger in the overtaking car let loose a burst of gunfire. Julissa screamed as she hit her seat belt. The car skidded sideways, knocking her head against the window glass. Chris jerked the wheel all the way to the left and accelerated into a high-speed U-turn, over the low curb separating the four lanes of Lincoln Way. They bumped into the westbound lane, laying rubber on the road as they sped towards the ocean. Julissa swiveled in her seat and looked out the back window. The rental car's front bumper lay on the curb along with a part of its muffler. The black car was sideways on the empty road, pushing over the curb into the westbound lanes. Its headlights were still off. As she looked at it, she saw a muzzle flash from the driver's window. She ducked and heard the shot hit the side of their car with a bang.

"Jesus, Chris! Get us out of here!"

"I'm trying," he said, his voice low and calm.

The black car was farther in the distance now because Chris had gotten a head start in the new direction. The rental car's engine was roaring louder now without the muffler. She could feel the acceleration pressing her against the seat. They shot through a red light without slowing.

"I'll try to lose them in the park."

She turned to see out the front, gripping the inner handle of the door. They were pushing past ninety; the parked cars on the side of the road came up and shot by in a blur. There were loud bangs underneath the car. Either something was breaking loose down there, or the car was getting hit by shots they couldn't hear.

"Try to stay down."

She ducked low in the seat and watched. They were coming to another red light, skidding as Chris hit the brakes in preparation for the turn. There was a Shell station on the other side of the intersection, the area around its pumps lit in bright fluorescent light. A police cruiser was there, the cop just stepping into the car after coming out of the mini-mart. Chris laid his hand on the horn and made a right turn, taking them into the park at fifty miles an hour. At that speed the car could barely hold the turn. They careened into the left lanes of the road they'd turned onto and mounted the curb before Chris corrected by cranking the steering wheel to the right. The car jumped off the curb and slammed back onto the road. Chris followed the curves and brought them onto a smaller road that led into the park. Now there were no streetlights. He revved the engine, and again Julissa felt the press of acceleration as they picked up speed. She couldn't believe they made the turn without flipping.

She was trying to get back up to look out the rear window when she heard the siren.

"The cop?" she asked.

"Yeah."

Chris raced through the park, working mostly west through the stands of dark eucalyptus and past the old polo field. The police car was catching up and she realized it was because Chris was slowing down. They came down a hill and rounded a long curve through a meadow where she could see the road behind them for a quarter of a mile.

"They back there?" Chris asked.

"I don't see them. Just the cop."

The police car was nearly on their back bumper now. They heard the officer shouting through the bullhorn mounted to the squad car's siren, telling them to pull over.

"They must've hung back on Lincoln when they saw the cop come after us."

"What do we do?" Julissa asked.

Before he could answer, another piece of the exhaust system broke loose from the car's undercarriage. Still leaning to look backwards, Julissa saw the trail of sparks shooting back. They were dragging something made of metal, and as she braced herself, it broke off. She felt the hard jolt as it went under one of the back tires. Behind them, the cop swerved to miss the broken and sparking piece of metal that came scuttling out from behind their car. The cop never slowed, but their own car started to lose speed in a big way, fishtailing all over the road.

One of the back tires had blown.

"Hang on!" Chris shouted.

The car swerved to the edge of the road and hit the curb. This time, instead of mounting the curb and continuing, the left front tire blew. And that was it. Julissa was conscious of the roar of the engine and the red and blue lights reflecting off the mirrors as her side of the car flew up and slammed upside down into the ground; she saw in that moment the shadows cast by the blades of grass, and then they were rolling again.

The car landed with a bang of steel on what was left of its four wheels and rolled through the muddy grass at thirty miles an hour until it slammed into the mulch-covered embankment of a terraced flower garden. Julissa was never aware that the airbags had come out. She only saw, when they had come to a complete stop, that the white silk bags were draped around them, already deflated.

"You okay?" Chris said.

She nodded, just to see if her neck was broken. Shattered electronic equipment and broken glass lay everywhere. She ran her hands along her chest and up her arms but found no cuts.

"Yeah. You?"

Chris nodded. "Okay."

He unbuckled his seat belt and started to open his door, and that was when Julissa saw the cop. He was standing outside the shattered driver's side window, his right hand on his still-holstered Beretta.

"Sir, are you—"

That was all the cop ever had time to say to Chris and Julissa before his chest exploded in a geyser of blood. Julissa looked past the slumping cop and saw the black car, its headlights still dark, idling on the street behind the parked police cruiser. In a single motion she would replay for the rest of her life, Chris reached through the broken window and grabbed the Beretta from the cop's falling body, kicked open his door and dropped out of the driver's seat to the ground with one knee on the grass and both hands on the pistol, and fired five shots through the passenger window of the black car. Then he was up and running the hundred feet to the car with the Beretta in front of him. When he reached it, he leaned inside through the passenger window and fired three more shots. Then he turned to look at her.

"Are you hit?" he called.

She shoved her door open and stepped out.

"I'm okay."

There was nothing still intact in the wrecked rental car for her to bring along. She walked stiffly across the tire-marked grass to the black car. Chris opened the passenger door and pulled a dead man out of the seat and dropped him onto the grass. His face and head were so mutilated by gunfire she couldn't tell which of the men it had been. From his close-cropped dark hair, it could have been the Italian, Giovanni Greco, but she couldn't be sure. She recognized the dead driver, though, from the dossier she'd read on the plane. As Chris hauled him out, dragged him around the front of the car, and dumped him on the grass next to his dead companion, she got a look at his face and recognized Jonah Chapman, the British fugitive and alleged smuggler. She was still standing in the grass staring at his body, vaguely aware Chris was walking back to the body of the dead policeman and kneeling down to put the Beretta in his hand. Then he was back at the black car, holding the passenger door open for her.

"Let's go."

She got into the seat and Chris shut the door. The car smelled of powder smoke and cigarettes. There was an Uzi in the footwell underneath one of her sneakers. She looked at it and moved her foot. The inside of the windshield was misted with blood.

Chris pulled around the police car and drove away from the scene. When they were back into the anonymous, sleepy avenues of the Sunset District, they heard the sirens begin to converge on Golden Gate Park. She noticed Chris was still wearing the gloves he'd worn into the hacker's house.

"What now?" Julissa asked.

"I need a payphone."

"A payphone?"

"I need to call Avis. My rental car's gone missing."

An hour past sunrise, they were doing seventy miles an hour on Interstate 5, heading south towards Los Angeles. The sub-machinegun was locked in the trunk along with their few possessions from the hotel. Julissa had fallen asleep, her hand on top of Chris's, her red hair blowing in the strong wind coming through the shot-out driver's side window. In her mind as she slept, she fit the bleeding letters *A* and *I* into the beginning of every word she could, and in this dream, as in her last few hours of wakefulness, she came up empty.

Chapter Forty-One

The ocean was limitless blue from horizon to horizon: blue waves and blue sky overhead, broken only by the occasional patch of white foam where current lines brought opposing waves together in wet claps of spray. Where he was, the waves were widely spaced and running to the east northeast, the direction he was going, and there was no spray at all. He'd opened the overhead hatch for fresh air and had been running with the waves and wind at six or seven knots for the last eight hours.

He still didn't know where he was, but he had a good idea of where he needed to go. This was thanks to the battery operated AM/FM radio he'd found in one of the supply kits while he was taking stock of the boat. It was a cheap little radio receiver with a built-in speaker and a flimsy telescoping antenna. He'd been hoping to find a handheld GPS, but instead he'd found this. As an old-school naval officer, who had navigated ships around the world decades before anyone even dreamt of GPS, he knew exactly what to do with a tool like this. While sitting in the helm seat with the overhead hatch open, he switched the radio to receive on the AM band, extended its antenna through the open hatch, turned the volume all the way up, and scrolled through the AM channels listening for any kind of signal. He found one at 850 kHz—a signal so faint he could only discern music behind all the static, but he couldn't tell what kind of music it was. But it was real, which was all that mattered.

When he found the station, he carefully stood on the helm seat, head and shoulders poking through the hatch. Then he'd turned the radio in his hands so the antenna was parallel to the sea, the little silver ball on its tip pointing at the blue horizon. The signal came in just as strong as before. He slowly rotated three hundred and sixty degrees, moving his feet cautiously on the helm seat so he wouldn't fall down the hatch, holding the antenna out like the dowsing rod it had just become. When the antenna was pointing east northeast, the signal abruptly faded out. A hundred and eighty degrees in the other direction, west southwest, the signal faded out again. He listened to the wind blowing past, and the sound of the engine vibrating below him, and the gurgle of waves sliding past the fiberglass hull. He listened to the silence of the radio and looked at the horizon where the antenna was aimed. There was nothing there, but that wasn't important. He noted the position of the sun in the sky, and the angle of the waves lined up on the face of the sea, and ducked into the boat again with his hand shading his eyes so he could read the correct bearing on the bulkhead compass.

What he knew was that AM radio stations fade out when a radio's antenna was aligned horizontally with the earth and pointed directly at the transmission source. What he didn't know was whether the transmitter was in front of him or behind him. The only way to figure that out would be to motor along in one direction or the other and see if the signal strengthened or faded. Because he was already going basically east, and because the wind and waves were carrying him that direction anyway, he chose east.

Near sunset, he knew he'd chosen correctly. The music was clearer. For a stretch of ten seconds, he heard an acoustic guitar backed by drums, but when the singer's voice came in, static cut it off. The signal still faded in and out, but it was getting stronger. He turned the radio off to save the battery and steered by compass, wondering how much fuel the engine burned and how long the little boat could carry him. There were tarps on board and a pair of wooden oars, so he supposed if it came to it, he could rig a sail and work downwind. But he hoped it didn't come to that. With the engine running at 1500 RPM and the gentle, steady push of the wind and waves, he was making good speed on the course he wanted. He locked the wheel and climbed down the ladder to find something to eat in the boat's supplies.

At full dark, he stood on the helm seat again and looked at the stars. All he was sure of was that he was in the northern hemisphere. He saw the Big Dipper and followed the pointer stars in its outer edge to the North Star, which hung a little less than halfway between the horizon and the zenith above his little boat. By this he guessed he was at about forty degrees north latitude. He took his time making this estimation, adding up the degrees in a swath of sky by measuring up from the horizon by the width of his thumb. But even if he had his latitude fixed within a hundred miles, he still had no idea whether he was in the Pacific and heading east towards California, or in the

Atlantic and heading east towards Spain. For that matter, he could be in the Mediterranean, motoring to Greece or Albania, or in the Yellow Sea, plugging towards North Korea.

That last thought, at least, made him smile.

He settled into the helm seat and watched the night. After an hour or two, he slept in a fashion, waking every few moments to check the compass and the engine gauges, and then to scan the horizon, looking first for signs of the ship he'd escaped, and then ahead for signs of land. Just before dawn, he woke cold and stiff. He hobbled down the ladder and forced himself to stretch in the little aisle between the seats. Then he redressed his wounds, took another dose of the antibiotic and urinated into one of the empty water bottles.

As he was standing, he saw the sleeve of the Englishman's jacket poking through the aft hatch. No wonder small splashes of water came inside the boat in the following seas: the sleeve kept the hatch from sealing properly. He looked through the window to be sure no wave was on the verge of overtaking the boat, spun the wheel, opened the hatch, and pulled the jacket inside. Then he slammed the door and sealed it. Because the jacket was soaking wet, he could see a rectangular shape of something stuffed into its inner-liner pocket. He flipped the jacket's lapel back, unzipped the pocket and pulled out the little leather case of syringes the man had used. He opened it and saw four intact syringes, held in place by nylon loops.

He still had no memory of what had happened after the man had stuck one of these into his neck. But he had no doubt these could be useful. He took the case and put it inside the first-aid kit.

When he climbed back into the helm seat, the cloud on the eastern horizon had dissolved. The silhouette of an island lay directly ahead. Another smaller island lay a few miles to the north. He stared at the islands and waited for them to turn into clouds and float away, but they didn't, and he wasn't too surprised. He supposed he'd been expecting them. The closer and larger island looked to be ten miles wide and about equal that distance from the boat. If he kicked up the engine speed and had good luck with the currents, the trip would take under two hours.

A lighthouse blinked from the island's northern end, but the land there rose in cliffs directly from the sea. The waves looked small and gentle here in the middle of the ocean, but would be a different story altogether when they were slamming into cliff faces. Towards the middle of the island, short river valleys dropped from the central plateau; if he landed at one of the riverheads, he might find a sandy

245

beach and a way up without having to climb a cliff. He steered for the island's center, watching the horizon for boats and escorted on this last stretch of his journey by a pod of dolphins that came from behind and then slowed to swim alongside the lifeboat, keeping Westfield within their ranks until he was so close to the island he could hear the surf breaking on the beaches just ahead. The dolphins left him and went back out to sea, and Westfield turned the boat to motor six hundred feet off the shore, going south along the island. There were no houses, but towards the crest of the plateau, he saw a cut in the pine forest that might be a road. He went below and got an inflatable lifejacket, a bottle of water, and the first-aid kit, which was in a watertight yellow box. He clipped the bottle and the kit to the lifejacket harness, turned the wheel to point the lifeboat away from shore, and locked the helm. Then he climbed out the hatch, stood on the curved orange deck, inflated the lifejacket, and stepped over the side.

Chapter Forty-Two

When Chris figured it out, it came all at once, whole and unbroken. If he and Julissa had to spend the next ten hours proving it was right, and making additional discoveries that went along with it, it didn't change the basic completeness of what he'd just realized. He was sitting in a stuffed armchair in a room at the Sheraton, four blocks from Los Angeles International Airport, looking out the window at the fading light, and there it was. He sat frozen for two minutes, watching a plane materialize out of the gathering dusk, watching it grow from a light in the sky to a jumbo jet about to land, and then he stood and crossed the room, entered Julissa's adjoined suite, crossed to her bathroom, and opened the door without knocking.

She was in the bath and looked up at him, startled.

"What is it?"

"A.I.S.," he said.

"What?"

"A.I.S. What you switched off on *Sailfish* when we sailed across to Molokai. The automatic ship identification system. You turned it off so no one could track us."

Julissa stood, gathered her wet hair into a ponytail, and took the towel he was handing to her.

"I don't know if that's what he was trying to write on the wall, but if it was, I'll bet anything we can find him that way," Chris said. He leaned against the sink. "Look. We know he's coming and going by water, and we know he kills close to ports. He's hired smugglers who're spending time in ports. He's moving around on ships and every commercial vessel in the world has had an AIS for a decade. There are websites that track ships live, all over the world, any time they're within thirty or forty miles of a port. You can see exactly where the ship is and where it's going. You can get its name and IMO number."

"IMO number?"

"It's like the VIN number on a car, but for commercial ships. They never change, even if the ship changes hands or the company that owns it changes its name."

Now Julissa was getting it, the whole idea, complete and intact and ready to go. Chris saw the look on her face and realized if he'd kept the AIS system running while they escaped across to Molokai, so Julissa could watch its screen, she'd have thought of this days ago.

"We can correlate them," she said. "Find out what ships were in the harbors on the days the murders happened."

"And then use their IMO numbers to figure out who owns them, and if that doesn't give us any clue, we can use the Lloyd's of London registers to figure out who's been chartering and sub-chartering them."

Julissa wrapped the towel around her torso and tucked the corner between her breasts to hold it in place.

"Show me these websites."

They left the bathroom and went back to Chris's suite. Then they sat on the floor at the coffee table, Julissa looking over Chris's shoulder as he logged into one of the ship tracking sites.

"There's one problem," Chris said. "Most of these sites only have data going back a couple days. If there's no way to get the data they had ten years ago, this won't work."

Julissa nodded and they looked at the screen. Chris zoomed in on a map of Galveston. Colored icons indicated ships coming and going from the port, or tied up alongside the wharves. There were dozens of them—tankers, bulk carriers, tugs, container ships.

"I can get the old data," Julissa said.

Chris looked at her, and she went on.

"In grad school, at M.I.T., I knew a guy who was studying the way the web grows. He's been at it since '99. His lab takes a virtual snapshot of the entire web, every day, then maps the changes. He's got hundreds of thousands, maybe millions, of terabytes stored up."

"Can you get in touch with him?"

"He's still at M.I.T. We dated for about two years, but that was a long time ago. I ended it on friendly terms."

"What do you need to start?"

"My laptop. The list of all the murders and when and where they happened. A list of every other website you can find that has this kind of data. Dinner. Coffee."

"You got it." He started to get up, but she stopped him by putting her hands on his shoulders and pulling him to her.

"And you," she said. "I need you."

Chapter Forty-Three

Westfield staggered up the black-rock beach, slipping once on the wet stones and landing on his bad knee, but rising and moving on before another wave could hit him. He followed the edge of a fast-moving stream a hundred yards inland from the sea and then sat against the stone abutment of a washed-out bridge. He took off his mechanic's jumpsuit and sat naked and shivering on the stones, wringing seawater from the suit. The sea had been cold but the air was warm enough. When the wind finished drying him, he stopped shivering. Swimming ashore had made a wreck of his bandages, but the first-aid kit held dry replacements and new ointment. The Russian syringes were still there, dry and intact. He cleaned his wounds and looked at the bites before covering them over with new bandages. The infection was waning; the antibiotics were working.

When he had wrung all the water he could from the jumpsuit, he put it back on. He kept the first-aid kit and water bottle, but deflated the life jacket and left it under a flat stone. Then he climbed the abutment and found the track of an abandoned dirt road that led into the higher country of the island. He stood a moment before setting off, watching as the lifeboat motored away. He hoped it would be a speck in the distance before anyone came along and found him.

The road wound up switchbacks along cliffs ledged with pine trees. After a mile, he came to a paved road. If he'd had a coin, he might have flipped it, but he had nothing in the pockets of his jumpsuit. So he went right, because he was already facing that direction, and besides, it looked to be downhill. He walked past terraced fields planted with some kind of yellow flowering bush and divided by neatly built, low rock walls. When the sun rose high enough that he was no longer in the shadow cast by the high country, he felt the jumpsuit finally start to dry. He walked for half an hour and then sat down to rest on one of the rock walls, looking down the escarpment and into a protected bay he had not been able to see from the water. At the head of the bay there was a village of whitewashed houses with red tile roofs, all neatly lined along stone streets that led to an old wharf. Fishing boats and wooden sailboats bobbed on their mooring balls behind a breakwater. Fifteen minutes later, he came to a road sign that pointed down a narrower asphalt road that led directly to the village. The sign read *Fajã Grande — 1 km.* A smaller sign beneath it bore the symbol of a cross and said *Igreja Matriz de Fajã Grande.* Westfield looked at the words and decided they must be Portuguese, and that was when he realized he'd landed in the Azores.

He walked through the narrow stone streets of Fajã Grande. An old man wearing a tweed cap and sitting on a wrought iron balcony put down his newspaper and watched Westfield pass. He had been feeling good in the morning air and the sunshine, and had forgotten his jumpsuit was stained with blood. He was barefooted and limping, and hadn't shaved in days. He nodded at the man and continued through the village until he found the small central plaza where the church, Igreja Matriz, was built. The parsonage was behind it, and like the church and everything else in the village, it was a low whitewashed house, built flush to the edge of the street, with flowers in iron planters that hung from the brightly painted window sills. He stepped up to the parsonage door and knocked. Across the street, a bakery was turning out the smell of fresh malasadas and coffee. His stomach woke, and he wished he had some money. Then the door opened, and the parish priest dressed in black clerics stood looking at him over the gold rims of his spectacles.

"Good morning," Westfield said. "You speak English?"

The priest smiled. "Yes. Can I help you?"

"I'm an American—a sailor. I ran my boat onto the rocks just before sunrise and lost her because I fell asleep on watch. I don't have any papers or any money. I walked to this village from the beach where I swam ashore. Is there a computer I can use? With an Internet connection?"

The priest looked at him. "You need a doctor."

"No. I got scraped up in the wreck and again coming to shore. But it's nothing serious."

"I can take you to a computer. And I can give you some shoes and clothes."

"Thank you."

The priest opened the door the rest of the way and motioned Westfield inside.

Half an hour later, Westfield followed the priest, whose name was Father Leonardo Silva, through the rest of the village and along the waterfront. Westfield wore an old gray jogging suit and a pair of Nike running shoes that Father Silva had given him. Though he seemed to want to walk faster, Father Silva kept pace with Westfield. He carried a set of keys on a large brass ring.

"Where had you sailed from, and where were you going?"

"I set out from Halifax and my first landfall was supposed to be Gibraltar." He was pretty sure the Azores lay on the great circle line between those two points.

"What kind of boat?"

"A thirty-four-foot sloop," he said, thinking of the last boat he'd seen beam reaching across Puget Sound when he could still go to his house. Except now that he thought about it, he didn't miss his house at all. He had escaped with his life and, for the first time, he had a solid clue: he knew the name of the ship.

"She's totally lost, your boat?"

"Yes."

"I'm sorry. What was her name?"

"Tara," he said, and without any hesitation. "Right now I'm just glad to be alive."

"I wouldn't have set out alone across the Atlantic before November," the priest said. "You must be brave."

"You're a sailor?"

"Yes."

They walked in silence for another few minutes and then Father Silva pointed at the two-story whitewashed building in front of them. It clung to the seawall on one side and its well-tended lawn faced the street. The stone lintel over the door was carved with a Latin cross.

"The parish school," Father Silva said. "Of course the children are not here now. Summertime."

They went across the lawn to the door, where Father Silva used the keys from his ring to open the locks. Then he led Westfield inside and up the stairs. The classroom facing the ocean was also the computer lab. There were two desktop PCs on a table by the window. They looked four or five years old, but they would work fine, if there was really Internet.

"Do you know how to use them?" Father Silva said.

"Yes."

"I have to go back to the church. Confession begins soon. When you're finished here, will you lock the door?"

Westfield nodded. "I can meet you back at the church?"

"Yes. I'll be in the booth."

"Thank you, Father."

"Be sure to lock the door." He handed Westfield the key ring and left.

Westfield listened to the old priest's feet clomping down the wooden stairs. When he was gone, Westfield sat at one of the computers and turned it on.

Chapter Forty-Four

No single ship had been present in every port on the day of each killing. But ships belonging to one company, Lothian Lines, Ltd., had been in Galveston on the day Allison was murdered, in Naples on the day the twins were slaughtered, and in New Orleans over the two-day course of Robin Knappe's dismemberment and consumption. Those ships were the M/V *Tantallon* and the M/V *Dunnottar*. Other Lothian Lines ships had been in ports the day before or the day after killings on the rim of the Atlantic. There were no Lothian Lines ships anywhere near killings that took place in the Pacific. But here, Julissa found ships either belonging to, or time-chartered into, the fleet of Cathay Steamship & Freight Co., Ltd.

Chris was sitting across from her at the coffee table. He had been doing research on his laptop and taking pages of notes on a pad of hotel stationery for the last three hours. Their empty room service trays were on the floor and they were both on their third cups of coffee. It was two thirty in the morning.

"It's better than you think," Chris said.

"How's that?"

"Lothian Lines is an old steamship company, registered in the U.K. in 1840. Privately held. They restructured twenty years ago so Lothian's a wholly owned subsidiary of a holding company called Lothian Holdings, Ltd."

"Okay. I don't get—"

"Hang on, there's more. Cathay Steamship is also a wholly owned subsidiary of Lothian Holdings, even though it's a privately held corporation registered in Hong Kong."

"So they're under common control," Julissa said.

"Exactly. Lothian Holdings is just an umbrella that covers hundreds of other companies. Maybe thousands, I haven't gone through all the records yet. And there's one other thing."

Julissa had been taking a sip of her coffee, but she set the cup down.

"It looks like Lothian is investing in a lot more than just shipping lines." He paused and flipped back through his notes.

"Like what?" she asked, feeling she might know the answer.

"Lately they've been getting into biotech."

"Intelligene?"

Chris nodded.

"It's a publicly traded U.S. company, so it wasn't made into a Lothian subsidiary. They didn't have to. Three privately held corporations, registered in Delaware or Nevada, bought seventeen percent, twenty percent, and fourteen percent of Intelligene's stock right after its IPO."

"And all three were tied back to Lothian Holdings?"

Julissa's computer began to make a quiet chiming sound, which she ignored. She was focusing on Chris.

"That's right. With their fifty-one percent interest, Lothian didn't need to make it a subsidiary; it already controlled the board, which is all it would need if its goal was to keep tabs on Chevalier's research. Trails like this used to be hard to follow until ten years ago. Now most of these records are online."

"Where's the headquarters of Lothian Holdings?"

The look on Chris's face faded a bit.

"I don't know. It's a privately held company, so it doesn't have to list very much about itself. It doesn't have customers, so it has no interface with the public. But all companies have to name a registered agent so you know who to serve when you file a lawsuit. Lothian Holdings, Lothian Lines, and about a hundred other LLCs and corporations have the same registered agent. A guy named Howard Stark III, Esq."

"Our killer's got a mob lawyer."

"Sounds like it."

"Where is he?"

"A law firm in Edinburgh, Scotland," Chris said. "I don't know where the holding company is, but the shipping line's been in Edinburgh since 1840."

Julissa rubbed her temples with her fingertips and looked at the coffee table.

"1840?" she asked. "Really?"

"Yeah, I know," Chris said. "Chevalier said the creature might not age. I guess he was right."

Julissa finally noticed her computer was still chiming at her. She looked at the screen, and what she saw was every bit as surprising as the idea they would be going to Scotland to kill a centuries-old monster.

It was a message from Skype.

Someone with the screen name Captain_Westfield wanted to talk to her.

"Oh my god," Julissa said. "Oh my god, Chris! Come over here!"

Chapter Forty-Five

Father Silva had been alone in the confessional booth for an hour, using a pair of votive candles to read a book in French about Saint Damien. The booth smelled of polished wood and candle wax. He liked to read in the shadowed, holy hush of the old church. He did it often during his confessional hours, because in a village this small, and in these times of waning interest in his Church, he spent most of these hours alone. Now he heard the main door to the church open. The flames of his candles bent towards the confessional door, then sputtered out and smoked in the darkness. Footsteps worked their way across the church to the opposite side of the confessional booth. Father Silva marked the page in his book and sat back.

"Forgive me, Father, for I have sinned," said the man, in American-accented English. "It's been thirty-three years since my last confession."

"Thirty-three years is a long time," Father Silva said. "Did the computer work?"

"It did, thanks. I reached my friends."

"You want to confess?"

"Yes."

The man was silent a long time. Father Silva could hear the wind blowing past the leaves of the apple trees that grew outside the church steps. He waited for the man to start speaking.

"There's a lot. If another person comes while I'm talking, I'll stop. Is that okay?"

"Yes."

"In 1978, at the Sasesbo naval base in Japan, my wife Tara was killed and eaten. It happened while I was away. I hadn't seen her in two months and I never saw her again. She died in agony. And in fear. Alone with a creature who tortured and raped her, and drew out her death for over a day. I thought the killer was just an ordinary guy. A monster, but a man. Now I know it isn't a man at all. I also know how to find it."

The man spoke to Father Silva, in his slow and careful whisper, for two hours. Now and then he encountered men or women who assumed because he was a priest, and a believer in God, and a vocal witness of miracles, he would be easy prey for superstition, or stretched truths, or even outright lies. That people would try to take advantage of his faith—the trait it was his duty to nurture in everyone he encountered—didn't particularly disturb him. It was just a fact of human nature, and facts were things to be dealt with as they came. But as this man's story came, he didn't sense a lie: the man believed every word he spoke. And though the man had been a physical mess when Father Silva first laid eyes on him, it was clear he wasn't out of his wits.

When Aaron Westfield finished his story, the two of them sat in silence on opposite sides of the booth. Again there was only the sound of the wind.

"What do you want me to do?" Father Silva said.

"My friends will come in four days. That's how long it'll take Julissa to get a new passport for me. Is there an airport on this island?"

"Yes."

"Actually, I don't even know the name of this island. I'll need to tell them where to come."

"Flores. The farthest west of the Azores. On the day they come, I'll borrow a pickup and drive you to the airport to meet their plane."

"May I stay in the school until then?"

"Yes."

"You need help with anything? In the school, or in the church?"

"There's a fishing boat with an engine that won't run. Two mechanics looked, and neither had any luck. Maybe you could help the man who owns it? He hasn't been able to fish for several days."

Westfield agreed to try.

That was how Father Silva came to be walking down the waterfront in the waning afternoon of the day he met Aaron Westfield, carrying a cot and a sleeping bag to the old school. He thought about Westfield's story. He supposed he could use the computer and check to see if parts of the story were true. It would be easy to see if Westfield had been in the Navy, if his wife had been murdered, and if a girl had been killed in the American state of Texas recently.

But he had seen enough already that he didn't need more. After the confession, and after Westfield had sat in the front pew of the church to pray and to say the Our Fathers and Hail Marys which Father Silva had imposed upon him, he had taken Westfield back around to his house and had helped him change the dressings on his wounds. These were no ordinary wounds, and they told him much. They were bite marks, but not from any man. In the few places where the creature had bit into Westfield without tearing away an entire mouthful of flesh, he could see the imprint of its teeth. Though its mouth was no larger than a man's, its teeth must have been set apart from each other like those of a predatory animal, each a sharp needle. Afterwards, when he was out of Westfield's sight, Father Silva bit his own wrist, hard enough to leave an elliptical imprint of his teeth. He'd looked at this bite mark and thought about what he'd seen all over Westfield's torso. Whereas his own teeth left individual marks like the blade of a dull chisel, the thing's teeth had punctured Westfield's skin with hundreds of perfectly round holes. While rubbing in new antibiotic ointment, he had counted the wounds in one of the clearer bites. The creature had fifty-two teeth on each jaw. The smell of infection coming from the wounds told him the rest of what he needed to know.

Father Silva opened the door to the schoolhouse, brought Westfield's bedding up the stairs, and made a place for his guest next to the computers. He looked out the window to the harbor. Westfield was out there, wearing his dirty mechanic's jumpsuit again, sitting on the red-painted gunwale of the broken fishing boat. He was using a wire brush and a borrowed sewing needle to clean the engine's fuel injectors in a porcelain bowl of petrol. He had spread tools and parts across the deck. He had a kerosene lantern tied to the boom over the open engine compartment, though it was not yet dark. He must have planned to work into the night. Father Silva raised his hand to acknowledge Westfield, who raised his own hand in return.

Chapter Forty-Six

The young woman woke naked and in pain in the darkness, and screamed herself hoarse. Then she went on screaming until she passed out again from the agony of wounds she couldn't see and the terror of not knowing how she'd gotten them. Or where she'd been dumped, or what was happening. The last thing she heard as she fell down a hole inside her own mind was the echo of her raw cries reverberating through the deep and endless hallways of the cavern where she was trapped.

The second time she woke, she curled herself into a ball on the stone floor, her arms wrapped tightly around her naked legs, her spine bent so her chin was over the top of her knees. She shivered and stared at a darkness so deep she became unsure whether her eyes were open or closed. Then her other senses fell one after another. Her skin was no longer freezing, no tug of gravity pulled her against the broken stones. Where once there had been the distant drip of water echoing from the far reaches of this dungeon, now there was only a spreading silence. She was floating through ink.

In that blackness, she began to remember things.

Days ago she'd been in Brighton. She'd walked from the 11:47 London train to the Grand Hotel to meet a man named Kent who'd spoken to her on the telephone twice that morning. He had information about her latest MI6 piece in *The Guardian*, but of course he couldn't give it over the phone. She wouldn't have let him if he'd tried, but there'd been no need to stop him. He knew how to handle himself. It was clear he'd been an operator of some kind. He asked her to meet him and she agreed. He called a second time from a different phone and told her to go to the Lincoln Lounge on York Way, to ask for Mitch when she got there. The lounge was close to her office; she'd been there in five minutes. The barkeep, Mitch, slid her a business card. It was blank on one side and on the other, printed in neat lettering, it said,

GRAND HOTEL, BRIGHTON. ROOM 803.
AS SOON AS YOU CAN.

She'd never met Kent, but he'd left her a computer disk in a dead drop last year. That disk turned into a major story. As a rule, if she left her desk before lunchtime on a Friday to see a man willing to talk about torture programs, and black ops, and Diego Garcia, she didn't tell anyone where she was going. Not even her editor. Secrets deserved secrecy.

People like Kent knew it was her rule and relied on it.

Besides, the Grand Hotel was a lovely spot, one of the old Victorians, the kind where rich men stayed and the tabloid paparazzi slinked around with their cameras across the street. If his information was useless, she'd still be in Brighton for the weekend. It was warm, and there hadn't been much fog at the seaside, so it wouldn't be a total loss.

She made it by noon and he'd opened the door at her second knock. He'd been handsome in a pleasant, English way.

"Rachel?"

"Hope I'm not late."

"Not at all. Come on in and get set up, your laptop or whatever. You look just like your picture on the byline. Stunning, I should say. Such beautiful hair."

He'd almost reached out to touch her hair where it fell over her shoulder, and then he'd stopped himself. He smiled and looked down; it was kind of sweet. Then she'd made the mistake of walking past him, into the room. Because she'd been blushing, she left her back to him while she unzipped her shoulder bag to get her notebook. She remembered the blow on the back of her neck, his fist coming down on her vertebrae like a sledgehammer. He'd probably wanted that to take care of her, but it hadn't been enough. Instead of falling to the floor in a heap, she'd pivoted and leapt for the door. So he'd tackled her, and forced her to the ground, using his weight to pin her while he got his hands around her throat and squeezed.

Now, floating in the deathlike darkness, she remembered clawing and biting at his face. But it hadn't done any good. If anything, he'd enjoyed it. He'd choked her until she'd gone limp, and he'd choked her well past that until she'd been a second or two from death. After that, she didn't remember much. Just a few images. It was like walking in and out of a snuff film and seeing only the worst parts. In this scene, the girl is staring at her hands and ankles as the man binds them with duct tape, the sight slowly receding as her pummeled eyes swell shut. The next shot is a long ride in the foot well of an unseen vehicle, the girl's head banging against the dash. She cries out; a man laughs. Hours into the drive, she struggles to the surface for just a moment, forcing one eye open against its bloody bruise. The man looks down at her as he drives.

"You're perfect," he says. "You'll do just fine."

It's hard for the girl to talk. Her throat has been crushed somehow; even whispering is a struggle.

"My editor. Knows. Where I went."

"No," he says. "She doesn't. I checked your email, your phone. You told her you were going to Cambridge. To meet a source on the hacking probe. So you're on your own here."

He reaches down to cup her breast and she blacks out as she screams.

Then they were in a dark and cold city and he'd put a hood over her head before taking her out of the van. He used a saw-bladed knife to cut her ankles free, digging into the skin while he was at it. She could see her feet, the mossy cobble stones across which he was dragging her. A door opened. The same door boomed shut. Now the darkness was total and he was guiding her down steps. They descended forever, his hand crushing her arm above her elbow, the point of the knife between her shoulder blades.

"You think I'm taking you down here to do things to you," he'd said. "Rape you, kill you. Stuff like that. But you're wrong. I'm just bringing you. Whatever happens next is between you and him."

He cut her clothes off, and cut her wrists loose, and whipped the hood from her head. She stood frozen in the utter darkness, listening for anything.

When his fist fell on her neck the second time, it had worked exactly as he intended: she fell to the stone floor like a dead thing.

She floated in the darkness for hours, for days. She didn't know. At one point she came to earth again, skin upon stones, and she found her way to her hands and knees. She crawled across the cavern floor, tentatively, then faster. Ten feet, a hundred feet. A quarter mile. Her hands found a round stone the size of a melon and she held it and turned it in her fingers, her thumbs finding deep openings. It was too light to be a stone. She found the teeth, the hinged jaw, and knew what she held. She threw the skull away and listened to it bounce hollowly along the floor, rolling and banging down a slope for minutes as it went deeper into the ground. She lay on her side and went back into a protective ball, shutting her eyes against the darkness.

Everything dropped away. She was drifting, unbound.

But there was something above her. A pair of unblinking yellow eyes watched her from on high, like a spider in its web. They began to circle. As they moved, she could hear the click and scrape of claws on stone.

She began to scream again.

Chapter Forty-Seven

The chartered Learjet 45 landed on the main runway at Edinburgh International Airport at nine p.m. on the twenty-second day of July, 2010. Edinburgh lay so far north the sun wouldn't set for another hour. In the gloaming shadows of the rainclouds, the fields around the airport were a cool, deep green. On their approach, the North Sea had been gray and choppy. The jet taxied to its hangar and then Chris unbuckled his seat belt, got his bags, and stretched in the aisle. His back and neck were still sore from the car accident.

"Can I carry those?" Julissa asked.

"I've got them. You want to wake up Westfield?"

Westfield woke at the sound of his name. He had no bags except for the first-aid kit he'd taken from the *Tantallon*'s lifeboat, and he wore old clothes given to him by a Portuguese fisherman. They walked down the plane's metal stairway. The charter company had arranged for a customs and immigration inspector to meet them in the hangar. To Chris's intense relief, the inspector simply stamped their passports and welcomed them to the United Kingdom without going through their luggage. On the other side of the hangar bay, a smoke-blue Rolls Royce waited at an idle, its chauffer standing by the passenger door.

Less than two minutes after they stepped from the plane, they were in the car and on their way into the city.

"Nice way to travel," Westfield said.

He was sitting on the wide leather seat facing Chris and Julissa. To his right was a wet bar with its crystal decanters of whiskey and Calvados brandy. There was a soundproof glass partition between the driver and the passenger compartment.

"Edinburgh's probably the most dangerous place in the world for the three of us to show our faces," Chris said. "So I thought the fewer people we run into getting to our hotel, the better."

"Good idea."

"Also," Julissa said, "you saw how we just blew through customs. You only get that if you come in by charter. And we've got some stuff in our suitcases."

"Julissa stayed in L.A. to work out your passport. I rented a car and went across the border to Arizona," Chris explained. "Went to a gun show in Phoenix. Cash on the table, no ID."

Westfield nodded. He looked at each of them and then let his eyes rest on the other empty jump seat.

"Mike's not here," he said.

"They got him," Chris said. "And his family."

"It was bad?"

"Yeah," Julissa said. She was whispering. "I saw it. I mean, I didn't see it happen, but I saw it after, and it was bad."

"Do we know which guys?"

"No," Chris said. "It could've been the guy I shot on my doorstep. Or the guys we killed in Golden Gate Park. Or the man you dumped in the Atlantic."

"I hope it was one of those," Westfield said. "He helped us get here, though, didn't he?"

Julissa put her hand on Westfield's knee and squeezed gently. Chris put his hand on top of Julissa's.

"A lot of vengeance coming down," Aaron said. "A lot of payback."

Chris nodded.

They came into the soot-stained, stone heart of the old city just as the sun disappeared. They were driving on Princes Street, along the sunken gardens built at the foot of the Edinburgh Castle. The castle dominated the city from its volcanic crag, its crenellated battlements and ramparts now catching the last of the light, the Union Jack rippling in the stiff breeze from its pole atop the highest keep. They passed the gothic spire of the Scott Monument, then turned into the porte cochère of the Balmoral Hotel just as the last of the burgundy glow faded from the bottom of the rain clouds.

This was the city of the monster. Chris felt it in his heart, like a roomful of cold air. They were so close.

Julissa used the key Chris gave her to let herself into his room half an hour after they got to the hotel. As she stepped inside, she used her left hand to pull off the silk scarf she'd had over her hair.

"I went downstairs and bought us a bottle of whiskey. There's a shop just down the street," she said. When she saw he was looking at the scarf, she added, "I thought it'd be a good idea to cover my hair. But I don't know. There are a lot of redheads in Scotland."

She held up the bottle of eighteen-year-old Laphroaig, which was still inside its protective cardboard cylinder. During their four days in Los Angeles she had found a way to securely move funds from her bank accounts in Texas to an untraceable Swiss account by initiating a transfer through a series of proxy servers. Chris could tell she was relieved to have her own money. She had performed the same service for Westfield and had given him his new bank card when he stepped onto the plane in Flores.

She found two crystal tumblers in the bar by the window and raised her eyebrow at Chris. He held up his hand with the tips of his thumb and forefinger about half an inch apart. Julissa poured the whiskey and handed one glass to Chris. They sat in armchairs by the fireplace and waited for Westfield.

When they were all together, Chris spread a map of Edinburgh on the dining table. He used a red pen to circle the law firm, Stark McCallister Fanning & Stalker. It was a four-man firm near the end of High Street in Old Town, a few blocks from the castle and close to the old courts. High Street followed the spine of an ancient volcanic ridge for a mile, ending at the gates of the castle. Because the sides of the ridge were so steep, instead of cross streets, it was cut by dozens of winds and closes—narrow stone staircases that wound between, and underneath, the eight-hundred-year-old buildings that crowded up either side of the ridge. There was a close on each side of the building that held the law offices, and the map showed one of the closes led to a hidden courtyard behind the building.

"Looks like we could get in from all four sides," Westfield said.

"Maybe five."

Julissa rotated her laptop so they could see the screen. She had zoomed in on the building using satellite photos from Google. "The closes are so narrow I think we could jump from roof to roof and get in through the skylight windows on the top floor."

"That would keep us out of view of the street," Chris said.

"But first we need to figure out if he even uses the office. He might work from home," Julissa said.

"You got a picture of him?" Westfield asked.

"Yeah." Julissa took a manila folder and passed out the pictures she'd printed in the business center of their hotel in Los Angeles. The first photograph was at least twenty years old. Chris came across it in the online directory of the Scottish Bar Association, and it showed Howard Stark, III on the day he became a member of the bar. It was a grainy black-and-white photograph, enlarged too much for its size, and showed a young man in a pinstripe suit with a mane of blond hair combed straight back from his forehead. He had a square chin and wore heavy black glasses.

Westfield looked at the first photograph in the folder and then turned back to Chris and Julissa.

"I was kind of hoping it'd be Stark. The thing I saw on the ship. But this is just a man."

"Who ages like a man, if you look at the next picture," Julissa said.

The other photograph was only two years old. Julissa found it by searching Google, which had turned up a page from a magazine published by the University of Edinburgh. It showed Stark, his faced lined and sagging beneath his eyes, his blond mane retreated and grayer. The nose that supported his gold-rimmed bifocals had blossomed from an additional twenty years of whiskey. The caption under the photograph stated *Howard Stark, III, Esq., (Law '75), delivering the Annual Tetlow Lecture on Admiralty Law.*

"The important thing is to get the syringe into him without him noticing," Westfield said. "I wouldn't know they interrogated me if the guy hadn't told me what was up before he did it. The only thing I remember is him telling me, and then the needle. Then nothing."

"How long were you out?"

"I don't know. By the time I finally got to shave at Father Silva's house, I had maybe seven days of beard growth. That's starting from Galveston, the last time I shaved. Then I drove across West Texas and the thing got me early in the morning on the second night, in Carlsbad. I spent a little over twenty-four hours in the lifeboat. So that leaves up to five days I absolutely can't account for, other than snatches in the body bag."

"Jesus, Aaron."

"But I think if one of us just comes up behind him and gives it to him in the neck, he won't remember a thing. And then we can ask him anything we want and dump him in his own bed, and he'll never be able to raise an alarm that we're here and asking questions."

"So at the very least we'll need to know his routine and know where he lives. If he's got a wife or a girlfriend or a maid, we'll need to get her out of the way," Chris said.

"It sounds like a couple days' preparation, at least," Julissa said.

"It'll take a lot of ground work. We can use Google maps and satellite pictures all we want, but we'll have to get out there and go into buildings and figure out the space. So we gotta make sure we don't get caught while we're trying to lay a trap," Westfield said.

"We thought of that too," Chris said.

Julissa brought a suitcase to the table. She pulled out the shopping bags from Los Angeles, then opened the concealed compartment at the base of the suitcase, where Chris had put the disassembled guns. Chris handed Westfield a shopping bag and a plastic bag full of gun parts.

"Can you put that together?"

"What's it supposed to look like when it's done?" Westfield asked.

"A Micro-Uzi."

"Jesus Christ, where'd you buy that?"

"We got it off the guys Chris shot," Julissa said. "The other two are just regular Glocks. They all load nine millimeter and we have four hundred rounds in the other bags."

"What about the rest of this stuff?"

Westfield reached into the bag and pulled out a man's wig and a pair of sunglasses. There was also a prepaid cell phone with a wireless earpiece, a pair of compact binoculars, and a Timex watch.

"Don't tell me we're going to synchronize watches," Westfield said.

Before the end of the night, they did.

Chapter Forty-Eight

Julissa stood on the parade ground in front of the castle gates. Behind and above her, the cannons of the Half Moon Battery kept watch over Old Town. She used the high-powered lens of her camera to look down the Royal Mile as she walked, stopping now and then to actually take a picture. Summer crowds of tourists strolled Lawnmarket Street with their shopping bags, or stood in groups around kilted bagpipers. Men were assembling a bandstand just below the castle walls; banners fluttered on every lamppost from the castle to Hollyrood Palace, a mile down the ridge. Behind that, the extinct volcano Arthur's Seat echoed the castle in ridges of exposed rock and green grass and brambles of heather.

Julissa wore a blonde wig, black jeans, a tight-fitting sweater and leather boots with good soles. Other than the camera, she carried a small black backpack. She expected she might be running today. She looked at the hands of her watch. It was ten seconds to one o'clock.

She counted down the last five seconds. When she reached zero, an artillery piece mounted high in the castle fired with a sharp crack. This was the One O'clock Gun, fired daily through the decades so ships at anchor in the Firth of Forth could set their clocks.

It wasn't just the ships that set their clocks according to the gun.

She was on the south side of Lawnmarket, at the traffic circle in front of a coal-blackened Scottish kirk. She picked up her camera and looked across the traffic circle and down the High Street, focusing on the door to Ensign Ewart pub. Three and a half minutes later, which was about average, Howard Stark, III came out the door, stepped around a crowd of tourists, and walked down the High Street towards his offices.

Julissa cupped her hand over her mouth and spoke into her wireless mike.

"He's on his way."

"Got it," Chris said. "Will you have time?"

"Just."

She shoved the camera into her backpack, and ran.

Chapter Forty-Nine

Four minutes after one o'clock, Westfield walked out of the darkness of James Court, a narrow alleyway running between the old buildings pressed nearly wall to wall along this part of the Royal Mile. Chris was at his side. Ten steps from the end of the alley, they saw Stark pass on the sidewalk. They came out of the close and fell in behind him, walking fifty feet away. A couple pushing a child in a stroller was between them for half a block, then stopped at the window of a pub. Chris and Westfield stepped around them and closed the gap just as Stark reached a red-painted door and raised a ring of keys. The glass transom over the door was painted in gold script: *Stark McCallister Fanning & Stalker, Counselors at Law.*

Westfield was wearing a light summer jacket and reached into his pocket to feel the syringe. He held it in his fingers and used his thumbnail to pop the plastic cap off the tip of the needle. He looked at Chris and nodded.

Stark found the key—a piece of wrought iron that may have been hammered on a blacksmith's anvil in the eighteenth century—and slid it into the keyhole. As he turned it in the lock, Chris stepped around to Stark's right shoulder and Westfield came to his left. Pressing up to Stark, Westfield used his left hand to jab the needle into Stark's neck, pushing the plunger with his thumb. Just as quickly, he pocketed the syringe, took the key from the unlocked door and pocketed that. Then he and Chris had their hands under Stark's armpits and they moved him through the open door. The building had a whiskey shop at the street level and the door through which they'd stepped opened on to a stair landing that would lead up to the law firm's offices. Past the offices, on the sixth floor, was a vacant space under construction. Stark jerked twice in a weak attempt to get away, then went limp. They had to hold him up to keep him on his feet. The stairs were narrow and barely wide enough to fit the three of them abreast.

Westfield looked at Chris, who put his hand to his ear and spoke to Julissa.

"We're in the stairs and on our way up."

Over his own earpiece, Westfield heard Julissa's response. He could hear the wind blowing across her microphone and her voice was nearly breathless.

"I'll be there," she said.

Chapter Fifty

Julissa jogged across Lawnmarket at a crosswalk, then wove through the crowd until she got to the Ensign Ewart. She walked down the steps into the sunken pub, nodded at the bartender, passed the row of men on stools sipping their pints, and headed for the ladies' room. She stepped inside, closed the door behind her and turned on the light. There was a door to a janitor's closet crammed between the tilted toilet bowl and the wall. She opened this door, stepped over a mop bucket and into the dank, chemical-smelling space, closed the closet door, and in the darkness fumbled until she found the handle for the sliding door at the back. This opened onto a dimly lit stair landing. She slid the door shut, then bounded up the stairs, using the hand rail as a pivot point at each landing so she could swing around and start up the next flight of steps without losing any forward momentum. She hurtled up the stairs to the fifth floor without meeting anyone.

At the top, she stood on the banister, leaned over the empty space above the descending stairs, and unlatched the dormer window that looked north, towards the Scott Monument and the Firth of Forth. The weighted window slid two feet and jammed, but it was enough. She jumped and got her head and arms through, then found finger holds on the underside of the sill. She pulled herself out and stood on the angled slate roof. She ran east, parallel to the Royal Mile but five floors up, running just past the roof's ridgeline. She vaulted over a cluster of Tudor-style clay pot chimneys, ran down the mossy slate slope and leapt over the five foot gap where Milnes Court cut between the old buildings. She landed a foot away from the edge of the moss-slick edge, but her boots had good traction and she never even paused. She ran up the steep incline of the new roof, over the crest and down towards the dark crevasse where James' Court close made its passage between this building and the next. This was an easier jump; the next roof was newer and had a rougher texture to its slate so she could run without fear of sliding over the edge and off a hundred foot drop to paving stones.

She stopped at the skylight she had marked with a blue chalk X two nights before and knelt down, breathing hard. No more than a minute had passed from the time she last spoke to Chris and Aaron. Now she keyed her mike and spoke to them again, her voice breathless as she gasped for air.

"I'm at the skylight."

"We're almost to the landing," Chris said.

"I'll be there."

Julissa took off her backpack, reached inside it, and took out a diamond-bitted glass cutter and a plastic suction grip bar. She spat on the suction cups, stuck them to the middle of the skylight, then used the wheel of the diamond cutter to etch along the lead soldered edge of one of the skylight panes. When she had gone all the way around, she braced her knees on the roof and pulled hard on the suction handle. The sound of the pane breaking loose reminded her of stepping on a frozen puddle. She lifted the pane free and set it gently on the uphill side of the skylight so it would not slide away. Then she pulled the release trigger on her suction grip, put it back into the backpack, and pulled on a pair of heavy-duty leather gloves. She looked at her watch. It was 1:06 p.m. Exactly two minutes had passed from the time Chris and Aaron had stepped out of James Court in pursuit of Stark.

She shouldered her pack, grabbed on to the frame of the skylight, and lowered herself until she was dangling by her arms. She could feel the sharp remnants of the glass against the leather palms of her gloves. The floor was six feet beneath her. She let go and dropped, landing on her feet and falling to a crouch so she hit the wooden floor with almost no sound at all.

They'd discovered the top floor of this building was being remodeled. Stacks of clean sheetrock took up one corner. The walls were bare studs with exposed electrical conduits. There was a table saw and a water-cooled tile saw. Julissa stood, turned around quickly to be sure the work crew was truly gone, then walked to the door. There were three sets of deadbolt locks, all of which could be opened from the inside without a key. She flicked them back one by one, then pulled the door open.

Westfield and Chris were coming up the last flight of stairs, supporting Stark in between them.

"You okay?" Chris said.

"I'm fine. Anyone see you?"

"Nobody on the stairs," said Westfield. "I can't say whether anyone saw us on the sidewalk."

They brought Stark into the room and lowered him onto the unvarnished wooden floor. Julissa closed the door behind them and locked it.

"Here," Julissa said. She handed out the black ski masks from her backpack. They each put one on. Westfield and Chris then slipped on their gloves.

"Let's see what we've got," Westfield said. He knelt next to Stark, took a digital recorder from his pocket, and pressed *Record.*

Chapter Fifty-One

In two days of searching the regular Internet and the FBI resources Julissa could access, they had been able to learn next to nothing about the contents of Westfield's syringes. The side of each glass syringe bore nothing but a Cyrillic stamp: *Серия-64*. Each tube was marked with metric graduation lines, and each contained exactly fifteen milliliters of a perfectly clear liquid. After spending half an hour figuring out how to type in Cyrillic, Chris translated the word as "batch". Nothing on the Internet gave any hint as to what Batch-64 might be.

The FBI had a little more. There was an advisory to the field offices warning counterintelligence agents to look out for something named Batch-64 or Lot-64. An unnamed source privy to the contents of Russian diplomatic pouches advised that Batch-64 was being delivered to embassies and consulates. The source claimed it was a hypnotic drug. Chris had been hoping for an instruction manual, but all they found was this.

Now he was watching the attorney twitch and writhe on the floor. Stark had never been entirely unconscious. His eyes were open but unfocused. If he could see, he probably wasn't seeing anything in the room.

"Where are we, buddy?" Westfield asked.

"Ensign Ewart," Stark said. It was almost a question.

"That's right."

"I usually have a pint of ale at lunch."

"I know."

"Just a pint. I think I went and had a bit more."

"You did, but that's okay," Westfield said. He looked up at Chris and nodded.

"You're the agent for Lothian Lines," Chris said, just jumping into it.

"Our first shipping line, that's right."

"Who's we?"

"My father was the agent before me. His father before him. And so on."

"Who owns it?"

"We don't have a name for it."

"But you work for it?" Julissa asked.

"Yes."

"All the Starks have?" she said.

"All the Starks, always."

"Where does it live?"

"Edinburgh."

"Where?"

The man's hands groped the air, gripping nothing, then holding on to nothing tightly and carefully as he brought his hands to his lips.

"You spill any?" Westfield asked.

"A little."

"You want me to get you another one?"

"That'd be good."

"The thing that owns Lothian Lines, where does it live?" Julissa asked.

"It's not just a thing. He's not just a thing."

"What is he, then?" Julissa said.

The man shook his head. "I don't know. He's old. Not old like a man. Old like a rock, or..." He trailed off, maybe searching for the word.

"Or what?" Julissa asked.

"Like a fossil. Like something you'd dig up."

"Are there others?" Chris asked. "Others like him?"

"He was looking for them. He'd go to the old cities and look for them. Maybe he thought he'd be able to smell them, or just feel them with his thoughts if they were nearby."

"Did he find any?" Chris asked.

"I don't know. I take care of his finances."

"Okay," Westfield said. "But where do we find him? We want to talk to him."

"You don't talk to him. He talks to you. Or through you. He can reach out and touch you." The man touched his left temple. "Here."

They all looked at him in silence. He went on.

"But you don't want him to do that, touch you that way," he said. "Especially you."

He was looking at Julissa when he said this. His eyes focused briefly and then filmed over.

"You know where to find him, though," Westfield said.

The man was silent, working with his hands in the air. Chris thought that if they were in a bar, he'd be tearing his soaked cardboard coaster to shreds. Maybe that's what Stark thought he was doing.

"I know how to find him."

"Tell us," Julissa said. She knelt next to him and brought her lips close to the man's ear. "Tell me."

"You'll need a key," Stark said.

His hands, soaked with sweat and shaking, moved up to his collar. He loosened the knot of his tie and then started to unbutton his white shirt. Julissa looked up at Chris and he saw what might have been fear in her eyes, though he couldn't see the expression on her face because of her mask. The man unbuttoned the shirt all the way to his navel, then fumbled at a leather cord around his neck. The key was beneath his undershirt, ancient-looking and forged of bronze.

"You would need a key like this."

Chris glanced at the key, then reached into his pocket. He found a brass and nickel two-pound coin. He stepped over to Julissa's backpack, getting her camera. As he walked back to Stark, the attorney said, "If you had a key like this, you could go to him."

"Where's the door for that key?" Chris said.

Now he knelt next to the man and gently took Stark's hand from the key. He placed the coin on Stark's chest for scale and began to snap close-up pictures of the key, turning it so he had pictures of both sides and from different angles.

"Advocate's Close," Stark said. "Halfway down Advocate's Close from the High Street. An iron door on the right as you walk down."

"And that's where he lives?" Chris said. "Just off of Advocate's Close?"

"Not where he lives. But where you can find him."

"Is there a number on the door?"

"No. But there's a carving in the lintel stone above the door. A ship."

"What about alarms or guards?" Westfield said.

"He doesn't need any. You'll see."

"Is he there now?"

"He comes there in between. He sleeps a lot."

"In between what?" Julissa asked.

Stark looked at her again, his eyes suddenly swimming up from beneath the strange surface of the drug and focusing on her.

"Redheads," Stark said.

"Why redheads?" Julissa asked.

"I don't know," Stark said. "I think it's because they're different. Because there's something he needs and he can only get it from them. But I don't know what it is. I don't want to know what it is."

"Let's take it from the beginning," Chris said. "Go back to when you first met it, and tell us from there."

Chapter Fifty-Two

Stark's eyes slowly opened.

The light was over his head, bright as the sun. He squinted and recognized the room. This wasn't his bedroom. He was in his office chair with his cheek planted on his blotter, staring across the broad oak and leather surface of his desk. The light was his reading lamp. An inch from his nose was a crystal tumbler from the wet bar with two fingers' worth of whiskey. The bottle that had poured the whiskey lay uncorked on its side farther down the desk, empty.

There was a second empty tumbler with a red lipstick stain on the rim.

When he slowly sat up, he saw a dry crust of vomit down the front of his white shirt. His tie was gone.

Was it a weekday?

He swiveled in the chair, and though the wooden shutters were drawn across his windows, he could see it was dark outside. His watch confirmed it was one a.m. Then he noticed a tube of lipstick on the edge of his desk, weighing down an empty Durex wrapper. He stared at that for a long while, his head still buzzing with whiskey. He sat in the silence and tried to remember what he'd done in the last twelve hours. Had he picked up a girl and brought her back to the office after his partners had left? He'd started doing that more often, especially now that he was almost divorced. But he'd never woken up like this.

Standing wouldn't be a good idea yet.

Instead, he felt for his wallet. Normally, he carried three hundred pounds in notes. But that money was all gone. There was a receipt from the whiskey shop downstairs for the empty bottle on his desk. He didn't remember buying it, but if he'd drunk all that, even with some help from the girl, he probably wouldn't remember. The receipt was for eighty-two pounds. He must have paid the rest of the money to the girl. At least he'd used a condom, he thought. There was no telling what you might get from a girl, even a good-looking young one. He unbuttoned his shirt and felt for the key. That was still there, so everything was okay. He leaned back in the chair and tried to think of what to do. He could throw his shirt in the trash can, wadded around the Durex wrapper, the lipstick, and the empty bottle. The cleaning ladies would get it in the morning. Then he could call a cab. It was only a mile home but that was too far to walk tonight, and he didn't like walking down the closes at night anyway. He was probably safer than anyone in Edinburgh—after all, he had the key to the door, he had the numbers to the offshore accounts, he arranged the voyages—but he knew what was in the closes at night. And he knew no one, not even Howard Stark, III, would be safe if its blood was running high.

Its blood had been up a lot this year.

Yes, he thought. Throw everything into the trash, call a cab and go home. Lock the doors and go to bed. He looked at the tube of lipstick and felt a little twitch down in his lap. He wondered what the girl had looked like, and what they'd done together. He felt stirrings of memory but there was nothing solid. Surely she had been very young, because he always picked them young. He had never hurt a girl, at least not that he remembered. Working as he did, he sometimes wondered about it, though. Anyone would, after spending that much of his life with the thing. Of course he wondered about that kind of power. He also thought about how far it went with them before it was satisfied, if it could ever be satisfied. It had been a long time since he'd walked all the way to the bottom of its abandoned lair off Advocate's Close and through the ancient bone pile in the chambers beneath Old Town, the dripping darkness of old caves and stone-lined passageways a thousand years older than the oldest wall in Edinburgh, his employer circling in the shadows just beyond the light of his flashlight, its voice coming from above him, behind him, underneath him, telling him what to do and how to do it. Some of the bones down there were gnawed to splinters, as though it kept returning to them, circling back for another taste.

Suddenly he wanted to be out of here, out of Old Town. He stood, walking shakily to the corner of the desk to get the lipstick. But he never made it.

Some thought stopped him, a flash of an idea, an image. He couldn't say.

He turned again to the window. The shutters were still closed but behind them the windowpane was open and he could feel the cool night air moving into the room like a rolling wall of fog. The window had been closed a minute ago, he was sure of it. He looked at his watch: two a.m. He steadied himself against the desk and looked around the office: the ceiling, the shadows in the corners near the door.

Where'd the last hour go, Stark?

Maybe he'd just misread the watch the first time. But then again, maybe not. He knew about this sort of thing, about the way some seconds could become swollen and engorged, and then devour the hour of which they were just a part, like a snake swallowing something twice its size. His employer could do this.

What do we do with things we don't want anymore, Stark?

The hair on his arms stood straight out. If he knew about time, he also knew about thoughts: not every idea that rose up and burst inside his own head was something he could claim to own. Thoughts jumped mind to mind like a virus; images burrowed body to body like worms. He'd seen landscapes of death he never could have imagined, felt stirrings his mind could never dream. All thanks to his employer, a thing that had lived in the base of his skull for forty years, and underneath the city for uncountable centuries before that.

That's right, Stark. What we don't want, we throw away. But first we break it, and we peel its skin off, and we take its heart in our fist and we squeeze. So that what we don't want, no one else can have.

There was a gold-plated letter opener on the desktop. He picked it up and held it close to his chest, his right hand shaking. In fact, his whole body was shaking, as though he had a high fever. His neck felt like he'd wandered into a hornet's nest. It rippled with bumps and hives, like some kind poison had been under the skin.

Then the tapping started: a closely spaced group of four clawed fingertips falling in succession against the wood. *Click-click-click-click.* He wasn't surprised. He knew how much it liked to toy with its prey, to build up the fear. Maybe, later, it could taste it in the meat. The brass door handle bent downwards and the door opened six inches. No shaft of light fell across the floor—it had put out the chandelier in the lobby.

Stark leaned against the front of his desk and tried to extend the arm holding the letter opener. But his hand was shaking so badly he dropped it onto the carpet. He fell on his knees to grab for it, and when he looked up, the door was fully open. A man stood there. Not a loping shadow, or a blur of vague smoke, but a man.

"Drop something, Dad?"

His fingers had closed on the letter opener but he let it go again.

"Ian?"

"You look like shit, Dad."

"I thought you were at—" he trailed off, trying to remember the name of the place. He drew a blank. "At school."

His son stepped the rest of the way into the office and squatted in front of him on the carpet. His motorcycle boot was on the dull blade of the letter opener; his hands were behind his back. His hair was greasy and matted, and his eyes were blank.

Ian had been with it: somehow, the creature had gone and found him and brought him north to Edinburgh.

"I was. At school. But I've been up here awhile. Talking. Learning," Ian said. His voice was dull and bland. "About you. Us. And now I came to watch the rest."

"Watch?"

Ian looked up and Stark let his eyes follow. The thing was on the ceiling, looking down at them. He saw its watery yellow eyes and its needle teeth. Its voice inside his head was like being strangled with a piano wire.

All the Starks, always, it said. *But only one at a time.*

In his mind, Stark took out a box and opened a locked memory. Something his employer had buried for him, buried well enough he'd forgotten he owned it. But now he remembered it all, so clearly he could taste the salted copper of blood in his throat from that long-ago meal. The meat had been so fresh it was still twitching as he swallowed it. He saw his own father. In this office, upon his knees on this carpet.

This was the end and the beginning, the closing of the circle. He knew what was coming next: Ian brought his hands from behind his back, and showed Stark the knife.

Maybe it was the same knife from forty years ago, and maybe not. It didn't really matter.

Stark tried to scream but the thing's voice exploded inside his head and cut him off.

What we don't want, we take its eyes out. We rip its jaw off and we pull away its tongue. And when we're done skinning it, Ian, we take its heart. And we eat it, Ian Stark. You and I.

Chapter Fifty-Three

They cut through Advocate's Close on their way back to the Balmoral Hotel. Midway down, right where it was supposed to be, they saw the door for the first time. The carving above the door showed what Westfield imagined was a three-masted schooner under full canvas in the midst of a gale. It was faded and lichen grew across the entire lintel stone. The door itself was cast from a single piece of bronze, reinforced with half-inch-thick strips of iron that had been through-bolted across the front at six inch intervals. The metal was blackened with old soot and dust, and in that dust there was a handprint just to the right of the lock where someone had pushed the door open. They all saw the claw marks there, five razor-thin streaks in the dust, tracks that cut to unblemished bronze.

Something had shoved through in a hurry.

They didn't linger, but went back to the hotel, converging in Chris's room where they locked the doors and drew the window shades. They sat in the armchairs near the fireplace. Westfield looked into the empty fire grate and thought about the last thing Stark had said. Finally he turned to the others.

"It's not just a monster with claws and teeth," he said. "When I was on the ship and in the same room with it, I could feel it trying to get into my head. It wanted to find out about me, but it couldn't. I know that sounds farfetched, but it's true."

"You're saying it's a mind reader?" Julissa asked.

Westfield nodded.

"I was thinking about what Stark said. He told us it needed something it could only get from redheads, but he didn't know what it was. When I was on the ship, I had to listen to it kill a girl. I could hear it taunting her, dragging it out. It wanted to make her suffer as much as it could."

"What's that got to do with redheads?" Chris asked.

Westfield looked at Julissa. "You ever had any kind of surgery?"

"On my jaw, when I was a teenager."

"The anesthetic, it worked like it was supposed to?"

She shook her head slowly and he could see from the sadness on her face that now she understood why it went after her sister, why it targeted women like her.

"No," she said. She was almost whispering.

"What happened?"

"They gave me the normal dose and prepped me for it, and when they started cutting through my gums with the scalpel it was like they hadn't given me anything at all. It hurt so much, even after they tripled the dose and I was completely out, I could still feel them cutting in. For a long time afterwards, a year maybe, I'd dream about it."

Westfield nodded.

"Tara was that way."

"You're saying redheads don't react to anesthetic like other people?" Chris asked.

"Not quite," Julissa said. She was looking at her fingernails. "Redheads, a lot of us anyway, are hypersensitive to pain. It's something to do with pigmentation hormones, I think."

"That's what it needs," Westfield said. "I think it doesn't just want to kill them and eat them—it wants to get inside their heads while it's doing it and feel what they're feeling. It's not satisfied unless the girl's suffering enough—enough for it to hit a certain point."

"Like an orgasm," Julissa said, quietly.

They sat in silence after that, looking at the cold, soot-blackened fireplace.

After a while, Westfield went to his own room and got into the bed. In spite of all their gains they might never know the final answers. If they were lucky, they would find the thing and kill it, but they wouldn't learn everything they had to ask. If they were only searching for a man, they would probably be satisfied with that. They could kill a man and wipe their hands, and never wonder much what happened in his childhood, or what part of the country he'd grown up in. Those things wouldn't matter: he would be just a man who killed women for sport, and men like that weren't anything special.

Maybe he would be satisfied if he killed this thing but never answered any of the questions. It was still just a thing that killed women for sport; maybe it didn't matter where it came from. The only thing that really mattered was to kill it.

Westfield went out alone the next morning and walked through the shops of New Town until he found a hardware store that sold brass stock. At a different store nearby he bought a small vise, a set of files, and an electric engraving tool that came with a dozen different bits for carving and grinding. He was back in Chris's suite by nine in the morning. They pulled a wooden shelf from the closet and used it to mount the vise over the claw-footed bathtub in Julissa's suite. Julissa had printed the pictures of the key, then used a ruler and a set of precision calipers to create a full-scale line drawing. The three of them worked through the morning, taking directions at times from Chris, who understood locks, but mostly working in concentrated silence. By two o'clock in the afternoon they had a rough cut of the key. Chris and Westfield took turns with an emery cloth, buffing the key to a fine finish, and then they oiled it with mineral oil. When they were done, Westfield held the key and compared it to the pictures.

"You think it'll work?" he asked.

Chris shrugged.

"It'll open the door. It's what happens next that worries me."

They would leave the hotel after three in the morning, when the last of the pubs had closed and the drunken crowds had finished stumbling home. It would be empty in the Old Town. Westfield watched as Julissa used black electrical tape to fasten an LED flashlight to the barrel of the sub-machinegun. She looked up at him, but there was nothing to say.

They watched the sun trace its long arc across the northern sky, and they waited.

Chapter Fifty-Four

Somewhere in the city a church bell was ringing the hour.

Julissa sat in the chair by the fire and counted to midnight. When the bell tolled the last hour, she rose and stood a moment next to Chris, who was asleep in the other chair, and then she quietly let herself out of his room.

The hallway was empty.

Earlier, she'd seen a janitor's supply closet at the end of the hall, near the stairwell. It was locked, but poorly. She took her Visa card from the pocket of her jeans and slid it into the doorjamb, twisting the knob to the left while she pressed the card down. The door popped open and she stepped into the closet and turned on the light. After their visit with Stark, Aaron had left the empty Russian syringe in her backpack. She took it out of her pocket now and looked at the jury-rig she'd fashioned from a nylon shoelace and a Velcro strap from her camera bag. It wasn't much to look at, but it worked, with the shoelace fastened to the thumb-button of the plunger with a couple wraps of duct tape.

She'd practiced with it in the bathroom when Chris and Aaron were finishing the key, and it had worked fine. Now she scanned the shelves in the janitor's closet, looking for something more potent than the tap water she'd used for practice.

There was a gallon-sized, grimy bottle of industrial drain cleaner on the top shelf. She climbed a stepping stool and took it down, turning it in her hands to read the label on the back. But the label had been dissolved by the contents of the bottle.

That's gotta be a good sign.

She knelt on the floor and poured a tablespoon of drain cleaner into the bottle's cap. Wisps of smoke rose from droplets that spilled on the concrete floor. She dipped the needle into the cap and drew the fluid into the syringe by pulling back the plunger. She strapped the syringe to her wrist, pulled the sleeve of her sweatshirt over it, and wrapped the shoelace around her finger. Then she put the drain cleaner back on the shelf, switched off the light, and went back down the hall to Chris's room.

Chapter Fifty-Five

Chris woke at fifteen minutes to three, when Julissa put her hand on his cheek. He stood from the armchair and stretched.

"Westfield?" he said.

"Just called him. He's changing his bandages one more time."

Chris took Julissa's shoulders and pulled her to his chest so that he was holding her against him, the soft curve of her breasts against his ribs. He kissed the top of her head, letting his face rest there for a moment in the warmth of her hair. Then he put on his jacket, tucking his pistol into the waistband of his pants.

Westfield was waiting for them by the elevator, his hands in the pockets of his jeans.

They walked across the empty lobby and out onto Princes Street. Crossing Waverly Bridge above the train station, they could hear a crew of workmen talking as they coupled train cars on the tracks down below. Then they crossed the cobblestone traffic circle at Market and Cockburn Streets, stepped under the scaffolding of a construction site, and entered the tight confines of Advocate's Close. They climbed the stone staircase and stopped at the door. Dewdrops in the lichen covering the carved ship glowed in distant light from the street lamps on High Street. Chris took out the key and held it in his left hand, then drew his pistol and held it in his right hand. Julissa turned on a small flashlight and aimed it at the door. He turned and saw it was the flashlight taped to the barrel of the sub-machinegun. Westfield was just behind her and to her right, his pistol drawn but pointed at the base of the door.

"Okay," Chris whispered.

He fit the key into the lock, slowly, feeling the faint taps as the pin tumblers lifted and settled over the newly filed ridges of the key. Then he turned the key clockwise and felt the lock's internal plug rotate with it. There was a click, and the door opened inwards an eighth of an inch. Chris put his hand where the creature had put its claws, and he pushed. The door swung on oiled hinges. He felt the rush of cold air coming around his feet and understood immediately, even before Julissa stepped forward and shone her light onto the stairs, that they were standing at the mouth of a cave.

Nothing rushed up to meet them except the dank smell of cold air. There was a smell like roots and earthworms. The stairs went down at a forty-five degree angle inside of a vaulted passageway that was only wide enough to allow them to walk single file. The stones overhead were carved into arches. They were standing in Advocate's Close with Julissa's light pointing down the passage. The light was only good for a hundred feet and then it was useless.

Chris pocketed the key and turned on his flashlight. He held it in his left hand with the pistol braced above it in his right hand. He walked down the first three steps and paused when he felt Julissa's hand on his shoulder.

"I think Aaron should close the door when we're all inside," she whispered. "So no one wanders in."

Chris nodded and walked down another two steps, then heard the quiet *click* when Westfield closed the door. With three lights shining down the tunnel he could see farther, but the shadow of the dropping tunnel stretched long past the reach of their light. The beam of his flashlight settled on a black box bolted to the solid rock wall up ahead. As they approached it, all three of the beams focused on the little box.

"Wireless internet repeater antenna," Julissa whispered. "Probably to bounce the signal around the corner and up to another antenna at street level."

"Wireless," Westfield said. "Jesus."

"All the modern conveniences," Chris said. He let his light follow the black electrical cable that came out of the box and followed the stairway downwards, secured to the wall at intervals by U-bolts.

Chris knew it wasn't just an animal they were stalking. It sent emails. It took digital photographs and flew around in helicopters. It had a lawyer in its pocket and a fleet of ships that spanned the globe. But the smell in this cave didn't tell him they were walking into the penthouse of an international shipping magnate. The stench of rot and mud and old death told him they were walking into something else. This creature could live in their world, but its hand hadn't shaped it. When they got to the bottom of these stairs, they would see how it lived when it was alone. *We're going into its nest*, Chris thought.

Its lair.

He walked downwards. The stairs were slick with damp and mold, but as they went deeper the air became drier. After six hundred and twenty steps the passageway leveled, curving to the right. There was another wireless antenna. The passage was barely two feet wide and wasn't high enough to stand up straight. He knew he was so amped up he would probably fire his entire clip if he saw a rat. He paused to steady himself and again felt Julissa's hand on his shoulder. She didn't say anything and he didn't look back. When he started to move again she kept her hand at the small of his back, a light press of her fingers to let him know she was there. When he made it around the curve, the floor dropped away again into another set of stairs. This passage was no wider, but the ceiling here was shorter, made of flat slabs of stone instead of arches. The small pools of light from the three flashlights wavered unsteadily on the ceiling and the steps as they went down.

Chapter Fifty-Six

For Julissa, the strangeness began the moment she stepped off the well-traveled steps of Advocate's Close and into the tunnel beneath the city. First there was the push of cold air and that smell, like a handful of wet earth taken from the place where a dead thing had been buried long ago. It was a dead smell, but it was more than that. It was sickeningly fecund; something was growing very well down there in the dark. After Aaron closed the door behind them, and the darkness was complete except for the dim circles of their flashlights along the dripping ceiling and mossy steps, something started to grow in her thoughts.

At first it was just a whisper.

Like hearing snatches of a conversation while walking on the streets of a foreign city, the language so different from her own she couldn't tell where one word left off and the next began. And then it was gone.

She held the sub-machinegun's pistol grip tightly, but kept her finger away from the trigger. They walked down the steps in silence and when they were deeper under the city, images began to take shape in her mind. She saw a young redheaded woman walking out of the water and onto the wet sand a few moments before sunset. She saw this from inches above the water, charging in towards the shore as if riding a powerful current. The girl turned to look at the waves, one hand behind her neck to feel the knotted strap holding up her bikini. Julissa's vision liquefied as she went beneath the surface. She saw taloned white hands gripping into the wave-rippled sandy bottom, clumps of Sargasso weed rolling in the current, a sand dollar. She watched the hands claw along the bottom, dragging her towards the shore; she could feel the small humps of sand sliding beneath her belly, the scratch of seaweed rolling down her bare leg.

Ahead of her, Chris stopped and she nearly bumped into him.

The vision in her mind disappeared.

Then, for a second, she saw the inside of Allison's condominium in

Galveston. She saw it from the outside looking in through the third-floor window. She saw her sister pass through the kitchen with a glass of wine, walking towards her bedroom wearing a pair of panties and a tank top. Superimposed over this image of Allison was a pair of glowing yellow eyes, a transparent reflection on the glass of her dead sister's window.

That image faded too.

They reached the bottom of the staircase and began to walk through a narrow, curving passage. Chris stopped and she put her hand on his shoulder, needing him. He paused and leaned back into her touch to acknowledge it.

She was seeing the creature's dreams. It must have been asleep or falling back to sleep, its mind wheeling through images and broken thoughts, waiting to settle on something.

She put her hand on the small of Chris's back and tried to clear her mind. If she could feel its thoughts, maybe it could feel hers. She focused on Chris's back so she wouldn't look at the tunnel or the steps. She opened her mind like a blank screen for the creature to cast its images upon, in the hope that none of her own thoughts would flow back out. This was like jumping into deep, cold water: she regretted it right away, but it was too late to take it back. She hooked her finger through one of Chris's belt loops and let him lead her down the next long stairway.

But she didn't see the steps at all.

She was kneeling on a ledge at a mountain pass overlooking an ice-bound fjord, shivering in the cold and striking flints together above a small pile of tinder. When a spark smoldered in the tiny nest of shredded birch bark, she was leaning close to it and blowing, adding stripped twigs to the growing flame until the fire caught. She piled on larger sticks from the heap of firewood next to the ring of stones, and knelt by the fire until she knew it needed no more tending. Then she turned and went into the cave behind her, walking through the darkness without any need for light.

She had left her prey back there, on a stone shelf at the far end of the cave. She gathered up the child and walked back to the fire. The child was already dead, its skull crushed. This was one of a pair that she'd caught; she'd already eaten the other. It was still wrapped in a swaddling cloth made of the skin of some animal. A bear, maybe. She removed the animal skin and threw it off the edge of the cliff and took one of the bigger branches from the wood pile to make a spit to cook the child. She sharpened the stick with the edge of a broken rock, skewered the child, and propped the stick next to the fire so the meat was close to the flames but not in them.

From her spot on the ledge she could look down and see the squalid encampment on the bank of the fjord where she had taken this prey, but she knew the small band would move on when they discovered they were being hunted.

It was no matter. She could follow them from a distance if she wanted to. She could track them through the mountains in the snow and pick them off one by one whenever they strayed from each other; she could rush into their camp in the middle of the night and take them all at once. It didn't matter if they threw stones or spears. She was too fast for them.

Or, if she felt like it, she could crawl into the back of her cave and make a bed of pine needles and skins, and seal herself up with a wall of rocks and sleep until spring or the spring after that and then come out to see if the world had brought better pickings. Or see if any of the Others had returned. She watched the child cook next to the fire and watched the thin lines of smoke rising from the camp far below her and listened to the howls of wolfs rising from the ledges behind her. The wolves could smell the meat cooking, but they could also smell her own scat and they knew better than to approach. She liked the lonely sound the wolves made, and the way the meat smelled when it sizzled, and the memory of catching this child and its older brother in the snow. She wondered if there was Another somewhere in the mountains on the far side of the ice, looking down on the same camp from its own fire and its own prey.

Julissa bit her tongue until it bled, and by doing so finally shut out the dream.

She swallowed a mouthful of hot blood and spit, unhooked her finger from Chris's belt, and felt in the darkness along the stock of the sub-machinegun, switching its safety off. She felt her pockets for the extra clips and swept her light around, seeing this part of the passage for the first time. She still felt cold from the dream, numb from the glacial wind of whatever place and time she had just escaped. She looked around.

Here and now, they were coming towards the end of this tunnel. She felt the gun again with her fingers to be sure it was set for automatic fire. The dream had been pounding at her with such ferocity when she finally closed it out that she knew they were almost on top of it. There was a chamber up ahead; she told herself that she was not afraid, that she was here with people she loved. They had come to settle a very old account.

Chapter Fifty-Seven

When they reached the bottom of the second set of stairs, Chris thought they might have come down as much as a thousand feet. Because the curve between the flights of steps had led them to the west, he thought they were probably directly underneath the castle. Ahead of him the passageway appeared to open into a chamber. He walked until he was five feet from the end of the narrow passage and waited to feel Julissa behind him. Then he stepped into the chamber, swept his light to the left and saw Julissa rush out to cover the right. Westfield came last, his light searching the high ceiling.

They were in its dining room, or perhaps its dining room from a thousand years ago. A waist-high flat rock took up the middle of the long rectangular hall. The vaulted ceiling reached up fifty or sixty feet above them at its peak, carved from solid rock. The walls were lined with stone pillars. But it was the floor that held Chris's attention. It was littered with bones: rib cages and skulls and individual leg bones, all of them gnawed and broken in pieces to get at their marrow, whole femurs split lengthwise down the middle and gnawed apart at either end as if by a dog. A few of the skulls still had locks of long red hair hanging from patches of dry scalp, and there were braids and plaits of red hair swept along the base of the table stone in the middle of the room. A cast iron brazier sat on the middle of that stone, its cold ashes littered with chunks of half-cremated bones. In the corner farthest from where they had entered was a pile of discarded corsets and petticoats, moldering woolen and silk dresses, tartan hoop skirts, cotton bloomers, and leather shoes, all of them ripped and shredded and stained. There was even an age-yellowed wedding dress, slashed across the middle where it was stained black with the blood of its last occupant now dead a century or more. The far side of the room opened to another passage, this one wider than the one from which they had entered.

Chris walked around the table stone. He kept away from the pillars and checked behind each one as he passed it. There were old bones, and behind one pillar was an entire skeleton hanging from its skull on an iron spike, its dry skin dangling in ribbons from its feet. But there was no creature hiding in the shadows.

Westfield had passed on the other side of the table and had gone to the mound of clothing. While Chris covered the entrance to the next passage, he glanced sideways and saw Westfield use his foot to lift the wedding dress to the side.

There was nothing beneath it but more old clothes.

"You didn't really think you could talk to Stark without talking to me, did you? I've owned him since before his grandfather was born."

Westfield swung around, searching with his light and his gun.

Chris and Julissa were doing the same, the lights arcing wildly in the dark chamber. Shadows and bones. There were tunnels coming out of the ceiling, passageways leading out of the highest parts of the walls. It could be anywhere.

"You hear that?" Julissa asked.

"I don't know," Chris said. "It might've just been in our minds."

"But we all heard it, or felt it," Westfield said.

There was a hard metallic slam from the stairs they'd descended. It had cut them off somehow, dropped some unseen portcullis or gate. That much was clear.

"Stark told you to come here because I told you to come here."

Behind Chris, Westfield fired a shot at one of the tunnels in the ceiling. The gun blast was deafening in the stone chamber, and in the ringing silence afterwards Chris could barely hear Westfield's words.

"Thought I saw..."

"You saw nothing."

The creature's words hadn't lost any volume; it might have been speaking aloud, but it was also speaking directly inside Chris's head.

What are you? Chris thought.

The answer rushed into his mind like a flood of dirty water.

Hungry.

That message must have been just for him, because neither Julissa nor Westfield reacted at all. But Chris almost fell to his knees from the force of the thing's thought.

"Get each other's backs," Julissa shouted. "Come to the center and get each other's backs."

They all moved to the center of the room, just behind the table stone. They stood in a triangle, shoulder to shoulder, their lights searching the walls and ceiling.

"Call out if you see—" Westfield trailed off and then started firing his pistol. Then he was screaming wildly.

Chris turned to see Westfield on his back, his face bloodied. Julissa was kneeling over him. Something white ran along the far wall in a blur, disappearing into one of the tunnels before Chris even got off a second shot.

Empty cartridge cases clinked across the stone floor.

Westfield writhed under Julissa's hands and screamed.

Chris's light searched the overhead tunnels, the stairwell, the wide passage way on the far side of the room. There were too many places to check.

"Julissa!"

"He's still alive but it tried to take out his eyes—"

Chris heard something behind him, a rustle like old leaves. He turned, raising the gun. The thing that hit him was just a blurry vacancy, a shape his eyes couldn't see because the creature was standing there in his mind like a buzzing electric current, blocking everything.

Later, he would remember little except for the yellow eyes.

Chapter Fifty-Eight

Julissa was trying to stop the bleeding on Aaron's neck and face, trying to keep him still. She had taken his gun from him so he wouldn't accidentally shoot her for her efforts, and had set her own gun aside. He was screaming and the blood was flowing between her fingers, hot and too fast. She pulled off her scarf and began wrapping it around his neck, and that was when Chris started to fire his gun from behind her. She dropped the scarf and fumbled for the Uzi, bringing it around just as Chris hit the stones beside her. She fired at the first thing she saw, blasting apart the skull of the skeleton hanging from a hook behind one of the pillars. Then she looked at Chris's face, putting her fingers on his lips. He was still breathing and was not bleeding much except for a trickle from his left temple.

Westfield screamed again, a gargled shout that sounded like her name.

She turned, but the thing had her from behind. It ripped the Uzi away from her with its taloned hands even as it was carrying her across the floor and up the wall. As it reached the ceiling, it slammed her head into a rock and she blacked out for a second, coming-to in time to see the scene in the room she was leaving, lit by three flashlights on the floor: Chris was struggling to sit up, Westfield was still screaming.

Then it was dragging her down a stone tunnel by her ankles, fast.

"They actually brought you to me," the thing said.

It came to a stop and seemed to hover over her. There was still a little light from the opening of the tunnel. Its eyes glowed like a pair of embers.

"They brought you down here with nothing but some guns," it said. *"They might as well have put you on a plate."*

She was paralyzed, either with fear or because it was immobilizing her somehow. She could feel its fingers moving over her sweatshirt, the press of its talons against her flesh. It traced a claw along the underside of her breast and found her nipple.

"*We'll do it here. They'll want to listen.*"

Chris screamed, from somewhere far back.

"*Julissa!*"

There was a flash of light and then it was darker again. Chris was searching the ceiling for the right tunnel and had passed it over. The leering thing above her felt all this too; it was there in her mind, dancing around the edges of her terror. And it was there between her thighs, pressing against the seam of her jeans. Hard and sharp, like the broken bones in its tunnels. If it entered her, it would rip her to pieces. When she remembered the syringe, it sensed that too.

But it wasn't fast enough.

She brought up her wrist and shoved it towards the thing's neck. It tried to back off the needle, but she had her other arm around its back, feeling the sharp ridges of bone that came out of its spine. She felt the needle sink in.

You fucking animal, she thought. *Here's a trick right out fucking Wild Kingdom. I look like a redhead, but I've got a stinger.*

She flicked her wrist back, pulling the shoelace taut with her middle finger. The plunger sank all the way in, and she rode up with the creature as it bucked backwards and howled. Then it was off of her, the sharp ridges of its spine tearing her hand as it snapped around and ran down the tunnel. She could hear its leathery feet slapping the stones as it sprinted away on all fours.

Now the howling was real and not just in her mind. An inhuman wail. Like an animal caught in a fire. She struggled to her knees and felt in her pocket for the second flashlight. It was a tiny keychain light with a single LED bulb. She pushed the button and looked around. There was a pile of bones next to her. She found a shattered femur, sharply splintered in the middle.

What the hell.

She stood and began to follow the thing's screams, slowly at first. But when its howls quieted as it drew farther ahead, she broke into a run.

Chapter Fifty-Nine

"It was the middle one."

"What?"

"The middle one," Westfield said. "It took her up that one. I saw." His good eye was bulging.

Chris moved his light from Westfield's bloody face and scanned the ceiling. He could hear the thing's howls. They might have been filtering down from that tunnel, but it was impossible to say. The wall beneath the opening of the tunnel was rough enough to climb, maybe. He found Julissa's submachine gun and slung it over his back. Then he found Westfield's Glock and gave it to him.

"In case it comes back."

"Just go, damn it. Don't waste time on me."

Chris went to the wall, put his flashlight in his mouth, and looked up. The tunnel entrance was twenty feet up. Rough stone, an iron hook jutting from the wall halfway up. Not much else. The thing roared again, the kind of sound you might hear coming out of the jungle at night. And Julissa was in there with it. That got him moving. He clawed his way up, his head throbbing from where the thing had hit him. When he got to the iron hook, he leaned his weight against it and adjusted the flashlight in his mouth so it wouldn't drop. Then he kept climbing, knowing he was just at the edge of his limit and the only way to get up was to keep moving. If he came to a stop, that would be it. And if he fell and landed the wrong way, that would be it for all of them. He punched upwards, slicing his fingertips on the rock in search of holds. In fifteen seconds he was standing on the iron hook and moving up past it.

When his fingers found the lip of the tunnel entrance, he hoisted himself in a smooth chin-up, kicked his legs over the side, and rolled in. The tunnel was just high enough to stand. He took the light from his mouth and brought the gun around. He didn't look back at the chamber below to see how Westfield was doing. He just took off down the tunnel, running at a crouch with the gun out, trying to see ahead through the shadows so he wouldn't be caught on his flank by a side passage.

Chapter Sixty

It was going up, leading her along with its screams.

For five minutes she'd been running through switchbacks and stairs as the tunnel punched upwards through the rock beneath Edinburgh. She wasn't too clear on what she'd do if she actually caught up to it. Maybe beat it with the bone she was holding, maybe stab it in the face with the sharp broken end. It was in a lot of pain, and thought it was dying. She could feel it thinking of its own death as it scuttled along the tunnel. But it still had the strength to outrun her. She'd given it a taste of something it had never known.

Fear.

She could feel its fear spreading through the dark tunnel in waves, could feel it as clearly as she could hear its howls. She didn't know if it could feel her thoughts, but maybe it could. So she thought about peeling the skin off its face with a sharp rock. About using the bone in her hands to pry out its eyeballs and stomp them on their stalks with the heel of her boot. She thought about the way it would scream and twist if she and Chris impaled it on a pole and stood back to watch it die.

Ahead of her, it screamed and ran. It tried to pull out of her mind but she clamped down on it and would not let it go. Holding on to it was like having a handful of earthworms. Filthy and squirming. But she squeezed her mind down on it anyway.

What I shot into you, you're as good as dead. But I'm gonna catch you first.

It yanked in her mind and slipped away, but it left her with an image. She knew what it knew: Chris was running up the tunnel behind them, armed.

The tunnel was narrower now, the steps finer. The stone stairs were polished, the walls were paneled with oak. She passed a locked doorway, then another. They must have been in the sub-basement of some building in Edinburgh. She could still hear the sharp slap of the thing's hands and feet on the stone. It was a bend or two ahead of her on the stairs. And now she could hear Chris pounding his way up the stairs behind her.

It would be a hell of a thing if he came around a corner with an automatic weapon and confused her in the shadows.

"Chris!" she called. She was nearly breathless but the sound carried well in the tunnel. "Keep coming. But don't shoot me in the back. I'm chasing it."

He called out her name, and nothing had ever sounded so good as his voice.

Now she passed a window set in the wall. The warped leaded glass looked over a fast-running stream. Trees bent in the dawn rain, the sky a smear of gray. She kept running up, the stairs curving into a spiral. Somewhere above, she heard a door open and slam.

"It went through a door, Chris!" she said. "Hurry!"

The door was at the top of the stairs and was made of heavy hardwood, studded with bronze. It was locked. She listened to Chris thunder up the stairs and waited. When he rounded the last curve he saw her and kept running, and she saw the way his eyes moved from her head to her feet and back up again. Checking her, making sure she was all right.

"Thank god," he said.

"Shoot it," she said. "Shoot the lock."

"Stand back."

She stepped back onto the stair landing. Chris leveled the Uzi at the lock from a foot away and fired a long burst at it. Then he kicked the door in and it swung open in an arc of smoke and wood splinters and a clattering of broken metal. He put a new clip into the Uzi and handed it to her, taking the Glock from the waist band of his jeans.

"Let's go," she said. And she didn't wait for him, but started for the door.

He stopped her with his hand on her shoulder.

"What'd you do to it?"

She held up her wrist and let the sweatshirt slide down so he could see the syringe.

"You didn't tell us—"

She nodded and finished his sentence. "Because the more of us that knew, the more likely it'd find out. Let's go."

They stepped through the doorway together, Julissa covering the left and Chris taking the right. The room was long with a soaring ceiling. Book shelves rose to the exposed rafters. Windows between the bookshelves looked down on the stream. At the far end of the room was a fireplace big enough to walk into. In front of the fire place was a thick

Persian rug. There were a couple of leather armchairs on the rug facing the fireplace. The thing was on the rug, naked and writhing.

They could see it easily now. It was in too much pain to play any mind tricks. It couldn't cloud their vision. Standing, it would have been about six feet tall. It was leathery-looking, its face scrunched like a bat's. As it flopped on the rug, Julissa saw its spine. Sharp protuberances came through the skin down the length of its back like something on an alligator. It looked up and saw them and went on writhing. There was a black mark on its neck where the needle had gone in; probably the drain cleaner had dissolved the blood vessels there and it was bleeding under its skin.

Julissa remembered the way the drain cleaner had smoked when she spilled droplets on floor of the janitor's closet. The thing was flopping and jerking like its blood was boiling, like something was burning holes through its heart.

"You want me to shoot it?" Chris asked. But he sounded like he knew the answer already.

"Only if it gets up. And then just in the gut to put it back down."

Julissa sat on the edge of the closer chair, her gun aimed at the thing's stomach.

There was a desk in one corner of the room. A computer on the desk, some papers. No telling what the rest of the house held. Coming up from the sub-basement to the top floor, she'd gotten an idea of the size of the place. At least fifty rooms, possibly more. Plus all the tunnels and chambers beneath the city. The thing must have been living in Edinburgh since the Stone Age. Maybe that's when it found the original Stark. After it was dead they could comb through everything they wanted, go through its files, sift through it all. They could take weeks or months and put it all together. If they wanted to.

They didn't need it to answer any questions. They only needed one thing of it, and it was busy doing it on the carpet in front of her. It was dying.

The thing writhed and screamed and looked at her. If nothing else, it was smart enough not to ask for mercy. Or mercy was an alien concept. Either way, it just did its thing on the rug by itself, and she watched. If she had to help it along, she would. They had to get back to Westfield and she didn't want to make him wait all day. But the thing died in five minutes, just thrashing on the floor, its mind wheeling through images of terror that it cast all around. When it was almost over, it lay still. Julissa nodded to Chris.

He knelt next to the thing and put the muzzle of his handgun to its temple.

It was alive, barely, but still crashing through images. Young women, begging for their lives. She saw Allison, Cheryl and Tara. A hundred others. The ice in the fjords from some long-ago time. Its mind quieted. It settled on a last image. Broken ice drifting across deep and black water. A scene of eerie peace.

Chris pulled the trigger and the gun blast shattered all that and sent it away.

The room was still and quiet. The thing's final thought blinked out in Julissa's mind, just gone. The contents of the thing's head were splattered across the back of the fireplace. Gray and red; not so different from anything else.

Chris stood and put the pistol back into his waistband.

"We should see if we can find a rope or something to get Westfield up."

"Will he be okay?" Julissa asked.

"He was talking when I left him. He was sitting up."

"Let's hurry."

Chapter Sixty-One

When he'd been alone for ten minutes, Westfield got to his feet and leaned awhile against the table stone until the rushing in his ears quieted. His right eye wasn't working too well but he thought it might just be swollen shut. The thing had clawed him in the face but had been moving too quickly to do any real damage. At least it hadn't gotten into him with its teeth again.

He took the flashlight and the gun and walked out of the chamber through the arched doorway at the far end. This led into an even larger room. Cavern might have been a better word for it. The floor was humped and uneven. The ceiling soared overhead beyond the weak beam of his flashlight. It was supported in places by long stalactites that flowed into the ground.

He hadn't heard the creature's screams in a while now. Either it was too far away, or it was occupied doing something else.

"Get to her, Chris," he said.

He scanned the flashlight along the floor, looking for anything that might help him scale the wall to the mouth of the tunnel where his friends had gone. The floor was littered with rocks that had fallen from the ceiling. There were a few small bits of bone that must have come from the other chamber where all the skeletons were piled. But there was nothing here that would help him up a twenty foot wall.

He limped to the back of the cavern and stood looking at one of the stalagmites rising from the floor. Something had been interred inside of this one. The calcite flowstone was translucent, the color of dirty amber. When he held his flashlight up against it he could see the shape of the thing inside. He stared at it for a long while, moving around the stalagmite until he was sure. Something had propped this thing up on the cavern floor beneath a drip of mineral-laden water. To turn it into a statue, like some kind of burial rite. The stalagmite had formed around a skeleton, but the thing inside wasn't human. There were sharp protrusions coming from its spinal column, long claws on its feet. The skull was barely covered by the flowstone and easy to see.

Its eye sockets were huge and widely spaced, its nose just two slits in the thick bone. Its lower jaw had fallen open and its many teeth sparkled, encased by calcite crystal.

There were others like it in the cavern. Two more about the same age, judging by the size of the stalagmites surrounding them. He guessed the floor-to-ceiling flowstone formations might have held even older burials. But these were so large they were opaque, so he couldn't be sure.

His flashlight caught something near the base of the column. A droplet of fresh blood. He played the light around and found another, then another beyond that. He forgot the things entombed in the flowstone and followed the blood trail. In a little bit he came to a crevice in the far wall. The blood disappeared inside it. He dropped to one knee, aiming the gun and the light into the opening. Ten feet back there was a dirt-caked young woman. There was blood all around her, in her red hair, on her face. He thought she was dead, but then she raised her hand to shield her eyes from the light. Her mouth opened in a silent scream.

"Miss?"

There was a clatter from the other chamber. Rocks hitting the floor and shattering. Then a hint of light from back there. And a voice.

"Aaron?"

He had wheeled around with his gun raised, but at the sound of Julissa's voice he lowered it.

"Westfield? Hey, man, where'd you go?" Chris called.

"Back here," he answered.

"Can you walk?" Julissa asked.

"Yes."

He started towards the sound of their voices. There was a new sound now. A hollow clatter of lightweight metal.

"Julissa hopped a garden wall and broke into a caretaker's shed," Chris said. "Found an extension ladder. We stole it."

Westfield came into the thing's abandoned dining chamber and watched as Chris lowered the ladder from the mouth of the tunnel. He came over to the base of the wall and helped position the grooved rubber feet on the floor. He looked up and saw Julissa. She was just fine. A little blood on her forehead, but that was all.

"The creature?" he said.

"We'll show you," she said. "We got it."

He nodded.

"Forget that for now," he said. "There's a girl back there, in the cavern. She's alive."

Chapter Sixty-Two

Julissa dove off the side of the boat into the clear water of the inner lagoon, and then turned back to the boat. She was treading water with her feet while she checked to make sure her bikini hadn't slipped off in the dive. The water was wonderfully warm. And there was no one here. She took off her bikini top and tossed it back onto the *Sailfish*, then swam around behind the boat.

They'd sailed nine hundred and fifty nautical miles south of Molokai, dropping anchor in Palmyra's inner lagoon five days after returning to Molokai by chartered jet. Palmyra was perfect: an uninhabited U.S. possession controlled by a conservation group that couldn't afford to keep a permanent staff. They'd arrived in the night and had sailed back and forth offshore, waiting until first light to navigate the coral-strewn channel from the open Pacific into the lagoon. She put her head under the water, and even without goggles could see the corals and bright orange urchins, dozens of reef fish.

There was plenty to do. Mainly, they needed to figure out where they stood. They could be wanted by the F.B.I., the Honolulu Police, the Galveston Police, the San Francisco Police, Interpol, Scotland Yard. Or none of the above. It would take some delicate hacking to find out who was looking for them and how much they knew. And then erase it all.

Their funds were safe, anyway. She had seen to that before they left Edinburgh, had taken care of Aaron's too. But she was still traveling on Cheryl's old passport, and Chris was using an I.D. that could be compromised.

But the *Sailfish* had everything, including Inmarsat satellite internet reception. She looked up at the white dome encasing the antenna at the back of the boat. Then Chris came out in a pair of board shorts and stood at the rail, looking down at her.

"Swimming ashore?"

"I'll wait for you. So we can explore together."

He nodded and took a sip from his glass of orange juice. One of the things they needed to do ashore was see if they could find some fresh fruit. They had spent all of ten minutes in a store on Molokai before setting sail, just piling things in a cart. There would be coconuts here for sure. And fish.

"Got an email from Westfield," Chris said.

"What's up?"

"Rachel's coming along okay. She's still staying with him, and he's still in Edinburgh. Chiseling out the skeletons he found in the cave. See what he can figure out."

"What's to figure out?"

Chris shrugged. He'd felt the same as her: their job was done when the creature was dead. But Westfield had been unable to leave Edinburgh. He was keeping the creature's house under surveillance, exploring the tunnel network, rooting through files. He'd been upset when they learned the creature had killed Stark. He'd been looking forward to another round with the attorney, without drugs. The police had been all over the law firm's offices, so Westfield hadn't gotten a chance to go back in to examine the files kept there. But Julissa and Chris both believed if there was anything to find, he would eventually find it. He was stubborn that way.

If he found a spaceship down there in the caverns, that would be different. She would probably need to go back. But in her heart she didn't think it was like that. She thought Chevalier had been right: the creature was something old, something that branched off long ago. Chris thought so too.

Julissa floated on her back, her hands behind her head.

"You think Aaron's gonna find what he needs to find?"

"I don't know," Chris said. "I think sometimes there's no satisfaction. You just have to let it go."

"That's what I think," she said. "Jump in. The water's great."

"In a minute."

"Why wait?"

"Because I'm looking at you. You're beautiful."

She smiled and stretched out in the warm water, kicking lazily. She closed her eyes and listened to the water lapping against the boat. Even this early, the sun was hot on her face, a red dazzle behind her closed eyelids. There would be plenty of time here to take care of everything. Time to find out where they stood in the world, to fix whatever needed fixing. At least she didn't need to find out where she stood with Chris. That much was certain now. She heard the splash when he hit the water, and opened her eyes.

About the Author

Jonathan Moore and his wife, Maria Wang, live in Hawaii. When he's not writing, or fixing his boat, Jonathan is an attorney at the Honolulu firm of Kobayashi, Sugita & Goda. Before completing law school in New Orleans, he was an English teacher, a whitewater raft guide on the Rio Grande, a counselor at a Texas wilderness camp for juvenile delinquents, and an investigator for a criminal defense attorney in Washington, D.C.

Connect with Jonathan at:
www.jonathanmoorefiction.com

Six-guns vs. werewolves in the Old West!

The Guns of Santa Sangre
© 2013 Eric Red

They're hired guns. The best at what they do. They've left bodies in their wake across the West. But this job is different. It'll take all their skill and courage. And very special bullets. Because their targets this time won't be shooting back. They'll fight back with ripping claws, tearing fangs and animal cunning. They're werewolves. A pack of bloodthirsty wolfmen has taken over a small Mexican village, and the gunmen are the villagers' last hope. The light of the full moon will reveal the deadliest showdown the West has ever seen—three men with six-shooters facing off against snarling, inhuman monsters.

Available now in ebook and print from Samhain Publishing.

It's all about the story...

Romance

HORROR

www.samhainpublishing.com